Courting

Fate

Book 1 of
The Courtship Saga

A.R. Kaufer

ISBN 979-8-9867469-5-1
Cover image & design by: A.R. Kaufer
Background, *Courting the Stars,* & Moon by Cassie Evans
Courting Books Publishing
First edition, December 5th, 2022.

Kevin,
My love and my soulmate, my
moon and my stars.
This is for you.

Like a shooting star,

falling beyond

its control,

we fell in love.

Now we brace

for impact.

-A.R. Kaufer

Chapter 1

The shot echoes down the alley. Tensing at the sound, Rafe prepares himself for the worst and rushes forward, praying he's not too late. Rounding the corner, his heart pounding furiously in his chest, he nearly runs over the man responsible. As the shooter raises the gun, Rafe deflects his arm away. Using his training, he then stuns him to his knees before rendering him unconscious. Rafe makes his way to the alley with the man slung over his shoulder. He drops him at the sight of the woman splayed out on the ground with blood oozing from her shoulder.

He grabs the purse from the man's grip and finds her phone inside. He presses the emergency call button, informing the operator where they are. As he listens to the operator, he opens the wallet. Inside, he finds her ID and reads it before laying the purse beside her.

"Is anyone injured?" the operator asks.

Rafe kneels beside the woman, ripping her shirt open around the wound. He grimaces at the sight. "The woman was shot in the shoulder. I'll do what I can to stop the bleeding."

"An ambulance is on the way. You need to stay on the line with me—"

Rafe hangs up the phone, tossing it aside. He kneels over the woman, carefully removes her jacket, and wads it up before using it to apply pressure to the wound, grateful the alley is lit enough for him to see.

"Miss? Can you hear me?" he asks.

She looks up at him, her face ashen as she trembles. Though he doesn't know if she can hear him, he comforts her as best he can. Relief floods over him when he hears the sirens.

An officer has to drag him away so the EMTs can take over and stabilize her for travel. "I need your statement," the officer says as he opens his notebook.

"I have to go to the hospital—" Rafe tries, looking over his shoulder and watching as the ambulance pulls away. His hands clench as his worry flows through him.

"She'll be all right. They know what they're doing," the officer says casually. "Give me your statement, then you can go."

Rafe swallows hard, realizing he's right. He gives his statement, wanting nothing more than to get to the hospital.

Once finished, the officer hands him his business card. "Call me if you think of anything else."

"Do you know which hospital they took her to?" Rafe asks.

"Mercy General."

"Thanks." Rafe rushes to his car and drives to the hospital as quickly as he can, where he tells the nurse he's the woman's brother. She informs him the bullet grazed her shoulder, and she has been treated, now waiting is in an exam room for the doctor to come in. Once the nurse gives him the room number, he barrels down the hall to her. He takes a breath before going in.

At the sight of her, his breath escapes him. She's unconscious on the bed, her color still gone, while an IV and wires are hanging all around her. He pulls up the chair and sits by her bed. Studying her face, he sees her curly chestnut hair splayed out around the pillow, and her pink lips tremble as she sleeps. He gently brushes a curl off her face before he runs the back of his hand down her cheek, surprised at how soft her skin is. He pulls back and straightens up, cursing himself for the small violation.

He sits by her side all night, relieved when she wakes up around ten the next morning. The nurse steps in and takes her vitals. Rafe and the woman say nothing to each other as the nurse looks her over and asks a few questions, typing her responses onto her tablet, then leaving.

"Who are you?" the woman asks, eyeing Rafe with distrust. She studies his features. His dark brown hair is long enough for him to comb his fingers through. She blushes when she realizes he caught her staring. His silver-emerald eyes pierce into hers, but his expression is soft. Her breath catches at the sight, having never seen eyes that color and wondering if they are contacts.

Her eyes go back up to his hair, tracing the sideburns down to the stubble around his soft lips and chin before trailing from his lips up to his nose, stopping again at his eyes. She swallows hard.

"I apologize for startling you, Ms. Summers. I—" before he can finish, a uniformed officer walks in.

"Ah, Ms. Summers, glad to see you're awake. Are you able to give me a statement about what happened last night?"

"Yes, of course," she says, glancing at Rafe before returning her attention to the officer.

He pulls out his pen and notepad. "Whenever you're ready."

She clears her throat. Rafe reaches over to her bedside tray and hands her a cup of water. "Thank you," she says, sipping slowly through the straw then looking up at the officer. "I left work and passed by the alley. Before I knew what was happening, the man grabbed my arm and dragged me in. He shoved me against the wall and threatened me with his gun. He demanded my purse and phone."

Looking down as her hands clench the blanket, she composes herself before she continues. "I don't know why he shot me since I complied and gave everything to him. I couldn't stand on my own. I guess I passed out because I don't remember anything until I woke up here." She glances over, confused by the look of hurt on Rafe's face.

The officer finishes writing down her statement before giving her a reassuring smile. "Good thing you had this guy with you. He saved your life." He looks down at Rafe. "You already gave your statement, correct?"

"Yes, sir. Last night at the scene," Rafe answers, standing up. Ana is surprised at his height.

"All right." The officer closes the notebook, shoving it and the pen into his pocket. He pulls out a card and hands to her. "Call us if you need anything, or if you remember anything else."

"Thank you," she replies, taking the card and setting it on the tray table beside her. She picks up her cup, drinking more of the ice-cold water. He leaves as Rafe sits back down. "You saved me?" she asks, glancing at him.

"Yes. I apologize, I was about to explain when he came in. I heard the shot and followed the sound to see what had happened. That's when I found you. I called 911 and kept pressure on your shoulder until they got there."

"I don't know what to say, except thank you."

"You don't need to thank me."

Her head cocks slightly at the sincerity in his voice. "Please, you literally saved my life. Thank you isn't enough."

"Just glad I was passing by."

"Have we met before?" she asks.

"Other than last night, no."

She sighs. "I swear, I know you from somewhere."

"You've probably just seen me around town." He smiles at her, a light flickering in his eyes. "I'm Rafe, by the way."

"Ana," she answers, looking him over again. Envious of his tawny beige skin, she wonders if he is from the Mediterranean. She sees him studying her with a kind expression on his face.

"Nice to meet you."

The doctor steps in with a tablet in his hand. He reads it over before giving his attention to Ana. "Everything looks good, Miss Summers. How do you feel?"

"I'm okay," she answers softly.

"The bullet grazed your shoulder, so we cleaned the wound and bandaged it. We'll be releasing you shortly." He looks at Rafe. "The officer told me what you did, saving her. Thank you. Most people these days would've kept walking."

Rafe shakes his head. "I couldn't."

The doctor gives a small chuckle. "Thank goodness for that." He looks at Ana. "Do you have someone to give you a ride home?"

"No," she replies. "My roommate is out of town."

"I'll get her there," Rafe answers.

The doctor looks at Ana, relieved when she gives him a small nod. "If you need anything else, press the red button on your bed. Otherwise, the nurse will be in shortly to discharge you. Any questions or concerns?"

"No, sir."

"All right." He closes the cover on his tablet and leaves the room.

Wincing in pain, Ana clenches the sheet in her hand. Rafe jumps to his feet. "What's wrong?"

The pain on her face masks her confusion, as she wonders why this stranger is so concerned over her. "A spurt of pain. I'm okay now." She gives him a small smile.

"I should've asked you first," he says, sitting back down, "about taking you home. Apologies."

"No, it's okay. I don't mean to put you out."

His smile grow as he runs his hand through his hair. "It's no problem."

Her heart races at that smile, at his sultry voice. She is struck again by how familiar he is, sure she has met him before. "Thank you," she manages.

A nurse comes in. "I apologize for the delay. Between our computer system having issues and the flu going around, we're a little swamped." Ana cries out in pain again, and the nurse quickly looks over her chart. "I'll get you your next dose of medicine while you are waiting for your discharge. We'll get you out of here soon." She pulls out the syringe and plunges it into her IV. She makes a note on the tablet then steps out.

Watching Ana fall back to sleep, he decides this would be a good time to run down to the cafeteria and get a bite to eat.

Ana wakes up, groggy from the medicine. She and Rafe say nothing as they wait for her to be discharged. Finally, a nurse comes in, pushing a wheelchair. On the seat is Ana's paperwork, a copy of her prescription, and her remaining clothes. "I have her discharge papers."

Rafe looks at Ana. "Are you ready to go home?"

"I am."

He helps her sit up. The nurse brings her clothes over. "I apologize, but your shirt was in shreds."

Ana shakes her head. "I don't have anything else."

"Here," Rafe offers, removing his hoodie. He hands it to Ana. Taking it, she smiles at him and watches him leave to give her privacy. The nurse removes her IV and monitoring equipment, then helps her dress. Ana gets in the wheelchair and clutches her paperwork as the nurse wheels her into the corridor and to the exit. Rafe runs across the lot, gets his car, and pulls up to the curb. He jumps out and rushes to Ana's side.

She eyes his silver-blue sports car and tinted windows. "Is this brand new?" Ana asks, her voice thick with envy.

"Yep, just came off the factory floor two weeks ago," Rafe beams.

"Maybe someone else should take me home."

He immediately turns serious and kneels beside her. "Did I upset you? What's wrong?"

"No. I don't want to risk bleeding on your brand-new car, is all."

Relief washes over his face. He reaches in, getting a jacket and wrapping it over the passenger seat. "All good, see?"

She smiles at him as he helps her out of the chair. Keeping her head down, she winces as she moves towards the car. He gets her settled into the seat, helping her buckle up then closing the door. He gives the nurse a smile, gets in the car, and drives away without saying another word. They head onto the highway.

After a few minutes, Ana looks at him. "Um, don't you need to know where I live?"

"I saw your address on your ID," he explains while keeping his eyes on the road.

"Okay. That's not creepy, at all," she mumbles.

He takes a breath. "I looked at your ID when I called the police, in case they asked for your name. Plus, I wanted to be able to visit you at the hospital and make sure you were okay. I wasn't sure they'd let me into your room if I didn't at least know your name. I apologize for the intrusion."

"I understand," she replies, curious about him. The sense she knows him is gnawing at her, but she ignores it as the pain in her shoulder is throbbing.

The rest of the ride is silent. He parks outside her house. Rafe looks over the single story with cream siding and a dark colored roof. When she groans in pain, he looks at her. "Are you okay to get in or do you need help?"

She smiles at him. "I'm okay. Thank you." She folds her papers in her hands and starts to get out of the car. Her head is spinning as she leans out and vomits, pain consuming her shoulder.

He hops from his seat and runs to her. "What can I do to help?"

"I'm dizzy," she admits.

He gently grips her arms and lifts her from the car. Once standing, he keeps his arm around her waist for support, getting her to the front door. She hands him her key, and he gets them inside. Once she's on the couch, he goes to the fridge and gets her a bottle of water. He admires the setup, with the kitchen and living room being open. The kitchen has stainless steel appliances with dark granite counters and a round table with four chairs. He walks past it and back into the living room.

"Drink slowly," he says, handing it to her.

She takes the water, doing as he says. Between sips she takes deep breaths, trying to stop the room from spinning. Cheeks flush with embarrassment, she looks at him. "I'm sorry you had to see that. It's gross."

He sits next to her. "Ana, you were shot. I think it's okay if you throw up."

She looks down a moment then drinks another sip. Taking a long breath, she meets his gaze. "I don't mean to upset you," she says, worried.

"What's wrong?"

She looks away. "It's just… I don't really know you. I'm so grateful for everything you've done, but—"

"You want me to go?"

"I'm so sorry, but yes, I need to rest now. If you'll give me your number, I'll text you in the morning."

"I don't have a phone," he admits.

She yawns as her exhaustion is wearing her down. "You don't have a phone?"

"No."

"Hmm, okay." Her eyelids flutter.

"Could I stop by in the morning? I'll bring breakfast and check on you. I don't have to stay if you're not up for company then."

"That would be really nice." She smiles at him. "Eight o'clock?"

"I'll see you then."

He stands up, guiding her to lie down. She falls asleep immediately. He grabs the blanket off the back of the couch and covers her, gently stroking her forehead. Giving her one last look as he leaves, he gets in his car and worries over her the whole drive home.

He sighs in relief as he steps into his apartment. Blasting the hot water, he stands under the shower head and lets the water wash away his cares. He steps out and twists so he can see his back, flinching at the sight. Sighing, he gets dressed as the exhaustion seeps in. He brushes his teeth, then falls into bed. He's anxious about seeing her again and drifts off into a restless sleep, hearing the echo of gunshots and finding her on the ground, covered in blood.

Ana jerks awake, the nightmare fading as she sits up. Regret fills her as pain shoots from her shoulder down her chest and arm. Removing his hoodie, she walks into the bathroom. Her bandage is soaked with blood. Groaning in frustration, she carefully peels the bandage back. She grabs a washcloth and gently cleans the wound. The doorbell rings, but she ignores it.

"Ana?" Rafe calls out, walking into the living room, worried when she didn't answer the door. "Are you all right?"

Forgetting she's not wearing a shirt, she steps out of the bathroom. A cardboard drink holder in one hand, with a large bag of food in the other, he nearly drops everything at the sight of her. She jumps back into the bathroom, slamming the door harder than she had intended. He sets the food on the table and rushes to the bathroom, pressing his palm against the door.

"You're bleeding! Let me help."

"You just want a sneak peek," she says, muffled through the door.

"Ana, I swear to you, I don't. I want to see why you're bleeding. Let me?"

"Only because I can't get it to stop," she admits, opening the door. She's grateful to at least be in a tank top bra. He walks in and goes through her cabinet, finding what he needs. She watches while he cleans her wound, every movement quick and efficient. "Are you a medic?" she asks.

"No. I learned in the field, though," he says as he applies pressure, being careful not to hurt her. "At least, how to stabilize and treat lesser injuries."

"You served in battle?" she asks, her breath catching in her throat when he nods in confirmation. "Where did you serve?"

"I'd rather not talk about it, if that's all the same. I need to focus."

"Of course. Sorry."

He brushes his finger gently beside her wound before applying a new bandage. "Should be good now," he says. As she gently prods around the wound, her hand briefly touches his. He grabs her arm at the sight of the scar on her wrist. "What is that?" he asks. He looks down and grabs her other arm, shocked to see a matching scar. "Ana?"

She slams the hoodie back on, looking at him. "Don't ask about those. Don't ever bring them up again," she demands.

Swallowing hard, he nods. "Of course." He follows her into the kitchen. "I wasn't sure what you liked, so I got a variety."

Ana pokes around in the bag filled with donuts, bagels, and muffins. "It looks like you bought out the café!" She laughs. "Thank you. I'm in no shape to fix breakfast this morning." He offers her a pick of the different drinks he brought, and she chooses an earl grey tea, adding a bit of milk from the fridge. After putting it back, she picks up a box and sets on the table while they spread the food out. She smiles at the variety when they sit down to eat. "Thank you for everything." She picks up the box and opens the lid. She slides a phone across the table to him. "This is for you."

He picks it up, surprised. "You're giving me a phone?"

"I upgraded mine recently, wanting a bigger screen. I like to read books on my phone during my lunch break." She smiles at him. "That one still works. I'll help you set it up if you want. Least I can do."

"Thank you. I have a tablet, but I've never had a phone."

She laughs, only stopping when she realizes he's serious. "How have you never had a phone?"

Shrugging his shoulders, he grins at her. "Never needed one."

"Okay," she says, deciding not to press. As they eat, she sets up his phone and creates his account. He hands her his credit card to finish setting it up. "You know, you're pretty trusting."

"Not usually. I trust you. Although, if you went on a shopping spree with my platinum card, I'm sure I could think of a way for you to pay me back." Regret floods him when she shifts in her seat and flushes a deep red. "My apologies, that was in poor taste. I didn't mean—" he takes a breath. "I would never think that."

"It's okay," she says, finishing the set up. "Why do you trust me? You don't know me."

"You just seem like an honest person. Though, I know you lied to the officer when giving your statement. Why did you lie about the reason you were shot?"

The phone and card slip from her hands. She gets up and walks over to the kitchen counter, leaning over, unable to look at him. "What do you know about it?" she asks, her skin growing warm as she thinks he knows what happened.

"Nothing," he admits, getting to his feet and walking to her side. "Only that I saw the look on your face when you talked about it. What were you hiding?"

Keeping her head down, she runs her finger along the cool granite. "I don't want to talk about it." Relief floods through her.

"Did he hurt you?" Rafe asks, stepping closer.

She looks up at him. "He wanted to."

"Ana, I'm sorry."

"For what? You have nothing to be sorry for. You saved my life and are still helping me. Why are you apologizing?"

"I should not have brought it up."

"It's okay." She returns to the table and finishes her donut. His phone restarts, letting her know the setup is complete. When she has input his pin and added her number into his contacts, she hands it to him. "All done."

"Thank you," he says, smiling as he takes the phone. He puts it and the charger in his pocket.

"I called my boss this morning. I was worried he would be upset about me missing, but hearing what happened, he told me to take a few days."

"What do you do for a living?"

"Bank teller. It's pretty boring most days," she says with a chuckle, "but it's good hours and good pay. I was late last night because I had a meeting." Pain spirals down her arm and chest. She sucks in her breath and squeezes her eyes shut, waiting for it to pass.

"Are you hurting?"

She nods. "I need my prescription. I'm in no shape to walk to the pharmacy, though."

"I'll get it for you."

"You can't. It's a controlled substance, in my name. I have to get it myself."

"Then I'll take you."

"But you've already done so much for me."

"Please," he offers. She is startled by his kindness. "Let me help you."

"Thank you. Let me get dressed." She goes into her room, changing clothes and stepping back out. Overwhelmed

16

with pain, she leans against the wall. Rafe walks over and helps her to the couch.

"You're in no shape to go anywhere!"

"I have to. I need the pain medicine." She closes her eyes, taking a deep breath. "Give me a moment, then I'll be okay."

Worry drawn across his face, he watches her closely as he wishes he could take her pain. He's pulled from his thoughts when he realizes she's raised her hand. Helping her stand, he wraps his arm around her waist, then guides her to his car while she tells him which pharmacy.

———— ⚬ ————

They arrive at the pharmacy and wait in line. She's leaning against Rafe for support when a man accidentally bumps into her. At her cry of pain, Rafe sees red.

"I'm sorry," the man is saying when Rafe steps up to him, daggers in his eyes.

Ana grips his arm with both hands. "Rafe, please, don't." She tries to pull him away, unable to budge him even an inch.

Rafe takes a breath before looking down at her. "My apologies." He watches the man run off. "Are you all right?" he asks Ana.

"I'm fine. Please, go wait in the car. It shouldn't be too much longer. Please," she begs. Without a word, he turns on his heel and leaves.

A few minutes later, prescription in hand, she heads for the door. A sudden wave of light-headedness hits her, and she makes it to a chair in the waiting area where she plops down, holding her head in her hands. A hand grips her uninjured shoulder, causing her to jump. She looks up to find Rafe kneeling beside her, looking at her in concern.

"Come on. I'll help you to the car."

The room spins as she gets to her feet and the vomit threatens to rise in her throat. Standing up, the world goes black. Rafe catches her and carries her to his car.

⸺ ∾ ⸺

At her house, he carries her inside and gets her settled onto the couch. She comes to, asking for her prescription. He gets her a bottle of water and two pills, watching her swallow them, then lie back down. He sits in the recliner and checks out his new phone while she sleeps.

After an hour, Ana wakes up slowly, her head heavy from the medication. "What happened at the pharmacy?"

"You fainted," Rafe replies.

"I know that. I mean, why did you go toe to toe with that man? It was an accident, and he was apologizing to me when you stepped in."

"I'm so sorry. I heard you cry out, and I was overwhelmed. I wouldn't have hurt him; it was just an instinctive reaction."

"You scared me."

He looks down, ashamed for his reaction. "I never want to do that."

"Rafe?" He doesn't move. "Please, look at me." She gives him a small smile when he meets her gaze. "It's okay."

"Still, I'm sorry."

She lies down. "I'm gonna get some more sleep," she says, drowsy from the medicine.

He watches her a moment, then he feels her forehead to be sure she's not running a fever. He's thankful she's not as he pulls the blanket up and sits down in the chair beside her, starting to nod off.

The door opens, and a blonde woman he doesn't know walks in. She's dressed in dark jeans with a blue flannel shirt, her hair pulled back in a loose ponytail with bags slung over her shoulder.

"Ana?" she calls out, freezing at the sight of Rafe. "Who are you?"

"I'm Rafe. Ana's here on the couch. She was hurt last night by a mugger."

The woman drops her bags and runs around the couch. She falls to her knees in front of Ana, looking her over when she opens her eyes.

"Kara, is that you? You're home early."

"I was able to catch an earlier flight. Are you okay? What happened?" She looks to Rafe then back at Ana.

Ana shakes her head. "Hmm. The medicine... Too sleepy. Ask Rafe."

Kara looks up at him, her green eyes full of distrust. "Who is he? Why is he here?"

"He'll tell you," she says, falling back asleep.

Kara picks up her bags and carries them to her room. When she comes back in, she walks right up to Rafe. "Tell me what happened," she demands.

They go to the kitchen table, where he tells her everything from finding Ana in the alley to bringing her home from the pharmacy. "She's on powerful pain medication, which is why she's sleeping."

"Well, I'm here now," Kara says, getting to her feet and walking towards the door, "so you can go."

"Don't send him away!"

They turn to Ana, who is sitting up. Rafe runs to her and sits beside her. "Are you okay? How's the pain?"

"I'm okay. Kara, please, don't make him go."

Sighing, Kara walks over and sits on the other side. "Fine. He doesn't have to go. I'm sorry, sis. You know how much I worry over you."

"He saved me and helped me after. Be nice, please?"

Kara laughs. "I'll try. You know how I feel about men."

Ana glances at Rafe, before smiling at Kara. "He's okay, I promise."

Kara rolls her eyes. "You just met him!"

"I met him because he saved my life. Be nice."

Rafe is surprised when Kara looks at him, smiling. "Fine."

He returns the smile, disarming her temper then looks at Ana. "Are you sure you're all right?"

She brings her hand up, gingerly touching her shoulder. "It doesn't hurt as bad as it did earlier. I do need my next dose, though."

Rafe gets her medicine and water, while ignoring Kara watch his every move. After Ana's taken the pills, he helps her lie back down. He covers her with the blanket, surprised when Ana takes his hand. "What's wrong?"

"Nothing. I just wanted to thank you again." Her eyes glaze over as the medicine takes effect. "Hmm," she moans softly.

"Get some sleep. Let the medicine help."

She laughs, looking at Kara. "They gave me the good stuff." Kara chuckles softly. "Did you know Rafe saw me without a shirt on?"

"What?" Kara yells as she jumps to her feet. She stares at him. "What did you do?" she demands.

"No, no," Ana tries. "It's not like that." Her words are slurred. "I'm getting sleepy again. Kara, promise me you won't make him leave?"

"I promise," she relents.

"Rafe, you'll be here when I wake up?"

"As long as Kara allows it." Stifling a laugh when Kara rolls her eyes, he shakes his head at her. "Yes, I'll be here."

Ana closes her eyes, giving into the medicine. Kara looks at Rafe. "You must be something special."

"I beg your pardon?"

"I've *never* seen her look at anyone, male or female, the way she looks at you. And you're a total stranger, so it's probably just the medication she's on."

He tries to suppress the smile. "Maybe she likes me for my charming personality? Hmm?"

"Don't try that with me," she hisses at him. "I see right through you. Who are you? What are you doing with her?"

"What do you mean?"

"No, don't play stupid. Did you stage the mugging to meet her? Go viral on YouTube or something?"

He's instantly on his feet. "I don't even know what that means, but it's ridiculous. I would never do anything to hurt her."

"For someone who just met her, you seem awfully concerned about her well-being."

"I saved her life. I feel a need to protect her now, that's all. Once she's no longer under heavy medication, she will make the decision, to keep me by her side or send me away. I'll respect whatever decision she makes. Until then, I am not leaving."

Kara takes a step back. "Damn. All right. You can stay, but only if you pay for lunch. I need to eat."

Handing her his credit card, he smiles. "Order something for both of us. Whatever you want, I'm not picky."

"All right then," she says, looking over the platinum card. She pulls out her phone and goes online.

Rafe sits by Ana. He strokes her hair and watches her sleep. When the food arrives, Kara answers the door and gestures to Rafe. They go to the table, where Kara opens the bag and spreads out their order.

"Do you travel a lot?" he asks, picking up the chopsticks. He frowns, setting them down and going for the plastic fork.

"Sometimes. I'm a photojournalist, so it depends on where the action is. We're a small operation, mostly online. I try not to leave her too much, though."

"I see how much you care for her. How long have you known her?"

"We met freshman year of college, so going on five years now. I found lost her on campus. She was crying over her schedule, trying to find her class. I took her under my wing."

Rafe chuckles. "I'm glad she has a friend like you." She gives him a dirty look. He holds up his hand, gesturing peace. "I'm not being sarcastic, really."

She goes back to eating. "The friendship goes both ways. We take care of each other. What about you? What do you do for work?"

"I was an army brat. I traveled around the world with my parents. I enlisted at eighteen and served my four years. I lost my parents in a car accident last year, so now I live off my mother's trust fund while I figure things out."

"Sorry for your loss."

"Thanks."

"That explains the pretty blue car out front."

He smiles. "Jealous?"

"No," she replies flatly.

"By the way, I saw her wrists."

Kara drops her chopsticks, staring at him. "Don't ever bring that up."

"Kara—"

"Not to me or her. Do you hear me?"

"I don't understand. Who did that to her?"

Her jaw drops in surprise. "Are you serious right now?" He nods. "Rafe, she did that to herself."

"What? Why would she do that?"

As she's sitting up, Ana lets out a soft cry. Rafe runs to her. He kneels beside her and puts his hand on her arm. "Hey," he says, his voice soft and soothing. "Are you in pain?"

"A little. It feels… tight."

"Do you have an appetite?"

"I could eat a little."

Kara brings over a takeout container with Rafe's unopened chopsticks. "Sweet and sour pork, your favorite."

Rafe holds the container while Ana eats. Kara stands back, examining his every move as if questioning his true motive. She says nothing as she gets a bottle of water. "Do you need more medicine?" she asks.

"No, it's too soon." Ana yawns. "The food is making me sleepy, though."

"Get more rest," Kara says, taking the container and chopsticks.

"We have company. I don't want to be rude."

"You need rest, bonehead. Sleep while you heal."

Ana shakes her head. "I don't need to. I'm okay," she says, yawning again.

Rafe chuckles. He leans in, his face inches from hers. "You need to rest. I told you I will be here, and I meant it. Please, lay down and sleep some more." Reluctantly, she nods. Kara helps her lay back down, covering her with the blanket. She and Rafe return to the table.

"I don't know why she responds to you like that. Any time she's sick, I have to fight her tooth and nail to take her medicine or rest."

"Does she get sick often?"

"Thankfully, no. An occasional stomach bug or the flu. She's absolutely miserable to be around when she's sick." Kara laughs. "It's not funny really, because she orders me around like some little princess."

Rafe chuckles at the notion. "I find that hard to believe."

He throws away his trash and walks back to Ana, who is mumbling in her sleep. He grows concerned when she begins to shake. "No!" she cries out, waking up. She looks at Kara and Rafe, before dropping her gaze to the floor and sitting up. "Sorry."

"Are you all right? Were you having another nightmare?" Kara asks.

Nodding, she clasps her hands together. "He was shooting me."

"Ana," Kara says, walking towards her, "why did you come home that way? You know to avoid that street."

"I thought it was going to rain. It wasn't quite dark yet, so I thought I would be okay. Don't be mad at me. It's not my fault." She cries into her hands.

Kara sits beside her and wraps Ana in her arms, careful of her shoulder. "Oh, honey. That's not what I meant. I'm sorry."

Ana looks up at Kara and smiles. Kara kisses her forehead and helps her back down, pulling the blanket up. "Thanks, sis."

"Of course." Kara's phone rings. She walks into the kitchen as she answers it. She paces around, nodding her head and looking at the clock. Sighing, she walks over to Rafe as she ends the call. "That was my editor. He needs me on the next flight out to cover this scandal with the governor. It's making all the headlines, and he wants me on the ground for the press conference." She looks at Ana, sleeping peacefully, then turns her attention back to Rafe. "Normally, I would tell him to shove off, but I can't. We are shorthanded." She takes a deep breath. "I guess what I'm asking is, will you stay with her until I get back? Or as long as she wants you here, that is?"

He steps up, his gaze meeting hers. "Kara, I will stay with her. You can trust me. I mean that."

She scoffs, nodding to Ana. "I trust her. For some reason, she's usually a good judge of character." She goes into her room, grabbing her bags. "Good thing I had most of my stuff dry cleaned. My editor already has my flight booked. I need to go." She kneels by Ana and gently wakes her. "Sis, I have to go for work. Rafe is here. He's going to stay with you, okay?"

"M'kay."

"If you tell him to go, he will. Understand?"

Ana grunts and nods. Kara shoots Rafe an intense look as she stands up and goes out the door. He sits by Ana, pulling out his phone and turning it on, investigating the different features. He continues to be amazed by the technology he comes across. After a while, he leans back in the chair and falls asleep.

Chapter 2

"No!" Ana screams.

Instinctively, Rafe is on his feet as his eyes scan for any danger. Seeing none, he runs to Ana, and falls to his knees before her. "What happened? Are you all right?"

Staring at the floor, she slowly sits up. "I'm okay," she answers quietly. "Just a nightmare."

He sits beside her on the couch. "Will you tell me about it?"

"He… he was… he was hurting me."

Rafe takes her hand, squeezing it gently. "I'm so sorry. Can I do anything for you?"

"No, but thank you. It's stupid. He didn't even… why am I being like this?"

"You were scared and nearly killed. Your mind is trying to make sense of everything." He brings his hand up, nudging her chin so she's looking at him. "You have nothing to be afraid of. I'm here."

She wipes her eyes, giving him a reassuring smile. "Thank you."

He lets out a quiet laugh when her stomach rumbles. "Are you hungry?"

"Could you fix me some soup? Nothing else sounds good. There should be some in the pantry."

"Of course." Rafe rummages around in the kitchen and finds the soup in the pantry. He finds a pot in the bottom cabinet, pours the soup in, and opens drawers until he finds a serving spoon. "How's your pain?" he asks, stirring.

"It's okay," she replies.

A few minutes later, he pours the soup into a bowl and gets her a spoon. He walks in and hands it to her. "It's hot," he cautions.

She takes the bowl, setting it on a coaster on the coffee table. "Thank you."

"Ana, would you look at me?"

Shivering, she keeps her gaze on the floor. "I can't."

"Why not?"

"That man, he…" she shakes her head. "I thought he was going to…"

"You're okay, Ana. He didn't hurt you like that. You're safe now. So, why won't you look at me?"

"I'm ashamed," she admits.

Rafe sits beside her. "Why? Because you're scared?"

She nods. "Yes."

"That is nothing to be ashamed of. You want to know something? When I heard the shot, I was scared, too. I didn't know if someone was hurt or dying, if I would be too late. There is no shame in being afraid."

She looks up at him. "You mean that? You were scared, too?"

"I was." He smiles at her. "Now eat," he orders, winking at her.

She smiles back, picking up the bowl and eating slowly. While she eats, he goes into the kitchen and snacks on a muffin. Setting the bowl on the table, she lies back down. "Thank you, for everything," she says when he walks up to her.

He takes the bowl into the kitchen, rinses it out, and puts it into the dishwasher. He looks up when she sprints to the bathroom. He hears her retching and runs in, opening the door without knocking first. With one hand, she's trying to hold back her hair as her other hand grips the tank. Rafe grabs the hair tie off the vanity and gets her hair into a rough ponytail. He rubs her back as she finishes.

She looks up at him, her eyes glassy with tears. "I'm sorry."

"Are you okay?"

"I think I ate too much."

After she brushes her teeth, he carries her to the couch. He gets a bottle of water and some crackers. "Eat just a little, once your stomach is settled," he says, trying to hide the concern in his voice. She takes them both, nodding. She sets the crackers on the coffee table, slowly sipping from the water bottle. "Do you need another pain pill?"

"No, the pain isn't bad right now." She feels carefully around the bandage. The doorbell rings, and Rafe walks across the room. Opening the door, he sees two plain-clothes detectives, waiting patiently with their identification held up.

"We're looking for Ms. Summers. We have a few follow-up questions regarding her mugging," says the shorter of the two men.

Rafe steps aside, gesturing them in. He looks at the older of the two detectives. He's dressed in navy blue pants with a matching blazer and a white shirt underneath. His glasses hang out of the front pocket. He's short with a little weight on him. The younger detective has light brown hair, taller than the older but shorter than Rafe, dressed in black pants with a grey shirt.

"She's recovering, so please don't get her riled up."

The detectives exchange a look as they walk in. Introductions are made, and they sit, getting out their notebooks.

"Ms. Summers, I'm just going to get to the point. There are some parts of your story that don't match up with what the suspect is telling us."

"What do you mean?" she asks, staring at the floor and wishing it would swallow her whole.

"You told the officer that he demanded your purse and phone, and you complied. Then he shot you. The suspect admits to mugging you, but that he started," he clears his throat. "I apologize, but these are his words, not mine. He started groping you and grinding on you, then tried to get you onto the ground. He says that's when you kicked him in the groin, and the gun went off."

Her head goes lower, as she wipes her tears. "He's lying," she stammers, knowing they don't believe her.

"Ms. Summers, there was a surveillance camera in the alley."

At that, she's back in the bathroom, vomiting again. Rafe looks at the detectives. "Do you really have to do this right now?"

"Sir, she lied to the police. That is a crime—"

"She was attacked! Then you come in here, misleading us as if you want to help her."

"That's not what we did," the younger one tries.

"Then why not tell her there was a camera from the beginning? You see her as a liar and are only traumatizing her further. Do you not see how ashamed and humiliated she already is? I can't believe they sent two male detectives. This is ridiculous!"

"I didn't catch your name."

"Cause I didn't throw it," Rafe snaps back. "You need to leave. I will speak with her in private, and *if* she wishes to amend her statement, we will come down to the station to speak with a more appropriate detective." He walks over and slams the front door open. "Now go," he barks out.

The detectives look at each other, the older one shrugging his shoulders. They head for the door. "My apologies," the older one says. "We are just trying to get to the bottom of what happened that night."

Rafe snorts and slams the door behind them. Ana comes out of the bathroom, pale, trembling, and refusing to meet his gaze. He approaches her slowly. "I'm sorry they put you through that."

She hangs her head. "Please, just go."

"Ana—"

She chokes down her tears. "Please," she begs, turning away. "I can't…" she buries her face in her hands.

"If that's what you want," he says, walking to the table and grabbing his phone. "Call me or at least text me updates on how you're feeling, please. Or if you need anything."

"Why?"

He sighs. "Ana, I want to make sure you're okay."

"You heard what—" she looks down when her phone rings. She digs it out of her pocket and answers when she sees it's Kara. "Hey." She listens for a minute. "Glad you made it safe and sound. Where are you?" She continues to listen, glancing up at Rafe before turning away again. "Yeah, he's still here. He's getting ready to leave." She speaks quietly into her phone. "Because two detectives just came, and I'm upset right now." She rests her head against the wall, obviously not happy with whatever Kara is saying. "I know I'm recovering, but—" she hangs her head, relenting. "Fine." Rafe is confused when she hands him her phone.

"Hi, Kara."

"Look, I don't know what those assholes said to her, but she is not to be left alone right now."

"She's okay. She's up, eating, and drinking."

"I'm not talking about her shoulder. Just, please, don't leave her alone. Promise me."

Surprised at the desperation her voice, he agrees. "Yes, Kara. I promise, I won't." He hands the phone back to Ana. She finishes her conversation with Kara, slamming her phone on the counter. She lays her arms on the cool granite.

Her head goes down. "Please, don't go."

"I promised you I wouldn't." He walks towards her, concerned when she turns away from him. "Ana, talk to me."

She opens the prescription bottle and gets out two pills. She drinks them down, then walks over to the couch. "Thank you," she says, lying down and pulling the blanket up. The exhaustion claims her.

Sitting in the chair beside her, watching her sleep, his blood boils as he thinks of how the detectives treated her. He doesn't understand why she's so ashamed since she did nothing wrong. He turns on the TV, watching the news as he continually looks over at her. He turns it off when she sits up.

"Would you like something to eat?"

"No."

"Because you're not feeling well or because you don't want to?" he asks, concern on his face and in his voice.

"Rafe—" she tries.

"Which is it?"

Tracing her hand over the water stain on the coffee table, she gives in. "If you fix something, I'll eat it."

"I don't know how to cook," he admits. "We could order something. Like I told Kara, I'm not picky."

"Okay." She picks up her phone and places their order. She sets the phone on the coffee table.

"Ana? Will you look at me for a moment?"

Stretching, she gets to her feet. She goes into the kitchen to get a cold bottle of water out of the fridge. Drinking it slowly, she tries to build up the courage to face him. She places the bottle in the recycling bin then turns to him. She meets his gaze, but only for a moment. "I need to get cleaned up," she says.

She goes into her room to get clean clothes. In the bathroom, she stares longingly at the shower head, knowing she isn't up for a full shower yet. Instead, she starts the tub filling as she undresses. Even with only a few inches of water, she trembles at the thought of getting in, and she decides to sit on the edge. She dips the cloth in over and over, sponging herself off. It's the best she can do, given her current state. She uses some of Kara's body spray, gets dressed, and heads straight to the couch.

"Can I get you anything?"

Not looking at the source of those words, she sits down. "No, thank you," she replies.

Rafe looks over when the doorbell rings. He opens the door and takes the pizza and breadsticks to the table while

Ana gets paper plates. They sit in silence, with her picking at her food more than eating it.

"Please, eat one piece? So Kara doesn't kill me," he adds, giving her a grin.

She only nods and eats her piece. He puts the food away while she goes back to the couch. Sitting beside her, he sighs, wanting to ask her how she feels. He's surprised when she looks at him.

"Thank you for the food."

When she lies down, he stands up, and helps her with the blanket. "You're welcome." He looks at the clock. "Are you okay if I run home and freshen up? I shouldn't be more than an hour."

"That's fine."

Hating to leave her, especially since he promised them both, he goes for the door, needing to get clean.

At his apartment, he strips down and steps in before the water is even hot, getting the quickest shower he has ever taken. *This is what I should've done that night. It's my fault*—He shakes his head, clearing the thoughts out. Once clean, he packs his duffle bag and rushes back to her house. Without thinking, he walks in without knocking and is worried when he doesn't see her. He drops his bag beside the couch.

"Ana?" He sees the bathroom door partially open and the light on inside. "Ana?" he tries again, pushing the door open. She's unconscious on the floor. Kneeling beside her, he lifts her shirt and starts to remove the bandage, wanting to check her wound.

"Get off me!" she screams. "Please, don't hurt me."

"Ana, it's me. It's Rafe." She stops struggling. "You were passed out on the floor. I had to make sure you weren't bleeding again," he says, lowering her shirt back down.

He's concerned at how flush her cheeks are when she looks at him. "I'm sorry," she says, closing her eyes. "I should've known better."

"It's okay. The trauma you went through, I know you are still coping with it." He helps her stand and leads her to the couch. "You're safe now. I promise you."

"Why are you still here?" she asks as she sits. "You don't even know me, and you've been so kind. Why?"

A sad smile plays across his lips. "Because I know what an unkind world is like. We all need a little kindness sometimes."

"How can I ever repay you after everything you've done for me?"

"Just get better. Don't let all my hard work be in vain." He smiles at her. "Deal?"

She returns the smile. "Deal."

"Now, are you sleeping out here or in your bed?"

"I'll sleep in my bed. I can sleep in Kara's if you want mine."

"The couch is fine. Softer than any army cot I slept on." He winks at her. "Or I could sleep in Kara's bed."

Ana giggles, shaking her head. "Do you want her to kill you?"

"No, but I knew it would make you laugh."

"Thanks, I needed that."

"Good night, Ana."

Rafe gets up, his neck sore from a night on the couch, and his hand instinctively reaches over his shoulder. He closes his eyes, sighing. Going into the kitchen, he turns the stove on, fills the kettle, and places it on the burner. There are pastries left from the previous morning, so he sets those out as well. He walks to Ana's room and knocks on her door.

"Ana, are you awake yet?" he asks.

"Yes, I'll be out shortly."

"Take your time."

He waits for her at the table and gets to his feet when she walks out. She's wearing tight black yoga pants with an oversized grey sweatshirt. Looking over the pastries while she decides what to eat, she sits beside him.

"Thank you for setting this up."

"Of course. Ana, I'm going to ask a favor."

"Okay," she responds quietly, wondering what he could want from her.

"Would you look at me, and tell me how you're feeling?"

She shakes her head. "You heard the detectives. You know what happened. I'm too humiliated." Her head hangs lower.

"You have nothing to be ashamed of. You fought off an armed thief. You were very brave to do so."

Her head jerks up at his words. "You think I'm brave?"

He nods, swallowing his bite of food. "I do."

She returns her attention to her plate. "Thank you," she whispers.

He smiles at her. "Any time. Now eat something."

Kara calls a short while later to check in, and Ana takes the call in her bedroom. Rafe sits on the couch, trying not to eavesdrop. He's on his feet when he hears Ana yelling.

"No, Kara. Listen to me. Enough, already. You know I won't—" silence. "I promise you, I'm okay. Why are you getting so upset about this now?" Silence again. "How in the hell did you get ahold of the police report?" She throws her phone against the wall, then walks out, leaning against the doorframe. Rafe sees her trembling, her face pale. He rushes to her right before she faints. He gets her on the couch then picks up her phone, seeing it's unlocked, and calls Kara back.

"Ana, I'm sorry—"

"What did you say to her?" Rafe demands.

"Well, hello to you, too," she retorts.

"She threw her phone then fainted. What happened?"

Kara takes a deep breath. "I read the police report, and I was angry that she didn't tell me everything. I'm worried. She's… fragile, Rafe. She needs supervision."

"What are you talking about?"

"Her scars, Rafe. She isn't safe by herself."

"Well, I'm sure as hell not going anywhere."

"I'll be back tomorrow night."

"Fine," he snarls, hanging up the phone. He sits in the chair, glancing over and seeing Ana still asleep. Guilt flows in him as he looks through her phone. Kara and Work are the only two contacts in her messages, and most of her other phone contacts are restaurants. He scrolls down, unable to believe he can't find a single person's name, besides Kara. Setting the phone on the table, he sees her arm sticking out from the blanket. He kneels down to put it back under when he sees the scar. Rubbing his thumb over it, he thinks on Kara's words. *She did that to herself. Why would she do this?*

Ana's eyes open as she jerks her arm away from him. "What are you doing?" she asks, sitting up.

"I'm sorry. Kara is worried about you," he responds, sitting next to her.

Ana scoffs. "She needs to worry about herself."

"You just went through—"

"Rafe, I swear to God. Tell me I went through something traumatic one more time, I will scream."

He takes a breath, counting to ten. "I was trying to comfort you, and apparently, I failed."

"No, you didn't. I'm sorry. I shouldn't be angry with you, not after everything you've done to help me."

"How can I comfort you? How else can I help?"

"Just being here is enough. Thank you for staying."

"I promised you I wouldn't leave. I'm sorry I touched your scar. I won't do it again."

"Thank you."

"How's your pain?"

"No pain at all."

"I'm glad."

"Rafe?" she asks, looking up at him.

"Yes?" Confused, he watches her gaze fall back to the floor. "What's wrong?"

"Please tell me I won't have to deal with those two detectives again?"

"You won't, I promise. Whenever you're ready to go to the station and give an official statement, I will be right there with you, and I'll make sure of it."

"All right. We'll go now."

Ana goes into the bathroom, thinking of the two detectives. She stares at herself in the bathroom mirror, trying to push herself to get ready to go with Rafe to the police station. She strips off her shirt and slowly peels away the bandage to check for signs of infection. The scream escapes her lips at the sight of her shoulder.

"What's wrong?" Rafe asks, bursting through the door.

She looks at him, shaking her head. "I'm completely healed. How is this possible?"

He rubs his finger gently along her shoulder, surprised there isn't even a change in skin color where her wound had been. "Not even a scar." He looks at her. "You've never healed like that before?"

She runs her finger over her wrist. "These took weeks to heal. This is too weird," she admits, shaking her head again. Her fingers brush his when she reaches up to touch her shoulder.

Clearing his throat, he pulls his hand down. "I'm going to step out so you can get dressed."

"Thank you." Ana grips the vanity, still trying to contemplate how she healed so quickly. Splashing water on her face, she takes a breath and goes to her room. She slips on black work slacks with a long sleeve blue blouse, not sure how else to dress for giving a statement. When she comes back out, Rafe is waiting by the door.

They arrive at the police station in the city, as her small town shares it with the county. The building is a dull beige color, in desperate need of a fresh coat of paint. Ana groans quietly when they walk inside. The station is busy with people filing complaints, prisoners waiting for transport, and phones ringing everywhere. Rafe takes her hand, leading her up to the desk sergeant. He explains why they are there.

Ana squeezes his hand when she sees one of the detectives coming down the stairs, a grin across his face. "Well, hello, Ms. Summers. Ready to give us your statement?"

Rafe protectively steps in front of her, turning to the sergeant. "Ma'am, please. There must be a female detective she can give a statement to. He and his partner already upset her."

The sergeant nods, gives the detective the 'take a hike' gesture, and makes a phone call. A few minutes later, a young blonde detective makes her way down the stairs, carrying Ana's case file.

Introductions are made, and they follow her into a private office so she can go over everything with Ana. She squeezes Rafe's hand the whole time she is talking. He says nothing, only squeezing back from time to time. When she's finished, the detective assures her everything is in order.

"We 'misplaced' your preliminary interview, so we only have this official statement on file. I understand your reluctance, but it really is important to be honest in cases like this."

Ana hangs her head with her cheeks going flush. "I know. I'm sorry."

"Ms. Summers, please. I'm not scolding you. I can't imagine how scared you were, or how awful your experience was. Call me if you need anything," she offers, handing Ana her card. "I mean that."

"Thank you." Ana takes the card and slips it into her purse. "May we go?"

"Yes."

Rafe escorts her from the building with his arm around her shoulders.

Back at the house, Ana sits on the couch with her knees to her chest, her arms wrapped around as she chokes back her tears. Rafe sits beside her.

"What's wrong?"

Wiping her tears, she lets out a sigh. "I'm sorry. Reliving that night was a bit much for me. I'm okay now, really." The pain in her eyes reveals her true feelings.

"I wish I had gotten to you sooner. I'm sorry I was late."

She lets out a small laugh. "Are you psychic? You say that as if you knew I was in danger." She's confused when he turns away. "Rafe, what aren't you telling me?"

"Nothing," he says. He walks outside and sits at the top of the stairs on the porch. Ana follows and sits beside him, waiting a minute before she speaks.

"I won't be mad, I promise."

Taking a breath, his eyes meet hers. "I saw you at the coffee shop that day. I heard them mess up your order. You told the girl it was okay, you were nervous about a work meeting, and could understand how she was feeling. I found out you worked at the bank across the street. I was going to introduce myself. I wanted to ask you out, but I was… I was delayed."

"You wanted to ask me out? Whatever for?"

"I sit in that coffee shop all the time, and I hear people say such awful things when their orders are messed up, but not you. You were so kind to the barista, and you're so beautiful I just… I felt like I had to meet you." He looks down at his shoes. "If you tell me to go, I'll understand."

She takes his hand, squeezing it between both of her own. "Why would I tell you to go? If you hadn't been so intent to meet me, I would've bled to death in an alley. I'm only here because you saved me. I can never repay such a debt." She leans up, kissing his cheek. "Thank you for saving me."

His heart pounds in his ears as he stares at her lips, his skin on fire. He's leaning down when a taxi pulls up, and Kara jumps out. Ana and Rafe both turn and watch her run up the walkway.

She tosses her bags to the ground, running up the stairs and hugging Ana. "I'm back. I told my editor to shove it. I couldn't stand being away from you, not while you're dealing with so much." She pulls back. "I'm sorry we fought. I was only curious about the mugging. I wasn't trying to violate your privacy."

Ana nods. "I understand. I'm sorry, too."

Kara looks at Rafe as he gets to his feet. "I see she hasn't gotten rid of you?"

"Not yet."

Kara smiles at him. "Love the attitude."

She takes Ana inside, Rafe scooping up her bags and carrying them in. Kara thanks him then jumps into the bathroom to clean up. Rafe sits next to Ana on the couch in awkward silence. She studies the lines on her hand as he stares ahead, thinking of something to say. Kara comes out and stares at them.

"Are you two okay?"

"Yes," Rafe answers as he stands. He picks up his bag. "I'm going to give you girls some space. I know you've got a lot to talk about."

"That's… actually considerate. Thank you," Kara admits.

"You're welcome."

Ana stands and walks up to him. "When will I see you again?"

"Whenever you want. Just call or text me." He turns for the door but is surprised when she takes his hand. She pulls him to her, hugging him.

"Thank you for everything."

He squeezes her, smiling as he pulls back. "Any time." He looks at Kara. "I mean it," he says, going out the door.

Taking her hand, Kara leads Ana to the couch, sitting together. "I'm sorry. I read the police report, and I couldn't believe you didn't tell me everything that happened. I was so worried. Still, I had no right to get angry with you."

"I understand. I wasn't keeping it from you. I planned to tell you once you were back. I needed some time to deal with it, and I didn't want you distracted from your job."

"You worry so much over everyone but yourself." Kara gives her a small smile. "How is your shoulder? Do you need help changing the bandage?"

Averting her gaze, Ana responds, "no."

"Okay. What's going on?"

Ana pulls down her shirt collar, showing Kara her wound has completely healed. "I don't know how it happened," she admits.

I thought that didn't work here. Maybe it wasn't that serious to begin with, or it was a fluke. Trying to calm her racing mind, Kara looks at Ana. "However it happened, I'm glad. I hated seeing you in pain."

"Are you ready for dinner? There's pizza from yesterday."

"Sounds great."

The next day, Ana texts Rafe.

Ana: *I'd love to do lunch tomorrow, if you're free.*

Rafe: *I am. What time?*
Ana: *I usually take my lunch at noon.*
Rafe: *Perfect. I'll pick you up at the bank.*
Ana: *See you then.*

Ana smiles down at her phone, as she thinks of seeing him again. She puts her phone in her pocket and leaves the breakroom. At her workstation, she unlocks her drawer, answering phones, and helping her customers until five o'clock rolls around. She shuts down her drawer, balancing the till with her boss. The fresh air calms her as she walks home, and thinking of seeing Rafe again brings a smile to her face.

———————— ⋯⋯ ————————

"My, don't you look nice today."

Ana walks past Heather, ignoring her obnoxious statement. Heather has her red hair in a short, layered bob. This only further accentuates her chubby cheeks. She preens over her manicured nails, scrutinizing Ana's appearance again.

"What's the occasion? I don't think I've *ever* seen you wear make-up before." She gasps loudly when Ana's cheeks flush. "Do you have a date?" Heather laughs. "Right."

"No," Ana mumbles, getting her till and going to her station. She's grateful Heather is working the drive-up, so she can ignore her most of the day. The customers start to trickle in, and Ana smiles as she waits on them.

She glances at the clock from time to time, as if willing the hands to move faster. A few minutes before noon, the bell rings as the door opens. Ana swallows hard at the sight of the younger detective.

"Ms. Summers."

"Detective Sheffield. How can I help you?" she asks, her voice devoid of any emotion. She looks at Heather when she realizes she is trying to eavesdrop.

"I'm glad you're here." He leans over the counter, resting on his elbow as he smiles at her. She tells the vomit to stay down. "I wanted to let you know, the man who *allegedly* assaulted and groped you," he looks at Heather as he says groped, "was released on bail this morning." He turns back to Ana.

Trying to hide her surprise, she gives him her work smile. "Thank you for letting me know."

His smile widens as he winks at her. "Have a good day now." He turns and walks out.

Trembling, Ana can no longer keep the vomit down. She runs to the ladies' room, crying as she throws up. She groans when her phone buzzes in her pocket.

Rafe: *I'm here.*

Ana: *I'm in the ladies' room. Today isn't a good day. I'm sorry. Could we try again tomorrow?*

Rafe: *What's wrong?*

Ana: *Something came up. That's all.*

Rafe: *Your co-worker said a detective was here. She said he made you upset. I'm not leaving until you come out here and tell me to go.*

Ana: *Give me a minute.*

Groaning again, she walks up to the sink and rinses her mouth. She fixes her hair and make-up as best she can, grateful Kara had used her water-proof make-up on her. With a deep breath, she collects her thoughts and walks out. Rafe is waiting for her right outside the door.

"Hi," she says softly.

"Hi, yourself. Was it one of them?"

"Sheffield," she answers.

"Prick."

Ana sighs. "Rafe—"

"I'm sorry. Let's go to lunch, and you can tell me what happened."

"I don't have an appetite."

"If you were in there doing what I think you were, you need to eat. I know you don't want to pass out, too."

"Rafe, please," she begs, turning away.

He brings his finger under her chin and gently lifts her head up, so their eyes meet. "Eat something for me? So I'm not worried about you."

She nods, pulling back. She walks over to the counter, relishing the look of utter jealousy on Heather's face as she stares at Rafe. "Bill, I'm going to lunch. I'll be back in an hour."

Rafe takes her hand and escorts her out. Once outside the bank, he releases her hand.

"Your snotty co-worker looked jealous, so I had to add to that."

Ana laughs. "Thank you."

They walk to the bistro at the end of the block. The server seats them outside, and they order drinks. Rafe gives Ana his full attention. "What did Sheffield want?"

"To tell me the man who shot me was released on bail."

"What aren't you telling me?"

Shifting in her seat, her eyes meet his. "It was the way he said it. He said the man who 'allegedly' attacked me and told me to have 'a nice day' more as a warning than being nice. Everything he said and did felt… wrong." She shivers. "Ugh, he creeps me out."

"I'm sorry you had to deal with him. However, you aren't walking to and from work anymore. I will take you in the morning, and Kara can pick you up. If not, I will."

"Rafe, you're being ridiculous."

Keeping his voice low, he refutes her. "He nearly raped and killed you. Perhaps I'm not being ridiculous enough."

Ana sits back as the drinks are served. They order their meal, and she stares at her fork, pushing down the memory of that awful night. They say nothing else until the server brings out their salads. Ana pushes the croutons around, not in the mood to eat. She looks up when she realizes he is watching her intently. She makes herself take a bite.

"You were going to tell Kara about this, right?"

"No, because I know she would respond like you are."

"It's only until the trial, which in a small town like this, should be soon."

She nods, realizing there's no point in arguing. Kara would be saying the same thing; she's outnumbered. "Thanks for bringing me here for lunch. It's nice to get away from the breakroom."

The server brings their pasta and the bill. Rafe says nothing but pulls out his card as Ana eats. He slides it into the bill holder and places it on the edge of the table.

"How much is my portion?" Ana asks, opening her purse.

"Lunch is on me." He's startled when she nearly drops her bag. "Ana?"

She swallows hard. "This is… just a friendly lunch, right?"

"Right. You can pay next time," he offers, seeing the relief on her face.

"Okay. Thank you."

They finish their meal, and he walks her back to work, resisting the urge to hold her hand on the way. "Can I see you again tomorrow for lunch?"

"I wasn't thinking when I texted you that. I have a phone conference, so it will be a working lunch. Thursday?"

"Sounds good." He leans down, kissing her cheek. "Just a friendly peck," he assures her, whistling as he walks away.

She blushes and goes into the bank. The rest of the afternoon is busier than usual, which Ana doesn't mind because it means Heather doesn't have time to grill her about the detective or Rafe. At five o'clock, she realizes she never texted Kara.

Ana: *Can you pick me up from work?*

Kara: *Can't. Stuck in the basement on a work call. Are you okay?*

Ana: *I'm fine. Worried it might rain.*

Kara: *Stay dry. See you in a bit.*

She looks at her phone as she considers texting Rafe. *His sole purpose is not to watch over me day and night. He's not my guardian angel.* She chuckles at the thought. *I can walk home without anything happening. He'll never know… It's just one night. I'll be fine.* She balances her till, saying good night to Bill as she goes to leave. She raises her hand to push the door open, then freezes in her tracks. Standing across the street, she sees the man who shot her. Hands in his pocket, he stares at her intently. She immediately locks the door, watching as he walks away.

"Bill, I'm waiting for a friend to pick me up. Can I stand here in the lobby until he gets here?"

"Of course. What's wrong?"

"I think I saw the man who shot me. He was waiting across the street."

"Do we need to call the police?"

"No. Let me call my friend to pick me up."

"All right."

She opens her contact list, pressing her finger over Rafe's name and praying he answers.

"Ana?"

"Hey," she replies. "I hate to bother you, but could you pick me up from work?"

"Tomorrow?"

"No, now. I'm sorry."

"Don't move. I'll be right there."

He hangs up and drives to the bank as quickly as he can. When Ana sees him pull up and jump out of the car, she can't help but feel relieved. Bill opens the door for her, and she meets Rafe outside. "Thanks, Bill. Good night."

"Good night, Ana. See you tomorrow."

She relaxes once she's safely in the car with Rafe. "Thank you for coming to get me."

"So, where's Kara?" he asks. He glances over when she doesn't answer him. "Ana?"

She keeps her eyes forward, staring at the wood trim on the dash. "She got caught up on a work call," she answers.

"That doesn't sound like Kara."

"Please, don't get mad at me."

"What does that mean?"

"I got back to work and forgot to text her. I didn't realize until it was five o'clock. I thought it would be okay, just for tonight. But when I went to leave the bank, I saw him standing across the street."

"Who?" Rafe demands.

"The man who shot me," she replies.

The car jerks as he pulls onto the shoulder, stopping the car and running his hand through his hair. "What? You were going to walk home tonight, *knowing* he was out there?"

"Rafe, please—"

"Damn it, what if you hadn't seen him? What if he had been waiting around the corner to do God only knows what to you? Did you even think?" His voice raises with each question, until he yells the last one.

"Just get me home."

"Ana—"

"Now!" she cries out. He jerks the car back onto the road, driving the rest of the way to her house in silence. Once the car has stopped, she rushes out, slamming her door. "Thanks for the ride," she yells back at him, running for the stairs.

Before she can make it up them, he catches her, grabbing her elbow. He immediately drops it when he sees the look on her face. "We need to talk about what just happened."

"There's nothing to talk about. I made a mistake."

"What mistake?"

She scoffs. "Thinking you were different, that you were nice. You don't own me," she spits out. "You certainly have no say over what I do or where I go."

"Ana—"

"Just stop! What would've happened if he'd been waiting for me? I'd be dead. So what? Why do you care so much?"

Rafe turns away, closing his eyes and counting to ten as his heart pounds in his ears. "Ana, please. You know Kara and I both care about you."

Light floods over them when Kara suddenly opens the door and stands above them on the porch. "Are you two trying to entertain the entire neighborhood? What is wrong with you? Both of you, get in the house, now."

They follow her inside. "Kara, I'm sorry," Ana tries.

"No. I will deal with you in a minute. Rafe, what is going on?"

Ana doesn't hide the betrayal on her face. Rafe runs his hand through his hair, looking at Kara. "The man who shot Ana is out on bail. She was supposed to text you after lunch to see if you would pick her up from work. She forgot, was going to walk home by herself, but saw him across the street from the bank."

Kara turns to Ana. "Please tell me he's making that up." She sighs when Ana's head goes down. "I know you are smarter than that. What were you thinking?"

"I wasn't. I was tired and just wanted to get home. I'm sorry. Please, don't be mad at me." She cries into her hands. Rafe pulls her to him, wrapping his arms around her.

"We're not mad at you. I was angry at what could've happened, and so is Kara. It scared us."

She hugs him back, burying her face in his shirt. His heartbeat thuds quietly in her ear, his warmth spreading through her. She pulls back and looks at him. "I messed up. I'm sorry."

"We all do. After all, we're only human," Rafe says.

For some reason, Kara finds this particularly funny. Soon, all three of them are laughing, breaking the tension in the room. Ana goes to the kitchen to cook dinner. "It's my turn," Kara points out.

"I want to. I think it will help calm me down."

"I won't argue. I hate cooking," she admits, laughing again.

"I know, you always try to get out of it when it's your turn," Ana teases. "But you know how much I love it."

"Be my guest." She looks at Rafe then back to Ana. "Are you two okay now?"

"Yes," Rafe answers, walking over to Ana. "How can I help with dinner?"

"Ugh, you're joining us?"

Ana laughs. "Sis, be nice."

Kara bows, backing up to her room. "As her majesty commands." She laughs harder when Ana sticks out her tongue. Kara rolls her eyes then goes into her room.

"Sis?" Rafe asks.

"Oh, it's something we call each other. We've been best friends so long, we really feel more like sisters," she explains as she's fixing their dinner.

When the food is ready, Ana calls out to Kara, and she joins them, freshly showered and wearing her favorite Pink Floyd pajamas. Rafe is happy to watch Ana eat instead of pushing her food around. He leans back in his chair, fixating on something Ana said. Kara stands up when they've all finished and takes the dishes to the sink. She nearly drops the plate in her hand at Rafe's question.

"What did you mean, when you said so what, you'd be dead?"

Kara turns around, watching them. "Did you really say that?" she asks.

Ana looks from Kara to Rafe, then down at the table. "I didn't mean it, obviously. I was angry and said something stupid."

Kara dries off her hands and walks over to Ana, sitting beside her. "You know how much you mean to me, right? I would be devastated if anything ever happened to you. Why would you act like no one cares about what happens to you?"

"I didn't mean it," she defends herself. "Rafe was angry, and I said the first thing that popped into my head."

"Ana, I know we don't know each other very well, but I'd hate to lose you, as well. You are such a beautiful woman, and the world needs more people with your kind of light to shine."

She shakes her head. "Why would you say something like that?"

"I don't under—" Rafe starts.

"I'm not beautiful. I am as plain as they come. Why would you call me that?"

"Ana, you are the most beautiful woman I have ever seen."

Kara's eyes go wide, but she collects herself. "Ana, he means what he's saying. He cares for you. We both do. Please, be more careful. Your mistake today could've cost you your life."

"I know, Kara." She looks from her to Rafe. "I'm sorry. Please, don't be mad at what I have to say. I'm so grateful for all you've done for me these last few days, I really am, but this won't go anywhere. I don't date. I would love to be your friend, but it will never be anything more than that. I promise you."

Hiding his pain with his smile, he nods at her. "I understand. That's what I want, too. Friends?"

"Yes." Ana nods and gives him a smile back.

Kara continues rinsing the dishes and loading the dishwasher. Once she finishes, she goes to her room to give them privacy. Rafe looks Ana over.

"I'm sorry I was angry."

She nods. "You already apologized, it's okay."

"I know, but I felt it was warranted. I didn't mean to scare you or upset you, either."

"You were right, though. I wasn't thinking. I'll do better."

"We both will." He winks as he gets to his feet, smiling when she hangs her head and laughs. "I'm going to head home. What time should I be here in the morning?"

"Quarter after eight."

"I'll see you then."

She watches him leave then goes to her room, sitting on her bed as she holds a plush shark to her chest. *He's sweet and warm with me, and I see how much he cares. God, he's so good looking!* She blushes and giggles at the thought. *He makes my heart race, but I don't date. I won't get hurt. I owe myself that. I need to protect myself. Even if he*—shaking her head, she clears out the rest of the thought.

Rafe strolls into his apartment and clicks on the light. He goes to the fridge, getting out a bottle of water. Leaning against the counter, he drinks it down as he processes what she said. *I know she feels it. How can she deny this… whatever this is between us? I'm conflicted, I know what I have to do… still…* He takes another drink. *I won't push her. She will learn to trust me, to open up, or she won't. I can't make it happen. Even if I could, I wouldn't want to. This needs to be her choice, not mine. Rowenne will understand…* Rafe thinks of home, eager to return.

He tosses the empty bottle away then dumps the contents of his bag into the washing machine before going to bed.

Chapter 3

The next morning, he pulls up to her house a few minutes after eight. He's wearing dark jeans and a short sleeve black t-shirt, with the same silver rings and silver cuff on his wrist he always wears. It feels weird to ring the doorbell instead of simply going inside. He smiles when Ana opens the door.

"Hi," she says, rushing back towards her room. "I'm just about ready. Sorry."

"No rush," he replies, stepping in. She comes back out a minute later and grabs her purse off the coffee table. He walks her to the car and opens the door for her. She gives him a look but gets in.

"This is a really nice car."

He chuckles. "Thanks. Nicest one I've ever owned." He glances at her. "You don't drive?"

"No."

It's a quiet, short drive to the bank. He parks in front. "Kara is bringing you home, right?"

"Yes."

"Okay. Call or text me if anything changes."

"I will. Thanks for the ride." She smiles at him before leaving the car. Glancing back at him one more time, she goes inside and gets her station set up. Happy when her phone conference is over, she resumes at her till. It was really something Bill should do, but he passed it off to Ana with a vague excuse about wanting her to take on more of a leadership role. She's grateful when the afternoon goes by smoothly.

By the time she's finished balancing her drawer for the evening, it's almost five-thirty. She hurries out the door, worried that she's left Kara waiting. But she doesn't see Kara or her car. She pulls out her phone.

Ana: *Where are you?*

She stares at her phone, as if willing Kara to respond. Quarter to six, and still no answer to her calls or texts. Rather than waiting any longer, she leaves the bank and heads for home. She's near the end of the block when Rafe's car pulls up next to her.

"Ana!" he calls out through the open window. "What are you doing?" He jumps out of the car and runs over to her. "Why are you walking? Did you lie to me this morning?"

"No, I swear. Look," she says, getting out her phone. She shows him her calls and texts to Kara. "I don't know why she's not answering."

Rafe's eyes go wide as he looks at Ana. "You don't think the mugger—"

"Get me home, now. Please!"

They hop in the car, and he punches it, rushing to her house. He tells her to stay in the car with the windows up and the doors locked. Using her key, he lets himself in.

"Kara?" he calls out. She's not in the living room or bathroom. He's going for her room when she comes up from the basement. She freezes at the sight of him, then removes her ear buds. "Are you okay?" he asks.

"I'm fine. Why are you here? Where's Ana?" she asks, looking behind him.

"You mean the girl you were supposed to pick up from work?"

Kara looks at the clock on the microwave, swearing under her breath. "The battery in my clock downstairs must've died. I've been in the basement, developing my pictures." Her phone is on the counter. She picks it up and groans at the missed calls and texts from Ana. "I left this here to charge."

"Rafe?" Ana calls out, walking in.

"It's okay. Come in." He turns back to Kara. "She was walking home when I picked her up."

Kara runs to Ana, hugging her tight. "I'm so sorry. The clock in the basement stopped. I had no idea it was so late."

"It's okay, Kara. I'm fine. You two are taking this way more seriously than you need to." She lets out a nervous laugh.

"No, Ana. It is serious," Rafe says.

Kara shakes her head. "I can't believe I'm saying this, but I have to agree with him. You could've been hurt or killed. Why didn't you call him when you couldn't get ahold of me? Why would you walk home?"

Ana turns away, clasping her hands together. "I didn't want to bother him," she admits.

Rafe steps over to her. "I told you, it's never a bother. Friends help each other. You say you want to be friends, right?"

"Okay, you're right." Embarrassed, she goes to her room and sits on the bed. Rafe follows her, leaning in the doorway. "Can I come in?"

"Yes."

He steps in, admiring the floor to ceiling bookshelves that cover her walls. "You must read… a lot."

"I love books."

"I can see that."

"What do you want?"

He jumps at her sharp tone. "I wanted to check on you, to make sure you're okay. I'm worried, now that he's out on bail. You have to be more careful."

"You're right," she admits, getting to her feet. "Can I have a hug?"

He hesitates for a moment before pulling her into his arms. She slumps against his chest and lets him stroke her hair, enjoying the weight of his arms around her. Suddenly, she starts to tremble. "Hey, what's wrong?" he asks.

"I haven't been taking this seriously because I knew the moment I did, it would terrify me. Thinking about what could've happened, I'm so scared now."

"It's okay." He kisses the top of her head. "You're safe now. Kara and I won't let anything bad happen to you. You know that, right?"

"I do. Were you waiting for me to leave work?"

"Yes and no. I was at a meeting with a friend nearby, and I got this gut feeling. I don't want you to think I'm stalking you."

"It's okay, Rafe. I know you are." She grins up at him.

He smiles back. "Get some rest. I'll see you in the morning."

"And again at lunch."

His smile grows. "Yes, and again at lunch. You will be sick of me by next week, don't you know."

"Never," she answers, laughing. She walks him to the door.

At his apartment, he walks around in a daze, unable to stop thinking of holding her in his arms, the feeling of her head against his chest, the mint and rose smell of her hair. He gets a cold shower before turning in.

Rafe picks Ana up and gets her to work, safe and sound. He arrives at noon to take her for lunch. They arrive at the bistro.

"Can we eat outside?"

Rafe shakes his head. "Ana—"

"It's a beautiful day, and I've been stuck inside all day with tinted windows. Please?"

"It's dangerous."

Ana laughs. "Why are you so nervous? It's just lunch outside. He's not going to try anything in broad daylight with witnesses."

"You don't know that."

They compromise, sitting inside by the window. The server takes their order and walks off. Ana looks at him. "So, what do you do when you're not stalking young girls?"

"Lower your voice! That's not funny," he says, shaking his head as he grins at her.

She smiles at him. "I thought it was."

"I read, watch news on my tablet, go to bookstores and cafés."

Ana lets out a quiet groan. "I haven't been to a bookstore in ages. There's only one here, and it's on the other side of town. Kara refuses to take me; she thinks I already have too many books."

"No such thing."

"Thank you. That's what I say. What do you like to read?"

The server brings out their meal. Rafe takes a sip of his lemonade, thinking for a moment. "I like Shakespeare and Tolkien. As far as American writers, I rather enjoy your Stephen King. His works give me goosebumps."

"I love all of those, too. I mostly read fantasy series, poetry, mystery, and true crime."

"True crime? And you still tried to walk home alone last night?" he teases.

"Hey, just because I read true crime doesn't mean I expect it to happen to me."

They continue discussing their favorite books as they eat lunch. Walking with her back to work, he can't help but wonder how she's really feeling. He sees how hard she tries to mask them. She's going for the door when he takes her hand.

"Promise me you will not walk home tonight, that if Kara doesn't show up or anything happens, you will call me."

She nods. "I promise, Rafe." She glances down at his hand holding hers. He pulls away.

"Thank you." He hops in his car and takes off. Ana goes inside. She unlocks her drawer, counting down the hours until her shift is over. On her last break at three-thirty, her phone vibrates on the table. She picks it up, seeing a text notification.

Kara: *I have to go into the office tonight. Can Rafe pick you up?*
Ana: *Yes, that's fine.*
Kara: *Thank you. I'm trying to make nice with my editor, after I told him off.* :)
Ana: *No worries*

She texts Rafe about picking her up, and he responds right away, of course saying yes. Five minutes until closing, Rafe comes in. He flashes her a smile as he goes into the restroom. The bell above the main door jingles again. Everything freezes as she realizes she is face to face with the man who shot her. Her shoulders fall, but she recovers quickly and puts on her work smile, pretending she doesn't recognize him.

"Evening. How can I help you?" she asks, amazed at how steady her voice is.

"Don't try that with me. You know exactly who I am."

Her smile fades away, and she purses her lips. "What do you want?"

"Empty your drawer," he demands, shoving a bag at her. She looks down at the gun in his hand.

"Yes, sir." She opens it up, removing all the money and shoving into the bag. She slides it across the counter to him. Rafe catches her eye as he leaves the restroom, assessing the situation. Keeping her attention on the man before her, her body trembles in fear.

"Sorry it has to be this way," he says, smirking as he raises his arm. Rafe charges at him, tackling him to the floor before he can pull the trigger. They wrestle, Rafe trying to free the gun from the man's hand, and the man struggling to get out from underneath Rafe's strong frame. Both go still when the gun goes off.

"Rafe!" Ana cries out, running around the counter and rushing to his side. "You're hurt," she cries, quivering at the blood covering his shirt

"It's not my blood," he says, sitting up. "The thief was shot, not me." He looks at her. "I'm okay."

Neither one of them speak on the ride back to Ana's house. Their minds are busy reliving the past hour, the ambulance arriving, the paramedics carrying the body away, the police taking their statements. They walk inside, where Rafe breaks the silence.

"I'm sorry, could I use your shower?" he asks.

"Please. There are clean towels in the linen closet there. Are all of your clothes ruined?"

"Everything below the waist is fine. My shirt and jacket are ruined."

"Give them here." He takes them off and hands them to her without a word. She bites her lip at his muscled torso before turning away. "I'll throw the shirt in the wash. I still have your hoodie. I just washed it yesterday."

"Thank you."

"Help yourself to anything you need in there."

In the bathroom, he strips down and turns the shower as hot as it'll go. Ana's mint and rosewater body wash fills his nostrils. He cleans himself, feeling guilty when her scent causes him to react, and he pours more body wash into his hand, cleaning himself all over, thoroughly.

While Rafe is cleaning up, Ana realizes her clothes had also gotten bloody when she was clinging to him in the bank. She strips down to her underwear, pre-treats everything, and throws it all into the washing machine. Then she goes into Kara's room to use her shower. She's wrapped in only a towel when she runs into Rafe on the way to her room.

"I'm... I um... I need to get dressed."

He nods, trying not to stare at her petite frame, the towel snug on her damp body. "Okay. I'll be on the couch." She watches him walk over and sit down. Embarrassed, she runs into her room and slips on her yoga pants with a sweatshirt before returning to him.

"You saved me again," she says, standing before him.

"Yes," he answers, nodding his head, his voice emotionless.

She sits next to him. "What's wrong?"

"So much blood..."

Her hand comes up to her mouth, a small gasp escaping her lips. "Is it bringing up bad memories? From when you served in battle?"

"Yes," he admits.

"I'm so sorry. This was completely my fault."

Her words snap him back to reality. "What? Ana, no. Don't be ridiculous. This was his fault, not yours. You cannot blame yourself for what happened. Do you understand me?" He pulls her into his arms.

"I won't," she says, wrapping her arms around him. Her hands are on his lower back when she brings them up towards his shoulders. He pulls away, flinching in pain. "What's wrong? What did I do?"

"I'm sorry. I have scars on my back. Please, don't touch them. I should've told you about them sooner."

Without realizing she's doing it, she gently rubs the scar on her wrist, looking at him. "I can understand that. I'm sorry."

He leans down and kisses her forehead. "You owe no apology, as you did not know about them."

"Are they from battle?" she asks.

"From my duty, yes. I don't wish to talk about them."

"Hmm, sitting here, not wanting to talk about scars. Maybe we are two of a kind." She shakes her head. "Will you hold me? I can't seem to get warm." The two of them snuggle together on the couch, his arms wrapped tightly around her.

"Good God, what happened now?" Kara asks when she walks in and sees them.

Ana shoots her a dirty look over her shoulder. Kara sits in the chair beside the couch, waiting for one of them to explain. "The man who mugged me came in to rob the bank. He was going to kill me, but Rafe killed him instead."

Her mouth opens in surprise. "What? Are you serious?" she asks, bringing her hand to her mouth. "I'm so sorry, that's horrible, but I'm glad he's dead because that means you're safe now. Are you okay? Was anyone else hurt?"

"We're okay, just a little traumatized."

"Of course, you are. I can't even imagine. Have you two eaten?" Kara asks.

"No. There's plenty from yesterday, though. I can heat it up." Ana looks at Rafe. "Do you think you can eat?"

"I will if you will."

When she nods, he helps her up, taking her into the kitchen to take care of food while Kara showers and changes. Kara comes out, joining them for a quiet dinner. Ana watches Rafe, making sure he eats. He gives her a reassuring smile.

Once they've finished, Rafe looks at Ana. "I'm going to go. Will you be all right?"

"I'm fine. I have Kara. I'm worried about you being alone."

"I'll be okay. Really," he says.

"Still, call me if you need to talk. Since the bank will be closed tomorrow, I will probably sleep in. I don't care what time it is. If you need me, call me."

"Okay."

He hugs her and leaves. She turns to Kara. "Can we—"

"Sleep out here tonight? You don't even have to ask. I'm not leaving you alone." Ana sleeps on the couch while Kara sleeps in her recliner.

Ana dreams she's at the bank, the mugger standing before her. He brings his gun up, aiming for her, and she screams when he fires the gun and kills her. Kara shakes her to wake her up.

"Ana! It's a nightmare. You're okay now, you're safe." She hugs her tight, softly shushing her and muttering reassuring words in her ear. Ana opens her eyes and looks up at Kara.

"Sis?"

"I'm right here. You're safe now."

"Do you think Rafe is sleeping? He was traumatized, too. I'm worried about him. Should I call him?"

"Text him. If he's awake, he'll answer. If he's sleeping, well, you know."

Ana grabs her phone off the coffee table.

Ana: *Are you awake?*

Rafe: *What's wrong?*

Ana: *Nothing, just a nightmare. I wanted to check on you.*

Rafe: *Are you sure? I can come there.*

Ana: *I don't want to bother you, but I need to see you.*

Rafe: *I'm on my way.*

Ana gets up, going to her room to change out of her thin pajamas. She puts on her yoga pants and sweatshirt then walks back out.

"Why did you change?" Kara asks.

"Rafe is coming here."

"Ana—"

"He offered."

Kara sighs. "Fine. If that's what you want."

Ana runs to the door when Rafe knocks, and she opens it. As soon as he walks in, she falls into his arms, holding him tight. He takes her hand and walks her to the couch where the two of them sit side by side, hands still clasped together.

"Are you okay?" he asks, his voice full of concern.

"Yes," she replies. "I dreamed he killed me."

He strokes her cheek with his thumb. "I'm so sorry."

"Don't," she says. "You saved me."

Kara looks them over, debating. "I'm going to bed." She looks at Ana. "Wake me if you need anything." She glances at Rafe, unsure of how to feel about him, then goes into her room.

He holds Ana against his chest, trying to calm her pounding heart. "It really scared you, didn't it?"

"Yes," she admits.

"Me, too. It's over now, you're safe."

She pulls back, looking him in the eyes. "I don't know if it's because you saved me or because we went through this together. Maybe nearly being killed has made me realize life is too short." She stands up and moves toward him. One leg at a time she kneels on the couch, his legs resting between hers. "I'm sorry, what I said before."

"About what?" His chest is thumping so hard he has trouble focusing on her words.

"About us being friends and nothing more. I know we've just met, but," she tucks her hair behind her ear, "I have feelings for you. I want to see where this leads."

He stares into her eyes. "Ana, I'm going to kiss you. Is that all right?" he asks, his voice carrying his want to her.

"Please," she says with a smile.

He leans in, their lips meeting with a soft impact. Her heart is racing as her blood is consumed with fire. She grabs his hair as she kisses him harder. His head is swimming, and all he can hear is his heart drumming, threatening to burst right out of his chest. He pulls back, breathless while she gasps for air. Their eyes meet and so do their lips again. He brings his hands up against her back, pulling her into him.

They break apart, panting, and resting their foreheads together.

"Rafe?" she breathlessly asks.

"Yes?"

"I told you how I feel about you. How do you feel about me?"

He chuckles softly. "This didn't answer that for you?" He tries to kiss her again, but she slides off his lap and sits next to him. "Ana, I told you in the beginning how I feel about you. What else do you want me to say?"

"I don't understand. I'm so plain. How can you be attracted to me?"

"Why do you think you're plain? Why do you have so much self-doubt? You are breathtakingly beautiful. I kept my feelings in check after you said you only wanted to be friends. Truth is, I fell for you the moment I laid eyes on you. Getting to know you, learning about you, has only deepened those feelings even more." A few tears fall down her cheeks. "What did I do? Why are you upset?"

"No, these are happy tears. No one has ever said anything like that to me before, not even close. Kara is my best friend and sister. She tells me how pretty and sweet I am, but I've never had any interest from boys," her hands clench as she looks away, "unless they were being mean. That's why it's difficult to believe you could feel that way."

"Look at me, please." He waits until she raises her head, meeting his gaze. He leans in, planting a gentle kiss on her mouth. "I mean it. Every word."

She bites her lip, staring at his, then leans forward and kisses him. She lays her head against his chest, bringing her feet up onto the couch.

"Will you be able to sleep some more?" he asks.

"I think so."

"I'm right here. I'm not going anywhere. You're safe now, mia estrela."

"What does that mean?"

"I called you my star. Is that okay?"

She smiles, nodding. "It's really pretty. I love it."

He returns the smile, pulling the blanket over her. "Good, now get some sleep." He turns off the lamp. She lays her head in his lap, nodding off while he gently strokes her hair. He sits there, thinking he won't get any more sleep. Or so he thinks when he yawns as the sleepiness creeps in. He lies down, repositioning her so she's sleeping on his chest. Holding her wrapped in his arms, he falls asleep.

"What the hell?" Kara yells, walking out of her room and seeing them asleep together on the couch.

Jolted awake, Ana nearly falls to the floor. Rafe holds her steady and helps her to her feet. She looks at Kara. "What's wrong?" Ana asks.

Kara opens her arms, gesturing to them. "This! You two, that's what."

"Sis—"

"Uh-uh. Don't try that with me."

Rafe takes Ana's hand, bringing it up to his chest, clutching it between both of his. "Kara, we are a couple now."

Shocked, she takes a step back. "Excuse me?"

Ana nods. "It's true. I asked him last night. This was my decision, I promise."

Kara takes a deep breath, weighing the situation as she looks at Rafe. "Ana, please go to your room for a moment. I need to speak with him in private."

Ana tenses up, stepping protectively in front of Rafe. "About what?"

"Trust me, please?" Kara asks, her voice softened.

Ana looks from Kara to Rafe, who gives her a reassuring nod. She swallows hard, then goes to her room. Rafe steps over to Kara. "Go on."

She snorts. "As if I'd need your permission. Look, I won't do the whole 'hurt her, and I'll have to kill you' cliché. I'd say we are well beyond that, but you have to know, she's never dated, never had a boyfriend. You will take this slow, do it right, or I will cut off your favorite appendage and shove it down your throat. Understood?"

Rafe stifles a laugh, trying to look serious. He takes a moment to respond. "Yes, Kara, I understand. I promise you, hurting her is the last thing I want." His eyes close at his words, before he takes a breath and looks at her.

Kara walks over, knocking on Ana's door. "We're done." She goes back to her room to get dressed.

Ana approaches Rafe, her hands clasped tightly together. "Everything okay?" she asks, her voice small.

Rafe smiles at her. "Oh, yes. It will take more than your roommate threatening me with bodily harm to scare me away."

She gasps. "Did she really?"

He laughs as he hugs her. "It's okay. I am grateful you have someone like her, someone who is protective of you and cares for you so." He caresses her neck. "I need to go."

"Do you have to?"

"I need to go home, shower, and change into fresh clothes. I'll pick up breakfast and come back. Is that okay?"

"Of course. I'm sorry."

"It's okay, mia estrela. I'll be back before you know it." He leans down, looking into her eyes. She nods, gripping his neck as he kisses her.

She runs to her room, changing into jeans and a long sleeve shirt. She joins Kara in the kitchen. "Rafe is bringing us breakfast."

"All right."

Ana and Kara are waiting in the kitchen when he walks in, drinks in one hand and donuts in the other. Kara runs over, grabbing a coffee. "Thanks."

"Sis!" Ana says, laughing. She goes to Rafe, helping with the food. They set everything on the kitchen table. Rafe hands Ana a cup.

"Chocolate peppermint boba tea."

Kara gags. "How do you drink that?"

"It's better than coffee," Ana says with a laugh.

Kara gasps, pretending to be offended. "How dare you say such a thing?"

Ana and Rafe laugh. "Because it's true," Ana replies.

Kara shakes her head, eating another donut hole. "Hmm. These are great. I guess you can't be too bad. You can stick around, at least until I get tired of junk food."

Ana laughs. "That will never happen." She looks up at Rafe, still unable to believe how he feels about her. She tries making sense of it, but she doesn't understand how someone so attractive and brave could be interested in timid, quiet, bookworm her. Rafe catches the worry on her face.

"Mia estrela, what's wrong?"

She shakes her head gently, giving him a shy smile. "Nothing."

"What did you call her?" Kara asks.

"Mia estrela. It means—"

"I know what it means. I was surprised, is all. Where did you learn it?"

"Maybe in my travels, or perhaps in a book. I'm not sure."

"Where did you say you were from?"

Ana turns to Kara. "Why are you interrogating him all of a sudden? Can't we just enjoy a nice breakfast?"

"It's okay, Ana. I'll answer her questions." He looks at Kara. "I was born in California, but we travelled all over the world because my father was a captain in the army. He retired a few years ago, then I enlisted. I did my tour and got out, only to lose both of my parents in a car accident. Anything else you want to know?" He glances down when Ana takes his hand, giving it a gentle squeeze.

Kara keeps her face blank, her thoughts unreadable. "Not right now."

"Okay, then." He gives Ana his attention. "Would you like to do something this afternoon? We could go to the museum or the bookstore."

"I would love to, but I am not in any shape to go anywhere yet. I'm sorry."

"Ana, I want you to listen very carefully to me. You need to understand this from the beginning. If you ever don't want to go somewhere with me, or do something I am doing, or anything along those lines, you never have to apologize or explain yourself. Tell me you understand."

She looks at him. "I'll try. I can't make any promises, but I do understand what you're saying."

He nods. "Okay. Do you want me to stay with you today, or do you want the time with Kara? Either one is fine."

"I'd like to spend the day with both of you."

"Sweetie, I have to run into the office. There is an issue with the operating system, and none of the IT people can figure it out. Mr. Markson asked me to take a look."

Ana looks at Rafe, laughing. "She refuses to ask for help. So, when she started the job, whenever she had an issue, she would research how to fix it herself."

"I'll bring home Chinese," Kara offers.

Ana smiles at her. "That sounds good."

Kara goes into her room, shoving her laptop into her bag and pushing her hair out of her face. She grabs a hair tie off her dresser and pulls her hair into a loose ponytail, then wraps her blue flannel shirt around her waist. On her way out the door, she gives Ana a peck on the cheek.

"Be good, sis," she says, shooting Rafe a warning look on her way out.

"I like her," he teases.

Ana laughs. "She's definitely something not of this world. I think the mold broke when they made her."

"I hope."

She laughs again. "Be nice." She gathers dishes and utensils as Rafe cleans up the trash. They get the kitchen straightened up then go into the living room and sit on the couch. He stares at her lips, nearly moaning when she bites her bottom lip.

He gently grips her face, searching her eyes. She gives him a smile, nodding slightly. He pulls her to him and kisses her. She climbs onto his lap, her mouth on his as her fingers strum through his hair. She pulls away, walking over to the window and holding her hands behind her back as she looks out.

"I'm sorry," he says.

She turns to him, surprised. "For what?"

"Whatever I did that made you pull away."

"No, it's me. I've never dated before. This is all so new to me." She lowers her head. "I'm also still trying to deal with everything that happened with the man who shot me. I'm sorry if I disappoint you."

He stands up, walking over and lacing his arm around her waist. "What did I say about apologizing? No, you aren't disappointing me. We witnessed a man die. We both need time to cope."

"Thank you," she says, laying her head against his chest.

"Ana, are you going to be okay? You been through so much in a short amount of time."

She looks up at him. "I think so. I know how to cope, how to compartmentalize, and I'm trying not to disassociate," she says with a quiet laugh.

"Whatever you need, you let me know. I will help however I can." He leans down and kisses her forehead.

She stands on her tiptoes to reach his lips with hers. "Do you want to talk about what happened?" she asks, leading him to the couch. "I know it upset you, too."

He shrugs. "I've seen worse."

"Rafe, please, don't do that." He looks at her. "I know you've been through hell that I can't even imagine. Please, don't bottle everything up."

"Was I scared? Yes. Do I regret killing him? No. He hurt you, and I would do it again in a heartbeat. Anything else?" he asks, no emotion in his voice or eyes.

Ana leans away from him and crosses her arms tightly across her chest. "You don't have to be an ass about it," she mutters.

"You wanted to know how I was feeling, and I told you."

"You sounded like a robot." There are small round imprints on her arm from the strong grip of her fingers. "Like you weren't taking it seriously. Like you weren't taking me seriously," she adds, looking down.

Rafe sighs and pulls her hands away, forcing her body to relax a little. "I'm sorry, I didn't mean to do that. I didn't realize how hard it is for me to talk about this stuff. You have to know it's not about you. Please, don't think I would not take you seriously."

"I just want to be here for you."

"I know," he says, nodding. "What about you? Is there anything you want to talk about from that night?"

"The gun to my head. I knew you were there, and I thought that was it. I thought for sure he was going to pull the trigger, and I would be killed right in front of you. I didn't want you to see that."

"You were about to die, but you were worried about me? That's too much, mia estrela!"

She blushes, sneaking a peek at him. "I was already starting to fall for you, even if I was denying it myself."

He leans down and kisses her. "Well, I'm glad you're not denying it anymore." He grins at her.

She snuggles up to him, laying her head on his chest. "Did you get any sleep last night? Before you came over here, I mean?"

"No. I laid in bed, playing the scene over and over in my mind. I tried to fall asleep, but I couldn't."

"I didn't want to sleep. I knew I was going to have nightmares. Kara and I slept out here so I wouldn't be alone, but I still had them. I didn't think anything would help."

"But I did?"

She smiles at him. "Yes, you did. Besides Kara, that's the first time I've ever slept next to anyone."

His heart aches at her words. "What about your parents?"

She shakes her head. "I never knew them. I'm an orphan. I grew up in a foster home, until I was removed at the age of ten."

"Why were you removed?"

She looks down, debating how much she is ready to reveal. "It was nothing," she answers quietly.

"It's okay, you don't have to tell me, not until you're ready." The look in his eyes is sincere, and it calms her down.

"It just..." She takes a breath, holding it in and then letting it out. "It just wasn't a good situation, so social services removed me and placed me somewhere else." There is a pause between them while he waits for her to share more. A panic creeps into her, an unsettled yet familiar feeling that comes anytime someone shows an interest in getting to know her. She continues, afraid that if she doesn't the tears will come. "I'm sorry, I'm not used to opening up like this. I guess I'm afraid you'll learn something about me and see me differently."

With one quick move of his hand, her face is only inches from his. "Ana, I want to know you. Everything about you, I don't care what it is."

"How can you say that? How can you be sure?"

"Because I've seen how pure your heart is. How do you have such a big, full heart in a tiny body? You are a warrior. You were attacked, twice, and you've hardly cried. You are incredibly strong."

The tears start to fall, and she turns away from him. "Maybe you should go," she manages to get out between ragged breaths.

"What? Why?" he asks.

"Because I can't stay strong much longer. I don't want you to see me like this."

All he can think to do is wipe away her tears and pull her into his arms. "Ana, I want to be here for you. I want my words to soothe you, my arms to comfort you. Will you let me do that?"

In his arms, she unravels, allowing herself to cry freely for the first time since the mugging. The whole time, he strokes her hair and quietly reassures her. When the flow of tears slows down, he hands her tissues, and she blows her nose. As she wipes her face, she wonders how she got so lucky to have met someone like him.

They spend the afternoon watching a nature documentary that Ana has seen dozens of times but never gets sick of watching. Any time a cute animal comes on the screen, she giggles, and he watches her, captivated. When a snake is about to eat a mouse, she buries her face in his shirt, clutching it tightly. He strokes her hair and assures her when the scene is over.

Kara comes home with Chinese food. She laughs as Ana tries teaching Rafe how to use the chopsticks. In the middle of dinner, Ana's boss calls, and she goes into the other room to answer it. After some time has passed, Kara and Rafe exchange a worried look when she hasn't come back out. They rush to her door.

"Sis?" Kara tries. "Are you okay? Who was on the phone?"

"Go away," Ana pleads.

"You know I will come in there. Talk to us."

Ana opens the door, leaning against the frame and looking at them. Her eyes are red, and her cheeks are damp. "That was Bill, my boss. He said the bank sees me as a 'liability' after what happened. He had to let me go."

"Oh, Ana." Kara grabs her arm and pulls her in, hugging her tight. "That's bullshit. Is that even legal? I can't believe they would do that to you. You've worked your ass off for that place for three years."

"They fired you because of what someone else did?" Rafe asks, still not believing it himself. "That is ridiculous."

"You know what, maybe this is a blessing in disguise," Kara says, wiping a tear from Ana's cheek. "I wasn't looking forward to you going back there on Monday anyway. Take some time off, and recuperate from what you just went through."

"Kara, that's not fair to you."

"We may not be rich, but you know I have never worried about money. We will be fine. Take a few weeks, even a month if you need to."

"She's right. I think it's a good idea."

Kara turns to Rafe. "Don't think you're earning any points with me."

"Who said I'm trying to?" he snaps back.

She rolls her eyes at him and ushers Ana back into the kitchen, hoping she can get her to eat a bit more. Rafe excuses himself to the bathroom, and Kara uses the opportunity to voice her concerns.

"I say this with love, but you need a break from him. This isn't... healthy, spending so much time with someone you just met. Tell him you have plans tomorrow. It's Saturday, so you and I can do whatever you want. We can go to the bookstore."

"Believe it or not, I had already thought of that." Kara fails to hide her surprise. "He and I have both been through so much, we could use some time apart. I don't want to come across as clingy or needy," Ana says.

"Good. It's settled." She smiles and picks up another piece of sesame chicken with her chopsticks.

Rafe joins them. "I'll head home now. I know you two would like some time together. I am busy tomorrow, but could I take you to lunch on Sunday?"

Ana smiles at him. "I would love that."

She walks him to the door, holding his hand, and reluctant to say goodbye for the evening. But she knows Kara is right.

"Thank you for today. Text me tomorrow?" she asks.

"Of course, mia estrela," he says. One last kiss, and he leaves.

Kara comes out of the bathroom and finds Ana sitting on the couch. "He's gone?" she asks.

"Yes. I'll see him Sunday."

"I'll be honest, I'm kind of surprised at how well you're handling all of this. I hate to admit it, but I think Rafe is a big part of that."

"I'm confused about my feelings for him."

"What do you mean?"

"I've never been in love and had never been kissed. He is so gentle with me, asking my permission before kissing me—"

"You've already kissed?"

"Yes."

"Ana, you need to take this slow. As you said, this is all new for you. I know it's passionate and amazing. You have butterflies in your stomach. More importantly, though, is the getting to know each other."

"We talked today. We kissed a little, but we mostly talked."

"I'm glad to hear that. I don't mean to get too personal, but I've never asked this before since you weren't interested in dating. How do you feel about sex?"

"Kara!"

"I'm sorry, but when I tried to bring it up before, you would go flush or change the topic. Since you are seeing someone, I just want to help. Are you thinking about having sex with him?"

Ana jumps to her feet, turning away. Kara stands next to her, trying to look in her eyes. Ana can only stare at the floor. "Please, stop."

"I didn't mean to upset you. It's just... I don't know how much you know or even what you know, since you didn't have loving parents to sit down and talk about this with."

"I don't want to," she admits, keeping her head down.

"You don't want to talk about it?"

"I don't want to... to have sex."

"What do you mean? Until it's a long-term relationship? Or until you're married?"

"Ever."

"Ana, look at me." She doesn't budge. "Please." Ana lifts her head, meeting Kara's gaze. "Why do you feel that way?"

Ana wraps her arms around her stomach and walks over to the window. She loves looking out at the few trees that are in the park, before she closes her eyes. "Because I won't like it."

"How do you know? Have you done it before?"

"No."

"Then why do you think you won't like it?"

"Maybe I should break up with him now, before he gets any more attached to me than he already is."

"Ana!" Kara cries out, exasperated. "What are you talking about?"

"I'm getting cleaned up and turning in." She turns on her heel, going to her room and gathering fresh clothes. Her heart is racing as she thinks of what she's endured. Opening the door, she finds Kara blocking the doorway. She walks in, taking the clothes from Ana and setting them down.

"Ana, please talk to me."

They sit on the bed, Kara holding Ana's hand. Ana takes a breath. "I told you a little about my foster father, that he hit me. I told you about him breaking my ribs, that I was finally taken away from him."

"Yes."

"I never told you why he did it."

"I never knew there was a reason."

"He would come into my room at night," Ana starts, staring at her comforter and clutching Kara's hand. "He never…" She shakes her head. "But he did other things." Unable to contain it anymore, she breaks into tears.

"Oh, my God. Ana! Why did you never tell me this?"

"I was too ashamed. I didn't want you to be disgusted by me. Rafe can never know, not any of this. He would hate me."

"That won't happen. I would never feel that way about you. I won't tell him, Ana, I promise. But if your relationship gets serious, you may want to. I've seen the way he looks at you, the way he takes care of you. I don't think any of this would change that." Kara smiles, a sad smile, and touches Ana's cheek affectionately. Then her eyes flash with confusion. "But wait, why did that make your foster father break your ribs?"

"I told on him to a teacher. I didn't know she had a crush on him. She would call him in for parent-teacher conferences all the time, and she would ask me questions about him. I didn't put it together. So, instead of alerting the authorities, she called him."

Kara gasps. "You needed help and your teacher—" Without finishing her sentence she pulls Ana into her arms. "I'm grateful that son of a bitch is dead, or I would kill him myself."

"I am, too." She pulls back. "Can I get cleaned up now? I really need to, after talking about that."

"Of course."

Ana gets a shower, crying as she stands under the hot water and lets it wash away her fear and shame. She dries off and slips on her pajamas. Lying in bed, she stares at the ceiling as she fights the ghosts from her past who will not let her rest. She turns her thoughts to Rafe, to being held in his arms as he strokes her hair, and finally drifts off to sleep.

At two in the morning, the quiet of the house is broken by Ana's screams of terror. Kara runs in. She wakes her up and sits on the edge of the bed, waiting for her to calm down.

"Nightmare?"

"Yes."

"The bank?" Kara asks. Ana nods. "Do you want me to sleep in here with you?"

"No. I'll be okay. Thank you, though."

Kara hugs her again and leaves. Ana pulls her phone from the charger.

Ana: *Are you up?*
Rafe: *Yes. Everything okay?*
Ana: *Just a nightmare.*
Rafe: *I'm sorry.*
Ana: *It's okay. Were you already up or did I wake you?*
Rafe: *I was already up.*
Ana: *You don't sleep much, do you?*
Rafe: *I sleep enough. Speaking of which, you need more sleep. We'll talk tomorrow.*
Ana: *Fine.*
Rafe: *What's wrong?*

Ana slams her phone on the nightstand. She goes into the kitchen to get a drink of water and clear her head. *I don't know why I got so angry. I guess I thought he would be up for talking, since he's not sleeping, either. He's right. I should at least try and get more sleep.*

She's sitting on the bed when her phone vibrates. She picks it up, seeing she has three new messages.

Rafe: *Are you okay?*
Rafe: *Please talk to me.*
Rafe: *What did I do?*

Her anger rises at his response. She quickly types and is about to set her phone back down when he responds.

Ana: *Nothing. It's no big deal. Good night.*
Rafe: *It was a big deal, otherwise you wouldn't be ignoring me. I'm worried about you.*
Ana: *I'm fine. Good night.*
Rafe: *What did I do that upset you?*
Ana: *Nothing. GOOD NIGHT.*

She turns her phone to silent and lies back down, falling into an uneasy sleep. Images flash in her mind of the mugger, her foster father, the group home she was put in after. She wakes up in a cold sweat and looks at the clock. It's only five. Sighing, she prays for a few more hours of sleep.

Chapter 4

Ana's cooking eggs and toast for breakfast when Kara walks into the kitchen, still in pajamas with her hair in a messy bun.

"Morning, beautiful," Ana teases.

Kara returns the greeting with a crude gesture. "Don't start with me. We're not all early risers like her highness."

Ana laughs, blowing her a kiss. "If you say so."

Kara takes her coffee and sits at the table. "You're in a good mood this morning. Get more sleep after your nightmare?"

"Yep."

"Good."

Ana fixes up the plates and carries them to the table. They're halfway through their meal when the doorbell rings. Kara goes to answer it and finds Rafe standing on the porch, looking frantic.

"I thought you were busy today?" Kara asks.

"Is Ana all right?" he asks urgently.

Kara opens the door wider, so he can see Ana at the table. He walks in. Ana meets him in the living room. "What's wrong?" she asks.

"I should be asking you that. I called and texted this morning, and you never replied. Why are you ignoring me? What did I do?"

"Oh, no, Rafe. I'm so sorry. I silenced my phone last night and got up to make breakfast without even looking at it."

He closes his eyes in relief. "I was worried about you."

Kara makes a gagging noise and sits back down at the table to finish her breakfast, after Rafe gives her a stern look. Ana takes his hand. "I didn't mean to worry you so much."

"I'm sorry. You probably think I'm nuts, showing up here like this." Kara chokes down a laugh. Rafe ignores her.

"I don't think you're nuts. I was angry last night because I wanted to talk, and I felt like you were blowing me off. But I shouldn't have left it like that."

"That wasn't my intention. I wanted you to get some rest."

"I know that now. I thought talking to you would help me sleep."

"Already bored with him?" Kara inquires.

Rafe turns to her but bites his tongue, thinking better of it. He looks at Ana. "It was a misunderstanding. I'm sorry. Do you forgive me? Do you think I'm crazy?"

"Crazy? Hmm, that depends. Do I have one or two missed calls and texts, or do I have fifty-seven voicemails?"

He laughs. "I called and texted once, each."

"Then yes, we're all good. You're not crazy."

He leans down and kisses her. "I do have to go. You girls have fun today." He kisses her again, then leaves.

She walks back to the table, looking at Kara when she sighs. "What?"

"Okay, that was actually kind of sweet. Don't get any ideas, though. That doesn't mean I like him."

"You will." Ana looks away.

"What's wrong?"

She sighs. "I had this feeling when I first woke up at the hospital that I knew him from somewhere. I kind of forgot about it, but today I had that feeling again, that I'd met him before."

"Met him or saw him? Maybe you saw him at the coffee shop or the grocery store?"

"No, I know I've met him before."

"If you had met him, I'm pretty sure you would've mentioned something like that to me." Kara shakes her head. "I'll get dressed, then we'll head out."

Ana gathers dishes and cleans up, her mind reeling as she tries to think of where she knows him from. Kara walks out, dressed in her faded, ripped jeans, an oversized Metallica shirt, and a red flannel shirt tied at her waist. Ana looks down at her dark jeans and solid blue long sleeve shirt.

"I wish I could be more fashionable like you."

Kara stops in her tracks. "I've known you for five years. Not once have you mentioned anything about fashion." She jerks her thumb towards the door. "Is it because of him?"

"No, but you both dress to represent who you are. He has his leather jacket and silver jewelry, you've got your band t-shirts. All my clothes are so bland, they say nothing about my personality. Well," she lets out a small laugh, "unless my personality is bland."

Kara doesn't return the laugh. "Ana, we've talked about this. You don't self-deprecate. Right?"

"Right."

"Now, do you want to do some clothes shopping after the bookstore? There are a few cute boutiques nearby."

"Maybe."

Once inside the bookstore, Kara goes to the photography section while Ana walks up to look at fiction new releases.

"Hey, cutie. I haven't seen you here before."

She looks up when she realizes he's talking to her. She looks him over. He's taller than her, thinning strawberry blond hair and a ripped flannel jacket with jeans. She goes back to reading the flap of the book in her hand. "No, thanks," she replies. She puts the book down and quickly walks to the literature section.

"There's no reason to be rude."

Regret hits her as she realizes her mistake. They are in the corner, out of sight. She's trapped with a wall behind her and shelves on either side. She pulls out her phone, sending Kara an SOS and telling her where she is. Turning to face him, she has a death grip on her phone.

"You're right. I'm sorry," she offers, smiling as she tries to buy herself some time.

He steps up to her. "What kind of books do you like to read? Mystery? Sci-fi? Oh, I know… *romance.*" He smirks at her.

She swallows hard. "I like literature and mysteries. You?"

"You look like a mystery, one I would love to unravel, head to toe."

Her knuckles are white from gripping her phone, praying for Kara to find her. "You seem like a nice guy, but I have a boyfriend."

He laughs. "I'm sure you do. Anyway, what say we get out of here? We could go back to my place for an in-depth discussion of our favorite genres."

Ana's breath catches in her throat. She thinks of nodding, that she could follow him away from the shelves, but realizes she can't see over them, and she doesn't know where Kara is or if anyone else in the store. "I'm sorry, but I can't. I'm here with my friend. She's probably looking for me." She takes a step forward, trembling when he blocks the way with his arm. "Please let me pass."

"You're so polite, aren't you? I bet you are quite naughty in the sheets," he whispers in her ear.

Her face flushes red. She begs the tears not to fall, to not give him the satisfaction of seeing her like that. She calms herself down. "I will scream if you don't move," she threatens.

"Go ahead. I would love to hear you scream."

Before she can react, Kara grabs his arm and flips him onto the floor. She puts her boot on his chest. "What are you doing?" she demands.

He puts his hands up. "It was just a little harmless flirting."

Kara looks at Ana, seeing her watering eyes and flushed face. "Leave her alone! I am going to move my foot. You even look in her direction, I will run your favorite appendage down a cheese grater. Do you understand?"

He nods his head, shaking under her. "Yes!"

She moves her foot. He jumps up and runs from the store. She grabs Ana and pulls her into her arms. "I'm so sorry! My phone was at the bottom of the bag. I didn't hear it go off. I just happened to check it."

They walk over to a plush seat and sit down. "It's okay," Ana tries.

"No, it's not. What did that creep say to you?"

Ana shakes her head, crying into her hands. "It doesn't matter. Thank you for saving me from him."

"Never in a million years would I have thought something like that would happen at a bookstore."

Ana gets a napkin out of her purse and cleans her face. "Can we just go, please?"

"Are you sure you don't want to look around? I'll hold your hand and stay with you, I promise. Don't let some loser ruin our day."

She nods her head. "Okay." They walk around, looking at hardcover books. Kara tells Ana to pick out five, that she's buying them for her. "Kara, you don't need to do that."

"I want to. Let me buy my best friend some books. Please? I want to do something for you."

"You already did, just bringing me here and spending today with me." She laughs when Kara pouts. "Fine, I'll get one."

"We're not leaving until you pick out three books, at least." She smiles at her, taking a tote bag off the hanger. "Now."

Ana laughs as she takes the bag. "All right," she relents. They walk to her favorite section, fantasy, and Ana runs her hand across the spines on each shelf, quickly glancing at the titles. She picks one up. The cover has a beach at night. "Two worlds, one love," Ana reads. She smiles at Kara. "I've been waiting for this one."

Kara pays and takes the books to the car. They grab lunch at a café then go into the clothing boutique. "What do you want to look at first?"

Ana laughs. "You know how much I love my t-shirts."

Kara takes her hand. "You were quiet at lunch. Are you sure you're all right?"

"I am. Can we just shop?" She regrets asking when she sees the hurt on Kara's face. "I'm sorry. I appreciate that you're worried. I guess I'm still trying to deal with... everything."

"It's why I asked."

"You are such a wonderful friend. I don't know how I would get by without you."

"Same for you, sis. Now, shirts?"

They pick out a few graphic t-shirts, then Kara takes her to the nicer clothes. She picks up a pink shirt with lace sleeves. Ana shakes her head, but she picks up the blue one next to it. Kara nods. They continue looking.

Ana picks up a dark red blouse, smiling at Kara. "I think Rafe will like this one."

"I agree. I know you went through a lot as a child, but how come you were never interested in dating before now?"

"Because no one seemed interested in me." She shrugs her shoulders. "It's all right. I'm glad I met Rafe, even if it wasn't under the best of circumstances. I feel like I can trust him."

"You barely know him."

"You said it yourself, I'm usually a good judge of character."

"True."

They pick up dinner and head home. Ana goes into her room, putting her books on her desk then hanging up her new clothes. She walks out to Kara, who is sitting on the couch. Ana plops down next to her, startling her. They laugh.

"Thank you, Kara. For everything."

"Of course! Anything for my little sis. You know I'm here for you."

"Me, too. Although I feel like you do all the heavy lifting."

"That's not true. Coming home to you after I've been away is the highlight of my day. You make sure I've eaten, have clean clothes ready for me, ask about my trip. You know this goes both ways."

Ana smiles at her as she stands up. "Ready for dinner?"

"Always."

They laugh as they go into the kitchen. After dinner, Ana gets a shower and slips on her pajamas. Phone in hand, she sits on her bed. She stares down at the screen and wonders why Rafe hasn't texted her all day. Was he thinking about her? Finally, she works up the courage to text him first.

Ana: *I missed you today*
Rafe: *We saw each other this morning.*
Ana: *I know.*
Rafe: *Apologies. That sounded rude. I missed you today, too. Did you have a good time at the bookstore?*

Her hand clenches the phone in response. She wonders what would've happened if Kara hadn't been there. *Why does everyone have to save me? First Rafe, now Kara. Maybe I should take a self-defense class. I need to be stronger. I don't want to tell him what happened. He'll only get upset and then what?* Taking deep breaths, she calms her racing mind.

Ana: *Kara insisted on buying me books. We had lunch and did some clothes shopping.*

Rafe: *I'm glad you had fun. Do you have plans tomorrow or are we still on for lunch?*

Ana: *Lunch would be great.*

Rafe: *I'll pick you up at eleven*

Ana: *See you then.*

She puts her phone down and snuggles back against her pillows. She shivers at the thought of the man blocking her path and tries to push the incident from her mind. Picking up one of her new books, she hopes it will distract her until she falls asleep.

Kara runs in as Ana is screaming and thrashing about the bed. Kara sits on the edge, grabbing Ana's shoulders and shaking her awake. Ana bolts upright, looking around and breathing heavy. She grabs Kara, who climbs into bed and holds her tightly.

"What was this one about?"

Ana looks down. "It's stupid."

"The creep at the bookstore?" She watches Ana nod. "It's not stupid. He scared you. He literally cornered you and wouldn't let you leave."

"You weren't scared of him. I think… I want to learn how to fight, to defend myself."

"It's not a bad idea. I'm sure there's a self-defense class you could take, but it breaks my heart that you feel you need to." Kara looks down at her hands. *I never wanted you to learn how to fight. It's not what Rosalina would want.* Kara takes a breath. "You should get more sleep.

"Good idea. I don't want to look tired when Rafe picks me up for lunch."

"All right." Kara kisses her forehead and helps her lay back down. "Get more sleep, sis."

Ana watches her leave. She picks up her phone and rereads her texts with Rafe. At the sight of his name, she smiles and bites her lip. She puts the phone down and falls back asleep.

In the morning, she finds a pair of dark blue jeans and the new red blouse laid out on the dresser. Placed on top of the outfit is a note from Kara that says she had to run into the office, but she had left make-up for her in the bathroom. Ana looks at the clock. It's a little after eight, which means she has plenty of time to get a few things done around the house before she gets ready.

At a quarter after ten, she is standing before the mirror. *Why am I nervous? We've had lunch before.* As she towel-dries her hair, she realizes that she's going on a first date, that this will be their first time out together as a couple. *No wonder Kara picked everything out for me.*

She looks down at the array of make-up Kara left for her, unsure of where to begin. The only piece she feels confident about is the lipstick, but she manages to put on foundation, eye shadow, and mascara as well. She scrunches her curls a few times, smiling as they bounce, and leaves the bathroom feeling almost giddy about her new look. But while she gets dressed, the nerves start to creep in, and she wonders what Rafe will think of the make-up with her new clothes. Glancing at her reflection again almost sends her into the shower to scrub it all off.

Ana shakes the anxious thoughts from her head, grabs her purse, and sits on the front steps to wait. At precisely eleven, Rafe pulls up outside. She walks down the steps, and he meets her at the passenger door, opening it for her. The look of surprise on his face at the sight of her causes her to blush and smile.

"Mia estrela, this is a new look."

"Kara picked it out. Do you like it?" she asks sheepishly.

His smile grows. "I love it," he says, leaning down and kissing her softly, "but don't misunderstand. You are always beautiful."

He helps her into the car and shuts the door. They arrive at the Italian restaurant by the bookstore. Ana looks over, trying to forget about the day before. They go inside and are immediately seated near the bar. Their server arrives, telling them the specials and taking their drink order. Ana is surprised when Rafe takes her hand and places above his knee. She bites her lip, trying not to stare at him, then blushes when he winks at her.

"For a small town, you have some pretty good restaurants."

"Locally owned, locally sourced. Everything here is good."

"Everything?" he asks, his eyebrow raised.

She blushes again. "Thank you for bringing me here."

"I thought we both could use a break from Chinese."

Ana laughs. "It's Kara's favorite. What can I say?"

"And you?"

She gestures around the restaurant. "Italian. I could eat it every day."

"Me, too."

"You told Kara you were living off your inheritance. What do you do during the day?"

"I work out at a local gym. The owner is a good friend of mine. I read, and I watch news on my tablet. Sometimes on my new phone."

"Why didn't you have a phone?" They stay quiet when their meal arrives. Ana looks at her plate, wondering if she asked something wrong when he still doesn't respond. She decides to change the subject. "Do you like to play video games?"

"I play Ring of Sky."

"Oh, yeah. That one is pretty cool. A dragonborn searching for the ring of holding. I really like it, too. Kara says I play it too much."

Rafe chuckles. "I'm sure you don't."

They enjoy the ride back to her house, with music playing on the radio. She smiles at Rafe, who mouths along with some of the songs. She places her hand over his when he is adjusting the gear shift. He gives her a quick smile before turning his attention back to the road. Once they arrive back at the house, she gets a bottle of water and sits with him on the couch.

Rafe looks her over, admiring her honey-copper eyes. "Ana, can I kiss you?"

She smiles. "Yes."

He leans down, gently gripping her neck as their lips meet. He gently pushes her lips open with his tongue, exploring her mouth as she holds him tightly. His other hand trails up from her leg to her stomach. She pulls away, gasping for air and going to the window. Rafe walks up beside her.

"What's wrong?"

"I'm sorry," she says, biting back tears.

"Did I do something?"

She shakes her head. "It's not you."

"Is it because of your foster father?"

Her skin is cold as she loses her color. She sucks in her breath. "How did you know that?"

"It's not hard to guess." He brings his hand under her chin to gently guide her face to his. "You are a such a strong and incredible woman. You are a survivor and a warrior, do you know that?"

She tries to lower her head, but he keeps his hand under her chin. "Rafe, please, I'm not—"

"Mia estrela, you know it's the truth. Don't ever forget it."

"Speaking of being a warrior, I want to learn self-defense," she says, not ready to talk about her past. "I want to learn how to protect myself."

He smiles at her. "I could teach you."

"I know."

"I won't go easy on you, though."

"I wouldn't want you to."

"When do you want to start?" Rafe asks.

"As soon as possible."

"Let me text my friend." He digs his phone out and presses a few buttons, waiting a moment. "Tomorrow?"

She leans up and kisses him. "That would be great."

"Ugh, what a day!" They both turn towards the voice as Kara walks in. "Ana, you look great."

"I liked everything you picked out for her," Rafe says. "She looks stunning."

Ana blushes as she takes his hand, squeezing it. "Thank you." She smiles at Kara. "He's going to teach me self-defense."

Kara raises her eyebrows and gives them a skeptical look. "He is? Are you sure he's qualified?"

Ana laughs and rolls her eyes. "Stop, he'll be great."

"I guess it's for the best. I won't be able to help. I have to go on assignment again. I won't be back until Friday."

"New York? Chicago?" Ana teases, knowing Kara doesn't usually travel that far. She grows concerned when Kara doesn't respond. "Sis, where are you going?"

"Paris."

"Ah! Lucky!"

"Ana, it's not a vacation. I'll be staying in some crappy little hotel and spend most of my time in traffic or taking pictures of the protests. I'll bring you something back, though. I promise."

"When do you leave?"

Kara glances at the clock. "Half an hour."

"What?"

"I'm sorry. My editor sprung it on me last minute."

"I understand."

"I thought you said this was a small paper?" Rafe asks.

Kara laughs. "My editor is paying for this trip himself, trying to get us more exposure, both in print and online. I just hate that I have to go."

"Don't worry about Ana. I'll keep an eye on her."

Kara rolls her eyes and goes into her room. When she walks back out, Ana and Rafe are kissing on the couch. She drops her bag with a loud thud to get their attention. Ana jumps to her feet.

"I don't know what traffic will be like, so I have to head out."

Ana hugs her. "Please, be safe."

"You, too, sis." Kara looks at Rafe. "I guess I can trust you for that?"

"You know you can."

Once Kara's gone, Ana sits back down with Rafe. She glances at him as she climbs onto his lap, kissing him as her fingers ruffle through his hair. He wraps his arm around her waist, pulling her tighter to him.

Without thinking, she brings her arms around his neck and lets her hands rest on his upper back. He's instantly on his feet, gripping her tightly so she doesn't fall.

"My apologies," he says.

"No, I'm sorry." She kisses his neck. "I was lost in the moment and forgot about your scars. I know what it's like, to not want anyone to touch them. Please, forgive me?"

He kisses her. "Nothing to forgive. It was an accident. I'm not mad," he says, sitting down. He holds her on his lap. "It's okay. Really."

"If you want to go, I'll understand," she says softly.

He takes a breath as he crooks his finger under her chin, raising her face to his. He leans in, kissing her. "Mia estrela, I don't want to go anywhere, until you tell me to."

He plants a soft kiss on her mouth. Nervous, she takes a breath before meeting his gaze. "Are you staying the night?"

"If you want me here while Kara's gone, I will. I'll have to run home and pack a bag."

"I don't want to bother you."

He takes a breath, then he leans in, kissing her. "Ana, you're never bothering me. Okay?"

"Okay."

"I'll sleep on the couch, and tomorrow we'll have a date day. How does that sound?"

"Wonderful." She giggles when he plants kisses on her neck and chin.

He stands up, putting her on her feet. "I won't be long."

While he's gone, she changes into Kara's Pink Floyd pajamas. She laughs, not even sure if she's heard any of their music. She folds laundry and mops the floor while waiting for him. When Rafe walks in, Ana smiles at how natural it is for him to enter as if he owns the place. She stifles a laugh, knowing Kara would kill him if she saw it.

He carries his duffel bag over, letting it fall by the couch. "Cute PJs. I like their music." He tilts his head when she's blushing. "Ana?"

"I don't know if I've heard any of their songs. They're Kara's."

Rafe laughs and sits beside her on the couch. "Well, let's listen to some." She gets out her phone, opening the music app, and typing in their name. They listen to a few songs. "And?"

She smiles. "I do like them." She leans up and kisses him. "Kara has the newest Duty of War game. Wanna play?"

"Sure."

She grabs the controllers off the charger and turns the TV on while he makes himself a cup of coffee. "Have you played it before?"

"Once at the game store. They had a demo set up."

She climbs onto his lap as he turns on the TV. "Oh, I'm sorry," she says suddenly.

"For what?"

"You probably don't enjoy playing war games, I wasn't thinking. We can pick something else.

"Ana, I want to play this. If I didn't, I would've said something. I don't hide like you do." He smirks at her.

She hits his shoulder. "Jerk." They laugh as the game starts. Ana groans. "Do we have to sit through the cut scene? Yes, robot aliens have invaded earth. So realistic."

"How do you know I'm not an alien robot?"

"Hmm, I guess I don't," she plays along. She turns to him, bringing her hand to his chest. "Is this a heartbeat or some fancy device from another world?"

"Who says it's not both?" He chuckles when she shakes her head.

"You're being mean," she says, giving him a playful pout.

"Speaking of mean, are we playing versus or co-op?"

"Co-op."

"You better not get me killed."

She gasps. "How dare you? Give me a minute, and you'll see exactly what kind of player I am!"

The game starts. He laughs as she mows down armies of robots, scales buildings, and levels up. Each time the grenade indicator flashes, she yells out, "Pomegranate!"

"What does that mean?" he asks. "I thought pomegranate was a type of fruit?"

Ana pauses the game and explains how the word grenade came about. "It's a little inside joke Kara and I have. I'll yell 'pomegranate' when the grenade indicator flashes." She cocks her head. "I'm surprised you didn't know that, being in the military."

He lets out a nervous laugh. "I didn't use grenades during my time."

They beat the level and play two more before they realize they hadn't had dinner yet. Rafe orders a pizza, and they play and eat until neither of them can keep from yawning every few minutes.

Ana gets ready for bed while Rafe changes into black pajama bottoms and a tight-fitting light grey t-shirt. When she comes back out, he's standing near the door, waiting for her. She draws in a quick breath at the sight of his muscular torso and runs her fingers over his chest.

His head swoops down, his lips on hers as he presses her against the wall. His hands are on her back as his tongue explores her mouth, brushing along her teeth and tongue. She pulls away, gasping for air.

"Rafe—"

At his name, his mouth crashes onto hers. She grips his shirt in her hands, pulling higher on her toes. He slowly pulls back, studying her face.

"Why did you stop?"

"You said my name. I thought—"

"I needed air," she admits, giggling as her cheeks blush.

"Apologies. Do you need to sit down? I could get you some water or—"

"Rafe, I'm okay," she says, laughing again. "I'm not a child."

"If you could see how red your face is."

"You're a really good kisser," she confesses.

Now it's his turn to blush. "Ana—"

"Seriously, you are."

He gives her one more kiss and steers her towards her bedroom door. "Maybe that's what you'll dream of tonight."

"So mean." She laughs. "Night, Rafe."

"Night, Ana."

She lies in bed, imagining she's back in his arms, tasting him, his body pressed against hers. He tastes like coffee mixed with toothpaste, mint and coffee. She loves the combination. The kiss plays over and over as she falls asleep.

—◦—

"No! Stop!" Ana screams. "Please, don't!"

Rafe rushes in, quickly scanning the room for danger. He sees her on the bed and tangled up in her blanket. He runs over to her, shaking her awake. "It's okay. You're safe."

Her eyes jolt open as she sits up, looking around. "I'm sorry. I meant to tell you about the nightmares I have. I didn't mean to scare you."

He sits on the edge of the bed, pulling her onto his lap. "What can I do to help?"

She leans into him, wrapping her arms around his neck and laying her head on his shoulder. "Stay with me. Please?"

"I'm right here, Ana. I promise you, I'm not going anywhere. Do you want me to sleep in here tonight?"

Her body tenses. She looks at him, hesitating before she speaks. "Would you sleep on top of the blanket?"

"Of course. I'll hold you until you fall asleep, then I'll go back to the couch. Deal?"

"Deal."

They lie down together. His arms wrapped around her fills her with a warmth that calms her and allows her to drift off to sleep.

—◦—

Ana wakes first, realizing she's still in his arms. She slowly makes her way out of bed, careful not to wake him, and heads toward the bathroom with fresh clothes. His bag is sitting open on the floor by the couch. A bottle of body wash is poking out, so she picks it up and smells it. She smiles at the scent and takes it with her to use in the shower.

Rafe walks out to find her cooking eggs and sausage for breakfast. "Sleep well?" he asks.

She smiles at him. "Thanks to you."

He gets dressed for the day as she finishes cooking, then gets out the OJ and makes his coffee while she plates the food. They sit at the table. He grows concerned when she's not eating.

"What's wrong?"

"Nothing." She loved the feeling of being in his arms but waking up with him in her bed had left a knot in her stomach. Thinking of her foster father climbing into her bed, she gets to her feet. "Be right back." She runs to her bedroom, shutting the door and sitting on the bed while clutches her pillow to her chest.

When a few minutes have gone by, Rafe walks over and knocks softly. "Ana, what's wrong?" He waits for her response. "You don't have to tell me. Will you come eat?"

"In a minute," she replies. Hearing the concern in his voice, she gives in and cries into her hands. Then she composes herself, grabbing a tissue and cleaning off her face before she walks into the kitchen. She takes a bite, noticing he had heated it up for her. *God, he's thoughtful.*

"Are you all right?"

Swallowing her bite, she glances at him before studying her plate. *I don't know if I'll ever really be all right.* "I'm fine. Sorry." She continues eating.

"What would you like to do today? We could go to the museum or hit the outlet mall. It's only a half hour drive."

"Let me finish getting ready and think about it?"

"Of course." They stand up, Rafe pulling her into his arms and kissing her forehead. "Why do you smell so good, mia estrela?"

She looks up at him, roses in her cheeks. "I... I used your body wash."

"It's not my body wash."

"What? What do you mean?"

"If it smells that good on you, I want you to have it."

He lets her go so she can get ready. He gathers dishes and takes care of them, smiling at the thought of her using his body wash in the shower. Clearing his throat as the heat spreads through him, he pushes the image away. She walks up to him, pulling her hoodie on.

"Is it okay if we walk around the mall and grab lunch there?" she asks.

"Perfect, like you."

"I can change, put on something nicer—"

He laughs, kissing her brow. "Ana, you look perfect," he assures her.

She's confused to find her purse open on the table by the door, because she never leaves it that way. Her wallet is sitting on top. Inside, she finds a folded stack of twenty-dollar bills with a note from Kara telling her to have a good time while she's gone. Ana smiles and slips the wallet back into her purse. She takes Rafe's hand as they leave the house.

At the mall, they walk through a few clothing shops and a music store before finding themselves in a jewelry store. He looks at silver rings while she looks at pendants. An antique-style Celtic cross catches her eye. The center stone is the same color as Rafe's eyes, and for a moment she considers buying it. Then she sees the $500 price tag. Rafe walks over to see what she's looking at.

"See anything good?"

"Everything in here is pretty."

"Not as pretty as you," he says as they walk out.

She gestures down the hall. "I need to use the restroom. I'll be right back."

She goes in, thankful there isn't a line. She washes and dries her hands, looking herself over in the mirror. Self-conscious thoughts would creep in every time they walked by women who look from Rafe to her, as if wondering how someone like her could be with him. *I don't deserve him. Everything about him is better than me. He's served his country, he's handsome, he has friends. He is everything I am not. We don't make sense.* She brushes her hair, then smiles as she walks out and sees him waiting for her. He takes her hand, leading her to the steakhouse.

She has a cheeseburger while he chows down on his ribeye. He's happy to see her eat. "What?" she asks.

"Nothing. Just staring at you."

She sighs. "Do I have something on my face?"

He leans in to inspect when he kisses her suddenly. "You do now."

She covers her face and giggles, enjoying his playfulness.

Ana goes into the kitchen. "Do you want a water?" she offers as she walks to the fridge.

"No, thank you."

She gets one and drinks it before joining him on the couch. "So, I've decided I'm going to start looking online for a new job. I know you and Kara want me to wait. Honestly, between putting out résumés and hoping to hear back, it could be a few weeks or even a month anyway."

"Any particular job you have in mind?"

"I loved working at the bank, but it was enclosed and small. I think I would like something in a brighter, more open environment. The job itself? I'm not picky."

When his phone vibrates, he digs it out of his pocket, reading his text. "Oh, we are set up to train tonight at seven. Is that okay?"

"I can't wait to get started. What should I wear?"

"Your yoga pants, sneakers, and a tight t-shirt should be fine."

"Tight, huh?" she teases.

"Ana, it's strictly for training. You'll see why," he responds, his tone serious.

"Okay." She clears her throat.

"Do you and Kara have anything special planned for Saturday?"

"No," she answers, nervous. "Why would we?"

"I must be mistaken."

"About what?"

"Remember I looked at your ID? I thought it said your birthday is this Saturday." Regret washes over him as he sees the color drain from her face. "I'm sorry. Should I not have brought that up?"

"It's okay. Um, I don't celebrate it."

"Why not?"

"Because the last time I celebrated my birthday, I ended up in the hospital."

"Oh, God. Ana—"

She pulls away and paces in front of the window. Before she can protest, Rafe pulls her into his arms, warming her body and soul. She looks up at him. "How do you do that?"

"What?"

"Make me feel so safe? Being in your arms, I feel like the world can't touch me."

"I don't know. I'm glad I do." He kisses her forehead.

She wraps her arms around his neck, then pulls back suddenly. "Is that okay? My arms on your neck like that?"

"Yes." His hand trails down her side then caresses her stomach. "Will you tell me what happened? Was it something your foster father did?"

She runs into the bathroom, locking the door behind her. Rafe stands outside the door, listening for sobs or objects being thrown around, any sound that might help him understand.

"Are you okay?" he asks.

"I'm fine," she responds. The nauseous feeling in her stomach is settling, the panic in her chest is fading, but the memories are still fresh in her mind, triggered by him. "I need a moment, please?"

He wants to tell her to open the door, to talk to him. He takes a breath. "Okay. I'm out here whenever you're ready to talk to me." With nothing to do but wait, he decides to make a cup of coffee. When at last she comes out, he's sitting at the table halfway through his second cup. "Are you okay?"

"We need to talk about us."

He gets to his feet. "Okay." He walks to her, watching her features as she thinks of what to say.

"When I was a child, my foster father was hurting me. I told on him, and he broke my ribs." She meets his gaze. "I was taken away, and he was arrested. Still, I can't..." she looks away, collecting herself before facing him. "I don't know how serious this is going to get, or where we're going as a couple. We don't need to answer that right now. It's just that... I've never... I'm not—"

"Ana, we won't have sex until you're ready, whether that's next week or on our wedding day, if that's where this relationship goes."

"How did you know?"

"I could read it on your face and in your body language."

"I've never... I've never had sex. I don't believe in sex without love or with random people. I don't care if other people do, it's just not my thing. I'm sorry."

"You have no reason to be sorry. If you want the truth, I've never done it either."

"But you're so good looking." The words fly from her mouth, and she's immediately embarrassed. "I mean, you were a soldier. You traveled the world. I thought that's part of what you guys do."

"Not me. I was never interested in that."

"I'm sorry, I find that difficult to believe."

"You don't trust me?"

"It's not that. But I don't doubt you've had women throw themselves at you."

"They have. None ever caught my eye. Until you."

"Maybe it was the bullet wound that made me sexy." She grins at him.

He laughs, rolling his eyes. "Of course, that's what it was." He leans in and kisses her. "Mia estrela, I want you to feel comfortable talking to me about anything. I won't judge you, and you won't scare me away. I need you to believe that."

"I do. Same for you."

He brings his hand up, gently rubbing her shoulder where she had been shot. "I almost lost you before I even found you."

"My guardian angel," she says with a smile.

A look of guilt flashes across his face. He catches himself. "Always." He walks to the table, getting his mug and putting into the sink. "We need a light dinner before training."

They split a sandwich and have a small salad, then she gets changed.

"Is this okay?" she asks.

He examines her outfit. "Long sleeves?" When her head drops, he swears under his breath. "I'm sorry. Of course, long sleeves are fine. Everything you are wearing is fine. Except your hair."

She pulls it back into a tight ponytail, smiling when he nods in approval. She walks up, getting to her tiptoes to kiss him.

"Where is everyone?" she asks, following him into the gym. It's a little nicer than she had expected, with rows of workout machines and a few training rings.

"I'm friends with the owners. It usually closes at six, but they left it open for us. I didn't want you to feel a bunch of eyes on you while you're starting out."

"Thank you. I feel self-conscious even knowing it'll just be you and me."

He drops his bag and walks her into the training ring. "All right. First things first—your stance." He steps back making sure she is watching him. He separates his legs, planting his feet, and slightly bending his knees. She mimics the pose. "Good. If you're tight or rigid, they'll push you right over. Now, have you ever thrown a punch?"

Her eyes go wide. "No."

"Okay." He steps in front of her. "Punch me." She laughs. "I'm being serious. Don't worry, you won't hurt me. I'm going to see how you move, then I'll block you." He gives her a moment, then grows concerned when she doesn't move. "What's wrong?"

"Maybe this was a mistake."

"Talk to me," he insists.

She looks down, clasping her hands together. "If I throw a punch, you're not going to laugh at me? You won't make fun of me if I do something wrong?" she asks, a tear rolling down her cheek.

He wipes it away, studying her face. "Never. Why on earth would you think that?"

"The kids in PE. They would push me around, steal my clothes, call me horrible names. They would make fun of the way I threw the ball or how I ran."

He sighs, pulling her into his arms. "Ana, why didn't you tell me this before we started? I would've reassured you. If you do something wrong, I'll correct you in the kindest way I can, I promise."

"Okay." She goes back into her stance, crooks her elbow and clenches her hand, then swings hard, aiming for his chin. He quickly grabs her wrist and deflects.

"Here," he says, taking her hand. He corrects the position of her thumb. "Remember, on top of your index finger, not wrapped around your fingers. That's a good way to break it. Your arm was right, as most people pull their arm back as if they are swinging a baseball bat. You did very well."

She's walking away when he grabs her hand, stopping her and pulling her back to the center of the ring. "Ana?"

"If you're going to over-compensate for what I went through, it's just as bad. I don't need your pity!"

"I don't understand. What did I do?"

"You don't have to exaggerate how good I did to make me feel better."

"But I meant it."

"Really?" she asks.

"Yes, really."

Embarrassed, she hangs her head. "I'm sorry."

"Ana, you have to stop apologizing. You also have to stop walking away from me. Talk to me about whatever is going on. Otherwise, how can I help?"

"It's not you."

"What do you mean?"

She shakes her head. "This isn't the place for that conversation. Can we continue training?"

He nods. "Again, but faster this time." She brings up her fist, only missing his chin by a few inches before he grabs her arm. He turns it behind her, pressing her back to his chest. "Do you see how quickly I took control?" He releases her. "I didn't hurt you, did I?"

"No."

"Ready to go again?" He smiles when she nods. They practice a few more times before getting a drink of water. He sees her eyeing the punching bag in the corner. He chuckles. "You're not ready for that."

She looks at him. "I was just looking."

"Ana?"

"Okay, I've never even seen one before."

Taking her hand, he walks her over to get a closer look. He places her palm flat on the bag. "You need to build up both your strength and endurance before we tackle this."

"Tackle it? I thought I punch it?" Rafe goes to correct her when she bursts out laughing. "Okay, you are too easy."

Shaking his head, they return to the training ring. As she continues working on her form, sweat dripping from her brow and her heart racing, Ana has never felt so alive. She thinks back to the night of the mugging, wishing she had been better prepared. Rafe notices the distracted look on her face, taking the opportunity and coming up behind her. He wraps her in his arms, pinning her arms to her side.

"What are you doing?" she cries out, struggling to break free.

He releases her then spins her around to face him. "What were you thinking about?"

Stepping back, she shakes her head. "Nothing. I—"

"You lost your focus. Do you see how easy that was for me?"

Her anger fades down as she realizes he's using her own weakness as a teaching moment. Reluctantly, she nods. "Yes, you're right. I was thinking about the night I was mugged."

"What about it?"

"Wishing I had already trained, that I could've fought back."

"But you did fight back."

"Not fast enough."

"What do you mean?"

"He was still able to… to put his hands on me, before I brought up my knee. If I could've defended myself faster—"

"Ana, the man had a gun, and you still fought back. You did nothing wrong that night, and none of this is your fault."

"Are we done for the evening?" she asks quietly.

Seeing how tired she is, he nods and leads her to his car.

***

She cleans up in Kara's bathroom while he uses the guest bathroom. Getting them both a bottle of water, she stretches her arm, knowing she will be sore in the morning.

"You okay?" Rafe asks, taking a bottle.

"Yes. My arms are tired, though."

"Do you feel like you're learning it?"

"I think so."

"You seem to mimic the movement pretty quick. That's good."

"When will we train again?"

"Wednesday. Since you're just starting out, we'll give your body a rest tomorrow. I'll be leaving around ten in the morning. A business meeting I'd forgotten about, regarding an investment. I won't be long."

"That's okay. I'll start my online job search."

"Do you want me to sleep on the—"

"Couch? Yes, please," she says quickly. "I'm going to get ready for bed." She runs to the bathroom and brushes her teeth. Opening the door, a small gasp escapes her lips at the sight of Rafe taking up the doorway.

"What's wrong?" he asks.

She smiles up at him, shaking her head. "Nothing."

"Okay. Good night." He leans down and kisses her before going to the couch. She leans with her back against the vanity, eyes closed as she tries to calm her pounding heart. She thinks about waking up in bed with him, about the nights her foster father would climb onto her bed, removing his belt... then she leans over the toilet, unable to hold the vomit down any longer. Rafe runs in.

"Are you ill?"

"No," she replies, brushing her teeth again.

"What happened?"

"Bad memories. It... It happens sometimes. No big deal."

"Will you tell me about them?" he asks, taking her hand and leading her to the couch. He sits down, gently pulling her with him.

"I'm not ready."

"Ana—"

"Please, don't ask me to."

"I won't. Was it something I said? Or did? I don't want to do it again, not if it upsets you so."

"No, it's nothing you did," she lies. She stands up, leaning down and kissing his forehead. "Get some sleep."

Chapter 5

Ana wakes up, happy to see that she slept until morning without having a nightmare. She walks out to find Rafe still asleep and stands over him, watching him. Her hand grips his arm as she leans down to kiss his forehead, when he grabs her shoulder and throws her onto the floor, landing on top of her.

"Rafe!" she cries out.

He freezes, not even breathing as he looks at her. "Ana," he finally says. "I'm so sorry." He pulls her to her feet, holding her as she trembles in his arms.

"It's okay," she tries.

"No, it's not."

"You were asleep, and I startled you. What you've been through, I should know better."

"If I had hurt you—"

"You didn't. Really," she assures him. She kisses his cheek. "I'm okay."

Holding her another minute, he reluctantly lets go. "I am sorry, mia estrela."

"I know. We're okay now. I'll make breakfast."

He stays beside her, watching her cook pancakes while he makes a cup of coffee. "This is really cool," he says, pointing to her Keurig.

She laughs. "Kara loves it. Says it's the easiest thing in the world for making a cup. I've used it a time or two."

"I thought you didn't drink coffee?"

"Oh no, I've used the hot water setting for my tea." She laughs harder. "Don't tell the Brits, it might start a war."

"Your secret is safe with me." He joins in her laughter and looks over at the pancakes cooking in the pan. "They smell great."

When they're done eating, she changes into her dark jeans with a navy-blue long sleeve shirt, then gets out her laptop and sets up at the kitchen table. At ten, Rafe kisses her forehead.

"I won't be gone long. I have my phone if you need me."

"Okay. I hope your meeting goes well."

"Thanks."

She watches him leave then turns her attention to her laptop. After an hour of staring at her computer, she looks around the kitchen and decides a change of scenery would be nice. She smiles at the thought of going to her favorite café to grab a boba tea. She packs her laptop into her bag and steps outside, then stretches in the sun and groans as her sore muscles groan back. She's near the café when she sees Rafe across the street, sitting outside the bistro.

His face is blocked by a woman with red hair. She turns, laughing. Ana is envious of her beauty. As Ana gets closer, she sees she is practically in Rafe's lap, her mouth on his ear as she whispers something. Ana's face is flush, her body warm as Rafe speaks softly in response. She stops in her tracks when his eyes meet hers.

Seeing the look on her face causes him to lose his smile. She turns and runs as fast as she can, her legs screaming the whole way. Once inside the house, she slams the door behind her and locks every lock before going to her room, collapsing on the bed.

I should've known. He was too perfect. I knew something had to be wrong with him. She jumps when her phone goes off.

Rafe: *It's not what you think. I'm outside. Please come out and talk to me.*

Ana: *NO!*

Rafe: *You're going to feel silly when I tell you the truth. Please, give me a chance to explain myself?*

Ana: *I'm turning off my phone. Lose my number.*

Staring at his phone, Rafe reads her last message again. A pain slithers across his chest as her words worm their way into his heart. Everywhere aches at the thought of losing her. *I never meant to hurt her like this.* He sits on the front step, waiting for her to give him a chance to explain. He won't give up on her.

An hour later, the door opens. He's on his feet, facing her. "Ana, please. Just hear what I have to say. If you don't like it, you never have to see me again. Please, mia estrela, just let me explain."

She opens the door further and steps back so he can enter. When he tries to take her hand, she pulls away and walks to the table, sitting down and staring at the placemat in front of her. He sits beside her.

"So, it was a good meeting?" she asks, anger in her voice.

He sighs. "Have you eaten?"

"Just say whatever you're going to say," she snaps.

"Ana, what do you think you saw?"

"I don't *think* I saw anything. I know what I saw. She was practically in your lap with her lips on your ear! Not very business-like, unless that's the type of arrangement you were making."

"Never speak of Lauren like that," he snarls.

She straightens up, looking at him. "I beg your pardon?"

Rafe counts to ten and takes a breath. "She owns the gym where we trained."

"I don't give a f—"

"She owns it with her wife, Samantha."

Ana looks at him, confusion on her face. "What? Really?"

Rafe nods his head. "Let me start at the beginning. I started working out at that gym a few months ago. One day, I was heading to the smoothie bar when I saw this creep hitting on a young woman, just trying to enjoy her workout. I ran over and pretended to be her boyfriend, hoping to spook him off. Had no idea she was the owner! She banned the creep but was thankful I was willing to help like that. She's a lot like you. She had a really rough childhood and is really shy. She's working on personal space and opening up. Today, she wanted to see how close she could be with a man without feeling like her heart would explode, since she deals with so many people at her gym throughout the day, sometimes forced into close proximity. That's why you saw that."

"And her lips on your ear?"

"Ana, they weren't. She was talking quietly to me about how she was feeling, embarrassed that she is working through this and didn't want anyone to overhear what we were discussing. It was also a business meeting, as she's asking me to invest in her gym. She wants to expand and possibly open another one in the next town over."

"She's absolutely beautiful," Ana says, her words dripping with jealousy.

"If you say so."

"You don't think she's the most beautiful woman you've ever seen?"

"No," he replies honestly.

"Why not?"

Rafe takes her hand, looking into her eyes. "Because she's not you."

Her face flushes red. "I want to believe you, I do. You looked so cozy together, though."

"Here," he says, fishing out his phone. He unlocks it and hands it to her. "Open the FriendBook app."

Ana does. She sees the pictures of Rafe with Lauren and Samantha, out having brunch. There are messages from Lauren thanking him for letting her message him so late after her nightmare, since Samantha was on a business trip. She tells him he's a great friend. Ana hangs her head and hands him back his phone. "I'm so sorry. I feel like the world's biggest idiot now."

"I should've told you everything up front. If I told you more about my plans, who I was with, it never would've happened."

"I don't need to know what you're doing or who you're with every second of every day."

"It was a misunderstanding. These happen in any relationship."

She looks up at him. "Are we—do you still want to be my boyfriend?"

He scoots his chair closer to her, leaning in and kissing her. "Of course, I do. Why wouldn't I?"

"I can't believe I was so stupid."

"Hey, if I saw you with a guy like that, I would've reacted much worse. It's okay, really." He kisses her again, pulling back when her stomach rumbles. "Have you eaten lunch?"

"No, and I don't think I can, knowing I ruined yours."

"We had already eaten. You need to eat something. For me?" She agrees and heats up leftovers. He watches her eat and starts to laugh. "Wait until Lauren hears about this."

"Oh, please don't! It's too embarrassing."

"I won't tell her. You'll get to meet her, though. She'll be at the gym tomorrow evening when we get there."

"Okay. Promise me you won't tell her?"

"I promise."

"Can we go for a walk? I was on my way to get a boba tea when…"

"Of course."

They hold hands as they stroll down to the café. Ana orders her favorite boba tea, and Rafe gets a large black coffee.

"I don't know how you can stand to drink that. It's so bitter!"

He laughs, taking another sip. "What can I say? I love coffee."

"I see that."

"Do you feel better now?"

She nods her head. "Yes, thanks to you. I'm sorry."

"Whatever for?"

"For the last message I sent you."

Rafe gets out his phone, presses a few buttons, then slides the phone back into his pocket. "I have no idea what you mean." He shoots her a grin.

"Thanks."

They're watching a movie and eating pizza when the doorbell rings. Rafe walks over and opens it slightly, not hiding his disdain.

"Detective Sheffield. What do you want?"

"I need to speak to Ms. Summers regarding her case. Is she here?"

"No."

"Don't lie to me," he says, absently tapping his jacket pocket.

"Excuse me? She gave her statement, and Detective Andersen has her information, if she has any more questions. That son of a bitch is dead, and he got what he deserved. You need to go."

"Whatever," Sheffield snaps as he walks away.

Rafe slams the door shut, then turns the deadbolt and slides the security chain in place. He spins around to see Ana standing behind him, her hand clutching the bottom of her shirt.

"Is he gone?" she whispers.

"Yes."

Rafe watches her body relax. She sits on the couch, and he joins her, taking her hand and stroking it affectionately with his thumb.

"Thank you."

"I told you, you don't have to deal with them anymore."

She lays her head on his chest, and they resume watching the movie. Glancing down at her, he realizes she fell asleep. Stroking her hair, he smiles when he realizes they are still holding hands. He closes his eyes, leaning back against the couch and falling asleep.

They jump awake when her phone rings. Ana grabs it and answers it, happy to hear from Kara. She goes into her room to talk and get dressed. Rafe gets a quick shower, then decides he's going to cook breakfast—or at least try to. Looking in the fridge, he decides on something easy, scrambled eggs and toast. A few bits of eggshell land in the pan, but he manages to get them out. Grateful the toast didn't burn, he plates everything up when Ana walks into the kitchen.

"You cooked breakfast?"

He laughs. "I think so."

"It looks great," she assures him.

They sit down to eat, and he takes a bite of the eggs, watching her face to gauge her reaction as she eats hers. He drinks his coffee, smiling at her. "Everything tastes okay?"

"These are the best eggs I've ever had."

He watches her gobble them down and can't help but laugh. "I'm glad you like them. I was feeling kind of useless, with you doing all of the cooking."

"You always help clean up and do dishes after. It's not as though you sit there, expecting me to wait on you hand and foot."

"I would never!" He laughs. "So, how's Kara?

"Ready to get stateside. Otherwise, she's okay."

"Did you tell her about the detective last night?"

"No. I'll tell her when she gets home. No reason to upset her," Ana says, gathering dishes and going to the sink.

"Probably for the best. Are you ready for our next training session?"

"Yes, I do have one question though."

"What's that?" he asks, walking up beside her.

"How long until I can kick your butt?"

He throws his head back and roars with laughter. "Oh, sweetheart. Never!" he cries, leaning down and planting kisses all over her face and neck. She pulls away, playfully hitting his shoulder.

"Jerk!"

He nibbles her neck then helps her with dishes. She goes to her room, getting dressed in dark jeans and a long sleeve shirt. She walks up to him, looking intently at his lips.

"What are we doing today until training?" he asks.

Clasping his hand in hers, she leads him to the couch. With her hand pressed against his chest, he sinks down to the couch and sits, waiting for her. She sits on his lap, one leg straddled on either side of him, the way she did when they had their first kiss. She leans in, devouring his lips. He brings his hand up to the small of her back, pulling her into him. A small moan escapes her mouth, exciting him.

The taste of coffee fills her mouth. She pulls back to catch her breath, pressing her forehead to his. He smiles at her then steals a gentle kiss. It grows in hunger as her hands stroke through his hair. His tongue probes the inside of her mouth while his hands explore along her back with soft caresses

She holds the back of his head, kissing him with everything she has. Her body melts into his, as a wave of desire rushes through her. She breaks the kiss, and he caresses her face, then runs his fingers down the front of her neck, down her chest and side. She moans and writhes under his touch.

"Please," she begs.

"Ana—" he whispers, out of breath.

"Yes?"

"We need to stop."

She gets to her feet, suddenly self-conscious. "What's wrong? What did I do?"

"It's not you." His face is flush.

She stifles a laugh. "Oh… I don't—"

"It's okay," he says, smiling at her. "I just need a moment."

She goes to the fridge and gets them each a bottle of water. He drinks it as he tries to calm his entire body down.

He looks at her. "God, you're beautiful." She looks down, her cheeks flushed. "Don't hide your face."

"Are you okay?" she asks, trying desperately not to laugh.

"Yes. I am now." He stands up and kisses her forehead. "For someone who doesn't have much experience, you are an amazing kisser."

"I would say the same for you." She bites her lip.

"What's got you so happy?"

"I should be apologizing because I know we aren't ready to… I shouldn't be smiling like this."

"So why are you?" he teases.

"I never thought I would want anyone that way. And I certainly never thought anyone would want me."

"Ana, it's taking everything I have not to throw you over my shoulder, carry you into your bedroom, and give you everything you want. That's how much I want you." He leans in and plants a gentle kiss on her lips. "Believe me, mia estrela. You don't know the affect you have on me."

"Hmm, I think I have a pretty good idea," she teases back. "Kiss me again, please?"

His arms engulf her, and he leans down, his lips meeting hers. "Like that?"

She smiles as she nods, and he kisses her again. "Meeting you was the best thing that ever happened to me," she quietly admits. "I still can't believe it."

"I'm here, and I'm not going anywhere."

A pain webs through her chest at his words. She wonders if she can believe him. Rather than dwell on her doubts, she suggests they finish watching the movie they started the night before. They snuggle up on the couch, and his fingers trail across her arm while the movie plays. When it's over, she goes to the kitchen to make lunch. He follows her and leans against the counter, observing quietly as she cooks spaghetti.

"You weren't kidding when you said you love to cook."

She smiles at him. "It's something I've always enjoyed. Well…" she looks down. "Anyway, if you don't cook, what do you live on?"

"Sandwiches, soup, and hot pockets, mostly."

She laughs. "Hot pockets? Those hardly count as food."

"We can't all be masters in the kitchen like you."

She sticks out her tongue. "You did just fine this morning."

"In exchange for me training you, perhaps you could teach me to cook?"

The last word is barely out of his mouth before she squeals and kisses him hard. "I would love to!"

The water boils over, and she turns her attention back to the stove with the biggest smile on her face. She drains the noodles and adds olive oil with a teaspoon of butter.

"I find your offer acceptable," she says, trying to keep a straight face. He barks with laughter.

"Acceptable? It's too late, Ana. You showed your hand prematurely. I know you're dying to teach me."

She laughs. "Well, I couldn't help myself. I love to cook."

"As much as Kara loves to eat?"

"Be nice! She would murder you if she heard that."

"She could try," he says with a chuckle. While Ana pours on the spaghetti sauce, he gets out two plates and forks, trying to be useful. They enjoy a quiet lunch, discussing the movie and stealing glances at each other. When they're done eating, he looks at the clock. "We have a little time. Play some Duty of War?"

"Yes, please." She puts away the leftover food then fires up the game. Rafe watches her more than the TV. He laughs at her reactions, how she jerks with the controller and yells at the TV when an enemy is in sight.

"Pomegranate!" she cries out. She mutters under her breath when the screen goes black. "We didn't get to cover in time." She looks at Rafe, sucking in her breath when she realizes he is staring at her. "Are you all right?"

"I am. I'm just watching my beautiful girlfriend play a video game. Something I never thought I would do."

She sets her controller on the table, then leans towards him. The desire in his eyes sets her heart ablaze. He pulls her onto his lap, and she runs her fingers through his hair. She kisses his forehead, his brow, his cheek. She hesitates, pulling away for a moment, but he leans in and kisses her passionately. Her breath and thoughts are lost as she gives in to him.

His hand grips the hem of her shirt, and he looks at her. Once she nods, he brings his hand under the shirt and rests his palm on her ribs. He looks at her again. She gasps softly then nods, and his hand continues higher. Her body tenses beneath his hand, and he pulls away, leaving space between them on the couch.

"I'm sorry," she says.

"No apologies, Ana. Remember?"

"But—"

"None. You did nothing wrong."

She looks down. "I ruined our moment."

He sighs. "No, you didn't. Besides, we need a break."

"A break?" she asks, getting to her feet. "What do you mean?"

"I just meant a break from being physical. We were moving too fast for you." He grabs her hand and holds her close. "I didn't mean breaking up." Nodding, she takes a few deep breaths, willing the tears not to fall. "Ana, how could you even think that?"

She walks to the window, wrapping her arms around her waist. "Because I sometimes wonder why you're even with me, as damaged as I am."

Rafe walks over, clamping his hand on her shoulder. "Ana, I am here by your side until you tell me to go. I told you, nothing you say will change how I feel about you. Every time you let me in, every time you tell me more about yourself, I see how strong you are. I see a woman who has survived so much, who is so beautiful, resourceful, and compassionate. I see the kind of woman I could easily love."

"Rafe—" she spits out, looking up at him.

"I know, we're taking it slow. I'm not saying it right now, but you need to understand how much you mean to me."

"I care for you," she confesses. "You mean so much to me."

When she smiles, he kisses her softly. "Now, let's get ready for training."

"Yes, Rafe. Thank you. I am blessed to have you in my life."

He kisses her forehead. "We both are."

On the drive to the gym, he holds her hand, glancing at her periodically to make sure she's okay. Once inside, Lauren is waiting for them near the training ring. Ana suppresses her humiliation as they approach her. Rafe introduces them, and they shake hands.

"Lauren's going to help tonight. I thought it would be good for you to watch two skilled combatants. We'll do each move twice. Once quickly, then again slower, so you can see each movement."

"That sounds great," Ana says.

Rafe and Lauren face each other in the training ring. "Ready to begin?" Rafe asks.

"Always," she says with a smile.

When Rafe lunges at Lauren, she grabs his wrist and turns to the side, pulling him to the floor. She's instantly on top of him. He helps her to her feet.

"See how I used gravity and his own weight to bring him down?" Lauren asks.

Ana nods. "Yes."

They do it again, but slower. Ana watches Lauren grab Rafe's wrist, twisting her body at the same time, and pulling Rafe to the floor again.

"Do you want to try?" Rafe asks.

"Would you do it once more, slowly?"

They do it again, then Lauren steps out to let Ana into the ring.

"We'll do it slow, so you feel the movement. Then we'll go fast. You'll be able to bring me down the first time, since we are moving slow. Are you ready?"

"Yes."

He lunges at her the same way he did Lauren. She grabs his wrist, twisting the same way and bringing him to the mat. When she turns back to smile at Lauren, he grabs her hand, pulling her to the mat and pinning her down. He steals a kiss.

"Rule number one when battling an opponent, never turn your back on them." He helps her up. "Ready to try it for real?" He notes the unease on her face. "You won't hurt me, I promise. Ready?"

They step apart, and she takes her stance. "Ready," she answers.

He lunges at her, much quicker. She barely has time to register his movement before reaching for his wrist. With a quick twist of her body, she brings him to the ground. He jumps to his feet. "Good job!"

Lauren shows Ana to break free of someone grabbing her wrist or arm, how to use the bottom of her palm to ram into someone's nose, and how to use her elbow against various soft points. Ana learns how to kick Rafe's knee out, sending him sprawling to the floor. They decide to practice the lunge one more time before calling it a night.

Rafe looks at Ana, returning her smile. "Prepare yourself!" he calls out, lunging at her.

Caught off-guard by her frozen, blank stare, he's unable to stop himself from hitting her in the face with his palm. She falls to the floor. "Ana!" he cries out and helps her to her feet. "I thought you were ready. I'm so sorry." He tries bringing her head up so he can inspect the damage. "Ana, I have to see. Look at me." She turns to run, but he grabs her arm. Her body goes slack as the blood drips from her nose and lip.

The room is spinning. Her body runs hot and cold, her hands are clammy, and she can barely focus. She leans over, resting her hands on her knees, and throws up. Lauren runs over, wearing nitrile gloves, and carrying towels and ice. She applies an ice pack to Ana's face and presses a towel to her nose to stop the bleeding. Once she's sure there's no serious damage, she looks at Rafe.

"She'll be okay. I think it's more shock than anything else. You didn't break anything."

"I don't understand what happened," he says, shaking his head. "I thought she was ready."

"I thought so, too."

"So, what happened?" Rafe asks.

"I don't know."

"I'm right here you know," Ana manages to get out.

"Then tell us what happened."

"No," she says as she loses consciousness.

Rafe puts her on his lap and continues holding the ice pack to her face. "Do you think she needs to go to the hospital?"

Lauren pulls the ice pack away, gently feeling around her face. "No. She just needs rest and to keep this on," she says, applying the ice pack.

"I'll get her home. Can I pay for the mess?"

Lauren laughs. "Wow. I've never had someone offer that before. No, thanks. I've got it. Just get her taken care of." She gathers up his bag and slings it over his shoulder. He carries Ana from the gym, getting her in the car and reclining her seat. Once at her house, he removes her clothes, leaving her sports bra and underwear on.

He takes her into the bathroom, wetting a washcloth to clean the blood from her face and body, then gets her dressed into her pajamas. Once he has her on the couch, he brings her two of her pain pills and a bottle of water. She wakes up enough to take them before going back to sleep.

Shit! Kara is going to kill me! I'm a dead man. He sighs, wondering how he will tell her about this. He showers and changes, sitting in the recliner by Ana. Pushing the chair back, he turns off the lamp and falls asleep.

⤚⤙

Ana wakes up to find her face is uncomfortably numb. She brings her hand up but quickly winces in pain at the slightest touch. Rafe is still asleep, so she slips into the bathroom quietly. There's a bruise under her left eye and her nose is swollen. The sight of her battered face brings her to tears. She's surprised when she leaves the bathroom and doesn't see Rafe. Assuming he's in Kara's bathroom, she slips into her room, hoping to avoid him. She opens the door and stops in her tracks at the sight of him sitting at her desk. Her head instantly goes down.

She's torn between continuing in or bolting but realizes she really has nowhere to go. With her head still lowered so he can't see her face, she steps in and sits on the bed.

"Ana, let me see," he demands.

She shakes her head. "No."

"Ana?"

"No!" she cries out, weeping into her hands. She cries harder from the pain radiating across her face.

"What happened? What is going on?" he asks in exasperation. "Will you not look at me because of how you look or because you're mad at me?"

"Why would on Earth would I be mad at you?"

"I hurt you, Ana."

"You think I'm mad at you? I'm mad at myself. I messed up," she admits.

"What do you mean?"

"I can't, please. You'll never want to see me again."

"Ana, you know that's not true. I told you, nothing you say or do will make me feel that way. Open up to me."

She brings her hands down and looks at him. He flinches at the sight. "You told me to prepare myself. Instead, I froze up." She looks down again, wringing the blanket in her hands. "I told you about my foster father breaking my ribs."

"Yes."

"He would come into my room at night and climb into bed with me. He... he never put himself in me, but he would touch my stomach and legs while he... with himself..." She shakes her head. "He would come in and say 'Did you have a nice bath? Did you prepare yourself for me?' When you said to prepare myself, I was hit with the memory of those awful nights. I froze." She looks at Rafe. "If you want to go, I'll understand." Her heart sinks when he stands up, but he doesn't leave. Instead, he sits on the bed beside her.

"I'm not going anywhere. I told you that. I'm so sorry for the hell you had to endure."

"How can you still be here? How can you look at me without being repulsed?" she asks quietly in disbelief.

"Ana, you were just a child. Awful things were done to you, but you survived and grew into the beautiful young woman you are. If anything, knowing what you've overcome makes me see how strong you are."

She cries into his chest. "How is this possible? Are you real?" she asks, looking up at him.

"I am." He smiles and takes a breath, looking at her bruised face. "You do realize Kara is going to kill me for this."

"Oh, crap."

"She doesn't get back until tomorrow. Maybe it won't look so bad by the time she gets here." He gently places his hand under her chin, turning her face as he looks her over. "God, I feel so bad for this."

"It wasn't your fault."

"Ana, it was. As your trainer, it is my responsibility to make sure you're ready. I got caught up in the banter of the moment."

"It was an accident. It won't happen next time."

"There won't be a next time," he says sharply.

"What? Rafe—"

"If you want Lauren or Kara to train you, go ahead. I can't."

"Please? I want you to do it."

"Mia estrela, I can't." He gets up and leaves the room.

She cries out. The tears start to fall, and she sits there, pulling her knees to her chest.

Rafe runs back in. "What's wrong? Are you in pain?"

She wipes her tears and looks up at him. "I've ruined everything!"

"Ana, you didn't—"

"This was my fault, I know. Please, don't punish me for it. Please."

"You think by not training you, I'm punishing you? No, mia estrela. I can't bear to see what I've done. I won't take a chance of hurting you again. That's why I won't train you anymore."

"Really?"

"Yes. I couldn't take it."

She reaches out for him. He grips her arm and helps her to her feet. He wraps his arm around her waist and walks her to the living room. He sits her on the couch.

"Would you bring me a pain pill and water, please?"

"Of course." He brings them over. She takes the pill then sets the water bottle on the table.

"Thank you," she says, lying down.

He sits on the edge of the couch, holding her hand until he can't stop yawning. Letting the exhaustion win, he settles back and falls asleep.

Chapter 6

Ana watches Rafe sleep for a minute before getting up and going into the bathroom. She braces herself to look at her reflection, then raises her head to the mirror. Her mouth opens in shock. There are no bruises. She touches her face to be sure, pressing hard in the places which should have made her yelp in pain.

She walks to Rafe and wakes him up. "What?" he cries out. He looks around, coming to and realizing where he is. He looks at Ana and smiles, almost falling back to sleep, then jerks up. "Your face!"

"I know."

"How is this possible?"

"I'm not sure," he answers. *The legend...* He stands up, caressing her face while he pushes down the thought. "I'm grateful you are better." He looks at her in disbelief.

"Me, too. But I don't understand why?"

His breath shudders. "As I said, I'm not sure. Now, do you have an appetite?"

She leans up and kisses him. "Yes. I'll fix breakfast."

He gets dressed while she cooks. "What time does Kara get back?" he asks as they set the table.

"Assuming no delays, she should be home this evening."

"Okay."

Ana stops, realizing what that means. "Then you'll go back to your apartment."

"Yes," he replies. She hangs her head. "It's okay. We'll see each other plenty. I can come over and annoy you while you're searching for your online job."

The thought of having Rafe keep her company during even a mundane task like job searching brings a smile to her face.

After they eat, she sits on the couch, suddenly drained of all energy and barely able to keep her eyes open. Rafe sits next to her, and she lays her head against his shoulder.

"Ana, what are we doing today?" He looks down when she doesn't answer. "Ana?" When he stands up, she falls over, her body completely limp. He kneels beside her, gently shaking her and growing concerned when she doesn't wake up. Remembering his field training, he feels her forehead and checks her wrist to find a strong pulse. Her breathing and vitals all appear normal. "What's wrong?"

He covers her with a blanket, deciding that if she doesn't wake up within an hour or two, he'll take her to the hospital. He watches the news and strokes her hair, constantly checking her vitals and trying to rouse her. After an hour and a half, she opens her eyes.

"What happened?" she asks, slowly sitting up.

"I was going to ask you the same thing."

"I don't know. I sat down, and it was like I had no energy at all. Do you think it was from healing myself?"

"That would make sense."

"This is so weird."

"Are you going to tell Kara?" he asks.

"No way. I don't want to freak her out."

"I think you should, but I support whatever choice you make."

"Thank you. Hmm, I am still tired." She lies back down, yawning.

"Rest. I'll be here when you wake up." He strokes her hair and caresses her face. She falls back to sleep.

—◦—

She wakes up when Kara comes in at five.

"Taking a nap?" she asks. "Are you sick?"

Rafe and Ana exchange a glance. "No, I'm fine," she says, getting to her feet to give Kara a hug. They squeeze each other tight.

"I missed you. I'm glad to be home."

"There's food in the fridge."

"How did you know?" Kara asks, smiling at Ana. They all go into the kitchen and sit together, eating leftover Chinese food.

"How was Paris?" Rafe asks.

"Chaotic. Oh, speaking of which." She walks over to her bag and returns a moment later with a clear pyramid paperweight with a miniature Eiffel tower inside. She hands it to Ana. "Told you I would bring you something back."

"I love it!" she exclaims, turning it upside down and shaking it. The silver and blue glitter swirl around. "It's beautiful." She takes it into her room and places it on her antique secretary desk, the one she found at a flea market a few years ago and had to have.

"Okay, what's going on?" Kara whispers to Rafe.

"Nothing."

"No. What happened while I was gone?"

Ana walks back out and senses the tension in the room as Rafe and Kara speak quietly. She sits at the table. "Everything okay?"

"That's what I'm trying to find out. What happened?"

"We can talk about it later, it's not a big deal. Right now, I'd rather hear about your trip and enjoy being together before you kick Rafe to the curb."

"All right." Kara tells them about the protesters she was photographing and the police violence that broke out while she was there.

"How did you avoid getting hurt?" Rafe asks.

"I got lucky. There were a few close calls. I got the pics I needed then got the hell out of there." She tells them about the food she ate and what little she did get to see. She yawns. "I need a good, hot shower."

"I'll take that as my cue," Rafe says.

Before either of them get up from the table, Ana looks at Rafe and clears her throat. "Do you have dinner plans for tomorrow?"

"No," he replies.

She looks at Kara. "I would like if the three of us could have a nice, quiet dinner here." Ignoring the look of surprise on Kara's face, she continues. "No cake, candles, gifts, singing, or balloons. Just dinner with the two of you. Please?"

Kara and Rafe instantly agree. Kara leaves them alone to say their good night. Rafe takes Ana's hand.

"What time?"

"Be here at five."

He leans down and kisses her. "I'll see you then."

After changing into her pajamas, she returns to the living room. Kara sits with her on the couch, holding her hand.

"Now, will you tell me what happened while I was gone?"

Ana nods, looking down. She tells Kara about the detective, the trip to the mall, and training, leaving a few details out, of course. "I need to sleep."

Kara chuckles. "I see how tired you are. Get some rest. Love you, sis."

"Love you, too." Ana hugs her then goes to her room. Thinking of seeing Rafe the next night, she falls asleep with a smile on her face.

Ana pulls the manicotti out of the oven while Kara gets the good dishes down. Ana sets the pan on the stovetop to cool, then gets a bottle of wine out of the fridge.

"I still can't understand why you wanted to cook your own birthday dinner?" Kara asks, regretting it as Ana flinches at the word birthday. "I'm sorry. It's just, we could've gone out or ordered in."

"I wanted to cook. I want today to be special. You're home, safe and sound. I have a boyfriend. I'm changing jobs. Things in my life are so different right now, and I want to celebrate that."

Kara smiles. "Good."

"While this is cooling, I'll get ready." Ana runs to her room.

There's a knock on the door, and Kara opens it to let Rafe in. He's dressed in black slacks with a charcoal shirt, running with glossy, black buttons. As usual, he has his leather jacket and silver jewelry. He smiles at Kara in her bohemian skirt and peasant blouse.

Rafe chuckles. "This is different."

Kara shoots him a grin. "I wanted to dress up for Ana's special day."

They turn when Ana walks out from her room. Rafe's breath sucks in at the sight of her.

She's wearing a navy-blue blouse with a V-cut neck and lace sleeves. Her pants are tight, black dress slacks. Her hair is braided and pulled up, forming a crown around her head. Rafe walks to her, taking her hands in his.

"Mia estrela, you look like the stars." She looks down as her cheeks flush. He gently cups her chin and lifts her face. "Can I give you a birthday kiss?"

She smiles and gives him a slight nod. He places a firm, loving kiss on her mouth. He steps back to admire her.

"Thank you. You look great. I love that shirt on you," she says, squeezing his hand.

He smiles when she leads him into the kitchen. He hangs his jacket over his chair. "It smells amazing! What are we having?"

"I made ricotta and spinach stuffed manicotti, with rosemary garlic bread. I made the loaf from scratch."

"I made the sauce!" Kara beams.

Ana laughs. "Opening the lid and pouring it from the jar doesn't count." Kara shoots her a crude gesture in response.

Ana brings their plates to the table, smiling when Rafe inhales his food. "I take it you like it."

He laughs and wipes his mouth. "It's delicious. In fact, this might be the best meal I've ever had."

She blushes, thanking him. Rafe picks up his wine glass. Ana cocks her head. "You want to toast?"

He nods, watching as Kara and Ana raise their glasses. "Happy birthday to the most beautiful woman in the universe. May this next year be filled with blessings, love, and new adventures."

Kara's eyes squint for a moment as she loses her smile. She regains herself, joining in. "To my sister, happy birthday." They clink their glasses and drink together.

When they've finished eating, Rafe takes Ana into the living room. Kara gathers their plates from the table and watches him kiss her, running his lips along her cheek and neck. She loves seeing Ana so happy but can't shake the uneasy feeling she has about him.

Rafe pulls back from Ana, smiling. "I have something for you." He jumps up and goes to his jacket, removing a small, wrapped box. He hands it to her. "I know you said no presents, but in my defense, I bought it before you said that."

She laughs, shaking her head as she opens it up. What's inside leaves her breathless. She gently lifts out the cross she had looked at when they were at the jewelry store. "Rafe, I can't. This is too much."

"I saw the look on your face when you were admiring at it. Please, accept it from me?"

When she nods, he opens the clasp and puts the necklace on her. He smiles as she gently runs her fingers over the knots and stone of the cross. "I've always loved the Celtic cross. It's such a beautiful symbol, and the stone is so unique."

Kara comes in from the kitchen to admire the pendant. She gives Rafe an approving smile then finishes loading the dishwasher before joining them to have another glass of wine. Rafe takes a refill while Ana politely declines.

"How is your search going?" Rafe asks Ana. "Find anything yet?"

Kara straightens up. "What search? What are you talking about?" They look at her, confused. She laughs, holding up her glass. "I'm sorry. Must be the wine."

Ana shakes her head. "Online searching for a new job."

"Oh, right." Kara sits back, smiling. "Any bites yet?"

"A few prospects. I'm not sure."

"You do hate trying new things. Anything outside your comfort zone usually sends you running for the hills." Kara stares at Rafe when he makes a weird face. He catches himself, flashing a grin at her. She glares at him before smiling at Ana. "You know you'll be fine, whatever job you take."

"I know. Thanks."

"I'm going to pack up the food," Kara says, picking up the bottle and her glass.

"I'll help."

"No, Ana. It's your birthday. I'll take care of it."

Ana looks up at Rafe, clutching the cross in her hand. "Thank you again. It's stunning."

"Hmm, like you, mia estrela?" He chuckles when she blushes. He nuzzles in, softly kissing her neck and chin.

"Rafe…" she says, breathless. He raises his head, staring into her eyes. Her lips part as she nods, and his lips crash on hers. She grips his neck, climbing onto his lap.

Kara chokes on her spit, running to her room to give them privacy. Rafe chuckles when he hears the door shut. He pulls back, bringing his hand to Ana's neck while his fingers strum up her chin and cheek, before running his fingertips along her mouth.

She runs her fingers over his chest and down his abdomen, smiling at the intake of breath when her hand is on his stomach.

"Ana—" he tries, swallowing hard. "We need to slow down."

"You don't want me?" she asks, biting down tears.

"That's not it."

She pulls away and walks to the window. Rafe takes a few breaths, commanding his body to calm down before he walks over to her. He's concerned when she won't look at him.

"It's okay," she says. "I understand. I'm disgusting, I know."

"You have to stop saying things like that!"

Kara runs out. "What is going on?"

"This is private," Rafe says.

"What did you to do my little sister?"

"I was telling her we need to slow down."

Kara gasps softly. "Ana?"

"I told you he wouldn't want me."

Rafe shakes his head, raising his hands as Kara is walking to him. "No. I said we need to slow down because we are supposed to be taking all of this slow." He looks at Ana. "I don't want to rush you into anything, into falling in love, into bed, any of it. You said yourself this is all new to you. I want us both to take our time, to enjoy it together."

Kara stops walking, genuine surprise on her face. She looks at Ana. "Sis?"

Ana raises her head to meet his eyes. "Is that really how you feel?"

"I swear on every star in the sky and the one standing before me," he says, taking her hand. "I do."

"I'm sorry. I was... I was caught up in the passion of the moment."

He smiles at her. "We both were. You know how much I love kissing you and feeling you on me?"

Kara gags. "I'll be in my room!"

Rafe winks at Ana, smiling when she giggles. "Be nice!" she admonishes him. "She did nothing wrong."

"Now, can I take you to lunch Monday then train Monday night?"

"You're going to resume training me?"

He nods his head, losing his smile. "You have to understand, though. I will be much more serious and careful this time. I won't hurt you again."

"What does that mean?" Kara asks, turning back to them as she was almost to her door. "He hurt you?"

Ana moves in front of Rafe, a begging look in her eyes. "Kara, please—"

"Answer me! Did he hurt you?"

"No!" Ana yells. "I hurt myself."

Rafe and Kara both freeze at her words. "What does that mean?" Kara asks.

"I made a mistake. Yes, Rafe's hand hit my face. It was my fault. I froze in place, and I hurt myself with him. He did *not* hurt me."

Kara takes a deep breath. She looks at Rafe. "What happened?"

"Ana took her stance, and I lunged. We had already done this move several times, but then she froze."

"Why, Ana?"

"It doesn't matter. Just please, understand. He didn't hurt me, not the way you were thinking he did."

Kara thinks it over a minute. "Fine. Good night, Rafe," she says as she walks into her room.

Ana collapses back against Rafe as relief washes over her. "Oh, I was worried how she would react."

"It's okay, mia estrela." He brings his arm around her waist and kisses the top of her head. "You're cute."

She looks up at him, confused. "Why?"

"The way you stood between me and Kara, protecting me."

She laughs. "You haven't tangled with her."

He roars with laughter at the thought. "Let's hope it doesn't come to that. Now, can I kiss you good night?"

"Please?"

He takes her hand, spinning her to him and planting his lips on hers. He caresses her neck as his lips part hers, then he pulls back. "Happy birthday, my shining star."

"Thank you." She watches him leave, smiling as she thinks of his birthday kiss.

Monday arrives with beautiful weather and not a cloud in the sky. Since it's a nice day, Ana and Rafe decide to sit outside for lunch at the bistro. While they wait for their food, Rafe notices Ana shifting uncomfortably in her seat.

"What's wrong?"

She nods her head towards the building across the street. Rafe looks over. "I hope he's not looking for me," she says, watching Detective Sheffield pacing.

Rafe swears under his breath. "He better not think of coming over here."

They watch him walk down the block. Ana sighs in relief. She smiles at Rafe. "Good. I'd hate to ruin lunch." Her smile fades when she sees how serious he looks. "What's wrong?"

"Ana, this has got to stop. You have to stop blaming yourself. You haven't ruined any of our time together." He watches the relief flash across her face. Running his thumb along her jawline, he gives her a reassuring smile. "I'm not going anywhere, mia estrela. As long as you'll have me, you are stuck with me."

She smiles at him. "I'm sorry." Swallowing hard at the look on his face, she stops. "Thank you, Rafe."

He leans forward and kisses her. Their food arrives. "Did you have a good birthday?"

"I did. You and Kara made it perfect."

"Are you looking forward to training tonight?"

"I am, as long as you are, too."

"What do you mean?"

"I know you're worried after last time. I know this isn't supposed to be fun, that it's serious. Even so, I don't want to spend an hour in the training ring with a robot, either."

He smiles at her. "You won't. You have to understand something, though."

"Okay."

"I take training as seriously as I do, because when I was training others, it was for war. I can't help but think of that." He looks down before meeting her gaze.

She takes his hand and gives him a reassuring squeeze. "I'm sorry. You don't have to train me. Kara or Lauren could. I never want you to feel like this because of me."

"It's okay. What I started to say was, I can't help but think of the war sometimes, but training you, I'll be making better memories."

"If you're sure?" She squeezes his hand again.

"I am."

He drives her home after their meal and walks her to the door. "I'll pick you up at quarter til seven."

"You could—" she clears her throat. "I'll see you then."

"What is it?"

"It's nothing," she says, giving him a reassuring smile. She leans up and kisses him.

She finds Kara in the basement, developing her latest set of pictures. After all their years of friendship, Ana has become an expert at helping her. Kara loads new film into her cameras while Ana clips the developing images onto the clothesline.

"Remind me again why you won't go digital?" Ana asks with a laugh.

"I do with my phone, sometimes. I really love all of this. Being down here, making something from nothing. It feels like making magic, watching the pictures appear out of thin air."

Ana smiles at her friend. "I understand. I'm going to read a bit. Rafe will be here around seven to pick me up."

"Training?"

"Yes."

"Do I need to chaperone?"

Ana laughs. "His other girlfriend might be there." Kara turns sharply and stares at Ana with her mouth open. Ana laughs even harder and tells her about Lauren. "She is really sweet."

"I'm glad you saw that instead of me."

"Kara—"

"The things I would've done."

"Oh, come on, be nice. I'm going to read now."

"All right."

Ana goes into her room, grabbing the book off her desk and lying in bed. She reads until six, then fixes dinner. Kara joins her at the table.

"Are you nervous about training?"

"No, I'm actually excited. I feel safer now, learning how to protect myself."

"I'm glad."

Ana glances at the clock. "Speaking of which, I need to get dressed."

Kara washes dishes while Ana changes. She laughs when Ana walks into the kitchen. "Is that my shirt?"

Ana looks down, blushing. "Do you want it back?"

"Nah. Keep it. I've got a hundred more. But why are you wearing my clothes? I mean, I know we've shared PJs."

Ana looks over. "I... I wanted to..." Kara walks to her, taking her hands. "I just wanted something different than the plain shirts I wear."

"Sis, you know anything of mine is yours. You never have to ask. I mean that."

"Thanks."

The doorbell rings, and Kara answers it, letting Rafe in. "If I have to say it…"

Rafe laughs, holding up his hands. "She'll be safe with me, I promise."

"Hmm. She better be."

Ana takes his hand and smiles at Kara. "We'll be back."

Rafe walks her to the car and opens the door for her.

———— ~•~ ————

When they arrive at the gym, he notices her looking around. "Lauren was meeting with another investor tonight."

"Okay."

They go into the center of the ring. For a while, all they do is work on her stance. Then he has her punching the air, working on her form. Finally, she stops and looks up at him.

"What?" he asks.

"You are scared you're going to hurt me." Not a question.

"I am," he admits.

"You won't. I know you won't."

He takes a breath. "We'll start out slow, not because I'm afraid to hurt you, but to make sure you have the movements down."

"Okay."

Pushing down the memory of blood dripping down her face, he lunges for her. Her footing slips, and he grabs her wrist to keep her from falling.

"Are you all right?"

"I need a restroom."

He walks her to the restrooms and waits outside the door for her. When he hears her retching, he quickly runs inside. "Are you sick?" he asks, pulling her hair back.

"I'm fine."

"Ana?"

She rinses her mouth at the sink. "I'm okay. Will you take me home?" As she speaks, she keeps her head down and her arms crossed.

"After you tell me what's wrong."

"I'll tell you on the way."

"Deal." He follows her out of the restroom and grabs his bag, tossing it in the trunk after he helps her in. He starts the car and leaves the parking lot. "Ana?" She doesn't respond. "Did I hurt you?"

"No," she replies.

"You said you would tell me what's wrong."

She says nothing the rest of the way back to her house, until he passes it by. "Rafe! What are you doing?"

"Talk to me, then I'll take you home."

"Please, take me home now!" she begs.

He turns the car around. When he pulls up to her house, she jumps from the car without a word and runs inside. Rafe debates going after her but decides he will talk to her in the morning.

Ana goes to the bathroom, getting a shower and going to bed. Kara knocks on her door.

"Ana, are you all right?"

"I'm okay. Tired from training. I'll see you in the morning."

"Good night."

Ana is cooking breakfast when Kara wakes up. Kara almost always wakes up after Ana does—she has a bad habit of staying up late to binge watch whatever new show she's hooked on. She's just started to drink her first cup of coffee when the doorbell rings. She gives Ana a confused look before she opens the door, then steps back and gestures Rafe inside. Ana looks up but immediately hangs her head at the sight of him. He walks over, putting his arm around her waist.

"How are you this morning?"

"Okay," she says, flipping the pancakes. "Do you want a coffee?"

"Keep doing what you're doing. I'll make it."

Ana plates the food. Rafe sits with her, drinking his coffee and staring at her.

"All right, what is going on?" Kara demands.

"I don't know, but I would like to know as well," Rafe answers.

They both look at Ana. "I'm okay, really," she says, keeping her head down and eating a bite.

"Sis, look at me."

"Can I just eat?" Ana asks, exasperated.

Kara looks at Rafe. "Did something happen at training last night?"

"Apparently, but I don't know what." Ana reaches for the butter, and Rafe gently grips her arm to pull up her sleeve. He gasps at the bruise around her wrist. "Did I do that?"

Ana looks from Kara to him. "Yes," she admits quietly.

"What happened?" Kara demands.

"It was an accident. I lost my footing, and Rafe grabbed me to keep me from hitting the ground."

"Is that why you're upset?" he asks, bringing her hand up and kissing along the bruise. "I'm sorry. I never meant to hurt you."

"I'm not upset."

"Ana," Kara is interrupted when the doorbell rings. "Crap. Now who?" She opens the door to find Detective Sheffield waiting. Rafe jumps to his feet, getting in front of Ana.

"What do you want?" Rafe asks.

"I need to speak with Ms. Summers about her case."

"The mugger is dead. What else do you need to know?" Kara asks.

His nostrils flare as he takes a breath. "I need to speak with her. I have questions."

Rafe approaches him. "She answered your questions. Either send Detective Andersen or leave her alone," he orders.

The detective scoffs. "I'm sure I'll catch her another time." He turns on his heel and storms off. Kara and Rafe both turn to Ana. Her face is buried in her hands. Kara runs to her, pulling her from the chair and holding her tight.

"Shh, sis. It's okay. He's gone."

"What does he want?" Ana asks.

"He says he has questions, but with the mugger dead, I don't see what it matters."

"Should we go to the station? Speak to him there so he stops coming here?" Ana asks.

Kara looks at Rafe. "What do you think?"

Failing to hide his surprise at Kara asking for his input, he thinks a moment. "If they need more information, they can send Detective Andersen. She took her statement and was very professional."

"Can we finish breakfast?" Ana asks softly.

"Of course," he says, kissing her hand as she sits. He sits beside her, watching her eat. "What are you two doing today?"

"I'm leaving for the office shortly. Ana?"

"I have an interview online at ten o'clock."

"All right. I have a few errands to take care of. Would you have dinner with me?" he asks.

"I'll cook. Be here at five?"

"Of course. I'll see you then." He kisses her forehead and leaves.

Kara sits across from her. "What is going on with you two? I feel like I need to put on a sweater after that interaction."

"I had a small episode at the center last night. I'm trying not to let him see that, not yet."

"Ana," Kara sighs, "I understand, but he seems to really care for you. I think you should let him in."

Her eyes go wide. "Really?"

"I know, believe me, I do. This is not what I thought I would be saying, either. He's good for you, though. You've eaten and talked and laughed more since you've met him than you have all year."

"I didn't notice."

"I did. That's why I'm saying this."

"Okay. I'll think about it. I need to go get some paperwork together for my interview."

"I'm heading to the office. I'll text you when I'm coming home."

Ana gets her laptop set up, getting her paperwork laid out. After the interview, she does laundry and housework, smiling at how well it went. She thinks this might be the job for her. It's a cute little print shop within walking distance. She had been worried about interviewing, but the owner had to stay home and asked if she could do it online.

At four, she begins meal prep for dinner. She listens to music as she cuts vegetables, makes her ricotta mixture, and layers the lasagna. She puts everything into the oven, getting a shower and changing into dark jeans with a pale pink long sleeve shirt. She had rolled her eyes at the sight, but Kara insisted the color looked good on her. After seeing herself in it, she couldn't disagree.

Five on the nose, Rafe rings the doorbell. Ana smiles at him and lets him in, then takes his hand and leads him to the table. He removes his jacket and sits. When she sets his plate down, he takes her hand and kisses her palm.

"Mia estrela, this looks incredible. Like you."

She blushes as she smiles at him and joins him. "It's just lasagna and garlic bread with fried zucchini."

She watches him devour his plate. She laughs when he asks for seconds. He fills his plate then sets it on the table before he walks up behind her, looking down. He leans down and kisses her on top of her head before sitting beside her.

"Are we okay?" he asks.

"We are. I'm sorry about last night. It's something I'm still dealing with, and I didn't mean for you to blame yourself."

She sees the urge to ask in his eyes, but he doesn't question it. "Well, I'm here if you need to talk. How did your interview go?"

"Really well. I like the company, and she seems like a good boss."

"What would you be doing?"

She tells him about the position and what it entails. Kara walks in right as they are finishing dinner.

"Gee, did you leave me any?"

Ana giggles. "Rafe had two plates, but there is plenty. You know I would never let you starve."

Kara laughs, fixing a plate and standing at the counter. "How was your interview?"

Ana tells her about it as she packs the food up. Rafe gathers their dishes and puts them in the sink. Kara decides to take her plate into the basement to eat so she can check on her photos. Ana rolls up her sleeves up to rinse dishes, then hands them Rafe to put into the dishwasher. She hands him the last one. With one hand putting the dish in, his other gently grips her wrist. He looks at her as he brings her arm to his mouth, kissing along her scar.

"I really wish you would tell me about these."

Her eyes go wide as she pulls away, running to her room and slamming the door. He steps up as he hears the lock click. He leans into the doorframe, his arm against the door.

"Ana, please, come out."

Kara comes up from the basement. "What did you do?" she asks, setting her plate on the counter.

He glances over at her, taking a breath. "I was kissing her scars, and, well—"

"You asked about them?" She sighs when he nods. "You really are a stupid man. Why would you do that?"

"I couldn't help myself." He faces her door. "Ana, please. I'm sorry. Will you come out and talk to me?"

"Good luck. She didn't talk to me for a whole week after I asked."

"Ana, I am truly sorry. Please, come out. I swear, I will never bring them up again."

The snicker dies in Kara's throat when the lock clicks. Ana opens the door slightly. "Do you mean that?"

"I do."

Kara is shocked when Ana steps out. She and Rafe return to the kitchen to finish cleaning up. Kara sits on the couch, looking up in surprise when she hears soft laughter coming from Ana. *Maybe he is good for her,* Kara realizes. *I still don't trust him entirely, though.* She watches as Rafe whispers in her ear, making her smile. He plants small kisses all over her face.

Ana walks Rafe to the door, saying good night and smiling when he kisses her goodbye, promising he will see her for lunch the next day. She watches him leave, then joins Kara in the living room.

"Are you okay?"

Ana nods. "I'm fine."

"I don't know why he did that."

"Kara…"

"He should know better!"

"Why are you so angry? He's curious about them. Why wouldn't he be? You asked about them, too."

Realizing Ana is right, Kara calms down. "I know."

"It's okay. I'm not mad at either of you. It's from a really dark time in my life that I never want to talk about."

"I understand. I don't need to know about them, as long as I know you're okay. That's the main thing."

She smiles at her. "I'm more than okay."

Kara shakes her head, returning the smile. "Get some sleep."

"You, too." She hugs her then goes to bed, thinking of Rafe planting kisses all over her face.

Ana gets dressed in her favorite jeans and a pale blue blouse Kara had bought her. She's fixing her hair when the doorbell rings. She smiles as she walks to the door, excited to see Rafe. Opening the door, she steps back in surprise. "Detective Sheffield, how can I help?" she asks, trying to keep her voice steady as a tremor of fear flows through her.

"I have questions for you."

"Then I will come down to the station later today," she says, pushing the door closed. He quickly grips the edge, stopping the door from closing, and forces his way inside. Her eyes go wide as she wonders what he wants with her. "You need to leave."

"Not until you tell me how you set that up."

She shakes her head. "I don't know what you mean."

"You arranged to have the mugger killed. How?"

"I swear, I don't know—"

He grips her neck, shoving her against the wall. "No. Tell me!"

"Why are you so angry?" she manages.

"Because he was my nephew." He loosens his grip, and she drops to the floor. "Well, more specifically, he was my wife's nephew. She is devastated."

"I didn't know that," Ana says, slowly standing up.

Sheffield paces. Ana glances at the door, then decides to take the chance. She sprints towards it when he grabs her wrist and throws her against the wall. *Rafe will be here soon. If I can just keep him talking, keep him calm, maybe it will be all right.*

"You aren't going anywhere!"

"No, I'm sorry. Please, tell me why you think I had him killed? He robbed the bank where I work at. I had nothing to do with it."

"Liar," he snarls, grabbing her arms and pinning her to the wall. He slaps her across the face, bringing his arm back and about to punch her when Rafe walks in. Everyone freezes then Rafe tackles Sheffield to the floor, getting his handcuffs off the detective's belt and cuffing him. Ana manages to get her phone out and call 911. Within minutes, the house is full with emergency personnel.

"Miss, you really should get checked out," the EMT insists.

"I'm fine," she responds. "I don't need to go to the hospital."

"I live here! Let me in," Kara demands. Ana looks over, seeing a uniformed police officer holding Kara back. Ana gestures for him to let her pass. Kara runs up to her and looks her over, trying to see where all she is hurt. "What happened?"

"Sheffield came for me. Rafe tackled him, and they just took him to jail."

Kara takes a breath then looks at Rafe, who is giving his statement. She gives him a small smile before giving her attention back to Ana. "Are you about to go to the hospital?"

"No, I'm fine."

"Sis—"

"Please, Kara. It's just a few cuts and bruises. And a headache. I'm okay, really."

"All right."

Once Rafe finishes giving his statement, he joins Kara and Ana, taking her hand and squeezing it tightly. He inspects her face, looking at the bandage over her eye and regretting that he didn't get to her sooner.

"Rafe, are you okay?" Ana asks.

"I'm fine, mia estrela." He looks at Kara. "Is it all right if I spend the night tonight?"

Reluctantly, she nods. "Yeah, that's fine." She watches Rafe kiss Ana's forehead, clinging tightly to her.

Chapter 7

Ana sits up and opens her eyes, smiling when she realizes her head is no longer pounding. She stands up and stretches before walking to the mirror. Her mind races when she realizes she's healed again. She pulls off the bandages, only finding smooth skin. Not a single bruise or cut is to be seen.

How is this happening? I don't deserve something like this. Why me? She gets clean clothes and goes to the bathroom, glancing at Rafe on the couch, still asleep. In the shower, she thinks back over the attack, grateful she wasn't hurt worse. Rafe saved her, and she wonders how she can ever thank him for everything he has done for her. *He was so scared, I could see it in his eyes. He truly cares for me, in a way I never thought any man would. I swore I would never date, that I would never be vulnerable, but he has broken through my walls.*

Kara walks into the kitchen, rubbing the sleep from her eyes. "Hmm, Rafe. What are you cooking? It smells—" she stops in her tracks at the sight of Ana, standing at the stove and completely healed. Clamping a hand over her mouth to prevent the scream, she runs to her. She runs her fingers over Ana's face and neck. "How?" is all she can ask.

"I don't know," Ana replies.

Rafe wakes up when he hears them talking. He stands up and stretches, freezing with his arms in the air when he sees Ana. He goes into the kitchen. "This isn't the first time."

"Her bullet wound," Kara replies. She looks at Ana. "I see you look better. How do you feel?"

"Fine. I'm not sore, and there's no pain." She finishes cooking the eggs as Rafe makes himself a cup of coffee. The three of them sit together at the table.

"I'm still in shock," Kara confesses.

"How do you think I feel? I don't deserve this."

"What do you mean?" Rafe asks, exhaustion creeping in.

"Of all the people on this planet, the military, the doctors, the people who risk their lives, they should have healing abilities like this. Instead, it's wasted on a nobody like me. It's not right."

"Ana, you aren't a nobody."

"Don't, Kara. Just don't. I have done nothing to earn this gift. Why me?"

Rafe and Kara exchange a glance. Kara turns back to Ana. "You are special. You are such a wonderful, compassionate person."

"I don't deserve it," she says again. "I don't. I should not have this. It should go to somebody important, not a nobody."

"Ana, you have never been a nobody. Why would you say that?" Rafe asks.

"It's what I heard growing up, that I'm useless, worthless, that I'm a nobody. I was told that I'm stupid. It's all I ever heard."

"You know none of that is true," Kara insists. "You know how much we care for you, how much you mean to us."

"It's wasted on me," Ana repeats, not hearing Kara.

Kara sighs. "Sis, I love you, but I'm going to murder you if keep on like this. I'm going to let Rafe take over." She gets up from the table and goes to her room.

Rafe takes Ana's hand, kissing it softly. "You have never been and never will be a nobody. I swear this to you."

She looks at him, hearing the sincerity in his voice. She nods. "If that's what you believe."

"It is, but what I believe isn't important. You need to believe it."

"I can't," she replies softly "It's not true."

"It is!" he cries out. "God, how do you not see how special you are? How do you not see everything about you is beautiful and amazing?"

"That's not true, Rafe. I am broken and twisted and dark. There is nothing light or beautiful within me."

"Ana, the charcoal of night contrasts against the pastel of sunrise shining through. You think you are consumed with darkness, but I see the light burning within you."

Her breath sucks in at his words, and she wonders where he read something so poetic. "Nothing you just said is true. Why on Earth would you believe it is?"

"Because I'm in love with you!" he yells. Everything freezes. Her breath catches in her throat, her eyes glued to his as his words sink in. He studies her face, looking for any sign of how she feels about him. Anything at all. She doesn't move, doesn't blink.

Then she takes a deep breath. "You love me?" she whispers.

"Yes. I love you, Ana."

She smiles at him. "I love you, Rafe."

He rushes to his feet, pulling her out of the chair as he kisses her intensely. She brings her arms up around his neck. He plants small kisses all over her face and neck before his lips are on hers again. He picks Ana up, carrying her to the couch and holding her on his lap as they continue kissing. She holds her hands against the back of his head, pressing him into her as much as she can. She pulls back.

"Say it again, please," she begs softly.

"I love you, mia estrela."

"I love you, too."

She devours his lips, probing into his mouth while her hands grasp at his shirt. He puts his fingers into the small of her back, gently pressing forward, causing him to smile as she trembles under his touch and the moan escapes her lip. She pulls in, kissing him harder.

Rafe pictures her in the hospital, all the tubes, the wires, thinking how close he came to losing her the night she was mugged. Then she was hurt and could've been killed by Sheffield because he was too close to see the danger.

He pulls back. "Ana," he says softly.

"Yes, love?"

He stands up, gently placing her on the couch. "I'm sorry. I have to go."

"What's wrong? What did I do?"

"It's not you. It's something I need to take care of." He leaves without another word, and she runs to grab her phone off her desk.

Ana: *When will I see you again?*
Rafe: *Soon, I promise. I'm sorry, mia estrela.*

She clutches her phone to her chest and lets out a sob. Kara comes running into her room. "What happened? Where's Rafe?"

Ana shakes her head as violent sobs shake her entire body. Kara pulls her into her arms, holding her tight. She gets her to the bed, sitting down with her and holding her until Ana calms down enough to tell Kara what happened.

"He just... left?" Kara asks, angry. "What the hell? I'm going to kill him!"

＊＊＊

Rafe goes into his apartment, his heart pounding in his chest. He throws his phone on the charger, then digs through the closet until he finds what he's looking for. Inside the box, he pulls out the leather journal. He sits down at the table, flipping through it until he finds the passage and reads it aloud.

"Legend has it there is a pair of soulmates, so rare in their bond, they heal each other with a single touch. He will die to save her..." Rafe sucks in his breath as he silently reads the rest.

No, no, no! This can't be happening. He slams the book on the table. *Fate wouldn't be so cruel.* He picks up the book, tosses it into the box, and puts everything back into the closet. Heading for the bathroom, he's suddenly shrouded in a bright, pure white light. He brings his hand up to shield his eyes before he disappears in a flash, leaving the apartment empty.

Rafe opens his eyes. He's on an exam table in a bright room, lying on his stomach with his wrists and ankles restrained. His shirt has been removed, and he can't move or speak. A man he doesn't recognize walks over and says something he can't quite make out. Intense pain trails down his shoulder blades, carving into the scars already there. He holds his breath as navy blue wings rise from his back. Almost wisps at first, they quickly solidify into feathers. The straps are removed, and he's slowly put on his feet.

He looks up at the man. "Why did you do that? You just destroyed everything I've been working for!"

Another man walks in, dressed in the guardian uniform of navy-blue pants and tunic jacket, adorned with silver buttons and gold lapels. His boots are black and well-polished. His chestnut brown hair is as well-groomed as his mustache and small beard. He unfurls his black wings slightly as he stares at Rafe with grey eyes, watching his every move.

"Rafe, where have you been?"

Cringing at the weight on his back, he leans against the exam table. "Where is Rowenne?" he demands.

The man stops at the name. "I'm sorry to be the one to tell you, but your father was killed in battle." He tries to read the emotions on Rafe's face at the news. "Where have you been?" he asks again.

"Rowenne sent me on a secret mission to find her."

"What? That's ridiculous. No one knows where she was taken."

"We scoured through the mid-wife's things again. In her journal, we found references to Earth. That's where I've been. I found Maeriana, and I'm so close to bringing her back."

"But the curse?"

Rafe shakes his head. "I'll bring her back, I promise. Whatever I have to do." He flinches when his left wing flutters slightly. "Oh, it's been a while."

"I thought perhaps you were being punished. Why else would Rowenne cut your wings off?"

"To blend in on Earth. They don't have them there. Now, I don't know how I'll explain them when I return. You blew my cover." Rafe shakes his head again, still dazed. "I can't place you. What is your name?"

"It's me, Declan. The travel must've hit you hard." He takes a breath. "Wait here a moment. I'll be right back." He steps out.

Rafe walks around the room, stretching his wings and smiling at the familiar sensations. *I've missed you. I don't know how I'm going to explain this, what she's going to think when she learns the truth.*

Declan walks in with a small wooden crate. He dumps the contents on the table and picks up a leather journal, similar to the one Rafe has in his apartment.

"Your father's journal." He scans through it. "He did send you on a secret mission, at the request of—"

"I need to get back," Rafe interrupts. "I need to. My mission is in danger."

"I see."

"How long have I been here?"

"Almost two weeks. The cryosleep always takes it out of us."

"Two weeks? Oh, no. I have to go back. If we want any hope of stopping this war, I need to go. Right now!" he cries out desperately.

"All right."

He gets Rafe a shirt. While he's doing that, Rafe grabs what he needs off the table beside him. He shoves them into his pocket, praying he doesn't have to use them. He gets his shirt on, his wings extending out the through openings on the back. Declan gestures to a door. Rafe opens it, unable to see anything inside except the bright light. The moment he steps through, he's back in his apartment. He crumples to the floor.

Rafe wakes up, dazed. He sits up then slowly gets to his feet, nearly falling backward at the unexpected weight. *Right, my wings. I'll have to hide those.* He tucks them in, throwing on his leather jacket to cover them, flinching as he does. Picking up his phone, his heart drops at the sight of so many missed calls and unread texts. *She will never forgive me. I don't blame her. I need her, though. I need this to work. Please, Ana, please forgive me.* He grabs his keys and heads straight for her house, praying she's home.

Dread fills his stomach as he pulls up to the house. His heart pounds in his ears. He walks to the door and rings the doorbell, each second feeling like an eternity as he waits to see Ana again. Kara looks through the peephole. She swings the door open, her jaw falling in shock.

"Where have you been?" she demands.

"Is she here? I need to see her."

"That's the first thing you say? Not where you've been or why you broke her heart?"

"Kara, please—"

"No! You destroyed her." She pushes him back, stepping out onto the porch with him. "I nearly lost her, Rafe. She has cried every single night you've been gone."

"I was only gone for two weeks."

"What the hell are you playing at? You've been gone almost four months!"

His mouth opens in shock. *Time difference. That explains so much.* "I—I was only supposed to be gone two weeks. I was unconscious for most of it and had no way to communicate. Please, Kara, where is she? I need to see her!"

"You need to go. She's in the basement, helping me with my pictures."

"I need to see her. I have so much to explain."

"I'll say it again. You *need* to go. She's been through enough. Last thing she needs right now is to walk in and see you standing—"

"Kara?" Ana's voice calls from the basement door. She sees the open front door and walks towards it. "Who are you talking to?" Gripping the doorway, Ana is unable to believe what she is seeing. At the sight of Rafe, tears fall down her cheeks. With slow, hesitant movements, she approaches him, reaching her hand to his chest to prove to herself he really is there. She pulls her hand back and slaps him across the face. "How could you?"

She turns on her heel to run away, but he grabs her hand. He pulls her to him as she sobs, wrapping her in his arms and holding her tightly to his chest. "Please, Ana. I can explain everything."

"I don't want to hear it!" she cries out as she struggles to break free of his grip.

"My scars are gone."

She stops struggling, looking up at him. "Really?"

"Yes."

"Prove it! Show me your back," she demands.

He flinches. "Ana—"

"No! It's the only way I'll even think about listening to what you have to say. Show me your back."

"As you wish," he relents.

He takes her hand, leading her to his car when Kara runs around to block them. "Where do you think you're taking her?"

Determination on his face, Rafe looks at Kara. "Move, now. I will bring her back here. I swear it."

Kara looks at Ana. "Sis?"

"Step aside."

Ignoring the cut of those words, Kara does as she says. "Please, don't disappear like he did."

Ana takes her hand and gives her a reassuring squeeze. "I won't. We won't." Ana and Rafe go to the car. "Where are you taking me?"

"Somewhere private. We need to have a long talk."

"Okay."

Once they're on the highway, she looks at him, studying his face and wondering where he has been these past four months. Part of her wants to throttle him for hurting her, and the other part of her... she longs to have him in her arms, kissing her along her neck and chin. Her breath shudders as she thinks of that day on the couch with him.

He drives her to the other side of town, full of abandoned warehouses and storage facilities. He finds a grassy spot where they can't be seen and lays his jacket on the ground, gesturing for her to sit. She complies.

"Before I show you my back, I need to tell you something. It's going to be difficult for you to hear. Honestly, you probably won't even believe me. However, it's the truth, and you need to know it."

"Rafe, you're scaring me. What is going on?"

He takes a deep breath. "Far from here, not just this planet or solar system, but far from this galaxy, exists a world similar to this one. It's called the Sea-Stellar Realm. In it, lies the Maristellar Kingdom. It was once ruled over by a king and queen, but ten years ago, the queen died in childbirth. The king, angry at the sudden loss of his wife, blamed the midwife. He was going to have her executed. In retaliation, she stole the baby princess and brought her to Earth. Since then, war has raged across the realm as the quadrants vie for the throne. The king was killed in battle, and now the war rages even worse. We need the princess to restore the throne and to bring peace."

"What does any of this have to do with me?" Ana asks in frustration.

"Maeriana, you are the lost princess. I need you to come with me. You can end the war and save thousands of lives."

She stares at him with wide eyes, thinking on what he said, before erupting into laughter. "What are you on?" she asks, standing up. "Are you high? God, Rafe. What the hell? I'm leaving."

"Didn't you want to see my back?"

Her breath sucks in as she freezes at his words. She knows she should run away, but her curiosity is too great. She looks at him. "Show me."

He gestures for her to sit, watching as she does. "Please, try not to scream at what you're about to see." She says nothing but watches as two blue wings unfurl from his back. Overwhelmed with shock and awe, it takes her a minute to take them in.

She gets to her feet, staring at them, still not believing what she is seeing. Now his words have weight. Before, she could blow him off, thinking he was crazy. Looking at his wings, she knows in her heart he is telling her the truth.

"This is too much. I can't do this!" she cries. She turns away, but he grabs her wrist and pulls her to him.

"Please, mia estrela. I'm still me, you are still you. Nothing has changed." She lets herself get wrapped up in his warmth. God, how she has missed this. She nearly screams when his wings wrap around them. "It's okay. You're safe."

She looks up at him, her body shaking as her heart threatens to escape her chest. "I don't understand. There are seven billion people on this planet. How did you ever find me?"

"I'm a guardian. My duty is to protect the throne and the royals, and we have sense about us, that helps us locate you. It took me longer than I expected, but finding you wasn't really that hard."

"I don't understand. All of those things you told me… about being in the army, having a car, and an apartment. How did you manage that?"

"Rowenne had my wings cut off. That was the first step. Then he gave me some baubles from our realm, not really sure what they would be worth here. They were practically priceless. I sold some to a museum, and I found a private collector. I used the money to get an ID, papers, the apartment, my tablet, and a car. As I went from place to place looking for you, I would spend my time in cafés and bookstores, watching TV and reading books. I learned as much as I could about this world, immersing myself in the culture so I could blend in."

"Why go through all of that? Why not just tell me the truth? Or knock me out and take me back?"

"The mid-wife who stole you was also a witch. She placed a curse upon you. I had to get to know you, earn your trust. You have to willingly come back."

"Wait, you said the queen died ten years ago? I… I can't be the princess! I just turned twenty-three."

He takes a breath. "There's a time difference between Earth and the Sea-Stellar Realm. It's… It's complicated. I assure you, you are Princess Maeriana."

She closes her eyes, afraid to ask. Her breath shudders as she faces him. "Did you love me at all?"

"I didn't count on that happening," he admits. He leans down, kissing her softly as his wings wrap tighter around them.

"What now?" she asks.

"Now you decide. Do you stay here or come with me?"

"You're asking me to give up the only life I've ever known. I know it's not glamorous, but it's mine. I can read when I want, watch TV or play video games. Kara and I spend so much time together, and I can't imagine leaving her behind. I've read enough to have an idea of what the life of a monarch is like, how lonely and demanding it is. It would be so different from the life I have now. What if I can't do it?"

"I'll be with you the whole time. As long as you'll have me, I'll be there."

"Really?" she asks, pushing down her doubt.

"I swear it."

"What will it be like once I'm there? I don't know how to be a princess. I have no experience, I know nothing of the people or the land."

"You'll have handmaids to help you with the culture, fashion, and the customs. You'll also have advisors to help guide you in your decisions. You will have time to learn the history and adjust. Once you are ready, you will be crowned as queen."

"Queen?" she repeats quietly. "Oh. It's too much. Why me?"

"Maeriana," she stiffens at her name, "you are the princess. You are royalty. I told you that you're special."

Thinking on his words, she pulls away. She walks around him and studies his wings. She brings her hand up to touch his feathers but stops herself and looks at him. "Can I touch them?" He nods. She gently caresses the plumage, amazed at how soft and warm they are. He lets out a small moan when she brushes her fingers across the space between his wings before she walks in front of him.

"I need to think. I know we don't have much time, that you said people's lives are on the line. Just a little time to think."

"Take it. Whatever you need."

Deep in thought, she turns away. She still can't believe what he's told her. *Except, I healed really fast. Except, he's standing before me with actual wings. Except, some small part of me always felt like I was destined for more. I say no and what, go back to video games and pizza? Do my job, watch TV? All these years I've escaped into fantasy, dreaming of faraway lands and beautiful kingdoms. I have the chance to actually experience it. I would be crazy to turn this down, right?* She walks up to him and steps up to her tiptoes, kissing him softly.

"I'll do it."

"You'll come with me?"

"Yes, I will come with you."

He kisses her again. "Oh, Ana. You have no idea how happy I am."

"We have to see Kara. I promised her I wouldn't just disappear."

"What are you going to tell her?"

"I don't know. I'll think of something on the way over."

"Good idea." He tucks his wings back in. She helps him with his jacket, making sure they are completely covered. They hold hands as they walk to his car, and she can't help but feel excited about her decision, about what her new life will be like. "I need to swing by my apartment and grab something. Won't take me a minute."

Once at his building, he runs in and grabs the journal. He's walking to the door when it slips from his hand, hitting the floor with a loud thud, and opening to the middle. His eyes scan over the page when he picks it up, and he gasps softly in surprise at what he reads. He tucks the journal into his pocket and runs downstairs.

When they arrive at Ana's house, she's nervous as they go inside.

"What's going on?" Kara asks. "He's still here?"

"Kara—"

Before Ana can finish, Rafe pulls out bindings that are glowing blue and wraps them around Kara's wrists. As she opens her mouth to protest, he wraps a matching gag around her face. She can breathe but not speak. He turns to Ana, getting out the journal and seeing the worry on her face as she stares at Kara.

"The bindings are safe, I assure you. I wouldn't have brought them otherwise. You need to know, she's the mid-wife who kidnapped you."

"That's impossible," Ana says in shock. "Look at her. She's the same age I am!"

"There's an explanation for that. We'll get answers once back at the kingdom. She will pay for stealing you."

Ana walks up to Kara. "Is it true? Are you the one who stole me?"

Kara stares at her with defiance in her eyes. She gives a single nod in response. Ana turns away, unable to believe it.

"Princess Maeriana, we need to go."

"Am I allowed to take anything?"

He thinks a moment and picks up her laptop bag. "Whatever fits in here, you can bring. Hurry."

She runs to her room, grabbing her journals, bookmarks, her Eiffel tower paperweight, and a few books. She slings the bag on her shoulder, taking one last look around her room. She wipes a tear as she walks out. "Let's go."

Rafe takes Ana's hand and gestures her to grip Kara's arm. He pulls a metal disc from his pocket and tosses it down. Ana watches a wall of light open before them, the size of a door. He grips her and Kara, taking them towards it.

"Welcome to the Maristellar Kingdom," Rafe says as they go through the portal. Ana loses consciousness in his arms.

Chapter 8

Ana opens her eyes as she slowly comes to. Focusing on the sounds and sights around her as she observes the sterile, white room she's in. She realizes she's lying on an exam table in a white gown, similar to what she wore in the hospital. Her head hurts at so much white.

"Princess Maeriana, you're really here."

She swallows hard as her head jerks up at the voice. "I'm sorry. Who are you?" she asks, looking him over. His deep brown skin contrasts the light grey pants and white tunic medical coat he is wearing. His blue eyes are staring at her, as if he can't believe what he's seeing. He puts his glasses on and watches her.

"My apologies, of course. I am Winslow. I run the Medical Center and help with travelers such as yourself. Now, how are you feeling?"

"Okay, I guess. A little tired." He studies her chart, and the harsh light reflects off the silver clipboard, causing her to turn away.

"That's to be expected. No other side effects from the travel? You aren't seeing double or having shortness of breath?"

"No, sir."

He lets out a quiet laugh. "So polite. I like that." A nurse walks in, wearing a pale blue tunic medical coat. He holds up the silver chart and a vial of blood, catching Winslow's attention. Winslow walks over to him, speaking quietly. Ana notices when the nurse points at her, and she leans closer to try and hear what they're saying. Winslow nods and waves him away, thanking him before returning to her. "The tests

confirm it. You are in fact Maeriana, Princess of the Realm."
He bows to her. "Welcome, Your Highness."

"Thank you. I'm sorry, but I don't know your customs.
What is a proper response?"

"You may address me, tell me I'm dismissed, or simply
nod."

"I see. Thank you, Winslow."

"Very good, Your Highness."

"Where are my companions?"

"Rafe is still recuperating. He knows better than to make
two trips together like that! Goddess help him." He shakes his
head. "The woman you were with is in the dungeon until we
could figure out who she is, and why he had her in bindings."

"I'm curious to know that myself," she replies.

A look of confusion crosses his face, but he decides not
to ask. "Your handmaid, Evren, will be here shortly. She will
help you with anything else you need, Your Highness."

"Thank you."

"I will check on Rafe now." Winslow leaves the room.

Ana gets to her feet, stretching as she looks around.
Surprised, she sees a keyboard and monitor, not expecting
such technology in the kingdom. She looks up when the door
opens, trying not to stare at the short, strange looking woman
who entered.

"Mi'lady, I am Evren, your handmaid. I am here to serve
however you may need." She approaches then bows to her.

Ana stares at her a moment, looking down at her and
noticing she is at least a foot shorter than Ana. She's taken
back by Evren's lavender skin, pointed ears, shocking blue
hair, and bright green eyes. "Thank you. I appreciate that."

Evren nearly steps back in surprise at her politeness but
catches herself. "What may I do to help, mi'lady?"

"I'm not sure. I don't know the customs or process here.
Do I have quarters and clothes? What am I supposed to be
doing now that they've confirmed my identity? When can I
see my friends?"

"I know, mi'lady. It's a lot to take in. I brought you some clothes, whenever you are ready to change." Ana notices the gold fabric with matching shoes in Evren's hands. "You can change in the washroom there," she says, gesturing to a nearby door and handing the items to Ana.

"Thank you." Ana takes the clothing and steps inside, shutting the door behind her. She sets the bundle on the vanity, trembling from head to toe as her nerves and fear overwhelm her. Stripping off the hospital gown, she sees a hamper of sorts, and tosses it in.

She looks over the gold slippers, similar to ballet slippers, and sets them on the floor. Then she picks up the gown and runs her fingers over the thin material, panicking that everyone will surely be able to see right through it. Taking the chance, she slips the golden gown on over her head and examines herself in the mirror. It molds nicely to her shape, covering her from her neck to her ankles. She's impressed at how thick it looks but still feels exposed in the light material.

She leaves the washroom, approaching Evren. "Thank you for the clothes and shoes."

"Yes, mi'lady."

"What now?"

"Would you like to see your quarters and rest?"

"I want to see Kara first." She sees the blank expression on Evren's face. "The woman that came with us."

"Oh. Of course. I'll have her brought up." Evren steps out into the hallway and speaks quietly with one of the guards. She returns to Ana. "She'll be here shortly, mi'lady."

"Thank you." Ana looks at her ears but quickly diverts her gaze. "I don't mean to offend, but are you an elf?"

"Yes, mi'lady."

"Are there many elves here?"

"Not in this realm."

"May I ask about your necklace?"

"It's a collar to mute my magic," Evren explains.

"I don't understand."

"I'm a slave, beholden to serve you."

Ana sucks in her breath. "I'm sorry."

"It's all right. You may ask me anything, mi'lady. You will not offend me. I am here to help."

"Thank you." The door opens, and a guard walks in escorting Kara. The guard steps back. Ana walks up to them. "Remove her gag," she commands, trying to sound in charge. He does as she orders. She looks at him and Evren. "Leave us."

"Mi'lady—" Evren starts.

"Now." They turn and leave. Ana walks up to Kara, who is watching her every move intensely.

"Royalty suits you, Ana."

She takes a breath. "Why did you kidnap me?"

"It's a long story. Look, your mother died in childbirth. Your father, who was a horrible king, blamed me and was going to have me executed. I took you away to save you from him."

"Why did you leave me once we were on Earth?"

"I didn't! I was knocked unconscious during the journey. Our space travel is much more advanced than Earth's but still not perfect. When I came to, you were gone. I searched everywhere for you. The portal must've separated us. It's rare, but it does happen. As I had no ID or paperwork, I couldn't very well file a missing person's report. I kept my head down, worked job to job, and kept searching. I counted my blessings when I saw the article about a local orphan going to college on a full scholarship. I couldn't believe I had found you!"

"How old are you?"

"Oh, I don't think you're ready for that one."

Rafe runs in, still in his Earth clothes. "Princess Maeriana, what are you doing? Don't speak to her! She could curse you or enchant you." Kara rolls her eyes.

"What do you mean?"

"She is a witch, remember?"

"Rafe, it's okay. Kara has done nothing but show me love and kindness in all the years I've known her. I believe her when she says she was trying to save me from an evil king."

"I won't deny he was cruel. Only the queen could keep him in check. Once she was gone, he was truly brutal. She isn't lying about that."

"Release her," Ana says.

"Your Highness, we can't. She must pay for what she did. She kidnapped a royal."

"I said release her. That's an order!" Ana barks at him. Reluctantly, Rafe walks to Kara and removes her bindings. Ana takes her hand. "Are you really my friend?"

She pulls her into her arms. "Everything I did was to protect you. I love you, Ana. You know I do."

Ana hugs her back, grateful to have her with her. She steps back. "Now what? Can you stay here in the palace with me? I'm not sure what your role would be, but I don't want you to leave."

"Yes. I will be your Sage." Kara falls to one knee, her head bowed. "I pledge my life to you, to serve you, and to defend you. May death find me otherwise." She stands up.

"Thank you." Ana looks at Rafe. "Can we see my quarters?"

"Yes."

When they go out into the hall, Ana gasps at the stark contrast between the sterile Medical Center and the palace itself. The walls are grey stone with white marble floors, and dark blue marble pillars with specks of silver and gold that tower up to the ceiling, which is painted blue with silver constellations.

"Evren, we are going to my quarters now," Ana says.

"Yes, mi'lady," she replies, looking at Kara. Kara turns away and bites her lip when she catches Evren staring.

Ana looks at Rafe. "The palace is more beautiful than I could have ever imagined."

He smiles at her. "I'm glad you like it, mi'lady."

The hall is long with several oak doors, dark trim, and large, gothic windows. They arrive outside her quarters. Rafe turns to Evren. "Will you show Kara to her room?"

Evren looks at Kara, the two of them exchanging a small smile. "Yes, sir." She gently places her hand on Kara's shoulder and leads her away.

Rafe unlocks the door and leads Ana inside. There is a fireplace on the wall to her right, with a gold and blue chaise in front of it. To the left is a mural on the wall with relief work of suns, moons, and stars, which makes her smile. In the center of the room is a bed bigger than any king-size bed she has ever seen. The floor is white marble with blue and silver rugs.

She is taken back by the gothic windows with individual golden panels. The wall is adorned with navy-blue and silver tapestries bearing her family crest. She runs her fingers over the crescent moon with a pink rose resting on the curve of it, then down the golden crown hanging from the moon.

"Is this acceptable, mi'lady?" Rafe asks.

Only able to nod, Ana smiles at him. She gasps softly at the fireplace in the back corner, almost big enough for her to step inside. She walks up to him. "It's incredible." She steps onto her tiptoes to kiss him, but he places his hand on her shoulder and gently pushes her back.

"Your Highness, we need to talk."

Hiding her embarrassment, she turns away and goes to the window. "Oh, wow." She can see the courtyard below, where there are a few small outbuildings, then a path leading out to the market. From there is the village with farmhouses, lumberyard, and a watermill. She admires the forest and plains, happy to see the world isn't so different from where she grew up. She looks at Rafe. "What do we need to talk about?"

"I have something to tell you." He swallows hard. "I apologize, in advance. I want you to understand, I had to do my duty. I did not accept the job lightly, but I knew it had to be done if we wanted to have a chance at stopping the war."

"Rafe, what are you talking about?"

"When you were kidnapped, there was a curse placed upon you. The only way to bring you back was in the arms of the one you loved. It was my duty to find you, get you to fall in love with me, and return you to the throne. I apologize if I've hurt you."

She steps closer. "I don't understand. You… you don't love me?" Her skin grows cold when he shakes his head.

"It was my mission, to earn your trust and make you fall in love with me. I had to do whatever it took to save our realm. Sometimes we must put our duty above ourselves."

She turns away as the tears roll down her face. "Oh, God," she whispers, wiping them away.

"Your Highness, please. Say something." He steps towards her when she doesn't respond. "Ana," he says softly.

She spins around, standing tall. "Do not address me so informally, Guardian!"

He bows before her. "Apologies, Your Highness."

She walks up to him. "Was any of it real?" She gasps when his eyes go down. "Oh, God. Take me home. Take me back to Earth. Now!"

"I can't, Your Highness. They sealed the portal permanently in order to protect the realm. There's no way back."

She hangs her head and wipes her tears. "I hate you."

"Mi'lady—"

"You're dismissed!"

Swallowing hard, he leaves her quarters. He knew she would be hurt and angry, but he thought he would have a chance to explain to her how important it was to return her to the realm. Kara and Evren walk in a moment later. When Kara realizes Ana is crying, she runs to her. "What's wrong?"

Ana falls into her arms. "Rafe never loved me."

"What? What do you mean?"

"He said he had to, in order to bring me here. He said he never loved me!"

"Oh, Ana, I'm so sorry."

Evren steps forward. "I apologize, if this is out of turn. He's not allowed to love you."

Ana looks at her "What do you mean?"

"It is forbidden for a guardian and a royal to fall in love. It's against the law. It is also against the law for a guardian to court anyone outside of their own race. Any guardian found to be violating either of these laws will be executed. It was enacted to protect the royals, since they are their closest protectors. It also prevents a guardian from usurping the throne."

Kara looks at Evren. "He's not a guardian. He doesn't have wings."

Ana laughs. "Oh, he has wings. Beautiful blue wings."

"What? Did he have those on Earth?"

"Not at first. After he returned to us, he showed them to me. Do you think... is it possible he loves me but can't admit it?"

"What did he say to you?"

"He said he made me fall in love with him because of the curse."

"What curse?" Kara asks, clearly exasperated.

Evren speaks up. "There was a rumor that the witch who kidnapped the princess placed a curse on her. She could only return to this realm willingly, in her true love's arms."

Kara shakes her head. "There was no curse!"

"What?"

They all turn to Rafe. Ana loses her breath at the sight of him. He's in his guardian uniform, blue pants with matching tunic jacket, his wings extended out. She nearly cries at the sight and has to turn away.

"What do you mean, Sage?" Evren asks. "That there was no curse?"

"I mean it's a load of hogwash! I didn't curse Ana. I only took her away."

Rafe clenches his hands as he realizes he hurt Ana for no reason. He pushes down his anger for doing so.

Collecting herself, Ana faces him. "What are you doing in here? What do you want?"

"I apologize for the intrusion, Your Highness. The archduke has requested you join him for lunch."

"And who is he?" Ana asks.

"You might call him a cousin, though not really. He was married to your mother's niece. Since she passed away, along with the king and queen, he has been running things in your stead, as he is the closest to a royal in the realm. He is Archduke, but he is also called Chief Steward."

"I see," Ana says quietly. She wraps her arms around herself, turning away. "Could I have a few minutes to myself, please?" she asks. "Tell him I will meet him shortly."

"Of course, mi'lady."

They all leave the room, giving Ana the space she has asked for. She walks over and sits on the bed, wiping her tears. *I'm trapped here. I'm trapped in a world I know nothing about. Rafe doesn't love me, and now I have to meet someone regarding a kingdom I know even less about. I think death would be easier at this point.* She clutches the cross Rafe had given her, which still hangs around her neck. The cold of the metal with the weight of it brings her comfort as she holds it. She stands up and goes into the washroom.

It's massive, with a double vanity, marble toilet, and claw-foot tub. She steps into the walk-in shower, unable to believe the sheer size of it. She washes her hands at the sink and is grateful that her new home has electricity and running water, unlike some of the palaces she'd read about in her books.

Out in the hall, her three companions are waiting for her. She opens the door and gestures Evren back in. "What I'm wearing isn't appropriate for meeting the archduke, is it?"

"No, mi'lady."

"Will you please help me dress?"

"Of course." She leads Ana to the closet. Opening the door, Ana walks in and loses her breath at the sight. The sheer size of the closet nearly overwhelms her. She steps forward, amazed at all the gowns, suits, shoes, and accessories. Evren picks out a pale pink gown with silver heels. Ana shakes her head.

"I'll wear the gown, but I cannot wear heels. I'll break my neck in those."

"All the ladies of the court wear them."

"Evren, please."

She nods and helps Ana into the gown and gets her silver slippers, similar to her gold ones. Ana looks down at her scars.

"Mi'lady, is something wrong?" Evren asks.

"Do you have something that can hide these?"

Evren walks over to see what she's talking about. "Where did those come from? Did someone hurt you?"

Ana looks at her. "Do you not have suicide here?"

"I don't know that word," Evren answers.

"Do people here kill themselves?"

"Sometimes. A guardian or royal guard is supposed to be willing to give their life to protect their ward."

"Oh, no. Um, do people kill themselves because they are scared or sad?"

"No, mi'lady." Evren goes to the dresser, getting out silver arm cuffs and handing them to her. "If I may, are you saying you did that to yourself?"

She hears the confusion in her voice. "Yes, Evren."

"May I ask why?"

"No."

"I apologize, mi'lady."

"It's okay." Ana sits on the ottoman so Evren can braid her hair. She picks out a small tiara and pins it in. Evren goes to a set of doors and slides them open to reveal a mirror running the length of the wall. Ana walks over, not recognizing herself. "Oh," she says softly, unable to believe the princess looking back at her in the mirror is really her.

"Mi'lady, are you ready?"

"Yes, Evren. Thank you."

In the hallway, she lowers her eyes to avoid meeting Rafe's gaze. Kara approaches her. "Keep your head high. Do not show fear or weakness. You are the princess, and this is your realm. Remember that."

She smiles at Kara. "Thank you."

The dining hall is a large, square room, windowless, but bright, full of round and rectangular tables, all dark wood to match the trim. Ana runs her hand over the grain of one of the tables as she's led to her seat. The smell of the food wafts in from the kitchen, and Ana's stomach growls. When the archduke is announced, everyone stands.

"Your Highness," he says with a bow. "I am Archduke Kane. I cannot express how joyful I am that you have been returned to us." He smiles at her, admiring her in her gown.

She nods to him. "Thank you, Archduke." He's not much taller than her, with short, light brown hair, neat mustache, and small beard. She notes his dark brown eyes studying her as she does the same. She would almost call him handsome. He sits beside her.

"I want you to know, I will happily relinquish control of the realm to you once you are ready. There will be no fighting or power struggles within this palace. What is happening outside is bad enough."

"Thank you, Archduke."

"Please, call me Kane."

She looks at Kara, who nods. "Thank you, Kane. I can assure you, it will be a long while. I have much to learn first. Please, continue in your duties as you have, with my gratitude."

Kara can't help but be impressed. She knows Ana loves fairytales and fantasy books, but now she is grateful for the knowledge they have given her. The first meal is brought out. Ana looks at her dish, trying to figure out what kind of stew it is. She looks at Kara, who shakes her head, and she watches as Kara waves her hand over her dish, which is then promptly removed. Ana does the same. The next dish looks better. She and Kara eat.

Kane turns to Ana. "If I may be so bold, may I join you for dinner this evening?"

Ana nearly chokes on her drink. She knew she would have to deal with suitors eventually, with their eyes on the throne, but she hadn't thought it would be so soon. "My sincerest apologies, Archduke. I have already made plans for this evening. Perhaps another time?" She can see the look on his face as he debates pressing it. "If that's quite all right with you," she adds.

"Of course, Your Highness."

Kara stifles a laugh and looks at Rafe, who has the same amused look on his face as she does. She rolls her eyes at him when he winks at her. She eats a few bites before stealing a glance at Evren, who is staring at her. Kara blushes and goes back to her meal.

"May I take you on a tour?" Kane asks Ana once they are finished eating.

"Yes, I'd like that. Although I am quite tired, I don't want to explore too much right now."

"Of course, mi'lady."

Kane places his hand on Ana's arm and leads the way. She sighs, wishing she were taking the tour with Rafe instead. She clears her head and pays attention as Kane points to each door, explaining they are studies, meeting rooms, then the kitchen and Medical Center. He points down the hallway.

"The library is at the end."

"Could we see it?" Ana asks.

"For what possible reason, mi'lady? It's nothing but books everywhere. It's incredibly dull."

"I would like to see it. Please, Kane?"

He sighs. "Yes, Your Highness."

He escorts her inside, with Kara and Evren following behind. Ana takes in the enormity of the library as she walks around the room. The walls are at least twenty feet high with the stacks running the length of the hallway. She's never seen so many books in all her life. Kara smiles at Evren.

"Books are her favorite thing. I knew she would love this."

Evren smiles. "Mine, too."

They turn their attention to Ana and Kane. He is sitting by a small fireplace as he fiddles with his pipe. Ana is still exploring the library.

She looks at Kara. "I could spend a thousand years in here and still not read every book."

"I'm glad you like it." Kane shoots Kara a look. "Mi'lady," she quickly adds.

Tired of messing with his pipe, Kane stands up and walks over to Ana. "Could we move this along, Your Highness?" he asks, the boredom apparent in his voice.

She looks at him. "Of course."

He laces his arm with hers. Unease washes over her, and she looks at Kara, who sees it in her eyes.

"You now, the princess has already had a long day. Between travel sickness and everything else, I believe she needs to rest now."

Ana looks at Kara with gratitude on her face. She turns to the archduke. "I am quite tired, if you don't mind."

"Of course not, Your Highness. We shall resume tomorrow."

Kara and Evren escort her back to her quarters. On the way, they pass Rafe, who walks with them.

"Are you okay, Your Highness?"

"Yes, Guardian," she responds coldly. At the door to her room, she gestures Kara and Evren inside, then turns to Rafe. "Can I help you?" she asks as he starts to enter.

"I am here to serve," he answers. "I am here as your protection."

She points beside the door. "Then do so from here. You are not permitted within my chambers until I say so."

"Yes, mi'lady." He watches her go in, his hands clenched.

Ana looks at Evren. "I'd like to rest for a bit. Is there something I can change into?"

Evren goes into the closet and walks out with a white cotton nightgown. It has gold and silver trim along the collar and hem with stars embroidered along the body. Ana sighs as she takes it, goes into the washroom, and strips out of her gown and tiara. The nightgown is warm and heavy, like being wrapped in a hug. She steps back out to the main chamber.

Evren gestures her over and walks up to the wall, pressing a button on the sun figurine. The wall opens. "These are my chambers, mi'lady. I am next door for anything you may need."

"Thank you." Ana watches Evren go into her quarters.

Kara steps forward. "Your Highness."

"Kara, please, stop calling me that."

"We have to. Not just because it's custom, but it's for our protection and yours. You have rivals here, threats. Do you want them to know who your friends are?"

Ana gasps. "No, of course not." She lowers her head. "You're right."

"Your Highness, never hang your head."

She smiles at Kara. "Thank you."

"Of course."

"Now, I need to lay down."

"Yes, mi'lady." Kara leaves the room.

Ana climbs into bed, hoping she will wake up in her house on the corner she shares with Kara, and this will all be a dream.

~•~

When Ana wakes up, she sighs, realizing she's still in her quarters, not on Earth anymore. She goes to the closet and looks through the gowns, unsure of what to wear for dinner. She walks over and knocks on Evren's door.

"Mi'lady," Evren says as she walks in, "you simply press the button. You do not need to knock."

"I respect your privacy, Evren."

"Thank you. How may I serve?"

"Am I expected at dinner tonight? Or is it possible to have food brought in here?"

"Once you told the archduke you had plans, he dismissed the court. You can have food brought here."

"Will you help me dress? I don't know the different styles. I'd hate to wear a ball gown to eat in my room." She smiles at Evren, who laughs softly.

"Of course, mi'lady." Hearing someone knock, Evren walks over and opens the door, looking at Ana. Ana gives her a nod, and Evren gestures for Kara to come in.

"Evening, Your Highness. How are you feeling?" Kara asks.

"Fine," she replies. "I was just about to get dressed for dinner. We'll be out in a moment."

"Take your time."

Ana follows Evren into the closet. She picks out royal blue dress slacks with a long sleeve silver blouse, then steps out to give Ana privacy. Ana strips out of the nightgown and lays it on the ottoman. She slips on the new clothes and walks back to the mirror. A shimmer flickers across it, causing her to cry out and turn away.

Kara runs in. "What's wrong?"

Ana runs to her, shaking her head. "The—the mirror! There's something wrong with it."

"What do you mean?"

"It shimmered!"

"Did you look at it after?" Kara asks.

"No!"

Kara takes her hand and leads her to the mirror. "Ana, look at yourself."

She raises her head, shock on her face. "Who is that?" She brings her hands up, running her fingertips over her mouth and cheek. She looks at Kara, tears in her eyes and confusion on her face. "What happened?"

Kara pulls her to the ottoman, holding her hands. "I'm sorry. I was only trying to protect you."

"What do you mean?"

Kara takes a breath. "Before we arrived on Earth, I put a spell on you, one that would make you appear plain. I was trying to protect you—" Ana pulls away.

"What? What gave you the right?"

"I had to—"

"Please, leave the closet. I will deal with you later!"

Kara runs out. Her body trembling, Ana approaches the mirror and looks herself over, still in shock at the beautiful woman looking back at her.

She goes to the dresser, picks up the cross Rafe had given her, and runs her fingers over it as she cries softly. She slips it on, thinking that she would give anything to be in his arms again with his warmth flowing into her. Unable to contain herself, she buries her face in her hands and weeps. She composes herself, knowing that part of her life is over. Hard as it is, she must push past the pain and focus on her new duties.

She steps out, ignoring Kara, and looking at Evren. "Everything I'm wearing looks okay?" Ana asks.

"Yes, mi'lady."

"Thank you." She gently tugs on her sleeve. "I still feel overdressed for eating in here."

Kara laughs. "They don't have yoga pants or sweatshirts here, Your Highness."

Evren nods her head, not really understanding what Kara is saying. She loves hearing her laugh and watching her smile. Evren leaves to request food while Ana looks out the window, still trying to take it all in.

This is mine. This is my kingdom, these are my people. Yet, it still seems so alien to me, so foreign. Will this ever feel like home? She scoffs at the thought. *I don't know what home feels like. I thought I did, wrapped in his arms.* She pushes down the tears threatening to escape. When Evren finishes setting up the food, she sits at the table and looks at the bowl before her.

"Evren, what is this?"

"Braised crowwa in sauce with vegetables."

Ana shakes her head then looks Kara. "What?"

"Think beef stew," Kara responds.

"Hmm. All right." Ana pushes the food around with her spoon, looking around the room and still trying to take it all in. The shock hasn't worn off, and as she's looking around the beautiful bedroom, she'd give anything to share it with Rafe.

"Your Highness, are you all right?" Evren asks.

Ana looks at Kara when she brings her hand up, wiping a tear from Ana's face. She didn't even realize she was crying. "I'm okay," she answers softly.

"You miss Rafe, don't you?" Kara asks.

"What?" Evren asks, looking down as her face goes flush. "Apologies, mi'lady. That was out of turn."

"That's okay, Evren." She looks at Kara. "It's probably better if we never discuss any of that. We don't know who could be listening."

"Very smart," Kara agrees.

They resume eating. Ana glances at Kara. "I want to ask you something, but I don't want to freak you out."

"What's wrong?"

"I'm exhausted, utterly exhausted. Is that normal? After traveling?"

"Yes, especially since it was your first time." Kara lets out a sigh of relief. "Don't worry me like that, Highness."

"I'm going to bed soon, to try and recoup my strength."

"Me as well, mi'lady."

"I didn't even think to ask how you're feeling."

"It's okay. You're upset with me, and you've had a weird, life-altering day. I understand. I'm fine, just a little tired."

"Evren?"

"Already getting it, mi'lady," she says, walking to the closet.

"Thank you."

Evren walks out with another nightgown, and Ana thanks her with a smile. She goes into the washroom and starts the water as she undresses. The water rolls over her like velvet as she stands under the shower head, relishing the feeling and staying in longer than she intended.

She turns the water off, drying, and getting ready for bed. Flushing at the sight of Rafe waiting for her, she walks to the chaise, grabbing the blanket and wrapping around herself.

"What are you doing in here?" she demands.

"Your Highness," he bows. "I am your assigned guardian. I will be in here tonight, as your protection."

Ana turns to Evren. "Is there no one else who can be assigned?"

"Mi'lady? They could, but then he would go into battle."

Ana shakes her head when she sees the worry on his face. Regardless of how she feels about him, she would never do that. "No, Evren. It's okay. Please, let's forget I said anything." She watches his expression ease into relief.

"Yes, mi'lady. With your permission, I will be turning in."

"Good night, Evren." She watches her go into her room, wondering where Kara is. She shakes her head and walks to the bed. Rafe sits on the chaise and watches her.

"I know you're not happy with this arrangement. My apologies, Your Highness."

Ana doesn't answer as she climbs into bed. She buries her face in the pillow, crying softly. Her body tenses when his hand touches her back.

"Mi'lady, are you okay?" Rafe asks.

"Please," she begs, "leave me alone."

"Ana—" he clears his throat. "Apologies, mi'lady. How can I help?"

"Go back to your chaise!" she cries out.

"Yes, Your Highness." He lingers another moment before lying down, hating himself more than she ever could.

Chapter 9

Ana wakes up to see Rafe is sitting on the chaise, waiting for her. She looks down, shame washing over her as she realizes she took his blanket the night before. She gathers it up and takes it to him.

"I'm sorry. I took this last night to cover myself," she explains as she hands it to him.

He smiles as he takes it. "It's fine, mi'lady." He folds it up and lays it on the chaise, then gets to his feet and bows. "How may I serve this morning?"

"What are your duties?" Ana asks.

"I am to escort you, watch over you, and protect you, even at the expense of my own life. I am here to serve you."

"My guardian angel," she says softly, turning away. She catches herself. "I don't need anything from you at the moment."

"Yes, mi'lady."

She walks over to Evren's door, knocking softly. Evren walks out. "Mi'lady, how may I serve?"

"What's on my agenda today? I'm not sure how to dress."

Evren looks at Rafe then Ana. "Your Highness, he is in charge of your agenda," she says, gesturing to Rafe.

"Guardian, you failed to mention that."

"Apologies. You have breakfast with the court, then your first lesson on history and culture of the realm."

She looks at Evren. "Please?"

Evren smiles, leading her into the closet and picking out a pale blue gown with silver slippers. Ana holds up the gown, examining the sheer long sleeves and beadwork along the bodice, admiring the full skirt. She slips out of the nightgown and puts the dress on. She's sitting on the ottoman, putting the slippers on, when Evren walks over with a silver circlet.

"May I style your hair?" Evren asks.

"Please."

Evren weaves small braids then pulls them back to form a halo. She slips the circlet on, pinning it into place. Ana goes to the mirror and smiles at the sight before her.

"Mi'lady, if I'm not being too forward. You are a beautiful princess. You will have many suitors, I am sure."

Ana sighs. "But because they wish to know me or because they are after the throne?"

"Apologies, I was not thinking of that."

"It's okay. It's part of life at court, I know. I don't want to think of suitors or love right now, since I still have so much to learn."

"Yes, mi'lady. Are we having breakfast here or in the dining hall?"

"Dining hall."

"Of course. I'll give you a moment," Evren says, stepping out.

Ana looks herself over again, thinking of what Kara did to her and pushing the anger away, knowing she needs her friend to help her adapt to everything. She can't believe how beautiful she looks, like the maidens in books she read, maidens from faraway lands who found their prince charming. Snapping herself out of it, she walks back into the bedroom and tries to hide her smile when Rafe sucks in his breath at the sight of her.

"Thank you, Evren. I believe what you picked out is perfect," she says.

"Of course, mi'lady."

Kara walks in. "Good morning."

Ana looks at her. "Where did you go after dinner? You left without saying good night."

"I could tell you were still upset with me, so I thought it best. My apologies, mi'lady. For everything."

Ana decides this is not the time or place. "Of course. We'll talk later. Now, we are going to breakfast."

Walking into the dining hall, Ana is grateful to not see the archduke. Kara sits on her left with Rafe on her right. Evren stands against the wall, as is her status. Ana hates how Evren is treated and vows she will find a way to improve her station. She enjoys her meal, after Rafe explains it is basically bacon and eggs with rustic toast.

A squire approaches their table and bows. "Your Highness, I present Prince Ascienne of the HelioStora Realm."

Ana looks at Evren, who raises her hand, slightly folding it. Ana stands up, watching the prince bow to her. She gives a half bow in return, glancing at Evren who gives her a small nod of approval.

"Mi'lord," she offers. "Welcome." She gestures him forward. His blond hair is past his shoulders, pulled back into a loose ponytail. A well-groomed mustache rests above his perfect lips. His blue eyes practically burn into hers with intensity. He's dressed in black slacks with a white shirt, trimmed in gold and adorned with embroidered suns.

"He's so handsome," Ana murmurs, blushing when she realizes she said it aloud. She looks up, grateful he didn't hear her. Kara smirks at Rafe before giving her attention back to the royals.

"Mi'lady, I was wondering if you would dine with me for dinner tonight?"

"Oh, my apologies. I already have plans." She sees the disappointment on his face. "Would lunch suffice?"

He smiles at her. "That would be perfect. Is here at noon all right, mi'lady?"

"Yes, mi'lord."

He bows to her. "I will see you then."

She watches him leave, followed by his servants. She looks at Kara as she sits down. "Well, he is quite attractive," Kara says.

Ana giggles. "I will meet him for lunch, but as I've explained to Evren, I have no time for suitors. Not when I still have so much to learn."

Kara glances at Rafe. "Who says you can't do both?" She smiles at the flicker of anger in his eyes. "Besides, you deserve a little fun."

Ana looks between them, rolling her eyes. "Kara, this is neither the time nor place."

"Yes, mi'lady." She stops eating. "Wait, who do you have plans with for dinner?"

Ana laughs. "Myself." She smiles when Kara joins in the laughter.

Ana's first lesson is held in the library. When she arrives, accompanied by Kara, Evren, and Rafe, another one of her handmaids is waiting for her.

"Mi'lady, I am Brienne," she says as she bows. Ana looks her over, seeing she is human, like her. She is dressed in a uniform like Evren's, a blue skirt and white peasant blouse covered with a crimson corset. Her platinum blonde hair is braided down her back, and her violet eyes are piercing, as if she is looking into your very soul. She's nearly a foot taller than Evren with a button nose and full lips. "I am here to serve."

"You are a handmaid like Evren?"

"Yes, mi'lady."

"Are all handmaids slaves?" Ana asks.

"We are. Once we are purchased, we are brought here to learn everything about the realm. Our purpose is to serve you and see to your needs however we can. We are here day or night."

"How many are there?"

"There are four others, but they were pulled to the Medical Center to train as nurses because of the war. We can call them back, if you would like. The decision is yours, mi'lady."

"No, they are better suited at the hospital." She shakes her head. "Slaves? It's not right."

"Mi'lady?" Evren asks.

"I'm sorry. We can begin the lesson whenever you want." She looks back at Kara and Rafe, who are sitting at the table in the last row. What she would give to be a fly on the wall and hear their conversation. She gives her attention to her handmaids.

"So, tell me, Rafe."

"Yes, Kara?"

"Why did you do it? Why did you break her heart?"

"I had to. The war was getting worse, with no end in sight. We needed to bring her back here."

"Do you love her?"

"Keep your voice down!" he hisses. "You know how serious they take that here."

She studies his face and considers her words before speaking again. "You broke her heart. You devastated her. She nearly died when you were gone."

"What are you talking about?"

"I came home from work and found her on the kitchen floor." Kara's voice hitches. "She drank vodka and took her pain pills. I called 911. The doctor said if I had found her a few minutes later, she wouldn't still be here."

"Kara," he reaches for her hand, but pulls back, "why didn't you tell me?"

"I didn't have the chance."

"Why are you telling me this now?"

"Because if I have to live with the guilt, so should you. Especially since this was your fault."

"They pulled me back here. I didn't have a choice. Wait, why do you feel guilty?"

"Because I wasn't enough. She was overwhelmed, and I didn't help her. She was so angry and lost without you. Then for you to break her heart all over again, for her to find out everything you told her was a lie—"

"Not everything."

"Still, you lied to her."

He scoffs. "And you didn't?"

"My lies were to protect her, to keep her safe. What you did to her was downright cruel."

He looks down. "I didn't want to."

"Rafe? I don't care. Regardless of your intentions, you hurt her. I have been doing what I can to comfort her, but now she has to see you every day and be reminded."

"I'm sorry. I truly am. You're right, Kara."

Ana takes notes and tries to follow Brienne's lesson as best as she can.

"The realm is divided into four quadrants. MoonFrost, NightFall, MorningStella, and the Maristellar Kingdom, the one we are currently in."

"Do they each have their own language or does everyone speak English?"

"English?" Brienne asks.

"Terra lingua," Kara calls out.

"Thank you, Sage." Evren smiles at Kara. "NightFall is the only quadrant not made up of humans. MorningStella is a beautiful metropolitan, warm, and to the southeast, NightFall is dark and cold, due east, and south of us is MoonFrost, which, despite the name, is mildly temperate."

Brienne continues the lesson. "The king and queen maintained peace throughout the quadrants, but once she died in childbirth, the king became reclusive. He would attack and demand compensation and taxes from the other quadrants, until the leaders decided they had enough and sent their armies instead. The king went into battle and was killed.

"As there were no living royals, none of the bloodline, the archduke was appointed Steward, Protector of the Realm, until a living royal could be located," Brienne explains. "He is not the king, nor is he considered a royal. His title gives him the power to run the day-to-day affairs."

"When a king or queen is on the throne, how do they change or write laws?" Ana asks.

Evren steps forward. "Well, it depends on the law. Most of our laws are over a thousand years old, with many being over two thousand. If a king or queen wished to enact a law or ratify one, they also need unanimous approval from the Celestial Council. The only other way is if a treaty were enacted."

"How would that come about?"

"If you were to bring peace to the quadrants, you would meet the capitol leaders, and you would write the treaty yourself. It would contain all previous, active laws, plus any others you would need to add to maintain the peace, for the kingdom as well as your realm. The treaty would have to be approved by the chancellor, who oversees our laws."

"Is he a member of the Celestial Council?"

"No. They confer with him and work together, but it is a way to divide the power, so we do not have a tyrant in charge. Once it's approved, the treaty would be copied by scrivers, then passed out to the leaders and dignitaries. They would have one day to read it over. After, you would meet to discuss it. If everything is agreed upon, and there are no issues with the treaty, it would then pass into law. If there are any objections or further additions, they would be addressed."

Rafe can't help but notice Ana is furiously writing everything down. He smiles at Kara.

"I'm grateful to see she's taken an interest," he says.

"Me, too," Kara replies with a smile.

"Anything you two would like to share?" Brienne asks, glaring at Rafe and Kara.

They stifle a laugh for being scolded like schoolchildren. Kara contains herself. "No, ma'am. Our apologies."

Ana turns and shoots them a stern look, before winking at Kara. A tray with breads, cheeses, and dried meats is brought in. Ana sits by herself while she snacks, going over her notes so far, while the others sit at the back table.

Rafe looks at Evren. "How is the princess?" he asks. "You can see her face while lecturing. Does she seem overwhelmed or is she okay?"

Evren smiles. "I think she's okay. She's taking notes and asking questions. That's better than some students I've had."

Brienne laughs. "You and me both."

When he realizes she isn't in the room, Rafe looks towards Ana's table. Not seeing her, he jumps to his feet and rushes to the hall, stopping short when he sees her behind a pillar, leaning against it, her head hung low.

"Your Highness!" He runs to her. "Why did you leave without telling us?"

She scoffs. "I could ask the same of you."

He takes a breath. "Mi'lady—"

She turns away, putting her hand on the pillar. "I just needed some air. I was feeling stifled in there. I'll be in shortly."

"Please, Your Highness. You need to eat, and I am not to leave you alone." His shoulders slump when he hears her sniffle. "Ana," he says softly. "I apologize, mi'lady. It slipped out."

"Please, get Kara," she begs.

He runs in and gestures Kara to come out. She follows him and sees Ana leaning against the pillar. Rafe nods his head and goes back into the library. Kara walks in front of Ana.

"Oh, Your Highness. Why are you crying?"

"I'm never going to be ready. There is so much to learn and do. I'm not cut out for this."

"It's only your first day learning, so of course you're overwhelmed. I know I'm supposed to say something like, 'it's your birthright. This is what you were born to do. It will all work out.' But you and I know better. All I can say is, please, don't give up. Study, train, and keep your head up. You know we are here with you one hundred percent, whatever happens."

"Thank you, Kara."

"Now, let's get you cleaned up and back inside. You need to eat." They step into a washroom, where Kara cleans Ana's face. She takes her back to the library. Kara sits and finishes her snack. Ana goes to her seat, picking at her bread and trying to make herself eat a bite.

"Eat a little, please," Rafe whispers in her ear before returning to his table. She does as he asks, looking up when Evren takes her dishes. The lesson resumes, and Evren brings over a tattered document, encased in glass.

"This is one of the original by-laws, written by Celestia herself. She was queen almost three thousand years ago."

"I'm related to her?"

"Yes and no," Evren says. "The bloodline is a little complicated." Evren places it back in the storage case then returns to Ana. "This palace is also three thousand years old. Celestia had it built here when the palace in MoonFrost was overrun and destroyed."

"How old is the realm?"

Evren sighs as she thinks. "Again, there is some discrepancy. With wars and destruction, a lot of the original history has been lost."

"I see. The war going on now? Will that end once I am on the throne?"

"That is the hope, but truly we do not know." Evren glances at Rafe, swallowing hard. "Once you are crowned, you could reach out to your allies. As you are—"

Rafe stands up and interrupts her. "Evren? We talked about this."

"Apologies, Guardian." She gives him a small smile.

Ana looks at the clock. "I need to change for lunch with the prince."

Brienne concludes the lesson, staying behind to reshelve the books and prepare for the next day's lesson.

Evren picks out a purple gown and shows Ana. She smiles at the sight. It has a square cut bodice, long billow sleeves with slits at the elbow and a ballroom skirt. Ana slips into the gown while Evren gets out a diamond and platinum tiara.

"Mi'lady, shall I fix your hair?"

"Please, Evren. Thank you."

She undoes the braids and brushes through the curls, then pulls a few strands back to make a halo before pinning the tiara in. "I believe this will be to your liking."

Ana goes to the mirror, stunned at her reflection. She thinks one day she will look in the mirror and not be taken back by what she sees. Taking a breath, she shakes her head.

They arrive at the dining hall. Evren takes her to a small table for two in the corner. "Evren?"

"This is appropriate, I assure you, mi'lady."

"All right."

She looks up as Rafe and Kara sit at the table to her right, far enough away to give her and the prince privacy. When Prince Ascienne walks in, she stands up. He gestures his entourage to stay back, then walks up to the table and bows to her.

"Mi'lady, that gown is spectacular," he says.

"Thank you, mi'lord." She gives a half bow, and they sit together.

"We are grateful you have been returned."

"May I ask why?" She sees the look of confusion on his face. "My apologies, I did not mean to confuse you. I simply meant, why is my homecoming something everyone is celebrating?"

He looks at Kara and Rafe then back to her. "Surely they told you about the war tearing through your realm."

"They have. They say everyone hopes that once I am crowned as queen, and the throne is claimed, the fighting will end."

"You don't agree?"

"I don't believe it will be that simple."

"Ah, I see." He gives her a small smile as their meal is placed before them. "Speaking of the throne."

"Mi'lord?"

He chuckles. "I am the youngest of eleven children. I have six older brothers and four older sisters. However, I do not wish for you to see me as... well, pardon my bluntness, as a Hans to your Ana."

She tilts her head. "I beg your pardon?"

"I've been told that is what your friends call you. I am not interested in the throne, though I know I have no way to prove that. I simply wanted to meet the future queen."

"How do you know about Hans and Ana?"

"When I was on Earth—"

She sits up. "You were on Earth?" Her voice is thick with excitement.

"Yes. For about two months. I went to New York to study painting. We have artists, but Earth has such a unique variety, I asked if I could go there to study. If we are not an immediate heir to the throne, we are expected to have other gifts so we may aid our king and queen. We do not sit idly all day."

"Tell me about your time on Earth!"

He laughs. "Mi'lady?"

She gasps softly. "My apologies. I forgot my place. I wasn't trying to order you—"

He laughs again, squeezing her hand before letting go. "No offense is taken. I know you just came from Earth. I'm guessing you miss it?"

"So much."

"I can understand. I did not grow up there but trying new foods and seeing the skyscrapers was incredible. I miss it, too, if I must confess."

"What does your realm look like?"

"We are closest to Astriasol."

"What is that?" Ana asks.

"Astriasol is the name of our sun."

"It's a pretty name."

"Not as pretty as you."

She swallows hard. "Thank you," she says, picking up her glass. She takes a sip, looking over at Rafe and Kara. As usual, Kara is absorbed in her food while Rafe is staring at them. She quickly gives her attention back to Ascienne. "Would you tell me about your time on Earth?"

"I will. I stayed in a studio apartment with a roommate. She had a daughter who loved cartoons, hence the Hans and Ana reference." He smiles when she giggles. "I will hear that song for the rest of my life."

"What was your favorite food?"

"You probably expect me to say something like pizza or Chinese, don't you?"

She laughs softly. "Is it that obvious?"

"Honestly, I liked cheesecake the best. If I could eat it for breakfast, lunch, and dinner, I would." Her head rolls back with laughter. "Do you think I am joking?"

"Oh, no, mi'lord. Of course not." She winks at him, laughing harder when he joins in. "Cheesecake for breakfast. I'm sure something could be arranged."

"What about you? Your favorite food?"

"Oh, no. Now you will think I am dull. Pizza was my favorite."

"There is nothing wrong with that."

"What sort of food do you have at your realm?"

"As we are closest to the sun, we are what you would call a tropical planet. We have seafood, tropical fruits, and other foods similar to MorningStella's cuisine."

Not wishing to look ignorant again, Ana doesn't ask. "Right, of course. May I ask? Why are you on this realm?"

"I have been staying in MoonFrost as part of an exchange program, if you will."

"Even with the war going on?"

"You sound like my mother," he says with a laugh. "I wanted to come here and study. Sometimes we travel between realms to learn history, culture, and traditions. It helps with maintaining peace in the galaxy while building up allies as well."

"That's brilliant." She blushes. "Apologies."

He chuckles softly. "Mi'lady, none are needed."

"What is your palace like?"

"It is made from sandstone, and it is almost six thousand years old. It is not near as big as this one, but it is quite expansive." He reaches into his pocket and pulls out a handkerchief. He hands it to Ana, laughing when she is reluctant to take it. "I do not blow my nose on this. It is a symbol of our realm, not a tissue."

"Thank you," she says, unfolding it on the table. The fabric is black with a gold sun embroidered on it. Around the sun are the words light, peace, and strength. "What does it mean?"

"This is our family crest. Our motto is 'light will bring you peace, peace will bring you strength, strength will enhance your light.'"

"That's incredible." He smiles at her, looking at her lips. He leans forward, but she turns away and sneezes.

"Apologies! Oh, I guess I am still adjusting to the air here, as well." She gives him a small smile.

"Understandable. I must be going. May I see you again?"

"Could we have lunch tomorrow?"

"I would love to. Until then, mi'lady."

"Good day, mi'lord."

As she watches him leave, she wonders if he really is as kind as he seems. She looks up when Kara sits down across from her. "Well, that went better than I expected. Are you seeing him again?"

"Yes. We are having lunch here tomorrow."

Kara smiles. "I'm glad to hear that. Now, Rafe was wondering if you would like to resume your self-defense training?" She's surprised when Ana laughs. "Mi'lady?"

"It's nothing. Yes, I will need to change first."

Rafe and Evren take her back to her quarters while Kara goes to inquire about the training center. Rafe inspects her room, and once he's sure it's secure, he returns to the door.

"Evren, I need to see my Captain. I will be back soon. Do not leave her side," he commands.

"Yes, Guardian."

As soon as Rafe is gone, there is a knock at the door. Ana opens it and steps back as Kane makes his way in. "Your Highness," he says as he bows to her. "I hope I am not imposing." He smiles at her, eyeing the cut of her gown.

"How can I help you, Archduke?"

"Please, mi'lady, call me Kane." He flashes her a toothy smile. She struggles not to roll her eyes. "I would be honored if you would join me for a private dinner tonight."

"In the dining hall?"

Her breath sucks in when he steps closer. "In my quarters, mi'lady."

She knows she has to play nice, with him technically in charge and running the kingdom. "I apologize, but I am not comfortable with that. I am still learning the many customs here and—"

"Oh, say no more! Understandable. I will see you in the dining hall at six." His smile grows.

She starts to object, to point out she had not agreed to dine with him, and she realizes she walked right into his trap. "That will be fine, as long as you understand my entourage will be with me."

"That is acceptable."

"Until then, thank you for stopping by." She sees the surprise on his face at being dismissed so abruptly.

"Of course, Your Highness." He bows and leaves. She goes to the closet, practically collapsing onto the ottoman.

"Mi'lady, are you all right?" Evren asks as she follows her in.

"I'm fine. Let's get dressed for training."

Evren gets out a pair of black slacks and a pale blue shirt. Ana smiles as she slips the black leather boots on. They walk out as Rafe returns.

"Ready, mi'lady?" He loves seeing her in her training clothes.

"I am," she answers.

They meet Kara in the training center, and Ana is amazed at the size of the room. There are multiple training rings on the floor with mats, one ring on a scaffold, and several training dummies lining the side wall. She looks at Rafe.

"What are we practicing today?"

He looks at Kara. "She will be teaching you."

Ana stops walking. "Why?"

"I am not allowed to engage with you like that. If I were to hurt you—" He cocks his head when she scoffs. "You know what I mean, mi'lady."

"No. This will not stand. You have been training me, and you will continue."

"Mi'lady—"

"That is my command."

"Yes, mi'lady."

They go into the center of the training ring and work on her stance and posture. She looks at Rafe, her frustration apparent. "Rafe, train me."

"I am."

"No. This is like the first time after you hit me. You are scared. Train me right!"

"Yes, mi'lady."

They practice the lunge move then he shows her again how to kick his knee out from under him. Kara and Evren watch, impressed at how well she picks up the movements.

She looks at the clock. "Evren, it's five. I need to clean up and get ready for my dinner with Kane."

"Yes, mi'lady."

Ana showers and goes into the closet. Evren picks out a silver gown with matching tiara and shoes. Ana sits on the ottoman as Evren fixes her hair.

"It looks great. Thank you, Evren."

"You are welcome."

"Evren, what sort of leader is Kane?"

"As far as I can tell, a good one. He is respectful to the troops and the court. He does what he can to protect the throne, even sometimes at his own expense. He has fought in several battles, even when it wasn't necessary."

"What does that mean?" Ana asks as she and Evren return to the main chambers.

Rafe and Kara enter. "Are you ready to go to dinner, Your Highness?" Rafe asks.

She turns, watching Rafe's eyes go wide at the sight of her. "Yes, Guardian. Thank you."

She walks with him leading the way, and Kara and Evren following behind. They approach Kane's table, and he stands up to bow, looking Ana over as he does so. He smiles at her. "Welcome, mi'lady. You look ravishing this evening."

"Thank you, Archduke."

He sits beside her. "We've been over this, Your Highness. Please, call me Kane. I insist."

"My apologies."

The first course is brought out. Ana looks at her pasta, her appetite waning as Kane stares at her. She makes herself eat a few bites before the plates are taken away and the next course is served.

"What did you wish to talk with me about?"

"I don't follow, Your Highness," he responds, drinking his wine. He snaps his fingers for a refill.

"You invited me for dinner. I assumed there was some business with the kingdom or the war to—" She stops herself. "That's not why you asked me here, is it?"

"I thought we could discuss the future. The future of the palace, the kingdom, the throne itself."

"I see. What plans do you have in mind?"

He chuckles at her question. "Right to the point. A woman after my own heart. I believe we can stop the war and end the bloodshed once we place you on the throne. In order to do that, though, I think you will have to prove yourself."

"What do you mean?"

"A pretty face in a pretty crown won't be enough to stop the violence."

She tries to hide her annoyance. "Yes, I understand."

He smiles. "I believe a demonstration of our power may save the kingdom."

"What would you suggest?"

"If we can capture one of the quadrant's generals, you could have him executed, publicly. Show that you will not tolerate treason."

She nearly chokes on her drink. Taking a breath, she glances over to see Kara and Rafe talking and laughing. She gives her attention back to Kane. "I will think on what you have said. Perhaps you are correct, though, that I may yet have to prove myself."

"I have another suggestion, as well. One that may ease the peace without such… drastic measures."

"How so?"

"You need a king. The kingdom needs a strong, reliable man. Someone they know and trust, to aid you in your affairs. I think I would be most suitable for that if you would have me. Would you be my betrothed?"

"Archduke, this is too much too fast," she says, getting to her feet. "My sincerest of apologies," she offers, running from the hall. Kara, Rafe, and Evren follow her to her quarters. Once inside, she rushes to the washroom, slams the door, and turns the shower on. She stands under the steaming water, sobbing and clenching her fists. *Is this what I have to deal with now? Suitors who only want the throne, lessons that I am never going to remember? Being in the same room with… with…* Unable to stop the tears, she gives in and buries her face in her hands. *How could he do this to me? How could he betray me like this? I have done nothing to deserve being treated this way!* She collapses to her knees, her tears running with the shower.

I have to stop this. I am the princess, heiress to the throne. I cannot behave like this anymore! I will shut off my heart and my soul. I will act and think logically, think only of this kingdom, this realm, and what I can do for it.

When she leaves the washroom, dressed in only her robe, everyone is waiting for her. "What?" she asks.

Kara walks over. "What happened? Are you all right?"

"I'm going to change and get ready for bed."

"It's not even eight yet."

"I am tired, Sage."

Kara flinches at the use of her title. "Yes, mi'lady. Of course. Anything we can do to help, we are here."

Ana shakes her head and goes to the closet. As she picks up a nightgown, she realizes she will have to apologize to Kane in order to keep the peace. She rolls her head back and groans, then changes into a lavender gown and silver shoes. From the shelves of crowns, she chooses a small silver one and places it on her head. She leaves the closet and looks at Evren.

"Is my outfit okay?"

Evren looks her over. "Yes, mi'lady. Where are we going?" she asks as Kara and Rafe walk over to them.

"Evren and I will return shortly."

Rafe steps forward. "Your Highness—"

"What, Guardian?"

He steps back, swallowing hard. "Please, be safe."

Ana looks at Evren, nodding. They go into the hallway. "Where are we going, mi'lady?"

"The archduke's quarters."

If Evren is confused, she doesn't say or let it show. She simply leads her there and knocks on the door when they arrive.

One of Kane's servants answers the door. "How may I help you, Your Highness?"

"I would like an audience with the archduke."

"One moment," he says, shutting the door.

Evren looks at her. "Mi'lady, you are the princess. You should've requested he come to you."

"He is running this kingdom, so I will afford him the respect that goes with it."

The door opens. Kane steps out, gesturing Evren to give them privacy. "Your Highness?"

"I wish to apologize for my behavior at dinner. If I may, I am overwhelmed by so much here."

"I didn't help that, I'm guessing. It's quite all right. Will you at least consider my proposal?"

She swallows hard. "Yes, Kane. I will think on it."

"Then all is forgiven. Anything I can do to assist, Your Highness?"

"No, but thank you for your kindness." She watches him go back into his quarters. She returns to Evren and follows her back to her quarters. Ana goes to her closet, and after she puts her nightgown on, she rests on the ottoman in the center of the room. She calms herself before stepping into the main chamber.

"I am retiring for the evening. Guardian, what is my agenda for tomorrow?"

"Like today, Your Highness."

"I see. Thank you." She uses the washroom then goes to bed. Ashamed of her tears as they fall, she buries her face in her pillow and cries herself to sleep.

Ana jerks up, crying out softly and standing up. Wrapping her arms around herself, she walks to the window, looking out at the kingdom and admiring the lit braziers. She sucks in her breath when she realizes Rafe is standing behind her.

"Guardian, do you need something?" she asks without looking at him.

"Only to know you're okay," he answers.

Her heart stops in her chest, her breath dies in her throat, and she cannot think. She draws in a breath, and everything moves again as she collects herself. "I'm fine," she replies coldly. "Just a bad dream. I'm quite used to them, after the last four months." In the reflection of the window, she can see the hurt on his face.

"I understand. Let me know if I can help."

"Rafe," she slips. She clears her throat. "Guardian, I said I am fine."

"Yes, mi'lady."

She watches his reflection as he sits on the chaise, realizing he will watch her until she returns to her bed. Staring out at a world she does not recognize, she wraps her arms tighter around herself and lays her forehead against the cool glass, her heart pounding in her chest.

"I'm not fine," she whispers to herself. "Not at all." She returns to her bed, burying her face in her pillow as she cries herself to sleep once more.

Ana wakes up, stretching, then knocks on Evren's door. She steps out a moment later, bowing. "Your Highness, how may I serve today?"

"I need dressed, please."

They go into the closet. "Would you like to pick your gown today? You did fine last night."

"That would be nice." She looks through, deciding on a pale blue gown with billowing sheer sleeves and a ballroom skirt. She holds it up, smiling when Evren nods. She gets dressed, then sits on the ottoman so Evren can braid her hair, braiding it into a halo before adding a platinum circlet with a diamond star hanging over her forehead. Ana goes to the mirror. "Oh, Evren. This is beautiful. Thank you."

"Yes, mi'lady." She steps out.

Ana turns and watches herself twirl in the mirror. She smiles at the sight before she steps out of the closet, stifling the smile when Rafe stares at her. "Guardian?"

He clears his throat. "Apologies, mi'lady. Are you ready to go to breakfast?"

"Where is Kara?"

"She will meet us there," Evren answers.

Ana eats her eggs and toast, watching Kara and Evren speak quietly.

"Is everything okay?" Rafe asks.

"Yes, why do you ask?"

He nods over to Kara, who is standing with Evren. "Kara's not eating with us."

Ana laughs softly. "I believe they have become… good friends."

"Of course. It's too bad that is all they could become."

Ana sets her fork down. "What does that mean?"

"It is illegal for them to be together."

"Because they are women?"

"No, because of their station. Kara is a member of court, Evren is a slave. It's forbidden."

Ana shakes her head. "It's wrong. All of it."

"Then fix it."

She shoots him an angry look, until she sees the grin on his face. Her expression softens. "Jerk," she says, smiling at him. "I plan to. I plan to make everything about this kingdom better."

"Good. Now, are you ready to go to the library for your next lesson, mi'lady?"

"Yes, Guardian."

In the library, Brienne has Ana's table set up with books containing the earliest known history of the realm. Ana sighs when she sits down.

"Mi'lady?" Evren asks.

"I know history is important, but I need to learn the customs here. I am terrified I am going to offend the wrong person." She tilts her head when Brienne and Evren exchange a look. "Oh, God. I already have? Who?"

"No, mi'lady. We are surprised because you are the princess. You need not worry over who you offend," Brienne responds.

Ana shakes her head. "I don't like that answer."

Evren steps forward. "Mi'lady, what she means is that whatever you say or do is given a certain allotment of grace.

Of course, you want to watch what you say and to whom, but everyone knows you are new here and still learning your place."

"Thank you."

Evren looks at Brienne. "We could start with customs today, then do a history lesson tomorrow."

Brienne agrees. She grabs a book, opens it, and sets it in front of Ana "This will help."

Ana picks it up, flipping through the pages and reading the different introductions and responses. "I'll never remember all of this," she says, dropping the book on the table.

"Mi'lady, that is why we are here. Please, do not hesitate to ask us anything, at any time. We truly wish to help you."

"Thank you, Evren." She looks over, thinking on Kane's words. *Would he be a good king? I will never marry for love, but if I am expected to marry, and if it would help the kingdom, I suppose I could do worse. Everyone here to seems to respect and admire him.* She shakes her head. *Am I seriously considering this?* She takes a breath, looking at Evren. "Is there a washroom nearby?"

Evren walks her down the hall, with Rafe and Kara following behind. Kara is concerned, so she goes into the washroom with them while Rafe stands guard in the hallway. Ana rushes into a stall and loses her breakfast

"Mi'lady, are you ill?" Evren asks, concerned.

"No," she responds, retching again. Kara holds her hair back and keeps her steady on her feet. Kara walks Ana to the vanity where she can rinse her mouth.

"Ana, please, what is going on?" Kara asks.

She shakes her head. "I'm okay. I was a little overwhelmed, is all. I'm sorry."

Kara takes her hand. "You owe no apology. You were thrust into all of this. I never wanted any of this for you. I'm sorry you were dragged back here."

"Kara, Rafe told me everything and asked me what I wanted to do. He said the decision was mine. I came here willingly."

"What?" Kara utters in disbelief.

"I want to be here, to help the kingdom, to stop the war." She looks down. "Had no idea I would get my heart broken in the process."

Kara pulls her in, hugging her. "I know how you're feeling. I'm sorry. Do you want to retire to your quarters?"

"No, I'll continue with the lesson."

"All right."

They return to the library, Rafe watching her every move with concern. When Kara joins him in the back, he leans in and keeps his voice low "Is she all right?"

"What do you care?" Kara snaps, her anger reaching its boiling point.

"I deserve that. Even so—"

"No," she says sternly, leaning forward so her face is inches from his. "After what you've done to her, you deserve worse. I would report you, if it would not hurt her in the process."

Rafe pulls back. "Kara—"

"Guardian, I am Sage to the Princess, a member of her court. You will address me as such," she hisses at him.

"Yes, Sage. Apologies," he relents, turning his attention back to Ana and her lesson.

"Evren, how is the crown obtained? I understand lineage and birthright, but if someone came in here, bested Kane, and demanded the throne, what would happen?"

"All power for that lies with the chancellor. If the chancellor agreed, they would be crowned willingly, and the new king or queen would take the throne. If the chancellor refused, they would be executed and a new one would be appointed by whoever is vying for the throne, to ensure their success."

"How would they have power to appoint the chancellor?"

"Like everything else, with force."

"It's that simple? Anyone can get the crown that way? Even when I am on the throne?"

"Yes, mi'lady. Unfortunately."

She looks at Rafe, anger on her face and rage in her eyes. Kara catches the look but says nothing. Ana turns back to Evren.

"It is law that it should be a royal on the throne, but if you have an army big enough, who is going to challenge you? Who will stand up to you? I wish things were different."

"I don't understand. What about the guardians? Isn't it their duty to guard the royals and the throne?" Ana asks.

"It is. However, the war has nearly wiped them out. There are so few now, it is why you only have one instead of the five to ten you should have."

"I see. I need to rest before lunch with the prince."

"Yes, mi'lady."

They escort her back to her quarters. Once Rafe has inspected inside, she turns to them. "I need an hour alone before lunch. Guardian, you are to stay here in the hallway. Sage, Handmaid, you are dismissed until then."

They all exchange a look and bow to her in agreement before walking away, except for Rafe, who takes up his post outside the door. Ana goes inside and sits on the chaise. She picks up the blanket and holds it to her face, inhaling Rafe's smell before wadding it up and tossing it to the ground, tears streaming down her cheeks. She wipes her tears. Someone knocks on the door.

"I said I do not wish to be disturbed!" she says as she opens the door. She is face to face with Kane. "Apologies, Archduke. I thought you were someone else. Please, come in."

He gives Rafe a smug look, then walks inside and shuts the door behind him, ignoring Rafe's objection. "Your Highness—" The door shuts in his face.

"Is everything okay?" Ana asks.

"For now. I wonder, will you dine with me in my quarters tonight? I am waiting on news from a scout, something you and I will need to discuss in private."

She sighs, catching herself. "My entourage will be in the room with us."

"Of course. They will be well taken care of, I assure you."

"That will be fine. What time?"

"Six, mi'lady."

"I will see you then."

"Thank you," he says, bowing. He leaves the room. She goes to the closet, climbing onto the ottoman and falling asleep.

Ana wakes up when Evren comes into the closet. "Mi'lady! You slept in your gown."

"I'm sorry. I didn't mean to."

"I'm not upset about the gown. Are you sure you are not ill?"

"I'm fine. Will you help me change for lunch with the prince?"

"Of course."

Evren hands her a gown. Looking down, Ana runs her fingers over the royal blue fabric, with long sleeves, a tight bodice. and billowing skirt. Evren steps out to give her privacy.

Once dressed, Ana returns to the bedroom right when Rafe steps in "Guardian?"

"Apologies, mi'lady. I wanted to see if you need anything."

"If I did, I would ask," she huffs at him. "Please, return to your post in the hallway."

"I am assigned to you, as such—"

"Are you questioning my authority?"

"No, of course not, Your Highness. I am simply pointing out where I should be."

"I know where you should be," she snaps at him. Her hands clench as her throat tightens. "However, I am too polite to say it out loud. Now please, go back into the hallway until we leave for lunch. I am dining with Prince Ascienne for lunch then Archduke Kane for dinner."

"Kane," he mutters.

Ana smiles at him. "He invited me to a cozy, private dinner tonight, hoping to woo me. Isn't he so handsome?"

Rafe clears his throat. "If you say so, mi'lady. I will be in the hall."

"Oh, no. Perhaps it is better to have you in here. Tell me, what do you think of the prince? Would he be a good choice for the throne?"

Rafe's eyes go wide with understanding. "Ana—" he says, stepping forward. He catches himself. "Apologies, mi'lady. I'm sure he is as good as any choice here."

She scoffs. "As if you would know." She looks up when Kara and Evren walk in. "Are we going to lunch now? I'm excited to see the prince."

"Of course," Kara responds.

Chapter 10

"Mi'lord, how are you today?" She looks up when he chuckles. "Prince Ascienne?"

"My apologies. I thought we were past the small talk."

She gives him a hurt look. "I was being polite."

"I'm sorry. I—" he takes a breath. "Everyone here is so full of pleasantries. After spending time on Earth, I was used to being treated like everyone else."

"Yet you have your servants trailing behind you."

He cocks his head. "Does that bother you?"

"Are they paid? Or do you own them?"

"Ah. You're asking if they are slaves. No, slavery is banned on my realm. They are trained and compensated to serve me."

"I apologize for jumping to conclusions."

"I understand. It's refreshing, actually, to meet someone who cares so much for the people around them."

"Thank you. I wish I could do the same here."

"You'll find a way." He smiles at her.

"I wish I had your confidence."

The first course is served. Ana looks at her salad but doesn't recognize any of the vegetables. Upon seeing her confusion, Ascienne picks through his, holding up various vegetables and telling her the name of each one. He smiles when she giggles.

"I'm glad you're having fun playing with your food," he says. She laughs harder but stops when she catches the archduke staring at her. She hadn't seen him come in. A lump in her throat, she turns her attention to back Ascienne.

"When do you return to your realm?"

He nearly chokes on his drink. "Eager to be rid of me?"

She smiles as she leans in. "Quite the opposite."

"Mi'lady, be careful. People may think we are more than friends, sitting like this."

"Would that be a bad thing?"

His smile grows. "Keep this up, I may ask for your hand in courting."

"I may not say no."

"Hmm. I think that is a chance worth taking." He stands up. "I must go. Will you have dinner with me tomorrow?"

"Yes, mi'lord. I would be honored."

"Until then, Your Highness."

Her face is flush as she watches him leave. She finishes her tea and walks over to Kara. "Are we training after lunch?"

"Yes."

They go to her quarters so she can change. She's humming as Evren picks out her clothes. "Mi'lady, you're in a good mood."

"I think the prince is wonderful. He can help me in so many ways, help the kingdom."

"That is good."

Ana slips on her boots, still thinking of Ascienne. *Slavery is illegal on his realm. Perhaps he can help me change the law. He will also be an ally against Kane and his schemes. I know everyone speaks highly of him, but I cannot shake this bad feeling about him.*

At the training center, Rafe takes her into the center ring. They work on landing punches and holding her stance. He brings over one of the training dummies.

"Friend of yours?" Ana asks.

Rafe chuckles softly. "No, but you are going to be well acquainted with him soon enough."

She stands back as Rafe goes through his routine. He starts with various hits to the chest and neck, finishing with a punch to the eye. His moves are quick and efficient, and Ana's heart quickens as she watches him. She bites her lip when a drop of sweat rolls down his brow.

"Your turn."

She laughs, straightening up when she realizes he's serious. "I beg your pardon?"

He gestures her over. He takes her hands and slowly goes through every movement he did. "You will do this every day until you are as able to work as quickly as I can."

She gasps. "That's impossible!"

"Mi'lady, this is the training routine guardian children do. You will be fine."

She turns away to hide her embarrassment. "I'm not a child."

Rafe sighs. "I didn't say you were, I was simply explaining—"

"Kara, I am ready to go back to my quarters."

"Yes, mi'lady."

Rafe moves the training dummy back then follows them to her room. She looks at them. "I'm having supper with Kane tonight, in his quarters. You three will join us. I want you here at five to help me get ready. Until then you're dismissed."

"Yes, mi'lady." Kara and Evren leave.

Rafe steps forward. "My usual post then?"

"Is there a problem, Guardian?"

"It's humiliating, mi'lady. I am to be with you, at all times."

"Perhaps you would rather be in battle?" Regret floods her as soon when he loses his color, but she refuses to back down. "Then don't argue with me!" She goes into her quarters, slamming the door behind her. Barely two steps inside, she collapses to the floor and sobs hysterically. Warm arms surround her, but she doesn't look up, only clinging tighter and blinded by tears.

"I'm here," he says reassuringly. "It's okay."

He takes her into the closet, closing the door behind him. He sits on the ottoman, holding her to his chest until she falls asleep.

Ana wakes up, disoriented for a moment, confused that she's in the closet.

"Mi'lady? Are you in here?"

"Yes, Evren. Come in," she says, standing up.

Evren and Brienne walk into the closet. "You fell asleep in your clothes again?"

Ana looks down, seeing she is in her training gear. "I guess so. I'm sorry. Can we just get ready for dinner?"

"Of course."

"Where is Kara?"

"In the hallway, speaking with Rafe."

"All right."

Brienne picks out a crimson gown with gold shoes while Evren gets a gold and ruby crown off the shelf. Once she's dressed, they walk into the hallway where Rafe and Kara are waiting. Kara is dressed in black slacks with a dark blue blouse.

Ana steps up to him, and Kara backs away. "I'm sorry," she says to Rafe.

"Don't worry about it, mi'lady."

"Thank you."

They walk to Kane's quarters. His servant welcomes them in. Kane has a small table for two set up in the middle of the room, with a table and three chairs in the back corner. Her entourage sits, and Kane takes her hand, kissing it as he bows.

"Your Highness, you look lovely this evening."

"Thank you, Archduke." She smiles at him. They sit at their table. "Tell me, have you heard from your scout?"

"My scout?"

"The reason you asked me to dinner—"

"Ah, that." He smiles at her. "I thought a nice, private dinner would be appreciated by you. Instead of being in the dining hall with all eyes on you. I thought we could use this time to get to know one another."

"Thank you for your consideration," she says, angry with herself that he bested her again. Looking at Rafe and Kara, she pushes her anger down. She gives Kane a small smile. "I am still learning and trying to find my place. I don't have time for anything else, I'm afraid," she tries.

"You have time for lunch with a certain young prince," he says, his voice thick with jealousy.

"He is an ally, and I have to keep the peace."

"Is that why you were practically throwing yourself at him?"

Her heart racing, Ana tries to figure out a way to excuse herself without risking insult. Before she can say anything, his hand is on her side, caressing his way up. She holds her breath.

"Your Highness, have you considered my proposal? We would unify this kingdom while sealing our right to the throne. Become my wife, help me set things right for the kingdom."

She gets to her feet. "I told you I need time to think. Please, do not push me about this."

He throws down his napkin, stepping up to her. "Why are you blind to what is right in front of you? We could stop the war with our union."

Rafe and Kara are getting to their feet, but she gestures them to sit down, as she does the same. "Archduke, please. I need time—"

He slams into his seat. "People are dying, Your Highness. Time is not something you have the luxury of. Chancellor Corbin will not crown you until you are knowledgeable about the realm. Or if you have a king by your side. We could marry and bring peace. Why do you fight it?"

Glancing at Rafe, she sucks in her breath when she realizes Kane saw it. She looks down at her plate. "It's too much too soon."

"I see. Well, while you are thinking, people are dying. But please, take your time. What does it matter how many die?"

"Archduke, please—"

"No. I have been fighting for this kingdom, shed my own blood to defend it. I have given everything. All I'm asking for is your hand."

"I'm sorry, I can't."

"Why not?" he demands.

"Because I will not be forced to marry. I gave up a life of simple comfort to come here, in the hopes of bringing peace. I may not have sacrificed what you have, but I have lost enough." She wipes her tears. "You will not command me. You said yourself, I can take power any time I want. The fact that I am still letting you run things should show that I trust you, with my kingdom and my life."

"I see. What will it take? Shall I walk you through the triage in the camp? Perhaps watching soldiers die for a princess who cares so little for them will change your mind."

"Please—"

"Oh, I know. I'll take you to the field. Let you fill up on the coppery smell of blood, caked on the rotting corpses while the sound of flies buzz around you as they consume the dead."

Ana runs from the room, running to her quarters and losing her stomach contents as soon as she's inside. She falls to her knees, retching again. Rafe runs in and carries her to the washroom. Kara follows them in and helps get her cleaned up while Evren sees to the mess.

Once Ana is clean and put into a nightgown, Rafe carries her to the bed and lays her down. He stands by while Kara sits on the edge.

"Will you tell us what happened?"

Ignoring Kara, she looks up at Rafe. "You made a mistake."

"What do you mean?"

"I am not the right choice to be here. I am no more a royal than you are."

Kara sighs in exasperation. "What happened?"

Ana turns on her side, pulling the blanket up and losing consciousness from being so overwhelmed. Kara stands up, gripping Rafe's arm and dragging him to the other side of the room. "What is going on?"

"I know as much as you do. Let me speak to the archduke, perhaps he can shed some light on the situation. Will you stay with her?"

"Yes, because unlike you, I know how."

"Kara, this is neither the time nor place."

"Go speak to the archduke."

"Yes, Sage."

Rafe glances at Ana one more time before stepping out.

When Rafe knocks, Kane opens the door, giving no effort to hide his contempt. "Guardian, what do you want?"

"The princess is upset and not speaking to us. I wanted to find out what happened, mi'lord."

"I told her the truth, explained how things are here while we are at war. I didn't realize how… sensitive she is to such things. She certainly doesn't have the stomach for this."

Rafe clenches his hand, taking a breath. "I apologize on her behalf for leaving so abruptly, as she was overwhelmed, again."

"I could see that. Fine, tell her I expect her here tomorrow for dinner, so we may continue discussing the future of the kingdom. You are dismissed, Guardian."

Rafe gives a half bow then walks back to Ana's quarters. He relays the conversation to Kara. "Is she going to be okay?"

Kara doesn't hide her surprise at the concern in his voice. "Yes, she'll be fine. I think between studies and suitors, everything so new. It was too much for her. I'm going to bed. Call on me if she needs me."

"I will. Thank you." Rafe watches Kara leave, then walks to Ana's bedside. She is still asleep. He sits on the chaise, praying she sleeps all night.

Ana wakes up and knocks on Evren's door. She steps out. "Morning, mi'lady. Are you feeling better?"

"I just want to get dressed," she answers flatly.

"Of course. Apologies." Evren selects a red gown with black embroidered roses. She braids Ana's hair and pins in a black diamond tiara. They walk into the bedroom.

"Mi'lady, are you ready to go for breakfast?" Rafe asks.

"Yes, Guardian." He and Evren exchange a look of concern but say nothing. Ana turns to Evren. "I would like something special to wear to dinner with Ascienne tonight."

"We can—"

"Apologies," Rafe interrupts, "but you are having dinner with the archduke."

Losing her color, she turns to Rafe. "I beg your pardon?"

"I spoke to him last night, to keep the peace and ensure he did not feel slighted after you left. He said you will dine with him tonight to continue discussing the future of the kingdom."

"I see. So, you were jealous?"

"I—What?"

"You knew I was having dinner with Ascienne! Why did you not speak up on my behalf?"

"Mi'lady, you have not been here, and the way things work—"

"Stop. Just stop." She shakes her head. "I hate it here. I hate this place, I hate how I'm treated," she looks at Rafe, "and I hate who I am stuck with."

He doesn't hide the hurt on his face at her words but becomes angry instead. "Then what do you want to do? Do you miss your video games and pizza? Lazing about while people here are dying?"

She gasps softly. "You sound just like Kane."

His expression softens at her words. "I didn't mean—"

"We're going to breakfast. You will figure out a way to get me out of dinner with Kane, as I already have plans. You made this mess, clean it up, Guardian!"

"Yes, mi'lady."

Ana sits at the table, staring at her plate. She looks up when Kane walks in, then watches Rafe walk over and speak with him. She shoves her plate away.

"Your Highness, what's wrong?" Kara asks.

"Everything."

Kara takes a breath. "All right. Unpack it all for me."

"No." She looks up when Rafe approaches. "Well?"

He shakes his head. "He commands you join him."

She looks at Kara. "Does he really have that much power over me?"

"For now. Once you are crowned queen, he will have none."

"So, I need to keep the peace until then. When is my coronation?"

"The date hasn't been set, but I would think within the next few weeks."

Her shoulders slump. "That's too much time to deal with him."

"Then focus on your studies. Once the chancellor feels you are educated enough, you will be crowned. That's why they are so important."

"All right. Evren?"

Evren steps over to her and bows. "Yes, mi'lady?"

Ana speaks quietly to her, then she nods and leaves the dining hall. "Mi'lady, where is Evren going?" Kara asks.

"To take care of a personal matter for me. Now, are we going the library?"

"Not until you eat something."

Ana looks down at her plate. Begrudgingly, she picks up the piece of toast and eats it in front of Kara. "Better?"

"I guess it's a start."

———————— ⚊ ————————

Rafe and Kara sit at their usual table while Brienne and Evren begin their lesson on the realm.

"How many planets are in this solar system?" Ana asks.

"For starters, they are called realms, not planets. There are fifteen realms in all, with six having inhabitants. Each of the six has their own monarch to rule over them. Some have governors or stewards for the cities. Here, you have leaders who rule over the capitol, one for each quadrant. They are supposed to answer to you, but they do not because of the war. Once there is peace, they will all answer to you," Evren answers.

"I see. When did my father pass away?"

"He was killed in battle nearly two years ago. We did not know anyone had been dispatched to find you," Brienne admits. "As Evren said, we have been working as nurses during the war."

"How does the chancellor decide I am ready for the crown?"

"We give him daily updates on your progress. Once you are educated enough on the history, the laws, and have a general understanding of the realm, he will set your coronation date."

"Of course."

Ana insists they have lunch brought into the library so she can continue studying until dinner. Rafe is not happy about her missing training, but he understands her urgency to learn. Relief washes over him when she eats without prompting. Kara has the same look.

They return to her quarters so she can change for dinner with Kane. Evren picks out a pale blue gown with silver beads. Ana gets dressed then Evren does her hair. They go to his quarters.

His servant opens the door and gestures them in. Ana swallows hard as Kane approaches her. "Evening, mi'lady."

"Archduke. I want to apologize for last night."

"Your guardian already did."

"Still, I wanted to do it myself. Regardless of how I felt or my reasons, it was rude. I am sorry."

"Thank you."

They sit. Wine is poured, and the first dish is set before them. "I cannot thank you enough, all you have done for your people," Ana says.

"Our people, mi'lady. You may not have grown up here, but this is your world, your realm."

"I appreciate that. I think perhaps you are right."

"Is that an answer?" He sees the confusion on her face. "Are you saying you'll become my wife?"

"Oh, no. I meant that you are right about this realm needing a queen. I believe once I'm crowned, and the throne is claimed, the fighting will stop."

"That shows how naïve you truly are."

"Archduke—"

"I meant everything I said last night. I will do whatever I have to. Would you like to tour the triage unit? We could go after dinner."

"You aren't asking me so that I can help bring peace to the wounded, you're asking me to guilt me into marrying you. I may be young and inexperienced, but I'm not as naïve as you think."

The back of his fingers brush along her cheek, and she clenches her hands. "But we would be so good together."

"Archduke, this is most inappropriate."

His hand lowers to her neck. "I feel your heart racing and see how flush you are. I know you want me. Do you deny it?"

Wanting to flee, she is frozen in place. Her heart pounds in her ears when his hand grips her knee. She looks at him, fear in her eyes. His hand slides slowly up her gown, resting with his thumb on her thigh, his hand clamped on her leg.

"Please, unhand me," she begs softly. She cries out when his hand squeezes tight. Her chair crashes behind her as she jumps to her feet, leaning forward to keep her balance.

Her hand flies across his face. "You do not touch me that way!" she yells at him.

He stands up and grabs her wrist, twisting it as he pulls her towards him. She cries out in pain. Rafe is suddenly behind him, his hidden blade extended and poised at Kane's throat.

"Unhand her," he snarls. "Slowly."

Unleashing his charming smile, Kane releases his grip. He turns to Rafe. "This was simply a misunderstanding. That's all. Right, Your Highness?"

Rafe looks at Ana, her face distraught with fear. "Your Highness?"

"I—it—" she turns and runs from the room. Safely in her quarters, she locks herself in the washroom and sits on the edge of the tub, sobbing into her hands. She jumps when Kara and Rafe bang on the door.

"Your Highness, please, come out," Kara begs.

"Tell us what happened," Rafe pleads.

Collecting herself, she goes to the door, steps out, and sits on the chaise. Kara sits with her as Rafe stands nearby.

"Are you okay? Did he hurt you?" Kara asks.

Ana shakes her head. "It started last night. He put his hands on me. I let it go, hoping I was misunderstanding his intentions. This time, there is no mistake. He put his hand on my knee," she looks down as her hands clench, "and brought it up to my thigh. I asked him to unhand me, but he squeezed instead."

Kara looks at Rafe. "What can we do?"

His shoulders slump, "Nothing."

"What?" Kara asks, incredulous.

"It's her word against his. She may be the princess, but she's still a stranger here. She isn't queen, and the guards are loyal to him. It's out of our hands."

"He knows he can do whatever he wants and get away with it. He knew if I made a complaint, it would make me look weak and helpless," Ana says softly. "He has the upper hand, and I can't avoid him. What do I do?"

"Keep one of us by your side, at all times," Kara advises. "Never be alone with him. I spoke with the chancellor last night."

"Why have I not met him yet?"

"It's to avoid favoritism, until you are crowned. I know, an out-of-date tradition. Anyway, your coronation date is set for a week from Friday."

"A week and a half? How in the world did you convince him?"

"I told him how hard you are studying, that you are making great strides. Now, don't make a liar out of me." Her smile grows when Ana smiles back. "Mi'lady."

"I'm going to see the archduke to see if I can't smooth things out," Rafe says. "What he's done is unforgivable, but we have to keep the peace until you are crowned."

"I understand, Rafe. Thank you."

He flinches at his name, as he'd gotten used to her addressing him by his title. He bows and leaves.

"Danger everywhere, Your Highness."

"Yes, Kara."

"We'll be prepared."

"Will you stay with me tonight?" Ana asks.

"Mi'lady?"

"I don't want to be alone."

"Your guardian will be here." Kara regrets the words when Ana hangs her head. "Of course, I'll stay here tonight."

"Thank you, Kara." She looks around the room. "Where is Evren?" She opens the door and finds her waiting in the hall. She gestures her inside. "Were you out there this whole time?"

"I wanted to give you privacy, mi'lady."

"There's no need. You're part of my inner circle, too."

"Thank you."

"Evren, please stay with her while I grab a few things," Kara says as she stands up. "I'm staying in here tonight. I don't want her alone while I'm gone."

"Yes, Sage."

Rafe and Kara return at the same time, while Evren is helping Ana get ready for bed. Kara sees the frown on his face and walks up to him.

"Well?"

He shakes his head. "The archduke is beside himself with anger. He says the princess 'overreacted' to an 'accidental' touch. He won't calm down."

"You don't think he would hurt her?"

"I honestly don't know. He's livid. I tried to smooth it over. I told him she was upset with herself for how she reacted, but he wants an apology from her."

"Are you kidding me?" Kara cries out.

Ana runs from the closet, wrapping her robe around herself. "What's wrong? What happened?" The anger is written all over Kara's face.

Kara takes a calming breath. "The archduke is upset by what happened at dinner and would appreciate an apology from you." She watches the color fall from Ana's face.

"This can't be happening. Tell me this is a sick joke," she says as she turns away, leaning her hand against the wall for support

Kara walks over, putting her hand on Ana's arm. "I'm afraid not, Your Highness. I am so sorry."

Ana pulls her arm away and goes to the washroom. She leans against the vanity, trying to process everything that has happened. The shame rises in her throat, until she can no longer contain it. When he hears her retching into the toilet, Rafe runs to her.

"Go away," she says, retching again.

"I can't leave you like this. Let me help you."

"I have no strength. I can't even stand," she admits.

He gets her to her feet and helps her to the vanity. He holds her up as rinses out her mouth then gets her to the chaise. He kneels before her.

"How are you feeling?"

"A little better. Thank you, Rafe, for your kindness."

Regret washes over him. "I have not always been as kind to you."

"I don't know what was real and what wasn't, but you have acted with genuine kindness. Even when I don't deserve it," she says, looking down.

Rafe brings his hand to her chin, gently raising her head. "You are welcome, Your Highness. Everyone needs a little kindness in an unkind world. You deserve that most of all. I mean that," he says, standing up.

"Thank you. Will you help me to bed?"

She puts her arm around his shoulder, and he gets her to the bed, then covers her with the blanket.

"Rest now, mi'lady. You'll feel better in the morning."

Kara climbs into bed and pulls her into her arms. "Like old times, huh?" Kara laughs.

"Yes. When you'd stay with me in the dorm, even though it was against the rules. Everyone thought we were a couple."

"You didn't care what they thought. Neither did I. You know I have loved you as a sister as long as I can remember."

"Me, too. Thank you, Kara. I couldn't do this without you. I'm sorry for how I've behaved."

"You had so much put on you. I understand. I love you, Ana."

"I love you, too."

"Are you two going to sleep any time soon?"

"Rafe, shut up!" Kara and Ana giggle.

With a smile on his face, he lies down on the chaise. Ana and Kara laugh again, finding comfort in each other's arms.

A cold sweat washes over Ana as she wakes up. She pulls away from Kara and goes to the washroom, trying to forget her nightmare. She washes off her face as her body trembles in fear. Biting back tears, she opens the door and comes face to face with Rafe.

"Are you all right, mi'lady?" he asks quietly, not wanting to wake Kara.

She keeps her head down. "I'm fine. Thank you."

He steps aside, letting her pass. "Mia—" he clears his throat. "Mi'lady, please. I know something is wrong."

"It was just a nightmare. I'm okay now." She climbs back into bed. Rafe sits on the chaise, watching her and Kara. He would kill the archduke if he could. To be so bold, as to put his hands on her, lights a fire in Rafe's gut. He falls asleep, dreaming of wrapping his hands around Kane's neck.

Chapter 11

Ana wakes up, stretching. She gently wakes Kara up.

Kara smiles at her. "How did you sleep?"

"Good, thanks to you."

"Anything for you, Ana. I mean that." Kara hugs her tight before getting out of bed. "I'll be back in a few minutes."

Ana watches her leave, yawns, and stretches then walks to Rafe, who she is surprised to see is still asleep. "Rafe? Wake up."

"Let her go!" he yells, jolting upright. He looks at Ana, realizing where he is. "My apologies, Your Highness."

"It looks like we both have nightmares."

He nods his head, standing up. He bows. "How may I serve, mi'lady?"

"What is the agenda today?"

"Breakfast, studies then lunch. If you wish to train after lunch—"

"You forgot something."

"Mi'lady?"

"My apology to the archduke." She sighs when anger flashes across his face. "I have to. You know I do."

He nods, turning away. "I don't like it," he admits.

"I don't, either. What was it you said to me? Sometimes we must put our duty about ourselves."

He turns back to her, admiration in his eyes. "You've changed so much, in a short time." He catches himself. "Your Highness."

She smiles at him. "Thank you."

"I have to change." He goes into the washroom.

Evren and Brienne come in and take Ana to the closet. She wears a lavender gown with silver shoes and circlet, wrapped in gold vines. When Kara returns, they all agree it would be better for only her to escort Ana to Kane's quarters. They arrive before breakfast and knock on the door.

"Who is here at this ungodly hour? For f—" Kane opens the door, stepping back in surprise. He bows. "Your Highness, what can I do for you so early in the day?"

"I would like to apologize for our misunderstanding last night. I'm sorry for how I behaved."

He looks at her and Kara, debating. He nods. "Apology accepted, mi'lady." He leans down to her. "Know this, if your guardian lays another hand on me, I will execute him myself."

Ana swallows hard. "He was fulfilling his duty to protect me. This was my fault, not his. Even so, he regrets his actions towards you."

He steps back. "Fine. I will see you later." He shuts the door hard behind him.

Kara puts her hand on Ana's shoulder, worried as her entire body trembles. "You did great, Your Highness. Let's go to breakfast."

In the library, Brienne has a few books of laws laid out on the table. Ana looks up at her, worried.

"Am I expected to memorize all of these?" she asks.

"No, mi'lady. However, you need to know as many as you can. While the chancellor and tribunal dispense justice, they do seek your input on certain cases."

Ana picks up the book and begins to read. It is a tedious morning filled with notetaking and questions. Such an influx of information leaves Ana's head spinning, and she is relieved when lunch is brought in. Evren hands Ana a message from Ascienne with her plate.

When she's finished eating, Ana stands and opens the letter as she walks to the fireplace, hoping to read kind words from the prince. She bites back tears as she reads it, then crumples the letter in her hands and leans her head against the wall as she wraps her arms around herself. A few moments later, she returns to the table and puts the message in her bag. She continues reading as if nothing at all had occurred.

The image of Kane putting his hand on her leg forces its way into her mind. She pushes the memory back, but it won't stay down.

"Mi'lady, are you all right?" Evren asks.

Rafe and Kara immediately look up. Kara stands when Ana doesn't answer. She's walking to her when she speaks up.

"Fine, I… I'm fine," Ana responds, barely above a whisper. Kara sits next to her and gestures to her handmaids to give them a moment.

"Your Highness, what's wrong?"

Ana stares at the book in her hand. "Kara, I'm fine."

"Please, talk to me, mi'lady."

"It's stupid."

"Ana—" Kara catches herself. "Sorry, Your Highness."

Ana shakes her head. "This is too much!" she cries out, getting to her feet. With a loud thud, she slams the book shut and grabs her bag before running from the library. Her entourage follows behind as she returns to her quarters.

"I want to be alone!" she says, slamming the door.

"What is going on?" Rafe asks Kara.

She sighs. "I was afraid this would happen. I think she is overwhelmed, and with what happened last night, it's too much for her."

"Kara, you don't think she would…" Rafe can't even finish his sentence. Kara bolts past him and bursts into Ana's chambers. She runs to the washroom, pounding on the door when she realizes it's locked.

"You can punish me for this later. Ana, open this door. Now!" Kara cries. "I need to know you're okay."

"Leave me alone."

"Open this door, or I will have Rafe break it down."

"Kara, go away."

"Now!"

"I—I can't."

"What do you mean? You won't open the door?"

"No, I mean can't."

Kara turns to Rafe. "Break it down," she commands, pointing at the washroom door. Rafe looks unsure, until he hears Ana's voice.

"No," she calls out weakly. "Don't come in here."

He rips the door off the hinges. She's sitting on the floor of the shower, with her back to the wall. Cold water is crashing down on her, soaking her and her clothes. Kara runs over and turns the water to warm. She steps into the shower, wrapping her arms around Ana. She nods to Rafe, who slides the curtain across and steps out. He and Evren grab dry clothes for Kara and Ana.

Once they're dried and changed, Kara helps Ana to the chaise and sits beside her. "Please, talk to me. What happened?"

"I feel so stupid now. I got overwhelmed and let it show. I can't do that again. I know I have people watching me, waiting for me to fail."

"Did something happen?"

She asks Evren to fetch her bag, then pulls out the message and hands it to Kara.

Princess Maeriana,

I hope this finds you well. I was looking forward to our supper together. I had intended to ask for your hand in courting. Instead, you have humiliated me with your actions. I know you spent the night with the archduke. He told me everything.

Apparently, I misjudged your character and your intentions, if you can so easily go to bed with a man you are not betrothed to while toying with the heart of another. I am returning to my realm at once. I do not think we will see each other again.

-Ascienne

"Oh, Ana. I am so sorry. We can fix this. We can—"

"No."

"No?" Kara asks in surprise.

"If he would not even grant an audience with me, if he could not even give me a chance to explain, he is not worth my time."

"You have been pushed into so much so suddenly. It's amazing you have held up as well as you have. Coming to this strange new place, dealing with the archduke, rejection..." Kara glances at Rafe. "I'm sorry I didn't see how overwhelmed you were. I should've done more for you."

"Kara, it's not your fault. These are my responsibilities now. I have to learn to handle it on my own."

Kara pulls her into her arms. "I was so scared when you wouldn't open the door."

"I know. I'm sorry."

"You never owe me an apology. I'm sorry, though, for addressing you by your nickname and having your door broken down."

"Hmm, twenty days in the stocks should suffice as punishment." She pulls back, laughing at the look on Kara's face.

"So not funny, Your Highness!"

Ana laughs harder. "If you say so." She wipes her eyes as she stands up. "I'm feeling a little better. I'll return to my lesson."

"Are you sure? If you need a day to yourself, everyone will understand."

"No, I don't have time. Although, I would like a break from those books. Maybe some training instead?" Kara nods and Ana takes her hand, Kara helping her to her feet.

Rafe approaches her. "Are you all right now, mi'lady?"

She smiles at him. "I am, thank you."

"I'm sorry," Rafe says as they walk into the training center.

"Whatever for?" Ana asks.

"I overwhelmed you with our training. I acted in a way I should not have. How would you like to train today?"

"You're the trainer, guide me."

"Yes, mi'lady."

"Show me again. Only, slower, please?"

He gets the training dummy and stands it up. He takes her through the movements, then steps back, watching her. "Go ahead," he softly encourages when she doesn't move. "You know there is no judgment here. Only correcting, I promise, mi'lady."

She goes through the movements, stopping from time to time when he takes her wrist or hand to correct her.

"Very good." Beaming with pride, he studies her face and sees she needs a break. "Now, are you ready for dinner?"

"Yes, Rafe. Thank you."

They walk into the dining hall, Kara on one side and Evren on the other. Rafe follows behind, scanning for any threats. They sit, and Ana looks over when the archduke walks in. He goes to another table, sitting with a few members of the court.

"Kara, what is this court called?"

"What do you mean?"

"Does it have a name? You know, like Court of Summer or Court of Gold?" Her mind drifts back to the books she used to read, and the magical worlds she had escaped into.

"No, mi'lady. Though, once you are queen, you could name it," Evren offers. "If you wish."

"Thank you. I will think on that." Her gaze meets Kane's. He ignores her, turning his attention back to the man beside him. Ana continues to eat.

He knows I will defend myself, so maybe he will leave me alone now. He looks angry. I wonder if I am the cause of that. She chuckles at the thought, then suddenly notices that her hands have turned cold and clammy. Her mouth is numb, and when she tries to take a drink, she realizes she can hardly swallow. She looks down at her plate in horror. *I've been poisoned.*

"Kara," she mumbles.

"What's wrong?"

Ana licks her lips, trying to speak. "Take my plate," she manages.

"Where, Your Highness?"

"Follow me and Rafe."

"What?"

She turns to Rafe and leans in close to whisper in his ear. "Do not show alarm. I need your help." She clears her throat. "I've been poisoned. I need you to take me to the Medical Center."

He nods, getting to his feet. Kara picks up the plate as he helps Ana walk out. They're almost to the Medical Center when she goes limp in his arms. He picks her up and pushes the door open as he runs in, greeted by medical staff. "The princess has been poisoned," he announces. "We need help!"

Two nurses put her onto a gurney and whisk her away. A woman in scrubs approaches him, clipboard in her hand. "Do you know what kind of poison?"

Kara hands her the plate. "She was eating this." The nurse takes the plate to run tests on the food. Rafe and Kara sit in the waiting room. Kara gets up and paces, worried sick over Ana.

"She was so calm and collected," she remarks.

"I know. She told me she had been poisoned as if she were talking about the weather. I couldn't believe how calm she was."

227

Winslow walks out a short while later. "She's going to be fine. It was Prince's Bane. If she had eaten anymore, it would've killed her. You can come back now."

He leads them to Ana's room and gives them privacy. Walking in, they are taken back by how white she is. Kara closes the door and watches Rafe approach Ana. He gently strokes her face with one hand, his other running his fingers through her hair. "Mia estrela," he says quietly. "I'm here."

"You do love her, don't you?"

"Kara—"

"Just answer the damn question."

"It doesn't matter. I know she doesn't love me. She can't, after everything I have done to her."

"She still loves you, Rafe. She clutches her cross and cries over you."

"You know our laws. It's forbidden."

"You *do* love her!"

"Kara—" he tries.

"You didn't deny it. You spouted the law."

"Whatever I feel about her is insignificant. She has to focus on her duty and her kingdom."

"Don't give up on her, Rafe."

"I will never give up on her, but I know there is no possibility of us. I accept that."

Kara sighs. "How do you not see that's the same thing?"

"Drop it. I can't do anything about it." He looks at her. "What would you have me do? Profess my feelings and get executed?"

She thinks a moment. "Well, it's a start." She flashes him a smile.

"Don't even—" he stops speaking when Ana moves. Kara walks over and takes her hand. Her eyes flutter a moment but stay closed. Kara sits next to her, looking at Rafe.

"She's so cold."

Rafe feels her forehead. "Is that normal?"

"I've never known anyone poisoned with Prince's Bane. I can't say for sure."

Rafe steps back, standing guard while Kara reassures Ana she'll be okay. Winslow walks in and takes her vitals. "It looks like most of the poison is out of her system. She'll sleep a few hours and is expected to make a full recovery."

"When can we get her back to her quarters?"

"We're making arrangements to get her back without being seen. We'll come shortly to get her."

"Thank you."

Winslow leaves the room. Rafe walks to Ana, putting one hand on her arm and the other on her forehead.

"Rafe, what are you doing?" Kara asks.

"If I tell you, do you swear not to breathe a word of it? Not to anyone, especially her?"

"I swear."

"Do you remember when she healed after being shot, then again after the detective attacked her?"

"Yes. What about it?"

He takes a breath and holds it, then releases it slowly. "It only works if I touch her."

"What?" Kara thinks a moment, then understanding flashes in her eyes. "The legend—"

"It's not. I promise you. I don't know what it is, but I know it's not that. It can't be."

"How do you know?"

"Because fate wouldn't be so cruel," he answers, looking down at Ana.

"If anyone could find a way, it would be her. You know it in your heart."

"That would mean she would have to know the truth, and she can't. You know she can't. I won't risk her."

Kara nods. "I won't say anything, I swear."

Winslow comes in to get Ana to her room. They use a back hallway and a hidden corridor to get her inside without being seen. Kara and Rafe are getting her settled into bed when Evren walks in.

"Everyone is talking about what happened. Is she okay?"

"I should've known word would get out," Kara says, her voice dripping with anger. "Probably whoever did it, to make her look weak." She looks at Evren. "Sorry. Yes, she's going to be okay."

"I watched you leave, but I didn't know what to do. I stayed in the dining hall until I heard what happened."

Kara walks over. "I'm so sorry. When she told us she was poisoned and needed medical attention, we just jumped into action."

"I understand."

Rafe looks at Kara. "I think she's waking up."

Kara adjusts her pillows, helping her sit up. "Your Highness?" No response. "Princess Maeriana?"

Her eyes open as she tries to focus. She sees Rafe and Kara. "What happened?" she asks, her voice rough and low.

"You were poisoned at dinner," Kara answers. "How do you feel?"

"I'm freezing."

Rafe grabs his blanket off the chaise and brings it to her, then stokes the fire and adds two more logs. He returns to her side.

"Better, mi'lady?"

"A little," she says through chattering teeth.

As she continues to shiver, Rafe looks at Kara and Evren. "Could you ladies find something to do for say ten to twenty minutes? Maybe out in the hall to keep watch?"

Kara nods in understanding. She takes Evren's hand, leading her from the room. Rafe locks the door behind them. He takes his jacket and shoes off before climbing into bed. He pulls Ana into his arms, holding her tight.

"I'm sorry, Your Highness. I know this is highly inappropriate—"

"Shut up and hold me, please. It's already helping."

"Yes, mi'lady," he says with a smile.

She wraps her arms around him, and he pulls her in closer. She breathes in his warmth and comfort. When she stops shivering, he starts to pull away, but she grips him tighter.

"Another minute, please?"

"Yes, mi'lady."

He holds her, never wanting to let go. He swallows hard when he knows he has to, literally and figuratively. Reluctantly, he pulls away.

"Thank you," she says, torn on her feelings for him.

"Of course, mi'lady. Glad I could help." He puts his jacket and shoes back on, then walks to the door, opens it, and steps out into the hallway. Kara grabs his arm and pulls him to her. "What's wrong?" he asks.

"Brienne just stopped by. There is speculation that Kane had her poisoned. I bet that bastard would do anything to get her out of the way so he can have the throne. Brienne is going to investigate further."

"What are we going to do?" Evren asks.

"For one, she will have a personal taster," Rafe decides.

"You know she won't allow that," Kara counters.

"She won't have a choice." He stands up. "Something is wrong." He goes inside as Ana is walking unsteadily towards the washroom, and he rushes to her when she collapses against the chaise. "What's wrong?" She mumbles something he doesn't quite understand. He gets her into the washroom, where she throws up. "Winslow said you may have some lingering poison."

"Would you get Kara and Evren? I need a shower."

He sits her on the floor with her back against the vanity, then leaves and gets their attention, gesturing them in. Kara gets her cleaned up while Evren gets her a fresh nightgown.

Kara holds her arm around Ana's waist as she helps her into bed.

Once she's asleep, Rafe sits on the edge of the bed. He looks at Kara. "If I had any proof it was Kane, I would dispatch him myself!"

"You and me both."

There's a knock at the door. Rafe walks over and opens it slightly, biting down his anger at the sight of Kane.

"Can I help you?" he asks, no emotion in his voice.

"I heard the princess was… ill. I wanted to check on her."

"She's resting now. I'll tell her you stopped by." He starts to shut the door, but Kane blocks it with his foot. He pushes Rafe back.

"I'd like to see to her myself."

"She's asleep. This is not appropriate. Please, leave," Kara says as she walks over. "She is in no state for company."

Kane sees Ana asleep in the bed. "Fine. I'll be by tomorrow." He leaves the room.

"Is he gone?" Ana asks quietly, not opening her eyes or moving.

"Yes, mi'lady."

She slowly sits up. Kara helps her while adjusting her pillows. "The nerve!" Ana cries out. "After all he's done to me."

"We don't know for certain it was him."

Ana looks at Kara. "We may not have proof, but I feel it in my heart. It was him."

"You never have to be alone with him again. I promise you that. We will all ensure it. Now, how are you feeling?"

"A little tired."

"Do you want to sleep some more?"

"No. I'm hungry. Could I get something to eat?"

"I'll get you a plate," Evren volunteers. "I'll be back shortly." Once Evren returns with food for Ana, Kara sits with her to her help her eat. Evren takes the empty plate and hands it off. She walks back to Ana. "Can I get you anything else, mi'lady?"

"No, Evren. Thank you for everything."

"Of course."

Ana tells Kara she needs more sleep. Kara and Evren retire for the evening. Rafe smiles at Ana. "Thank you," she says, holding up the throw blanket. "Please, takes this back."

"Yes, mi'lady."

Drifting off to sleep, she whispers, "I love you, Rafe." He freezes in place at her words, clutching the blanket in his hands, then walks over to her and sees she is sleeping. While he wipes a tear from his cheek, he strokes his thumb over her forehead.

"Stop!" Ana screams, turning in her bed. The dagger plunges into her side, and Rafe jumps to his feet, charging at the assassin.

His hidden blade extends out as he grabs the assassin from behind. She stops struggling when the cool metal blade is digging into her throat.

"Who sent you?" he hisses.

"Never," she replies, lunging forward and killing herself on his blade. He throws her body to the ground and rushes to Ana. Evren runs in.

"What happened?"

"An assassin. She's hurt, badly." He scoops Ana into his arms and runs with her to the Medical Center. They take her from him, and he paces the room, shaking in fear and anger. Kara and Evren arrive a few minutes later.

"Rafe, it will take time for them to take care of her. Go get cleaned up and changed. She doesn't need to see you like this," Kara says.

"You're right. I'll be back." He heads to his quarters.

"Could you see how badly she was hurt?" Kara asks.

Evren shakes her head. "No, but there was a lot of blood. They are cleaning her quarters now. I pray she survives this."

"I can't lose her," Kara says, her voice breaking. "I can't."

Evren pulls Kara into her arms, holding her tightly. "You won't. She's strong. She'll survive."

Kara wraps Evren tighter. "Thank you for being here with me. I couldn't go through this alone."

Evren pulls back, looking into her eyes. "I know this isn't the right time, but I have to say it. If it were up to me, you would never have to be alone."

Kara's eyes go wide in surprise. She leans down and kisses Evren then pulls away quickly "I'm sorry. Was that okay?"

"No," Evren replies.

Kara steps back. "I'm sorry. I—"

"It wasn't long enough."

Kara smiles as she leans down, pulling Evren into her arms and kissing her again. They cling to each other, holding each other tight then look into each other's eyes. Kara stiffens when someone clears their throat. She looks up to see Winslow standing in the doorway.

"You can come see her now."

"How is she?" Kara asks as they follow him.

"We stopped the bleeding and bandaged the wound. Thankfully, nothing vital was hit. She needs rest and time to heal."

Once in Ana's room, Kara sits by her side, holding her hand as Evren sits in the chair in the corner. Rafe walks in, and Kara smiles at him.

"She should be okay. Nothing vital was hit, but it's a deep wound and will need time to heal." She stands up. "I need to speak with Evren about something. We'll be right outside."

He nods in understanding. As soon as the door shuts behind them, he walks up to Ana. Pulling the blanket down, he lifts her gown up and peels back the bandage. He places his hand on the wound, waiting a few minutes then reapplies the bandage and covers her up. Kara sees him when he opens the door.

They all walk into Ana's room, and Rafe sits by her side, holding her hand. He wants to keep as much contact as he can. Out of the corner of his eye, he notices Kara and Evren are holding hands as well.

"Really?" Rafe asks.

"Shut up," Kara responds.

"What? I'm happy for you both."

Kara shakes her head. "We can't go public with it."

"I know. I explained it to Ana, and she didn't understand why it is illegal because of your status."

"She thought it was wrong?" Evren asks.

"Yes. She sees no reason for the law."

Evren's eyes go wide when she sees Rafe's hand on Ana's. "Are you—"

"No. Don't ask about this."

Kara looks at Evren, nodding. "Please?"

"Of course."

When the door opens, Rafe stands up and takes a step back. A nurse walks in, checks her vitals, and notates the chart. "She'll probably sleep the rest of the night, if you want to come back tomorrow."

"Someone just tried to kill her. You couldn't drag us away," Kara speaks up.

The nurse nods. "I understand. Of course, you are welcome to stay," she says as she leaves.

They stay with her all night. Kara sits by her, holding her hand. Rafe wants to but can't risk it with the nurse coming in every so often to check on her.

When Ana wakes up in the morning, Kara adjusts the bed to help her sit up. A violent sob escapes her lips when she turns slightly, causing pain to strike through her side and across her stomach like a flash of lightning. Kara strokes her hair and reassures her as tears stream down her cheeks.

Rafe runs out to get the nurse, who gives her the next dose of pain medicine and checks her vitals. Once the nurse is gone, Rafe walks up to Ana, gently caressing her arm. Her eyes fly open as she is consumed with pain. "I can't—" she gasps out. "Rafe—"

"Shh, mia estrela," he whispers, leaning down and stroking her hair. "Go to sleep. This is all a bad dream. You'll feel better soon."

"It hurts," she says as her eyes flutter, then she loses consciousness.

———————— ⌙ ————————

"What do you mean, we can't move her yet? She needs to be in her own quarters. She's too exposed here."

"Because you did such a great job protecting her there, right?" Winslow shoots back.

Rafe's hands clench into fists. Kara steps forward, gently pushing Rafe behind her. "Look, she will do better in her quarters. We need to move her there. Now."

Winslow shakes his head. "You don't understand. We can't risk the movement. Her wound could reopen. She needs to stay here a little longer. I'm sorry." He walks out.

Rafe walks back to Ana and leans down to feel her forehead. She opens her eyes and brings her hand up over his. "Hmm, my love."

He sucks in his breath, straightening up. "Good afternoon, Your Highness."

She sits up slowly, pulling her hand away. "I'm sorry. My brain is in such a fog from the medicine."

"It's okay, mi'lady. How do you feel?"

"Sore and tired. I want to go to my room."

"The doctor won't let you yet."

"Can't I make him?" she asks, smiling.

Rafe smiles back, shaking his head. "You need to listen to the doctor and do what's best—"

The door opens, and Kane enters the room. "Everyone is talking about the assassination attempt! I'm so sorry I wasn't there to protect you, mi'lady. I would've stopped the assassin in their tracks." He shoots Rafe a smug look.

Rafe wants nothing more than to hang his head, but he refuses to let Kane see him ashamed. Instead, he keeps his gaze. "I'm sure you would've, mi'lord."

"Guardian," he snorts, "I would like a moment with her."

"We're not going anywhere, sire," Kara says. "We promised her after this last attack that we would not leave her side."

"Look here, witch—"

"Enough!" Ana commands, sitting up and wincing in pain. "They will not be leaving. Say whatever it is you came to say."

He looks at them with disdain then walks to her side. When he tries to take her hand, she tucks it under the blanket, and he stomps his foot like a toddler about to throw a tantrum.

"Anyway, Your Highness, I am here because I would like to offer you the services of the royal guards." She opens her mouth to object, but he cuts her off. "They would not replace your *guardians*," he says the word as though it were laced with acid. "They would merely assist."

"I am grateful for the offer, but it isn't necessary. I can assure you, I'm in good hands."

"Your Highness—"

"I have given my answer. Was there anything else?"

"Since you asked, mi'lady, there is one other matter. It's... delicate."

"They aren't leaving."

"Of course. Rumor has it the assassin was sent from Prince Ascienne. They are saying you slept with him but would not marry him. I apologize for the crudeness, as I am simply repeating what I have heard. The assassin was his revenge for being denied the throne."

Rafe and Kara look at each other, shaking their heads at how low Kane would sink. Ana speaks up. "Do you have any proof to offer? That he was behind this, I mean."

"Well, no—"

"I thought you would've been smarter than to believe such childish gossip. I see now, I was wrong." She clutches the blanket, trying desperately not to cry out as the pain snakes through her side. "Thank you for your time, Archduke. You are dismissed."

"Mi'lady," he says, giving a slight bow and running from the room.

The moment he's gone Kara bursts out laughing. "That was amazing! I can't believe how you spoke to him."

Ana smiles at her. "Oh, I'm sure I'll pay for it."

"No," Rafe assures her, "you won't. We will not leave you alone again."

"Can he control that?"

"What do you mean?" Kara asks.

"Can he reassign Rafe or send Evren away?"

"No. Only you have power over your entourage. He can assign us tasks, which you have to approve, but he cannot command us away from you," Rafe explains.

She lets out a sigh of relief. "That's good." She reaches her hand to her chest and sits up in a panic. "My cross! Where is it."

Kara picks up a bag with Ana's belongings and finds the necklace. "Here you are, mi'lady."

"Thank you," Ana says as she puts it on. Her fingers wrap around the cross. "It's the only possession here I care about."

Hiding his pain, Rafe turns away and closes his eyes, then steps out of the room. Kara looks at Ana. "Do you feel healed enough to return to your quarters?"

She turns slightly, wincing at the tightness. "I think so."

A few moments later, Rafe walks back in with a hot tea in his hands. He brings it to Ana. "This is similar to chamomile."

She takes the tea, smiling at him. "Thank you." She sips it slowly, savoring the strong flavor.

Kara looks at Rafe. "She's ready to be moved."

Rafe retrieves a nurse. Under heavy protest, she removes Ana's IV and gets her ready to leave. Still murmuring under her breath, she leaves the room. Ana sits on the edge of the bed and puts her feet on the floor. Rafe is instantly beside her. She attempts to stand but falls into his arms.

"I'm sorry," she says, steadying herself. "I'm okay now. I can walk."

"Can you get dressed?"

"I think so."

Rafe hands her over to Kara and Evren, then leaves the room to give her privacy. He's pacing outside the door when Brienne approaches. She gestures him over.

"I've learned some of Kane's plans." They speak quietly until the door opens, and Ana walks out. Kara and Evren are on either side to help her. Rafe looks at Brienne.

"Good work. Let me know if you find out anything else."

She nods and leaves the center. Rafe walks to Ana, who shakes her head at the nurse approaching with a wheelchair. Ana looks at Rafe. Evren steps aside so he can help her walk to her quarters, which is where they are heading when they see Kane approaching.

"Shit," Ana murmurs.

Rafe chuckles. "Ditto, Your Highness."

They turn a corner and keep walking, ignoring his calls to them. He stomps up to them, but before he can say anything, Kara moves between him and Ana. "We are taking her to her quarters so she may rest in private. Please, do not interrupt us."

"I will be by later to check on her."

"No, you will not!" Kara hisses at him. "She needs her rest and to not be bothered. If she wishes to see you, she will send for you."

"You don't speak for her."

"Actually," Ana interjects, "she does."

"Hmph." He turns and stalks off.

Ana is shaking in Rafe's arms. "Are you okay, mi'lady?"

"Yes. Please, get me to my room."

Rafe inspects her quarters, leaving Ana with Kara and Evren, then helps her inside and into bed. Once she's settled in, he sits on the edge.

"I'm sorry, Your Highness."

"Whatever for?" she asks, clearly confused.

"You were hurt because I failed you."

"Rafe—"

"Your Highness."

She nods. "You did your job, Guardian. You saved my life. Please, accept my gratitude."

"Yes, mi'lady."

She gasps suddenly, clutching her side as another wave of pain washes over her. She grips the blanket, and Rafe takes her hands.

"Squeeze, mi'lady."

She cries and squeezes until the pain is easing. "Thank you, Rafe," she says, her eyes drifting closed.

He keeps his grip on her hands as he wills the healing to happen. He has no idea how it works, or if he has any control over it, but he has faith that it will work once more. Watching her sleep in peace, he closes his eyes as anger washes over him. *How could I let my guard down? How could I be so stupid? She was nearly killed because of me.*

"Rafe, you need your rest as well," Kara says as she walks over. "I'll sit with her."

"I need to heal her."

"You have done all you can do. You're pale and trembling, you should go rest. She needs you strong."

He hangs his head, realizing she's right. "Yes, Kara."

"Sleep in my bed," Evren offers. "That way, we won't disturb you, and you'll be right next door if we need anything."

He stands up and nods to her. "Thank you for your kindness." As soon as his head hits the pillow, he passes out.

"Thank you, Evren."

"Of course." She smiles at Kara.

They sit at the table and talk while Ana sleeps. Kara tells her about their time on Earth, and Evren explains the different realms she has served on. Kara glances over from time to time to check on Ana.

"Hmm, Kara?" Ana calls out.

She runs over. "Mi'lady, how do you feel?"

"Better, just tired."

"May I check your wound?" Kara lifts the blanket after Ana nods her head, then lifts her gown, and removes the bandage. "It's completely healed," she says, exhaling loudly in relief. "You should continue resting, mi'lady."

"I don't understand. How do I heal? Is it because I'm a royal?"

"No, mi'lady."

"You mean she doesn't know?" Evren asks. Her face goes flush when Kara gives her an angry look. "Apologies. It slipped out."

"What is she talking about?" Ana asks Kara.

"I can't, Your Highness. Please, it's for your own protection."

"Kara—"

"I promised him. He could be killed for it. Don't ask me."

Ana nods her head. "For his sake, I won't," she says, turning on her side.

"Mi'lady, please—"

Ana waves her away with her hand as her tears are falling fast. Kara gives Evren another angry look when she hears Ana sniffling. Evren returns to the table in the corner while Kara climbs into bed with Ana. She pulls her into her arms.

"I don't care if you have me executed for this, but I am not leaving you while you're crying."

"I would never!" Ana cries out and turns to Kara, realizing she was joking. "I'm sorry." Ana pulls her to her and holds her. "Please, tell me whatever you know, that Rafe is okay. I couldn't bear to lose him."

"I promise you, he is safe."

"Thank you."

"I'm surprised you still care so much for him, after he broke your heart."

"I wanted to hate him that first day here, when he told me he didn't love me. Now that I know what I have to do to fulfill my duty and keep the peace, I understand why he did it."

"You've grown so much in such a short time. I can't believe you're the same girl who cried because she couldn't find her class."

Ana smiles at her. "It's because of you and Rafe. I couldn't have done this without you beside me." She looks at the light coming in through the windows. "What time is it?"

"Nearly dinner."

"Oh. Do I have to go to the dining hall?"

"Probably better if you didn't. You want everyone to think you're still healing, right?"

"Right. Evren?"

She comes to Ana's side. "Mi'lady?"

"Please see to food for all of us."

"Yes, mi'lady." She leaves.

"Kara, does he still love me?" Ana asks, hope flickering in her eyes.

She swallows hard. "Please don't ask—"

"Just tell me."

"Even if he does, there's nothing to be done. The laws being what they are, if anyone even thought he was in love with you, he would be executed, and you could be punished. You must treat him as a bodyguard and nothing more. Otherwise, you put his life at risk."

Ana pulls away, sitting on the edge of the bed as she cries into her hands. "I love him, Kara. I still do. I know I shouldn't."

"Oh, Ana." She rubs her back, comforting her. "I'm so sorry. I know he was the first man you ever loved."

"And the last. I will never love anyone else."

"Until he turned out to be a coward, you had a chance with Ascienne."

Ana laughs. "Uh, no."

"Mi'lady?"

Ana sighs, looking at her. "I had other intentions with him, to help me and this realm."

"I see," she says. "Still, there are ambassadors, nobility, dignitaries. Don't give up on love."

"I won't," Ana says, though she knows in her heart Rafe is the only man she will ever truly love. She stands up and brings her hand to her side, impressed at how quickly she has healed.

After showering, Ana changes into a nightgown, at Kara's suggestion, so she can keep up the impression of recovering from her wound. Evren sits at the table, mending one of Ana's gowns. Kara leaves to freshen up.

There is a knock at the door, and Evren opens it, failing to hide her surprise. "Archduke, how may I help you this evening?"

Ana grabs the blanket and wraps it around herself. She leans against the back of the chaise, trying to appear in pain. Kane steps around Evren and walks in.

"Evening, Your Highness. Forgive the intrusion, but I just had to see how you were doing."

"Still recovering, but I am in very good hands. Thank you for stopping by."

He walks over and sits with her. He looks at Evren. "Slave, leave us," he commands.

She looks at Ana, who gestures to the table. Evren sits and continues mending while keeping a close eye on them. "She won't leave my side, but this will give us privacy. Please, continue."

"I would request you at dinner tomorrow night. My chambers at six o'clock. Just the two of us."

She scoffs. "In what universe do you think I would agree to that?"

He smiles, leaning in. "Because what happened to you yesterday was but a taste of my reach. I will gladly send my assassin to visit your guardian. Or perhaps Kara? Hmm?"

"You openly admit to what you did?"

He laughs. "The guards are loyal to me, and you have no evidence. I have all the power here. The sooner you realize that, the easier this will all be."

"What if I take back that power?"

His smile grows. "Oh, my offer to you from our first conversation? If you went to the chancellor right now, he would tell you that your coronation date is set and cannot be changed. Do you really think you will last that long with me as your enemy? Now, I expect you tomorrow night."

"I was stabbed by your assassin! I am still healing."

"Oh, don't be so dramatic. It's just dinner, mi'lady. You'll be fine." He gestures to Evren after Ana shakes her head. "Or I could kill her as well. She wouldn't be the first slave I've killed."

Ana swallows hard. "I will see you tomorrow at six. Until then, I do need to rest."

"Very good, Your Highness. Perhaps there is hope for you yet." He stands up, bowing to her for show before he leaves.

Ana brings her knees to her chest, shivering while pushing down her tears. Evren rushes to her.

"Mi'lady, are you okay?"

When she doesn't respond, Evren runs to get Kara. They walk in, and Kara hurries to Ana's side. "Princess Maeriana?" she asks, kneeling beside her. "What's wrong?" Ana buries her face into her legs and cries harder. Kara looks at Evren. "What happened?" she asks, then turns to Ana and strokes her hair.

"The archduke was here."

At Evren's response, she whips her head around. "You let him in?"

"No. He pushed past me. He commanded me to leave, but I refused. I sat at the table to keep an eye on her while they spoke. As far as I could see, he didn't touch her, but I couldn't hear what was being said." Ana pulls away from Kara and climbs into bed. She follows behind her.

Kara sits on the edge, caressing Ana's back. "Please, talk to me? What did he want?" The arrival of their dinner interrupts her. Evren goes to her room to get Rafe. He walks in, yawning and rubbing his eyes, then freezes when he hears Kara urging Ana to get up and eat.

"What's wrong?" Rafe asks Evren.

Kara shakes her head. "Please, Your Highness. You need to eat. After healing from such a wound, you need to keep your strength up."

"I wish she had killed me."

Rafe gasps. He walks over to Ana, looking down at her in concern. She is trembling in fear as she cries. He looks at

245

Kara and Evren. Kara takes Evren's hand, leading her to the window to look out. Rafe picks Ana up and carries her into the closet. She doesn't object, wrapping her arms and legs around him as he sits on the ottoman. He quietly reassures her as she cries.

Once she calms down, he pulls her back gently. "You don't have to tell us anything. Will you come eat?"

When she nods, he stands up and puts her on her feet. He walks out first and sits at the table while Ana wraps herself in a robe. When she joins Rafe at the table, Kara and Evren sit with them. They eat in silence, watching Ana. Rafe gives her a concerned look when she pushes her food around with her fork.

"I don't want to talk about it," she says.

"You don't have to," Rafe responds. "Please, eat."

She nods, taking a bite. Once they finish, Kara tries again. "Did he hurt you this time?" She jumps when Ana let out a nervous laugh.

"No, Kara. Nothing so sinister as that."

"Then what happened?"

"You won't like it." She takes a breath and looks away. "I'm having dinner with him tomorrow night. Alone in his quarters."

"What? No!" Rafe cries out, rising to his feet. "You can't."

"I don't have a choice. He has all the power."

"What did he say? Why did you agree?"

Looking at Evren, Ana shakes her head. "It doesn't matter. It's something I have to do. I tried to delay it. I told him I am still healing, but he said it was just dinner."

"We can't trust him," Rafe says as he sits down.

"I know. That's why you'll accompany me. You may not be allowed inside, but if you're right outside the door, I know I'll be okay."

He closes his eyes in shame. "I was in the same room with you and couldn't protect you."

"That was different. You have to sleep sometime, and she was a trained assassin."

"You were hurt because of me."

"Rafe, stop! You saved my life and killed her. It wasn't your fault. Please, stop blaming yourself."

"As you wish, Your Highness."

Ana yawns. "The healing really takes it out of me. I'm going to brush my teeth and get more sleep." As she's walking towards the washroom, she collapses against the wall. Rafe runs to her, holding her up before she can fall over.

"What's wrong?"

"I'm completely exhausted. This was the most serious wound yet. I think it took everything I had." She steadies herself against him and tries to walk. "I can't."

He gets her to the washroom and waits for her. She steps out a few moments later, gripping the doorframe.

"May I?" he asks. She looks at him in confusion. He brings his arms around her and picks her up. "Is this okay, mi'lady?"

"Yes, thank you."

He carries her to bed and tucks her in. "Do you need anything?"

"No, just sleep." She turns to her side and drifts off.

He joins Kara and Evren at the table. "She's resting now. What are we going to do? She cannot meet him alone. He will hurt or kill her."

"She seems determined to do this. I don't know what he said to her, but I don't think we can talk her out of it," Kara says.

"I have a question," Evren says timidly. They look at her. "If Rafe is the one that heals her, why is she so tired after?"

"It's not necessarily that I heal her. It's a little more complicated than that," he explains. "It's like she already has a healing ability, but I accelerate it. Doing so drains her energy."

"I see. She doesn't know it's you?"

"She can't."

Evren nods her head. "I understand. Don't worry, I won't say a word."

Rafe stands up and stretches before pushing the chaise closer to the bed. He plans to watch over her all night but doesn't realize how drained he is, and he falls asleep.

Ana wakes up as breakfast is being set up. Kara and Rafe are in the corner, engaged in a serious discussion. She sits up, grateful her strength has returned. Kara sees her and turns to Rafe, saying something that makes him angry as she walks over.

"Mi'lady, are you ready for breakfast?"

"If you'll tell me what's going on with you and Rafe."

Kara looks away. "Just a disagreement."

"What about?"

"Mi'lady, please," Kara tries, looking at her.

"Fine. Yes, I would like to eat."

Kara takes Ana into the closet, where she helps her dress in an outfit of black gossamer pants with a long sleeve crimson shirt. She hands her black flats. Ana looks herself over in the mirror.

"Thank you, Kara." They join Evren and Rafe for breakfast at the table. Ana looks at Evren. "May I ask you something?"

"Of course, mi'lady."

"Where are you from?"

"You mean my home world?"

"Yes."

"Vulcara. It is the fourth realm from the sun. On my world, elves are regarded as the highest of beings, regaled for their beauty and intelligence." She studies her plate. "I've only heard the stories, because I've never been."

"You've never been to your own world?"

"No, mi'lady. I was born elsewhere then sold shortly after."

"I'm sorry I asked."

"Your Highness, please. It's okay. I told you that you could ask me anything, that you will not offend. I mean that. I wouldn't have met Kara if I was on my home world."

Ana looks at them. "You two can't—"

"No, not publicly. It's forbidden," Kara says.

"Oh, I wish there was something I could do. I can't change that once I'm queen?"

Evren shakes her head. "The Celestial Council have firmly held that there is to be a hierarchy. Any threat to that, to the status quo, they will not abide by."

"Mi'lady, you have a realm to tend to. Please, do not worry about us."

"I would never forgive myself if either of you were executed."

Evren is confused, but Kara understands. "Oh, no! Only a guardian is executed for that. Though I would be stripped of my station and banished. Evren would be beaten then returned to you, her owner."

"That doesn't make me feel much better," Ana admits.

Kara shakes her head. "It's because your heart is too big for your body. Please, don't worry about us," she says again, giving her a reassuring smile.

Ana nods. "If you say so." She glances at the clock over Kara's shoulder, watching the seconds tick by until her dinner with Kane. Dread turns into a knot in her stomach, and ice water flows through her veins.

"Mi'lady?" Evren asks.

She looks at them, realizing they are staring at her. "I'm sorry. Did you say something?"

"You look flush. Are you ill?" Kara asks, taking her hand.

"I'm fine," she says as she stands up. Pulling her hand away and going to the washroom, she shuts the door, leaning over the vanity as she trembles uncontrollably. *I'd give anything not to do this. I hate that he has so much power over me. I know what he wants, he's made it quite apparent. The way he stares at me, the way he touches me. Nothing can stop it now.*

At that, she loses her breakfast into the sink. Kara swings the door open, angry until she sees Ana, and her heart aches for her. She wants nothing more than to protect her.

"Please, Your Highness. How can we help you?"

"There's nothing anyone can do. I have to do this myself." She rinses the sink and brushes her teeth.

"I refuse to believe that. Tell me why you agreed. We can help you."

Ana walks past her and sits on the chaise. As the warmth of the fireplace flows into her, she wraps herself in Rafe's blanket.

"You're not going."

She looks up at Kara. "Excuse me?"

"I don't care if you punish me for disobeying you, but you aren't going. I won't allow you to."

"Kara, please. You don't understand what is at stake."

"What did he say to you? Did he threaten you? Threaten us? Tell us how we can help!"

"Sage, you're dismissed."

Stunned, Kara doesn't move. "Mi'lady, please—"

"Go. Now."

Turning on her heel, she runs from the room. Rafe walks over and kneels in front of Ana. "She's just worried about you, mi'lady. We all are."

"Well, if Kane has his way, you won't have to anymore."

"You've given up!" Rafe cries out in realization. "You've accepted whatever fate has handed you. Why? You are a princess, a survivor, and a warrior. You must not give up!"

"Guardian, you are dismissed as well."

"Your Highness, you can't—"

"Now! That is my command."

He hangs his head, humiliated and angry that she would dismiss him so. He assumes his post outside the door.

Evren approaches Ana. "Will you need help picking out your outfit for dinner, mi'lady?"

"I will, yes. Thank you, Evren."

When lunch is brought in, she sends for Kara, who picks up a plate and takes it to the chaise, eating alone. She finishes her lunch and sets her plate on the small table by the door before approaching Ana. "Anything else, Your Highness?" she asks with a bow.

"Kara, please—"

"I live to serve."

Tears well up as Ana closes her eyes and hangs her head. She wipes her tears as Kara straightens up. "Thank you, Sage. That is all." Kara turns to walk away. "Sis, please. I need you," Ana says with a shaky voice.

Kara stops at the word sis. Her hands clench and her jaw tightens. "Your Highness?"

"Look at me, please." Kara spins around to face her. "I'm so sorry about earlier. I know you are worried about me. I love you, Kara. You know I do. Forgive me," Ana begs.

"Is that a command, mi'lady?"

"No, of course not." Her voice breaks as she answers.

"Damn it!" Kara exclaims as she runs to Ana. She pulls her from the chair and holds her in her arms. "I can't stay mad at you."

Ana grips her tight. "I'm scared, angry, and overwhelmed. I took it out on you and Rafe. I'm so sorry."

"I forgive you, mi'lady."

"As do I," offers Rafe.

"Thank you both."

Kara pulls back, looking at Rafe. "We know the royal guards are loyal to Kane, but what about the guardians? It's their responsibility to protect her and the throne. Can't they do anything to help?"

"When you left for Earth, there were, what? Around three hundred guardians?" Kara nods. "Because of the war and… well, there are only about fifty of us left. We're too stretched out. Since we can fly, we are used as scouts and messengers in the war. Declan may be able to help, but I don't see how."

"Who's Declan?" Ana asks.

"Captain of the Guardians. Their leader. He took over after my father was killed in battle. I learned all of this when they pulled me back here."

"Rafe, I'm so sorry about your father."

"Thank you, mi'lady." He clears his throat. "I know Declan very well. We can trust him. He is genuinely happy we found you, and he wants peace as much as we do."

"Go speak to him, please," Kara begs. "See if he has any evidence or anything that will help her."

Rafe looks at Ana. "Your Highness?"

"That is fine." She watches him leave. She looks up at Kara. "Thank you."

"Of course. Now, how far did you get in your studies today?"

Chapter 12

Rafe approaches the barracks and sees Declan speaking with two members of the royal guard. Declan waves him over. "You are dismissed," he says to the guards as Rafe walks up beside him. "Is everything okay?"

"Do you have somewhere private we can talk?"

"Come with me." Declan takes him into his office. The room is adorned with a cluttered desk, covered with maps and reports, two chairs, and a bookshelf. He gestures to Rafe, and they sit. "What's going on?"

"First, I apologize for asking. Where is your loyalty? The princess or the archduke?"

Declan is obviously taken aback by his blunt question. "My duty is the same as yours, to protect the throne and the royals. You know this."

"I have to be sure because Kane is up to something. I have a source inside, but I need to know if you have heard any of his plans."

"Hmm. Now it's my turn. How can I be sure where your loyalties lie?"

"You know what I just endured to bring the princess back. The trial I had to face. We don't have proof yet, but we know Kane is behind the attempts on Ana's... on the princess's life."

"My intelligence team says the same thing." Declan shakes his head. "I don't have much against him yet. I honestly just started building a case after she was poisoned. He has been very careful, but with the throne slipping from his grasp, he is getting sloppy. I'm going to need time."

"That's one thing we don't have."

"What is going on?"

Rafe tells him about Kane putting his hands on Ana. "He expects her to join him for dinner today. She's to be there at six o'clock and to come alone."

"She can't. You're right, that she's not safe."

"What can we do? I don't know if he threatened her or what he said, but she truly feels as though she has no choice. What can we do without causing an incident? She's still over a week away from her coronation. Until then, she doesn't have much power here. He knows this and is exploiting it, exploiting the loyalty the royal guards give him."

"You won't like my answer. She may not have a choice tonight. If she can just hold on until her coronation—"

"She won't make it. Not without our help. The attempts will only get worse. He will kill her for the throne, and innocent people could get hurt."

"I hadn't considered that." He thinks for a moment. "You are escorting her to his quarters at six? You'll be standing right outside while they eat, correct?"

"Yes."

"What if I were to happen by and talk to you? If something did happen, we would go in together. I would be a witness, and they would have no choice but to believe me."

"You would do that? It's a big risk. If it fails, you're putting a target on your back."

Declan flinches. "I've had one of those my whole life. How would this be any different? Honestly, I don't see any other option. Do you?"

"No."

"Okay. Then I will see you shortly after six."

"Thank you."

Rafe returns to Ana's quarters, a little relieved to know Declan is on their side. He knocks and enters when Kara says to come in. When Ana smiles at him, his heart aches, knowing the pain behind it, and that he is to blame. He gathers his thoughts and approaches her.

"Declan is with us."

She lets out a sigh of relief. "That is good to hear. What is the plan?"

"It's better if you don't know, mi'lady, so you can focus on the archduke."

"Yes, of course." She looks at the clock. It's half past five. She takes a breath and goes with Evren to get dressed, reassuring herself that Rafe will protect her tonight. Evren picks out a navy-blue gown with a silver slip. She fixes Ana's hair and finishes the look with a silver circlet, a diamond star dangling on her forehead. Ana gasps at how beautiful it is.

"This was your mother's favorite circlet."

"How do you know that?"

"She told me, mi'lady. She was wearing it the day I met her."

"You knew my mother?"

"Yes, Your Highness. I hadn't been here long when she passed. I was still in training, so I never got the chance to serve her. But she made a point to come down and welcome the new handmaids. She was beautiful and very kind."

"I wish I could've known her." She looks at the clock. "Could I have a moment?" Evren bows and steps out. *This is it. Even with Rafe and Declan, I know what is going to happen. I know what I have to give to save my friends, and I will do whatever I must to protect them. I only pray they can forgive me.*

Rafe escorts her to Kane's quarters. When Kane opens the door, his eyes go wide at the sight of Rafe. "You gave me your word we would be alone tonight."

"My guardian will stand watch out here. Someone is trying to kill me, don't you know?"

"Fine." He takes her arm and leads her inside. A table for two is set up with flowers, wine, and candles. He pulls out her chair and helps her sit. "How are you feeling, Maeriana?"

She looks at him as he sits beside her. "I was unaware you had permission to address me so informally."

He smiles at her. "Well, if I'm going to marry you or kill you, it seems silly to be formal. Don't you think?"

She sucks in her breath. "Kane, what has come over you?"

"Whatever do you mean, Your Highness?" he asks, the last two words thick with sarcasm.

"You spoke of peace, of wanting to unite the quadrants and end the war. Now, you have tried to kill me and threatened my friends. To what purpose?"

He laughs. "Are you so oblivious to what is right in front of you?"

"All I've heard from everyone is how great you are for the kingdom. Everyone speaks highly of you. What has changed?"

"Nothing. What they see is a façade, a means of keeping the throne. Truth is, I have no interest in peace. There's no gold in that. Besides, I love the feeling of riding into battle, my blade cutting through flesh and bone, watching the life fade from my victim's eyes." He takes a bite, looking at her. "Aren't you going to eat?" She stares down at her plate and nearly cries out in surprise when his fork picks up a bite of food from her plate. He picks it up and eats. "As you see, it's not poisoned."

She eats slowly, trying to bide her time. "I don't understand. Why do you pretend to care so much?"

"To hide how much gold I am making from the war. Plus, I know the throne will be mine soon enough. I thought perhaps they would declare you dead after ten years, but they didn't. I was worried that when the time came for me to claim the throne, you would show up to spoil my plans. I decided we had to find you, claiming it was to bring peace. I knew I could force my hand and either marry you or kill you, instead of worrying about an heir returning to take it from me. I do not have an army of my own to march here, only the army that serves the royals and the kingdom. I married that miserable wretch to gain the title of archduke, biding my time until I could take the throne."

"You married her just to kill her? For a chance at the throne?"

"Yes. As you see, you are still alive only because I wish it so. I could dispatch you any time. I haven't because I truly believe we could rule as king and queen. You are beautiful and well-regarded. With you on my arm, I could accomplish anything! Why do you fight it? Do you not see how good it would be for the kingdom, for the realm, for—"

"I will never marry you. I would rather be dispatched," she hisses at him.

He slaps her across the face, and she cries out, falling from her chair. He gets to his feet, spitting down at her. "You ungrateful bitch! After everything I have done for you and this kingdom, this is how you show your gratitude?"

"Please, don't hurt me," she begs as she clutches her side, pretending to still be hurt.

His eyes roll back in his head at her pleas. He pulls her to her feet. "That only works on someone with a heart, I'm afraid." He leans in and kisses her, pushing himself into her curves. She tries pulling back, but his grip is too strong. She wants to knee him in the groin or scream for help but knows she can't. *He will hurt them. He will kill them if I fight back. I have to endure this for them. I can't be weak.* She whimpers when he leads her to the bed.

"Whether I kill you or not, I will at least get to enjoy you." He tosses her on it, then pulls out his dagger and cuts through her dress. He rips it off, stopping when he sees her stomach. He rolls her over, looking at her in surprise. "How are you already healed?" he demands. He slaps her again. "Tell me!"

"No," she responds defiantly. "Do whatever you're going to do then kill me."

"Oh, darling. The only thing I'm going to do right now is take my time with you. No, I'm not going to kill you, not yet. I rather enjoy watching you writhe with fear under my touch. I love how it makes me feel."

He climbs on top of her. His hands run along her stomach as he kisses her and licks the tears from her cheeks, sending a wave of shame through her. She knows she can do nothing but give him what he wants. When he stands up and removes his shirt, she squeezes her eyes shut, pretending she is in Rafe's arms on the couch and watching a movie with him. She has to sacrifice herself for them; she knows this.

He slaps her again and snaps her back to reality. "Pay attention, darling. I want you to feel every moment of this."

Something shifts within her, and she realizes she can't give in, not now. She has fought so long and hard, swearing no one would ever hurt her the way her foster brother had. She prays for forgiveness from her friends then lets out an earth-shattering scream for help.

Rafe charges in and grabs Kane by the neck, throwing him to the ground. He's knocked unconscious by the impact. Rafe strips off his tunic jacket, unbuttoning his shirt then helping Ana to her feet. He removes his shirt and wraps it around her. While she buttons it up, grateful it falls below her knees, Rafe slips his jacket back on. He folds up her dress and carries it under his arm. Once they leave Kane's quarters, Rafe flags down a royal guard passing by. Rafe and Ana tell the guard everything that transpired.

"I am loyal to him, but she is our princess. I will go in and arrest him. You will be summoned in the morning to give your account to the tribunal."

"Thank you," Ana says.

"Mi'lady," he replies, bowing before going into Kane's quarters.

Her head pounding and feet unsteady, Ana leans against Rafe. "May I, Your Highness?" he asks. She nods. He picks her up and carries her back to her quarters, where he gets her safely inside. Kara and Evren rush to them.

"Oh, God," Kara starts. "Did… did he…" she chokes on her words.

"No," Ana answers. "Rafe stopped him."

"Where is the archduke now?" Evren asks.

"Hopefully on his way to the dungeons. We'll find out for sure tomorrow." He lays Ana on the chaise and kneels before her. "Forgive me, mi'lady, for asking this. Why did you wait so long to scream for help?"

She picks up the blanket and wraps it around herself. "Because I wasn't going to."

"What?" Kara cries out. "What do you mean?"

"When he came to 'invite' me to dinner, he told me he was the one behind my assassination attempts. He told me if I didn't come, if I resisted him or fought back in anyway, he would have you all killed." She stares at the floor. "Please, don't be mad at me."

Kara sits beside her, taking her hand. "Why would we be mad? You risked everything to protect us."

"But I couldn't do it! I gave in and cried for help. You're in danger because of me. I wasn't strong enough. I'm so sorry I failed all of you."

"No, Your Highness. We are in danger because of him. He sees us as threats, regardless of how you acted tonight. Otherwise, he wouldn't have felt the need to threaten us." Rafe takes her hand. "Please, mi'lady, believe that."

She nods her head, then falls into his arms. "I'm sorry. I know this is wrong, but I'm so scared right now. I can't get warm."

He picks her up and carries her into the closet as Kara runs over and locks the door to Ana's quarters. Rafe shuts the closet door behind him. "We can have privacy in here." He sits on the ottoman, holding her to his chest.

"I know you don't love me, but please, hold me right now and comfort me."

"Yes, Your Highness."

"Rafe, please. While we are in the closet, call me Maeriana or Ana. I need that right now."

"Yes, Maeriana." She trembles in his arms as her tears fall. He wraps his arms tighter. "We are taking such a risk doing this. If someone saw this, I would be executed, and you punished."

"How would I be punished?"

He swallows hard. "Twenty lashes the first time. If you were caught violating the status law again, you would be banished and stripped of your title. This is too dangerous."

"What are we doing that's so wrong? You are comforting me, the same way Kara or Evren has. We aren't lovers, aren't engaged in a physical relationship."

"It doesn't matter. Even the appearance of impropriety could result in our punishment."

She scoffs. "So, Kane can do all of these horrible things and walk free, but you could be killed just for comforting me? What kind of kingdom is this?"

"It's not always like this. You'll see. Once you unite the quadrants and have peace, you'll see how beautiful and amazing this kingdom can be."

"My coronation is one week from tomorrow. It feels like forever, and somehow like it's too soon. I'm not ready for all the responsibility, for everyone looking to me for answers."

"I'm not saying it will be easy, but you'll have your advisors, your handmaids, and your captains to help. You won't be alone."

She nuzzles into his chest. "Thank you for everything, for saving me from the archduke. I know what a risk that is to you. I'm sorry I put you in danger."

"Like you are now?"

She pulls back, smiling at the grin on his face. "Don't scare me like that."

His smile grows wider. "Yes, Your Highness."

"Jerk," she whispers as she snuggles against him. "I'll be warm in a moment, I promise."

"Take as long as you need."

They look up when Evren walks in. "Mi'lady, I—" she stops at the sight of them. Ana scrambles from his arms, and they both jump to their feet.

"Come inside and shut the door," she cries out. Evren does as she commands. "We are not in love, nor are we engaged in a relationship. He is simply comforting me—"

"Mi'lady, I know how you feel about each other. It's been my secret to carry. I would never report you, I assure you." She glances back at the door. "I know about forbidden feelings. I was coming to tell you that two members of the royal guard are coming to speak with you and Rafe. You need to get dressed."

"Thank you," she says.

Rafe leaves the closet and sighs in relief when he sees only Kara is in the room. "I wasn't expecting this until the morning."

"I know."

Ana walks out a few minutes later, wearing a gold dress with a diamond and gold crown. She and Evren decided to make her look as regal as possible, hoping it would make her story carry more weight.

Evren opens the door, stepping back as two members of the royal guard and the archduke enter. Ana pushes down her fear as she looks the guards over. The royal guard uniforms are silver and gold embossed leather armor draped over dark blue pants with a matching shirt. One guard has silver and gold arm cuffs and a navy-blue cape draped down his back. His blond hair is loose over his head with blond stubble gracing his lip and chin. He steps forward.

"Good evening, Your Highness. I am Ramin, Captain of the Royal Guard. Do you know why we are here?"

"I'm not sure."

"The archduke has made some rather serious complaints against you and your guardian, Rafe. How do you respond?"

Ana swallows hard, careful to choose her words. "What complaints has he made? I know of nothing wrong either of us have done."

"He claims your guardian grabbed him by the neck and threw him to the ground, rendering him unconscious. He said this was after you accused him of hurting you but that you said yes to being in bed with him."

Ana's stomach drops. "I agreed to no such thing," she cries out, then clenches her hands, calming herself. "He said my guardian hurt him? I ask to see the evidence." She smiles at Kane, knowing he is too proud to show any wounds.

Ramin's face squints in confusion. "Mi'lady?"

"Kane, if my guardian did as you claim, you must have some injuries. Let us see them as evidence," she commands.

His eyes narrow in anger. "Well, I—"

She clears her throat, plastering a smile across her face. "This was all just a… oh, what's the word you use? Oh, yes. A misunderstanding. Isn't that right, Archduke?"

Sneering at her, he takes a breath. He knows he's lost this match. "Of course, mi'lady. Just a misunderstanding. All is forgiven."

Ramin looks at him, surprised. "Are you sure, Archduke?"

"Yes. Thank you for performing your duties. You are both dismissed." The guards leave the chambers. Kane walks up to Ana, smiling when Kara and Rafe tense up. He turns his smile to her, leans in, and kisses her cheek. "I love how you taste, like wine and sweet sauce. I'll relish that tonight as I think of you while I'm in bed." He turns and leaves.

"God, he's disgusting. Are you okay, mi'lady?" Kara asks when Ana nearly collapses onto the chaise.

"I will be."

Kara sits beside Ana and looks down when she is shaking. "Do you need Rafe?"

"No," she says softly, glancing at him and Evren sitting at the table. "He's right. I can't turn to him for comfort. I'll get him killed if I do. Please, get me a nightgown while I shower."

"Yes, mi'lady."

Once in the washroom, Ana strips down then steps into the hot water, knowing it's no substitute for Rafe's arms. She cries in the shower then cleans herself up before changing into the nightgown Kara had laid on the vanity.

Leaning against the doorframe, the last of her strength fades. Kara grabs Ana and holds her up. "What's wrong?"

"I'm spent."

Kara gets her to the chaise. "You need to eat."

Evren runs to get food. Rafe smiles at her when she returns, handing him a plate.

"Thank you for thinking of me. I truly appreciate that."

She smiles at him then takes a plate to Ana. Kara watches her to be sure she eats it all. "Now, are you all right?" Kara asks.

"I'm worried about going for breakfast in the morning. What does he have planned?"

Kara sighs. "I didn't think of that. Whatever it is, we'll face it together. You know we are here for you."

"Thank you. Would you help me to bed?"

"Of course." Kara walks her over, gets her under the blanket, and tucks her in. Rafe brings the chaise closer then sits down, somewhat relieved knowing there are additional royal guards stationed in the hallway.

—◦—

Ana wakes up trembling, drenched in a cold sweat. She quietly gets up and goes to the washroom to splash cold water on her face, then returns to the main chambers and walks to the window. A gasp escapes her lips at the sight of two moons nestled with so many stars. She jumps when Rafe puts his hand on her shoulder.

"Everything okay, mi'lady?"

"Bad dreams," she answers quietly. She looks at him. "You know he's lying, right? I didn't... I would never..."

"Mi'lady, believe me, I know. Can I do anything to help?"

"No, Rafe. You're right. I won't ask that of you."

"Princess, please. I feel you trembling. Let me comfort you."

"I won't risk you."

"Then I'll risk myself," he says, pulling her into his arms and against his chest. He carries her into the closet, shuts the door, and sits with her on the ottoman. She wants to pull away, but she's overwhelmed by his warmth and can't help but nuzzle in, instead. He rests his chin on her head.

"I can't keep asking you to do this. It's not fair to my heart, and it's not fair to you. I won't see you hurt or killed because of me."

"It's my duty, mi'lady."

"Not to be killed because I was weak and needed comfort."

"You're not weak. How do you not see your own strength?"

"I'll try." She's tries to pull away, but he grips her tighter.

"Another minute please."

She laughs. "Of course."

When she stops shivering, he carries her back to bed.

"Good night, mi'lady. No more bad dreams."

"Thank you." She turns on her side, hoping she doesn't.

Walking into the dining hall, Ana is prepared for cold stares, suspicious looks, or even anger. Instead, people are smirking or laughing at her, speaking in hushed tones. She sends Kara and Evren into the fray to see what people are saying. Kara returns, clearly upset.

"Kane is telling everyone you two slept together last night. He's trying to scare away any potential suitors and make you look weak."

A thought pops into Ana's head, causing her to smile. "Do me a favor. Tell them this," she whispers into Kara's ear.

"Oh, mi'lady, you are wicked," Kara whispers back, stifling a laugh.

Ana watches as Kara walks back into the crowd and repeats what Ana said. The ladies flush with humility, and the men shift uncomfortably. Kara returns, and they eat in peace.

Ana watches the archduke enter and smiles when he is greeted the same way she was. In his confusion, he walks over and speaks with a member of the court. Anger flashes across his face. He quickly walks to Ana's table and doesn't bow or request permission before sitting next to her.

He leans in. "So, I guess you think you're clever, don't you? You are going to pay for this." He grips her leg and slides his hand up to her thigh.

She jumps to her feet. "Just because you can't... perform," she holds her ground, "does not give you permission to put your hands on me!"

Snarling, he lunges up from his seat and punches her in the eye, knocking her to the floor. Kara runs to her side and helps her up. She starts leading her to the Medical Center, with Evren trailing closely behind.

"Kara—"

"They need to document your injury."

Ana gasps. "Right."

They go inside, where Winslow quickly gets them into a room. He steps out so Kara can get Ana into an exam gown.

Rafe walks in a few minutes later. "What the hell happened? I was gone for ten minutes, and she was punched by the archduke? In front of the entire dining hall?"

Kara smiles at him. "Yes."

"Why are you happy about this?"

"Because my plan worked," Ana says, covering up with the thin blanket.

Kara sees the confusion in Rafe's eyes. "Don't you understand? He assaulted the princess in front of a hundred witnesses. He can't talk his way out of this. She didn't touch him. He has no defense for punching her. They'll have to do something now!"

Rafe chuckles. "Brilliant, mi'lady. Are you going to be okay?"

"I'll be fine. It doesn't really hurt," she says, giving him a small smile. Winslow walks in.

"Would you excuse us?"

Rafe, Kara, and Evren step into the hallway. Kara looks at Rafe. "Where were you, anyway?"

"I had to speak with Declan. He was supposed to meet me last night outside Kane's chambers, to be a witness if he hurt her. I thought he'd betrayed us, but he didn't show because he was stabbed in the upper back, and I know it's not a coincidence. Someone learned of our plans and reported it to the archduke."

"I'm sorry."

Winslow gestures them in. "She's nauseous, which is to be expected. I'm giving her IV fluid to help with that. Her occipital orb isn't broken, but we can expect extensive bruising and swelling, which will go down in a few days. She has a minor concussion, so we are watching that as well. We aren't admitting her, but I would like to keep her here for the next hour just to be sure."

"Of course."

Kara sits beside Ana, holding her hand. "How do you feel?"

She laughs softly. "Like I was hit by a bus."

"What is a bus?" Evren asks.

Kara and Ana laugh. Kara looks at Evren. "I'll tell you later."

Ana leans forward, hanging her head. "I think I'm going to be sick." After a moment, the nausea eases. "False alarm." She closes her eyes as she lies back down.

"Ana, you need to stay awake. You have a concussion."

"But I'm sleepy," she argues.

Kara raises the bed, so Ana is sitting up. She sits on the edge of the bed, gently shaking her. "Ana, stay awake."

She sighs, opening her eyes. "Fine."

"Just for a little while. Then we'll take you to your quarters so you can rest."

"I need to be reading. I have to be ready for my coronation. A delay is the last thing I need right now."

"Evren, would you continue studies with Ana?"

"Of course," Evren replies. She walks over and sits with Ana, discussing various roles in court and what their positions mean in relation to the kingdom. Winslow walks in.

"We've documented your injuries. You'll want to come back in the morning so we can update them for an inquisition. Otherwise, you may return to your quarters."

"We'll bring her here. Thank you," Kara says.

Rafe steps out while she and Evren get Ana dressed. He's pacing the hallway when a guardian approaches him. They speak quietly. Rafe tenses as anger flushes his face. "Where did they find her?"

He shakes his head as he tells Rafe what he knows. "I'm sorry to bring you this news."

"Thank you." The guardian leaves just as Kara and Evren step out with Ana. He walks over to help, but Kara shoots him a look to stay back. Reluctantly, he nods, letting them take her to her room and getting her into bed.

"They said for me to come back in the morning. What if this heals before then? How will I explain that?"

"We'll figure something out. I don't think you have to worry about that, mi'lady. Not this time."

"Okay." Kara adjusts her pillows, and Ana looks at Evren. "Could we continue with my studies?"

"If Your Highness is up for that, I would love to."

"I am."

Evren grabs a chair and brings it beside the bed. She sits with Ana, telling her myths and legends of the realm. "Of course, my favorite is the legend of the Crimson Queen."

"Oh. Who was she?"

"The story says she was the most fair, cunning, and brave queen the realm had ever seen. She went into battle with her troops, only to see her true love about to be killed. She rushed over to defend him and took the fatal wound."

"That's awful!"

Evren laughs quietly. "There's more. Patience, mi'lady."

"Sorry."

"As she laid there, great wings of fire erupted from her shoulder blades. They wrapped around her, not burning her but healing her with their magic. They turned to wings of soft plumage with crimson feathers. When she stood, her wings spread out for all to see. At the sight of her, every soldier dropped their weapon, and knelt before her. She brought peace and freedom to the realm."

"She sounds incredible."

"Really, Your Highness," Kara speaks up. "It's just one of a hundred legends we have. There are stories of dragons growing big enough to ride into battle, tales of gold and lost treasure at sea guarded over by mermaids, and so many more."

"Well, it's my favorite," Evren says quietly.

"Mine, too," Ana says, smiling at her.

Evren returns the smile. "Thank you, mi'lady. Would you like to hear the legend of Raden the giant, who battled a great purple dragon?"

"Wait, are dragons real?"

"They are, but they are small. A full-grown dragon could sit in your lap, though they are not pets. They dislike people very much," Evren explains.

"I see. Please, tell me about Raden?" Ana asks.

"He was a mighty warrior, and he hunted for a week before finding the dragon's lair. He battled the dragon for three days, but the dragon's assault was unrelenting. Raden had lost all hope when—"

Kara rolls her eyes. "Are you really telling her this story?"

"Kara! I am enjoying it," Ana says.

"Sorry, mi'lady," she says with a laugh. "Please, Evren, continue."

"Anyway, Raden let loose an arrow just as the beast opened its mouth. It wasn't enough to kill her, but it wounded her."

"Her? The dragon was a girl?"

"She was protecting her eggs, as he discovered. He saw the dragon watching him as he approached her nest. He laid down his sword and bowed to her, forfeiting his life, and she charged at him. She stopped before him and lowered her head, so her face was only inches from his. As a sign of trust, she closed her eyes. Just as he leaned forward and stroked her head, they heard a war cry from a group of hunters who had come to try their skill against the beast. Raden picked up his weapon to defend her and her eggs."

"I like that story!" she exclaims. She looks down. "I feel ridiculous being in this nightgown. I would like to get dressed."

"Your Highness," Kara says, "when they come to question you, we want you to look as hurt and vulnerable as you can."

"I know. I feel silly."

"You look silly."

Evren softly gasps as Ana yells at Kara. "Twenty days in the stocks!"

Kara feigns shock and pretends to cry. "Your Highness, why are you so mean?"

Ana laughs, and it's music to Rafe's ears. He realizes she hasn't laughed much since he'd brought her here. "Do I need to separate you two?" he throws in.

"Never!" Kara exclaims, she and Ana folding over with laughter. Everyone stops when there's a knock at the door. "About time. I wondered when they were going to get your statement."

Evren goes to the door, unable to believe her eyes as the archduke stands before her, alone. She turns to them. They all get to their feet to and walk over.

"I need to speak with Her Highness in private."

"No, sire. You most certainly do not." Kara says, putting her arm around Ana's waist. "You won't intimidate us. Why are you here?"

Ignoring Kara, he looks at Ana. "Your Highness, a word in private."

"Stay here," she says to Kara then looks at Kane. "I will walk over to you, but I will not be alone with you."

"Fine," he snaps.

Kara hesitantly lets go. Ana pulls away and approaches him, trying to keep her distance. "What do you want?"

He closes the space between them. "You humiliated me in front of everyone this morning."

"You did it first. How do you think I felt, walking into that? You started this by spreading that horrible rumor."

"It's too bad. If you hadn't fought back last night, none of this would've happened. Now I've had to pay my assassin for three jobs."

Ana steps back, looking at her friends. "You can't be serious."

"I warned you of the consequences. You didn't listen. You did this, not me."

"Call it off," she begs. "Stop them, please."

"Hmm. Perhaps if you join me for dinner tonight and do as I ask, maybe I will."

"They'll never leave me alone with you. You know that."

"Find a way, or they're dead."

She sucks in her breath. "How do I know after we're done tonight, you won't kill them anyway? What reassurances do I have?"

He laughs. "None. I don't give those. At least if you come to me, they have a chance to live. As you see, I am not locked up or in bindings. Even after your little stunt this morning, I am still free. Now you see how much power I have."

Hanging her head, she asks, "What time?"

"Six." He leans in, kissing her cheek. "Come alone," he whispers in her ear, "or all bets are off. I'll have my assassin start with Evren. Her ears would make a nice trophy."

"I'll be there," she replies, her stomach churning. She watches him leave, holding her breath until the door shuts behind him. Kara leads her to the chaise and sits with her.

"What's going on? What did he say?"

"He was boasting about being free. He says no matter what he does to me, he's too powerful for them to lock him up. He was rubbing it in my face that he's won this round."

"Is that all?" Rafe asks.

"Yes," she lies. "I'm tired. I would like to lay down for a bit."

"Of course, mi'lady." Evren helps her to bed, then joins Rafe and Kara in the corner of the room, out of earshot. "She's resting now."

"Good. Because she's hiding something. There's more than she is telling us."

"I got that sense, too," Rafe says. "I just wonder what."

"He said something to her, something that scared her. I could feel her trembling as I helped her to the chaise."

"Kara, what are we going to do?"

"She knows we won't let her out of our sight. She's safe for now. I thought I was going to vomit when he kissed her. God, he's disgusting."

"Believe me, I was ready to kill him myself."

Kara looks at Rafe, seeing the pain in his eyes. "I'm sorry."

"For what?"

"That you can't be together."

He glances at Ana before looking at Kara. "We aren't going to discuss that. Not now, not ever. Let it go."

"Yes, Rafe. Of course."

They wake her up at five-thirty to get ready for dinner. They're surprised when she says she wants to eat in the dining hall. "I want to face him. I don't want him to think I'm hiding in my chambers, scared of him," she says, walking to the closet.

While getting dressed, Ana removes her cross and places it on the dresser. She gets out a small notebook she had hidden in one of her drawers.

To my friends, if you find this, Kane won. Do not avenge me, do not risk your lives. I am lost, but the kingdom will need you. I'm sorry I couldn't tell you the truth, but he threatened to kill you all. Forgive me for my weakness.

She signs her name and puts the notebook back in the drawer, forcing a smile before walking out of the closet. Her smile grows when Rafe sucks in his breath at the sight of her. She walks up and takes his hand. "Thank you."

"Whatever for?"

She looks down at his hand, releasing it. "Everything." She clears her throat. "Shall we go for dinner?"

They're heading to the dining hall when she stops and leans against a pillar, pretending to have an issue with her shoe. Her movements are so quiet that her companions don't notice and continue walking, discussing what might be on the menu for the evening. As soon as they are far enough ahead, she turns and runs for Kane's quarters, knocking rapidly. He opens the door, looking behind her to be sure she is alone.

"I slipped away from them. Hurry, before they realize I'm gone!"

He opens the door and pulls her in, then posts two guards out front, commanding that he is not to be disturbed. He takes her to the smaller room with the table set up as it was the night before. Trying to stop from trembling in fear, she takes her seat.

He reaches over and eats a bite of her food. "Not poisoned, see?"

She nods and eats. He pours her a glass of wine, and she fails to notice he does not have any himself. She takes a sip, realizing he is staring at her. "What?"

"I can't help it. You are beyond beautiful."

She takes another sip, regretting it as her head begins to swim. She gasps softly but does her best not to let on. "Thank you."

"You know," he starts, "I've wanted the throne for as long as I can remember. I didn't see how it would be possible, even after marrying the wench and killing her, as we had a king and queen. But then your mother died, and your father was killed in battle. Before I knew it, I was running everything. I love having so much power and control. I desire to be king, to watch the people kneel before me."

"I'm sorry," she says, her words slurring.

"Why are you sorry?"

"I don't know," she answers, giggling. When he looks away to hide his smile, she pours some of her wine into the empty saucer beside her plate. She covers it with a table linen before he turns back to her. She takes another small sip. "Hmm. This is very good."

"I'm glad you like it. An expensive vintage but worth it."

"How are the guards so loyal to you?" she asks, smiling at him. "I mean, I know you're handsome. I'm not blind." She giggles again. "There must be something more."

He returns her smile. "You think I'm handsome. I like that." He looks down a moment. "Seriously, though. I pay them well, treat them with respect, fight alongside them, and rule with an iron fist. They respect and fear me."

"That's amazing," she says, batting her eyelashes at him.

"I thought so, as well." He stands up when he hears voices outside. "Excuse me," he says as he leaves the room. She pours most of her wine into the saucer, leaving a small sip in her glass. She covers the saucer up, careful the linen stays over the rim, and waits for him to return. As he does, she finishes her wine.

"Is everything all right?" she asks.

He sits beside her. "I believe your friends are outside, trying to interrupt our fun."

She pouts at him. "I didn't tell them anything, I swear."

"Oh, I know. I believe you." He leans in, nuzzling her neck with his lips. "I want you."

"I want you, too."

He smiles. "Good. That's what I want to hear."

She burps, giggling softly. "Excuse me. I think I drank too fast. Where is your washroom?"

He helps her to her feet, smiling at how unsteady she is, and leads her to the washroom door. She shuts the door behind her and walks up to the vanity. With the tap on as high as it will go, she makes herself throw up the wine, then rinses her mouth and splashes cold water on her face, drying off with a hand towel.

She opens the door to see him lifting the linen off the saucer. She runs back in, but he pushes the door open and slams it against her head.

"Stop!" she begs.

He takes her to the bed, ripping her gown off. He sits her down, then gets another glass of wine.

"You will drink the whole thing now. Or my assassin will pay your friends a visit... tonight. Do you understand?"

She takes the wine and drinks it down, then throws the empty glass at him. He ducks as it shatters on the wall behind him. He slaps her again. She falls against the mattress. He strips down to his shorts and climbs on top of her.

"Please, stop! Get off!" she screams.

"What do you think I am going to do to you?"

She looks away. "Please, don't... don't..."

He laughs. "Seriously? I thought you knew, after your little stunt this morning. No, I was wounded in battle in my younger days. Can't get it up, I'm afraid."

"That's why you were so angry. But I don't understand. The things you've said..."

"Oh, I'm going to enjoy you. Just not in the way you were thinking." He punches her stomach, moaning when she cries out. He punches her chest, leaving her gasping for air. "Yes," he moans.

"Stop!" she screams when he brings his hand up again.

"That's right. Beg for me." He slaps her across the face. He kisses her as his hand gropes her chest. She struggles to get away, only making him want her more as she writhes under him. "Oh, this is what I need." He caresses her face. "The wine should be taking affect any moment."

She stops struggling, looking up at him. "You're cute."

He smiles. "There it is. Now, kiss me." She leans up and kisses him, running her hands along his chest and stomach. "Yes. I love the feel of you." He's climbing on top of her when the door bursts open.

Rafe and Declan charge in. Kane grabs the blanket to cover himself and Ana. "What is the meaning of this? What the hell are you doing here?"

"We heard her screaming," Rafe says through gritted teeth.

"Of course, you heard her screaming, didn't they, darling?" He looks over when she giggles softly. "Maeriana, do you want me to stop?"

"No, please," she begs. Rafe hears the slurring of her words and sees her eyes are glazed over. He looks at Declan.

"She's clearly been drugged. She needs medical attention."

"I don't understand," Kane lies. "We ate the same thing for dinner. Oh," he gasps for effect, "I didn't drink any wine. I wasn't in the mood. She had a glass. Was she poisoned?"

Rafe's jaw tightens as he fights the urge to kill him right there. He walks over, wrapping the blanket around Ana, and picking her up. Ignoring Kane's commands, he carries her towards the Medical Center, with Kara and Evren following behind. Declan remains to question Kane about the wine.

"Where are you taking me?" Ana asks. "I want to be with him. He's my lover."

Rafe takes a breath. "You have been poisoned, mi'lady. We are taking you to see Winslow."

"Oh, I like him! He's nice."

"That's good."

"Rafe, why aren't you my lover?"

He nearly drops her, looking at Kara in shock. "I think the poison is affecting you still. Let's get you taken care of."

She caresses his cheek. "I know how you could take care of me."

Ignoring her comment, Rafe sighs in relief at the sight of the center. Once inside, the staff take her away. Rafe and Kara sit while Evren paces the floor. Kara looks at him. "Did he—"

"No, we stopped him."

She sighs in relief. "He is relentless."

"How did you know?" Evren asks. "When we lost track of her, how did you know that's where she was?"

"Part of it was my locating ability. Also, I knew she was hiding something after he spoke to her. Then for her to disappear so close to his quarters, it wasn't hard to guess."

"I'm just grateful Declan is on our side."

"Me, too. I have to warn you though, Kane will probably get away with this. He's concocted some story about his wine being poisoned."

Before Kara can respond, Winslow walks out. "You three again, I see." He looks at Ana's chart. "The potion used was Shadow of Suggestion. It makes the subject pliable, can cause them to become aroused, and they will have no memory after. We purged most of it out. She is resting now. You can come back."

They go into her room. Kara looks at Rafe. "Hold her hand. She needs you now."

"Yes, Kara." He sits by Ana's side, caressing her face, holding her hand, and waiting for her to wake up.

"Rafe?" she asks softly.

"I'm right here," he answers, pulling his hand away.

"What happened?"

"What's the last thing you remember?"

"The wine tasted weird and made my head feel funny. When he wasn't looking, I poured it into an empty saucer. I excused myself to the washroom, but he discovered what I had done. He ripped my gown off and forced me to drink an entire glass."

"God, mi'lady. I am grateful you survived."

She looks down, clenching the blanket. "You're not mad at me for what I did?"

"What did you do?"

"I lied to you all and ran away to him. He said he had an assassin on retainer. He said if I didn't come tonight, he would kill the three of you. I couldn't let that happen."

"Maeriana, you are the princess. You are what is most important to this realm. You cannot sacrifice yourself for any of us. No more secrets from now on. Whatever happens, you tell us. Regardless of what he says, or what threats he makes. Do you understand?"

"Yes, Rafe. I'm sorry."

"No apology necessary, as you were trying to protect us."

"Thank you." She lies back down. "I'm going to sleep some more."

"Get your rest. You'll feel better in the morning."

"You promise?"

"I give you my word. I will see to it myself, mi'lady."

He smiles when she falls asleep. He stays with her, holding her hand all night then nods off shortly before dawn.

Chapter 13

"Rafe?"

"Yes?

"I… I'm completely healed again."

"I'm glad to hear that. How do you feel?" he asks, sitting up.

"Exhausted, of course. I'm happy all of the bruises are gone."

"What do you mean, bruises? Where else were you hurt, besides your eye?"

She looks down. "I didn't tell you last night?"

"No."

"He was so angry yesterday at breakfast because he really does have issues… down there. He wasn't trying to…" She looks away, uncomfortable. "He gets off on causing pain."

"He hurt you?"

"He punched me in the chest, the stomach, and slapped me across the face."

"Your Highness! Why didn't you tell us this last night?"

"In my defense, I was hurt and had been poisoned."

"Of course. I'm sorry, mi'lady. Forgive me."

"After you healed me, of course."

"What are you—"

"I woke up to you holding my hand tight, stepping aside when the nurse entered then immediately returning to me. I'm not stupid. I know I only heal after you touch me. I just don't understand, why didn't you tell me?"

"We can't discuss it. I could be killed for it."

Her eyes go wide. "That's what Kara meant. I won't bring it up ever again, I promise."

"Thank you."

Winslow walks in to release her. "How do you feel?" he asks, looking her over.

"Better."

He notices her wounds are healed, but he says nothing as he makes notes on her chart. He and Rafe step out while Kara and Evren get her dressed. "So, she can heal?" Winslow asks.

Rafe takes a breath. "Well, it—"

"Never mind. We'll pretend I said nothing. Just get her to her room to let her rest. That's what she needs right now."

"Thank you."

"I want to get dressed and go to breakfast," Ana says once back in her quarters.

"You need to rest after all of that. Let us have breakfast here," Kara says.

"I will not cower in here!"

"That's not what I'm saying." Kara sits beside her. "You need to take it easy."

"I'm fine. I want to eat in the dining hall."

Sighing, Kara helps her up and into the closet, Evren trailing behind. Rafe shakes his head. *God, she's tenacious. How can she think she is small or weak? I wish she could see herself the way we do. Still, I wonder if bringing her was mistake. Not because I doubt her, but I worry so for her safety. Rowenne and I did not foresee something like this. We thought I would bring her here, put her on the throne, and there would be peace. We fooled ourselves into thinking it would be that easy.*

Ana steps out in a pale pink gown with gold shoes and a gold crown. He gasps at the sight of her and offers his arm, escorting her to the dining hall. The entire hall goes quiet when they enter. They go to their table and sit. Feeling particularly brash, Ana invites Evren to sit with them.

"Mi'lady, she can't—" Kara starts.

"If the archduke can get away with the horrible things he has done to me, then my friend can sit with me for breakfast."

Evren looks at Kara, who nods. She sits at the table, surprising everyone in the court. Everything goes back to how it was.

"I knew they wouldn't care," Ana says. When the first course is brought out, Rafe picks up Ana's plate and takes a bite. "Can I help you?" she asks, snatching it back.

"I'm making sure it's not poisoned."

"You most certainly will not!"

"Your Highness—"

"No. You all take enough risks for me."

"It's what we're here for, mi'lady."

"No. I won't let you get hurt or killed because of me."

"Did you hear a word I said?" Rafe asks. "You are the princess, you are what matters most. Not us. We are expendable."

Her eyes go wide at his last word. She looks down, eating in silence and grateful Kane is nowhere to be seen.

—◦—

At the library, Ana smiles at the stacks of books piled everywhere. She pulls out a book on myths and flips through, stopping when she finds a drawing of the Crimson Queen.

"Evren, look!" She calls her over.

They admire the picture. The queen is in silver armor with her wings of fire arching from her back. "She's beautiful," Evren says.

"I would've loved to meet her."

"She's not real," Kara points out.

Ana continues flipping through the book, seeing legends of merpeople, something that looks like a unicorn/dragon hybrid, and tales of adventure. She looks at Kara. "Can I take this book to my quarters?"

"Mi'lady, all of these books are yours, to do as you please."

"Really?" she asks, turning back and admiring row after row of books. "It's more than I ever could've hoped for."

Rafe smiles at Kara, pleased to see Ana so happy for a change. Kara shares the sentiment.

"Shall we continue?" Evren asks.

"Yes." She cradles the book in her arms, then sits at the table and looks around. "Wait. Where's Brienne? I haven't seen her in a while." She looks at Kara and Rafe, who both avoid her gaze. Gripping the book to her chest, she walks over to them. "What?"

"Mi'lady," Kara starts, "we couldn't find the right time to tell you."

"Tell me what?"

She takes a breath. "Kane had her killed."

"What? Why?"

"She knew what he was doing to you. She was trying to gather evidence against him, acting as a spy for us. She tried to stop him," Rafe answers.

Ana drops the book as tears are streaming down her cheeks. "Why didn't you tell me this sooner?"

Kara strokes her hair. "I'm sorry. We were trying to protect you. We were worried you may do something in anger, something that would make him hurt or kill you. Please, understand why we did it."

"One of my handmaids was murdered, trying to protect me, and you didn't think I needed to know?"

"Maeriana, please—" Rafe starts.

"How dare you keep this from me?" She runs from the room. As she's coming around the corner towards her quarters, she runs into Kane. She gasps and tries to run away, but he grabs her wrist, pulling her to him.

"Well, hello, darling. Where are your friends?" he asks.

She looks over her shoulder, surprised they aren't behind her. They are still in the library, yelling at each other for not telling her about Brienne sooner. "They'll be here any moment," she tries, swallowing her tears.

"Right." He drags her into a room she doesn't recognize. He picks her up and puts her on one of the many tables in the study. He pulls her legs apart and stands between them.

"What are you going to do?" Fear echoes in her voice.

"Hmm, whatever I want." He pulls his dagger from its sheath and runs the tip of the blade along her neck, down her chest, and between her legs. He makes small cuts along her arm.

"Please," she begs as he brings the knife to her side. He slowly sticks the blade in about an inch. She leans forward as she sobs into her hand. "Stop," she tries again.

He sets it beside her as he leans in and kisses her. When he brings his hand up to her chest, she pushes her knee into his groin, sending him flying backwards. She jumps off the table and runs out the door, not stopping to see if he is following behind. Clutching her side, she turns the corner and runs into Rafe. She nearly falls, but he catches her. Worry consumes him when he sees the fear in her eyes and the blood on her arm and gown.

"Ana, what happened?" he asks. Kane steps around the corner. Rafe gently pushes Ana behind him as he unsheathes his blade. He steps forward. "What do you want?"

"To finish what she and I started last night, of course."

"Why aren't you locked up?"

He laughs, shaking his head. "I'm afraid the royal guard and guardians are loyal to me. You can't touch me!" Kane sheathes his dagger, not wanting to take the chance there are any witnesses. He can get away with most things but not murdering the princess in broad daylight.

"Rafe, we have to stop him. He's going to kill me."

Rafe eyes Kane warily, guiding Ana past him, when Ana collapses against Rafe. He sheathes his sword and picks her up. As his back is turned, Kane pulls out his dagger and plunges the blade into Rafe's shoulder. Keeping his grip on

Ana, Rafe spins around and kicks Kane. He falls against the wall, his head hitting with a loud thud, then slumps to the floor. Rafe stares down at him, wanting nothing more than to put Ana down and snap his neck. The pain radiates from his shoulder, and he has to lean against the wall.

Kara and Evren run over. "What happened?"

"Get us to her quarters. We need to rest."

"Are you both hurt?"

"Yes."

They go to her quarters, where Rafe showers while Kara and Evren clean her in the tub. They get them into clean clothes and take them to the closet. He holds Ana in his arms while Kara and Evren are in the main chambers, keeping watch.

———————— ᴗ ————————

Ana wakes first, surprised to be in his arms. She looks up at him and debates pulling away. Instead, she snuggles in closer, relishing the warmth that washes over her as she holds him tighter. Her hand brushes his wing, waking him up.

"I'm sorry."

He chuckles softly. "It's okay."

They sit up together. "Were you hurt?" she asks.

"Kane stabbed us both. How do you feel?"

She stands up, turning away as she lifts her nightgown. She lets the fabric fall from her hands. "Healed. You?"

"Yes."

"Do… do we heal each other?"

"I'm a guardian, so I have accelerated healing."

"How does that work?" she asks, sitting back down.

"As long as it's not a fatal wound, or we aren't already too drained from battle, our body will naturally heal itself."

"I see. I never asked, how old are you?"

"Let's get Kara and Evren for this conversation."

"Okay."

They step out into the main chamber. "How do you feel?" Kara asks, getting up from the table.

"Better. We were talking about his accelerated healing. I asked him how old he is, then he said we need you."

"He's right."

"I don't understand."

Rafe takes a breath. "I am five hundred and twenty-three years old."

"What?"

"The three of us are immortal," Kara explains. "Guardian, Elf, Witch." She points as she says each word. She points at Ana. "Human."

"So, I'm not immortal?"

"No. The average lifespan here for humans is five hundred years."

"Why didn't you tell me this?" She looks at Evren. "You never mentioned this in our lessons."

"Kara instructed me not to," she answers quietly.

"What?" she asks, spinning to Kara. "Why not? When was I going to find out? When I started to age, and you weren't? What else are you three keeping from me? What other secrets?"

"Mi'lady, please—"

"To hell with all of you!" She runs into the closet, locking the door. *I don't want to be immortal, but I can't believe they are! This doesn't seem real. Why would they keep this from me? What else are they hiding? I can't trust them. My inner circle, my support, and I can no longer depend on them. What do I do now? Oh, God. Nothing feels real anymore.*

"Mi'lady, please. Come and talk to us," Kara begs.

"Go away!"

Ana walks over to the ottoman, lying down and covering herself with the blanket. Still recovering from the healing process, she falls back to sleep.

Rafe paces in front of the closet, shooting angry looks at Kara from time to time until she can no longer stand it. "What?" she snaps.

"I told you it was a mistake to keep this from her."

"You were worried about Kane—"

"Not Brienne! I stand behind that decision. I mean, about us being immortal. You should've told her sooner."

"What difference does it make?" Kara asks.

"Apparently, a lot. Or she wouldn't be so upset."

"She's upset because we were keeping things from her, regardless of our reasons for doing so."

Someone knocks at the door. Evren walks over, speaking quietly with a royal guard. She walks back to them, smiling. "What?" Rafe asks.

Evren goes to the closet door. "Mi'lady, please. I have good news."

"What?" she asks through the door.

"The archduke has been arrested and will face the tribunal."

Ana opens the door, looking at Evren. "If you are saying that just to get me out of here—"

"I'm not, mi'lady. It is the truth. Declan arrested Kane himself."

"I don't understand. I thought he was on Kane's side?" Ana asks.

"What makes you think that?" Rafe inquires.

"I don't know. A gut feeling, but I'm probably wrong." She clears her throat. "Anyway, what's he been charged with?"

"Everything. From the attempts on your life, assaulting you, stabbing you and your guardian. Apparently, Declan witnessed the whole thing. He was coming to help when Rafe knocked Kane unconscious. Now, Declan is going after him hard."

Ana leans against the wall as the relief washes over her.

"We ate lunch while you were in there. You need to eat as well," Rafe says.

"Don't pretend you care about me," she snaps at him. She goes back into the closet, slamming the door behind her. Sitting on the ottoman, she pulls her knees to her chest.

I shouldn't be mad at him. I see now. Even if we weren't forbidden, we could never be together. He would lose me, to sickness or old age. I thought if he loved me, I could find a way for us to be together, but it truly is impossible. Fate has played every card against us, stacked the deck in favor of the house. I don't have an ace up my sleeve, because while I could try and change the law for us, I can't change the laws of time. We never stood a chance. She cries into her hands.

"Mi'lady?"

She looks up in surprise as Kara walks in. She shakes her head. "Please," she says softly.

Kara walks over and sits on the edge of the ottoman. "What's wrong?"

Unaware that Rafe is leaning against the wall, listening to every word, she tells Kara the truth. "I realize now, even if Rafe and I could be together, it wouldn't last. He would have to watch me grow old and die. That's not fair to him. I've been trying to hold out hope, holding on to the chance that he may still love me. I see now, I truly have to let him go." She wipes the tears as they fall. "I don't know if I am strong enough to do it, because I love him so much."

Rafe hangs his head as a single tear rolls down his cheek. He wants nothing more than to charge in there, take her in his arms, and tell her exactly how he feels. He realizes she's right, though. When he's tried to pull away, to shut himself off from her, she would smile at him or pull into his arms, and she's back in his heart all over again.

"You have to," Kara says, "for right now, but don't give up. Love always finds a way. For the time being, focus on your duties, prepare yourself for your coronation. That is what you need to concentrate on."

"I know you're right, and I hate you for saying it, because I know it's the truth. My heart is shattering all over again, and I don't know if I'll survive this time. I can't. Help me, Kara. Please, take this pain."

"If there was anything I could do, I would take it. I swear."

"I can't unlove him. I can't hate him. I can't turn off my feelings. Sometimes I wonder if maybe he meant it when he told me didn't love me, not because it's forbidden, but because it is the truth."

Rafe straightens up, knowing what he must do for her. He wipes his face, collects himself, and walks in. "I'm sorry, Your Highness. I did not mean to eavesdrop, but everything you said is true. I don't love you, and I never have. I've only acted to fulfill my duty as your guardian. I know this is painful for you to hear, but you need to hear it. If you wish to request another guardian, I will understand. Even if I must go into battle, it is the least I can do for hurting you as I have."

"I want to request another guardian," she says. Closing his eyes to hide his pain, he turns away. "But I can't. There is no one out there I trust. I'm still angry with the three of you for keeping things from me, but I need you and Kara and Evren by my side. I will push down my feelings for you and focus on my duty as well."

He bows and walks out. The moment he's out of sight, Ana falls into Kara's arms, unable to stop the tears. "Shh," Kara says. "I know. Get it all out now. Then we'll clean up and get back to studying and training. That will be a good distraction for you."

"It would be so much easier to do this if I didn't have to see him every day. It's killing me."

"It'll be okay. Just focus on one task at a time, okay?" Ana nods her head. "First things first, let's get some food in you."

"I need to get dressed."

After lunch, Ana approaches Rafe, who sat on the chaise to give her space while she ate. He smiles at her. "How are you?" she asks.

"Okay. Healed."

"Good. Sorry I snapped at you."

"Quite all right, Your Highness."

"I would like to train with a sword and dagger." She looks up as they are all staring at her. "What?"

"Kane's been arrested. There's no need."

"He won't be the only one after the throne, Kara. I need to be able to protect myself." She looks at Rafe. "Please, train me."

He nods. "We'll start this evening after dinner. I want you to rest a bit more."

"I understand. Thank you."

Evren sits beside her, book in hand. "Until then, would you like to have another lesson?"

"Please."

She hands Ana the book. "This will tell you everything you need to know about your wardrobe."

Ana flips through, amazed at the beautiful gown, suits, armor, and accessories. She looks at Evren. "You know all of this?" Evren nods. "Thank you. May I ask how old you are?"

"I am eighty-seven."

"So, still a baby?" She smiles at her.

"Yes, mi'lady."

Ana sighs. "Less than a week until my coronation. I don't think I'll ever be ready." She looks at Evren. "What will change once I am crowned queen?"

"You will still attend training and lessons. Your word will carry more weight. No one will be able to come after you like Kane has and get away with it. You'll attend briefings with your advisors and councilors, discussing everything from day-to-day affairs of the kingdom to the war itself."

"Will the war end once I am queen? Once they realize the throne has been reclaimed?"

"That is what we are all hoping for, mi'lady. We can't say for certain, though. You know the greed that grows in some men's hearts."

"I do, unfortunately. Too well."

Rafe straightens up at her words and looks at Kara. She's curious as well and goes to sit beside Ana. "If I may, are you speaking of the archduke?"

"No, Kara."

"Who, then?"

"It doesn't matter. I'd like to continue with my lesson, please."

"Yes, mi'lady."

"What will I wear for my coronation?"

"Oh, you have the most beautiful gown for that. Would you like to see it?"

"Not yet. I'm… not ready."

"Of course."

"Is there a throne room? I've seen so little of the palace."

"Shall we go on a tour? Are you up for walking around?"

"Yes, please."

＊

She and Evren walk together with Rafe and Kara following behind. Kara looks up at him. "I know that wasn't easy."

"What?"

"What you did in the closet."

He shrugs her off. "I did what was necessary for her."

"You could've jumped on a grenade, and it wouldn't have been as painful to watch. I know you are hurting, too."

"Since when do you care about me?"

"Rafe, please. She has already grown up with so little, for her to lose anything else, I think is too much for her. I had hoped when you came in there, that it was to tell her the truth."

"Who says I didn't? You make assumptions about my feelings for her, but I've never told you how I feel."

Her eyes narrow. "You don't have to. I know the truth. You can try and deny it all you want, but I know what is there. I think it's wrong of you to deny yourself, to deny both of you, but I know why you did it."

"Can we drop it?"

"Fine."

They arrive at the throne room. The guards part and open the doors for her. Ana grabs Evren's arm, stunned by the majesty of the room. It has a high vaulted ceiling, ash grey marble pillars, and a dark blue carpet leading up to the two thrones. The thrones themselves are intricately sculpted and ornately decorated with gold, blue, and silver embellishments. They walk her closer to see them.

"I can't sit in it, yet. Can I?"

"Why not?" Evren asks. "You are the princess and heiress to the throne. It is your right to sit there."

Ana turns to Kara and Rafe, who both nod. She slowly approaches the thrones but turns away, thinking she doesn't belong there. She looks around the room, overwhelmed by its size and beauty. *This can't be real. This can't be for me. I'm no one, useless, worthless.*

Her lungs ache, and she realizes she had been holding her breath. She lets it out and makes her way up, trembling as she gets closer. She stands in awe as she looks at the thrones and pictures a king and queen sitting regally, dressed in their finest robes, crowns of diamonds and rubies on their heads. It's too much to take in. She runs down the steps and stops at the marble pillar, resting her forehead against its cool surface.

"I'm sorry, mi'lady. I should've walked up with you," Kara says.

"No, it's okay. I just realized, I don't belong here. This is meant for someone who will do great things, who isn't afraid to lay down their life, to sacrifice everything for their kingdom. I'm no one. I'm not meant to do this."

Rafe walks in front of her. "Do you really think I would've brought you here if I didn't think you were the right one? Not because of your name or your bloodline, but the right person for the throne?"

She looks up at him. "Why did you bring me here?"

"Because it was fate. You are meant to be here, to bring peace. I know you will. We believe in you, even when you don't believe in yourself."

"Mi'lady, if I may," Evren says, "you have been so kind, patient, and loyal from the moment I met you. If ever anyone was born to rule, it is you. You truly are your mother's daughter, in every possible way."

"Thank you, Evren."

"Shall we try again?" Kara asks.

Ana nods as Kara gets on one side with Evren on the other. They walk her up to the thrones when she pulls away. "I'm okay, really." She takes a breath then sits. A smile spreads across her face. Rafe approaches, clearing his throat.

"Rafe?" She looks over when he gestures to the throne at her right. "What?"

"That is where you sit."

"I don't understand. I thought the queen sits on the left."

"The person with the highest title sits on the right."

She blushes, looking down. "Now, I feel foolish." She looks up when he lets out a soft chuckle.

"Nothing to be embarrassed about, mi'lady. It's perfectly understandable."

She stands up and moves to the other throne. They all smile at her, Kara with a tear in her eye as she thinks of Ana's mother sitting on the throne. After a few moments, Ana gets to her feet and joins them.

"How do you feel, mi'lady?" Kara asks.

"Better."

"Good. Now, time for dinner then training."

Ana smiles as they arrive at the dining hall. There is no staring or nasty whispers like she was afraid of. They sit at their usual table. "Mi'lady, with the coronation so near, perhaps you should meet with members of the court."

"By myself?"

"I'll escort you," Kara offers.

They walk around, with Kara making introductions. Ana knows she will never remember so many names and titles, but she does her best and keeps the smile on her face. They return to their table as the first course is brought out.

Ana looks down, seeing the same meal she'd had at the archduke's the night he poisoned her. She immediately waves it away. Kara leans over.

"I thought you like that one?"

Ana shakes her head. They bring out the next course. She sighs in exasperation at the awful looking stew. She waves her hand again. They gather the dish and leave.

"Okay, what's wrong?" Kara asks.

"Nothing."

They bring out the third dish. She quietly groans at the pasta dish. Kara and Rafe jump up when she stands and runs from the hall. Evren follows behind.

"Mi'lady, what's wrong?" Rafe asks.

"I can't eat any of that."

"Why not?" Kara asks.

"Because last time I did, it was poisoned, or I was!"

Kara looks at Rafe. "Kane."

He nods. "You need to eat. I won't train you on an empty stomach."

She spins on her heel to face him. "I beg your pardon?"

"I'm sorry, mi'lady. It's my duty to protect you, even if that means protecting you from yourself."

"What I would give for some pizza!" Ana cries out as she returns to her quarters.

Evren looks at Kara. "What is pizza?"

"It's a popular dish where she grew up. I'll tell you more, later."

Rafe goes inside to inspect, surprised to see Declan waiting for them. He's leaning against the chaise, obviously wounded. Kara runs over to him.

"What happened?"

"The archduke. He hired someone to steal all of the evidence and attack me so I couldn't testify at the tribunal. They had no choice but to release him."

"No!" Ana cries out. "Please, no."

"I'm so sorry, Your Highness." In pain, he limps over to her. He winces as he bows. "I have failed you. My apologies."

"No, you haven't. It's not you. It's him. He's too clever for us, but we will find a way to stop him. Now, please," Declan's face goes from pain to surprise when she puts her hand on his arm and escorts him to the chaise, "sit and rest."

"Thank you, mi'lady."

"Have you eaten?"

He looks up at Ana, unable to believe the concern in her voice for him. "No, I have not."

"I will get us food," Evren offers and steps out.

Ana goes to the window, looking out at the kingdom below. She turns to Rafe, hatred in her eyes because she needs his comfort, but she knows she can't have it. Shooting him an angry look, she goes into the closet.

She wraps the blanket around herself as she sits on the ottoman, unable to stop shaking. Trying desperately to calm herself down, she closes her eyes then hears the door shut, thinking Kara did it to give her privacy.

Her eyes fly open when she's in his arms, pulled to his chest. "What are you doing?" she demands. "Your captain is not twenty feet from here!"

"Then let him execute me. I know how scared you are. Let me comfort you, the consequences be damned."

"Why? If you don't love me, why do you care?"

"Because I do want to be your friend. I want to be here for you, the way Kara and Evren are. Will you let me?"

"The risk—"

"I will take the risk and comfort you how I can."

"I can't keep doing this. You don't understand what it does to me, how it affects me so."

"I do."

"You can't possibly!"

"Believe me, Your Highness, when I tell you I do."

She sees the pain on his face and nods, leaning back into his chest. He wraps his arms tighter around, his wings surrounding them as well. Smiling, her breath escapes her. Her trembling stops as his warmth crawls through her. She pulls away, trying not to stare at his wings.

"Thank you." She watches him tuck them in.

They step out and sit at the table. Rafe gives her a look when she is pushing her food around. She sighs and eats. She's so tired, she doesn't want to train. Knowing Kane is free, she decides she has to. Evren takes her into the closet to change for training while Kara and Rafe help Declan back to his quarters. Evren mends a pair of pants while Ana changes.

⁓

They go to the training center. "Evren and I will go first, like I did with Lauren. If you feel up to it tonight, we will begin."

"Yes, Rafe," Ana agrees.

Kara sits with Ana on the floor, on a cushioned mat, while Rafe and Evren prepare themselves. "How long have you trained?" Rafe asks Evren.

"A few years. You?"

"Pretty much since I was born."

"Don't hold back."

"Oh, I hadn't planned on it," he says, returning her smile.

They raise their swords then take their stances. Evren makes the first move, stepping towards Rafe. He brings his sword up when she lunges, and he parries the attack.

Ana looks at Kara. "Can I really fight Kane like this?"

"You can do anything. You know you can. She's what, four foot four inches against his six foot one? Look at her. She's standing her ground against him. You can do this, Your Highness."

"Thank you."

"Can I ask, why do you think you will have to?"

Ana shrugs her shoulders. "I don't know. I feel like, this is what it will come down to, that I will have to face him with a sword."

Rafe thrusts forward, and Evren parries the attack. She steps back to put some distance between them as she is catching her breath. Lunging at her, she steps around and brings her sword down. He drops to one knee, deflecting her sword. He jumps to his feet, attacking until her sword falls from her hand. They look at Ana.

"Any questions?"

"Can you and I go next?"

Rafe thinks it over a moment, before giving her a nod. "That's fine."

Kara and Evren walk into the other ring, since Kara had asked Evren to train her with a sword, as well. Rafe explains he will slowly approach her, showing different ways to deflect and attack. He walks towards her, sword down, then brings it up, swinging towards her shoulder. He takes her wrist and shows her how to turn her sword to deflect. They practice a few times.

"Are you ready for the real thing?" he asks.

"Yes."

He quickly lunges, bringing his sword around. She brings hers up, deflecting his. He steps back.

"Good, again."

They go a few rounds. Then he turns and feints, before lunging at her. She parries, then brings her sword up towards his neck. He deflects it away.

"Very good, mi'lady." He quickly jumps back when she lunges after him, anger flickering in her eyes. "What are you doing?"

At his words, Kara and Evren run over to watch. Ana lunges again, nearly piercing his shoulder. She watches him as she circles him like a vulture. He parries then steps back to put distance between them. She moves in, swinging hard. He deflects and grabs her wrist, pulling her to him.

"What is the matter?" he asks.

She is consumed with anger, angry at him for... everything. He lied to her, brought her here where she has been attacked and nearly killed, scared to death, and forced to deal with so much change. "You," she snarls. "You are what's the matter. I wish I had never met you!"

"Where is this coming from? Why now?"

"You and Kara told me to. You said for me to push everything down, but I can't. So, if the choice is to hate you or hate myself, I choose you. I've hated myself for long enough. I hate you!" she cries out, pushing back and circling him again.

"Ana, please. Stop this."

"No!"

"How are you doing all of this?" he asks, deflecting her assault.

"I took fencing in college and was a member of the fencing club. I only asked to train as a refresher, as it has been quite a while since I held a sword. I didn't say anything, because I thought it would be fun to surprise you." She charges forward, hitting his sword so hard he falls to his knees.

"What do you want?" he asks, jumping to his feet.

"I win, I never see you again. You win, you stay as my guardian." He drops his sword when she charges at him again.

"Done. You win."

She stops in her tracks. "Typical," she spits out. "You won't even fight for me. That's what I thought."

"Do you not understand? Even if I don't love you, I care for you. I cried when Kara told me about the pills and vodka."

Gripping her sword tighter, she turns to Kara. "You told him about that? Why?"

Kara keeps her gaze. "I was angry at him. I wanted him to hurt the way I did, to feel what I felt."

Ana laughs. "He would have to care about me to hurt."

"Did you not hear what I just said? I do care for you. I was devastated when she told me that. I never wanted anything like that to happen to you. That you would try and kill yourself with pills!"

"I wasn't trying to kill myself. I just wanted to sleep. I wanted to sleep without nightmares of you," she explains.

"Me?"

"You would return. I would run to you, only for you to literally rip my heart out of my chest and toss it behind you!" she screams. "I was lost when you left," she says quietly.

"Maeriana, I am so sorry. You know I never intended for any of this."

"I know you never loved me. Because of that, my heart is destroyed. I will never love anyone else because of you!"

"I don't know. You were quite cozy with Ascienne."

She gasps softly as Kara turns red. "I beg your pardon?" Ana asks.

"I saw the message from him. If Kane hadn't intervened, you probably would've fallen into his bed."

"Rafe!" Kara cries out.

"You are the only man I will ever love!" Ana admits. "No matter how much I hate you, I still love you. Do you know how much that hurts?"

"Good," he says. *God forgive me for this. I'm going to hate myself, but it will be worth it if it finally gets her over me.* "Why don't you run to your closet and have a good cry? You'll feel better."

She screams in fury as she brings her sword up and charges at him. He quickly bends down to retrieve his sword, parrying in the nick of time. Fire in her eyes, she unleashes the rage within, and lunges relentlessly until she backs him into the corner, with her sword at his throat. "I win," she declares.

He drops his sword. "I'll see Declan at once to arrange your new guardian. I pray they do a better job than I have."

She freezes, staring at her blade at his throat, then backs away as the sword falls from her hand. "No. Please, no. What have I done?" she asks as she runs from the room.

Kara runs to Rafe, berating him for how he spoke to her. Ana runs into the hallway, heading for her quarters when Kane steps out from his. He grabs her wrist and drags her inside as his hand clamps over her mouth before she can scream for help.

"Your Highness," he snarls. She struggles to break free of his grasp. He takes her into the inner chamber, throwing her into the chair. "You are going to pay dearly for everything you have put me through. You don't deserve the throne! I have been taking care of this kingdom since your father's death. I have earned this. I should be king."

"You will never be king!" she screams. As he's coming at her, she screams for help. He reaches her, slapping her across the face and knocking her out of the chair. He snatches her from the ground and throws her against the wall. She crumples to the floor and looks up, seeing the pleasure on his face. She brings her legs under and backs away, trapped in the corner.

"Please, stop," she begs.

He walks over, looking down at her. "Darling, I'm just getting started." He offers his hand. She doesn't want to take it, but she's scared what he will do if she refuses. She brings her hand up and grips his. He helps her up, then slams her against the wall and pins her to it, his body covering hers. Caressing her sides, he leans in and kisses her. She tries to push him away, and he responds by punching her in the stomach, knocking the air out of her. He slaps her again, bringing his hand to her throat.

He leans forward, kissing her as his hand goes lower and unbuttons her pants. She goes tense, praying for help. She gasps for air as his hand tightens on her neck. He runs his fingers along the top of her undergarment then trail down when Rafe bursts into the room.

"Unhand her now!" Rafe cries out, sword drawn. Kane turns to him. Ana uses the distraction to kick his knee out from under him. He falls to the floor, arms and legs splayed out. She runs past him, and he grabs her ankle. She screams as it twists, causing her to fall. Rafe catches her and picks her up. They ignore Kane's cries to stop and run from the room.

Rafe says nothing as he carries a sobbing Ana to her quarters. He takes her into the closet, shuts the door behind him, and carries her to the ottoman. He looks her over, concerned that her pants are open, but focuses his attention on her broken ankle.

"Rafe, please," she begs as tears continue to fall. "I didn't mean it. I didn't mean the horrible things I said. I love you, and I don't want you to go. I don't know what came over me. Please, don't go. Not again."

"I'm not going anywhere, Your Highness. I think you've been holding so much in that it erupted. You needed to get all of that out. I'm sorry I was cruel. I thought it best to push you away, that it would help you move past me. I didn't mean it, either. Forgive me?"

"Yes, Rafe."

"Where are you hurt, besides your ankle?"

"Everywhere. He beat me all over before he… before his hand…" she cries into her hands. He stands up, taking off his jacket and shirt. He climbs onto the ottoman.

"I'm going to remove your shirt. Is that all right?"

"But… but not my pants?" she asks quietly. "Just my shirt?"

"I promise."

"Yes, then."

He unbuttons her shirt and tosses it to the floor. He lays her down, then holds her tight. "We need as much skin contact for the healing."

"I understand. I don't deserve it."

"Mi'lady—"

"No, it's okay. Thank you."

He holds her in his arms, her wounds slowly beginning to heal. "I'm going to ask once then we never have to speak of it again. Why were your pants open?"

Her breath sucks in. "He… he was going to… he had his hand and was about to touch me when you came in."

"I'm sorry."

"You saved me. Why are you sorry?"

"I brought you here. You were right about that, everything that has happened to you is my fault. I have failed you."

"No, Rafe. You haven't. You've saved my life. Thank you."

He kisses the top of her head. "Please believe me that I care for you and never meant to hurt you."

"I know."

They pass out from exhaustion.

Kara stands in the doorway, watching them sleep on the ottoman. She shakes her head as she walks over, covering them with the blanket. "How can you both be so stupid?" she whispers. "You have to see how you feel about each other." She returns to the main chamber, walks over to Evren, and takes her in her arms as they sit on the chaise. "I think they'll be okay. They're resting now. Healing takes it out of them."

"What happened in the training center?"

"Something long overdue. Trust me, they needed to get that out and clear the air."

Chapter 14

A few hours later, Rafe leads Ana out of the closet. She walks to the window and looks out while he joins Evren and Kara.

"Are you leaving us?" Evren asks.

He smiles at her. "No. Everything is okay now."

Kara looks at him. "Are you okay?"

"Yes."

"Rafe, I know it's forbidden—"

"Kara, don't start. We are at a place where she and I understand each other. I don't want to ruin that."

"Yes, Rafe."

He walks to Ana. "Are you fully healed?"

"I am, thanks to you." She looks at him but quickly averts her gaze. "I'm so embarrassed about everything."

"You should be."

Her head snaps up, a smile breaking across her lips as she sees his. She shakes her head. "Rude," she says with a laugh.

"Everything will be okay now. You are so close to your coronation and to finally being free of Kane. Once you are queen, you can imprison him or banish him."

"What do you think he is planning as revenge for this?"

"I'm not sure."

"This was all my fault," Ana says.

"No, mi'lady. It was mine. I drove you to anger, drove you away." He clears his throat then looks at Evren. "Would you get us a meal? Healing really makes me hungry."

"Of course."

Rafe looks at Ana, who gives him a small smile. "Me, too. I need to change." Ana goes to her closet, picking out pants and a blouse.

She gets her clothes on, looking in the mirror. *Please, let this be right. I don't need Evren telling me I'm in something like a fancy blouse with pajama pants.* She laughs at the thought.

"Are you okay, mi'lady?" Evren asks when Ana approaches her, looking worried.

"Yes. Is my outfit okay?"

Evren steps back and looks her over. "Yes."

She sighs in relief. "Thank you."

The food arrives, and they sit at the table. Evren and Kara sit close together and speak softly as Ana pushes her food around. She glances at Rafe, sees the frown on his face, and slumps her shoulders as she makes herself eat.

"You are good with a sword," he says, hoping to raise her spirits.

"Thanks. I didn't tell you sooner, because I did think it would be fun to surprise you our first night training. Instead, I got angry. I didn't mean for it to go so far."

"It's okay. I was surprised. You never cease to amaze me, Your Highness."

When they've finished eating, Ana walks over to her nightstand, picking up the book of myths and legends Evren brought back from the library. She sits on the edge of the bed, skimming through it.

There is a tale of a pair of soulmates, able to heal each other with their touch. Their love fuels their healing. If one does not love the other, the healing will not work. They are fated to be together forever.

She slams the book shut.

Rafe walks over. "Are you okay?"

"I'm fine, just tired. I think I'll turn in shortly."

He looks at the name of the book. "You found the legend, didn't you?"

"Fate wouldn't be so cruel," she whispers, repeating his own words back to him. "You're right." He steps back. "I heard you say it when you were healing me."

"Your Highness—"

"It's okay. I know it's not your fault. So many things are out of my hands. Believe me, if there was anything I could do to change it, I would."

"I know, mi'lady." He gives her a sad smile. He walks over to Kara. "She found the legend."

She gasps. "What did you tell her?"

"What could I tell her? She's angry now. Maybe you could speak to her?"

"Of course." She goes to Ana. Rafe looks at Evren.

"How are you holding up?"

"Okay. Like you, waiting for her coronation so we can finally put the archduke behind us. Every time he hurts her, it makes me sick. I am not a violent person, but I would hurt him if I could."

"I know. I understand the feeling. I have to restrain myself because I know that no matter the reason, I will be executed if I kill him. I'm not so worried about my own life, but how would she cope with my loss? Plus, she needs me with her to heal her and protect her. Though, great job I've done so far."

Her eyes go wide at his confession. "Rafe, you know I won't say anything. And no, you have not failed her. She is still alive because of you."

"Thanks."

Ana goes to the closet to change into a nightgown. She tells them good night then crawls into bed. Rafe approaches her.

"Do you need anything?"

"No. Just knowing you're still here is enough. Thank you." She turns to her side, ready for a good night's sleep.

He moves the chaise closer to her bed. Kara and Evren say their good nights and go to their quarters.

———————— ⇜ ————————

Ana sits up, a scream on the precipice of her lips. She swallows it down, looks around, and sees Rafe on the chaise beside her. She slips out of bed and goes to the washroom, where she splashes cold water on her face, unable to believe how pale she is. She steps out to find Rafe waiting for her.

"Bad dreams?"

"Yes," she admits.

"I hope they weren't because of me."

"No."

"Good."

She walks around him when he takes her hand and pulls her into his arms. She'd give anything to stay there, as she thinks of the legend. *There has to be something I can do. I would rather have five hundred years with him than none. If he loves me, I will find a way.*

———————— ⇜ ————————

There's a knock at the door, and Kara opens it. A royal guard hands her a message for Ana. Kara thanks him and takes the message to her, watching closely as she opens and reads it.

"It's from Kane. He's inviting me to the morning briefing at ten o'clock. Why now?"

"Maybe he's finally realizing you aren't going down without a fight, and that he may still lose the throne," Kara suggests.

"If only." Ana turns to Evren. "Would you mind laying out an outfit for me?"

Evren nods and does as she's asked. "Whenever you're ready, mi'lady."

"Thank you." Ana goes into the closet, shutting the door behind her. Evren has laid out an appropriate gown, shoes, and circlet. Ana dresses and looks herself over in the mirror, still in disbelief over how beautiful the clothes are as she runs her fingers over the silver-blue fabric. She checks to make sure the circlet is secured and is heading for the door when she hears raised voices. She pauses behind the closet door, listening in.

"What do you mean you haven't told her? Kara, her coronation is in three days."

"Between the attacks, and everything she has been through, I haven't had the chance."

"You have to tell her!" Rafe insists.

"Why does it fall to me?"

"Because you are her best friend. She needs to hear it from you."

Kara goes to the closet door. "Fine," she snaps, flinging it open. It slams back, knocking Ana off her feet. "Oh, my God! Are you all right?" Kara runs to her, helping her to her feet.

"What happened?" Rafe demands, standing in the doorway.

"She must've been right behind the door. I slammed it open, and it hit her."

"I'm okay, really," Ana says, rubbing her forehead.

"I am so sorry, Your Highness."

"It was an accident. Now, what were you two fighting about?"

Kara's eyes go down. "Oh, you heard that?"

"Half the kingdom heard it."

Kara shoots Rafe an angry look as she walks Ana to the ottoman. She sits down with her. "The night before your coronation, the archduke is hosting a masquerade ball in your honor. He expects you there, as his date."

"What?" She jumps to her feet, looking at Rafe then Kara. "How long have you known about this?"

Kara swallows hard. "A little while…"

"Do I have to go?"

"It's a tradition," Rafe answers. "Since he's the closest to a royal, you are obligated to go. Believe me, if I had my way, you would never see him again."

She sits down. "This can't be real. Tell me this isn't happening."

"We will be with you. You won't be alone with him."

She stands up and walks over to the armoire, mindlessly opening it and going through drawers. Rafe walks over. He sees the small notebook. Without thinking, he pulls it out.

"Don't—" she tries.

He opens it, reading the only entry. "What is this?"

Kara walks over, taking it from him. "When did you write this?" Kara asks when she realizes there is no date.

"The night Rafe and Declan came in," she answers quietly.

"You gave up?" Kara asks. "Just like that?"

"No!" Ana cries out. "I was saving you."

"That's not what this sounds like. 'Forgive me for my weakness' sounds to me like you gave up."

"I want to be alone."

"Ana, please. Don't shut us out now."

"Why do you keep calling me Ana? Do you forget your place?"

"I thought it would help you not be so overwhelmed."

"You're both dismissed."

Kara runs out, angry and hurt. Rafe puts his hand on Ana's shoulder. "She's right, you know. Don't shut us out, don't give up. We want to be here for you. We can't help if you don't let us in."

She opens her mouth to dismiss him again when he steps up to her. He lowers his hand, gently gripping her arm. As he leans down, Kara walks in.

"I'm sorry, mi'lady, but it's time for the briefing."

Ana steps back, looking at Rafe in confusion. "Thank you." She goes to Kara and pulls her into her arms. "I'm sorry."

Kara hugs her back. "It's okay."

Rafe looks at Ana. "Kara and Evren cannot come. They do not have the appropriate security clearance, as you would call it. Once you are queen, you can give it to them."

"I see. Thank you."

Rafe escorts her to a part of the palace she hasn't seen before. They go into a meeting room, already full of scrivers, councilors, advisors, and military personnel. Ana doesn't recognize the insignia on their uniforms. She makes a mental note to ask Evren about it later. Towards the back of the room is a huge oak desk, covered with maps, reports, and messages. Kane is studying a map when they make their way up. Ana glances at the side wall, seeing the table with water and tea. Kane sees them and smiles.

"Welcome, Your Highness. Thank you for finally attending one of these."

"Thank you for finally inviting me," she shoots back.

Rafe gestures her over, and they sit. Declan stands up first, trying to hide his rage at Kane. He gives accounts of the battlefront, the casualties, and a summary of how the armory is doing. He sits down. An older woman Ana's never seen before stands up. She goes over inventory for the palace. It goes this way for an hour, each person giving a report on happenings of the palace and kingdom. Ana struggles to keep her eyes open.

"Your Highness," Kane says, looking at her, "I would like your advice on something. Would you come up here?"

She stands up and carefully makes her way through the sea of chairs. "How may I assist, Archduke?"

He smiles at her. "We have had difficulty in battle with NightFall because they have superior archers. If we send our men straight in, they'll undoubtedly be taken out by a volley of arrows." He points at the board in front of him, with a diorama showing what it will look like on the field. "What would you recommend in order to reduce casualties and maximize effectiveness?"

Rafe sucks in his breath, realizing that Kane is trying to show everyone why Ana should not be on the throne. Declan and one of the admirals walk over to the desk, curious to hear her response. She studies the board, thinking for a moment.

"I would separate them into thirds," she says, ignoring the Archduke's chuckle. "Two lines of phalanx going here and here," she points, "with one line veering right and the other left. The third would sneak up from behind, effectively cutting off the enemy while reducing casualties."

"I'll be damned," Admiral Lanx replies. "Apologies, mi'lady."

"No apology necessary, sir."

He smiles and nods, rubbing his chin. "That's actually quite brilliant. Kane, why didn't you think of that?"

"This briefing is over," Kane announces. "Everyone is dismissed."

Once everyone is gone except the three of them, Kane grabs Ana's hand. "A moment, mi'lady. I insist."

Rafe steps up. "What do you want, Kane?"

"I want you, Guardian, to give us privacy."

"I will step back, but I will not leave."

"Fine," Kane snaps.

Rafe walks to the table. He remains standing, ready for whatever might happen. Kane turns back to Ana.

"Your Highness, you are full of surprises. If I had known you were beautiful and brilliant, well, things would've gone differently. Do you not see how good we would be for this kingdom? I would lavish you with jewels and gowns, hosting balls while I continue with the war effort." He ignores her scoff. "Join me."

"What are you playing at? You must realize by now you will never get your hands on my throne. You can't sleep with me, and you will never touch me again, so what do you want with me?"

"Oh, I'll get to touch you plenty as we dance the night away at the ball."

"I am attending, but not as your date. I certainly will not be dancing, with you or anyone."

"Why do you fight it? Surely you feel this flame between us. You are so passionate and beautiful, exactly what I deserve to have adorning my arm."

"You don't deserve me. No one does. After what you did to Ascienne, what you have done to me, I have decided to rule alone. I don't need a king. I will bring peace. I will save my people."

"Your people? You haven't been here long enough for them to be your people. It's why they will never settle for you on the throne. You may be the rightful heir, but they will not accept you. I'm going to ask nicely one more time. Reject me now, and it will be the last time I ask this way. Choose wisely. Will you marry me?"

"I would sooner jump off the battlement."

He raises his hand to hit her. Before Rafe can reach her, she grabs Kane's wrist and flings him to the ground. She stands above him, with her foot on his chest. "Don't ever touch me again!"

She runs to Rafe, who quickly escorts her back to her quarters. Trembling in fear, she knows she will pay dearly, but she was not going to let him hurt her again. Kara and Evren run over at the sight of them.

"What happened?"

Ana shakes her head. "Everything was fine, until he asked me to stay after the briefing." She looks at Rafe then stares at the floor. "He expects me on his arm at the ball, and he asked for my hand in marriage again." She looks up when Rafe goes tense beside her.

"What did you say?" Rafe asks.

"That I will not be his date for the ball, that I will not be his wife. He went to hit me, and I brought him to the floor. The same way you did the pervert in the bookstore," Ana says, looking at Kara.

Kara hugs her. "I'm so proud of you!"

"You should've seen her. He tried to humiliate her, asking about battle strategy. Instead, she impressed everyone in the room," Rafe says, beaming with pride.

Kara looks at her. "Where did that come from?"

"Um, reading Tolkien and playing video games."

Kara's eyes go wide then she bursts into laughter. "Oh, God. Only you."

Ana looks at Evren. "I'd like to change into something more comfortable and appropriate for training."

"Yes, mi'lady." They go into the closet. Evren lays out the clothes then leaves. Ana picks the blanket up off the ottoman and wraps it around herself, shivering. She hears someone knocking and opens the door, expecting Kara. Nearly dropping the blanket in surprise, she steps back as Rafe walks in. He shuts the door, taking the blanket from her, and wrapping her in his arms.

"Rafe—"

"No, mi'lady. I don't want to hear it. You stayed so strong in front of him. Kara is right, though. You have to stop hiding from us."

"You don't understand."

"Then tell me," he says, tightening his arms around her. She lavishes his comfort, making her feel safe.

She leans up to his ear. "I love you, and I know you know this. I'm saying it so you understand something. Every time you pull me into your arms like this, my heart flutters, and I can't breathe. Being with you is so comforting and so painful at the same time. I'm trying to push it down, but it won't stay down. I don't know what to do."

"We both have to push things down. I had to push down my urge to kill Kane when his hand came up. I know it's not fair to either of us, but it's how it is. I am sorry for hurting you, for breaking your heart. We have to do things we don't like."

"I know. I'm sorry I'm not as strong as you."

"Ana, I have had over five hundred years of training the mind and body. You just need time, then you'll be okay. You'll see." He looks at her. "I was so scared when his hand came up. I knew I would never get to you in time."

"Now you see why my training is so important."

"Are we having lunch here?" Evren asks when Ana steps out from the closet.

"Yes," she replies as her face flushes.

Kara walks over. "What's wrong?"

"Nothing," Ana replies, keeping her gaze lowered.

"What?"

"I just want to eat in here."

"Look at me," Kara says. She takes her hand and spins her around. "Why are you so flush?"

"I'm ashamed. I'm too scared to eat in the hall because I'm not ready to face him again."

"He hurt you, and he nearly killed you. You have absolutely nothing to be ashamed of!" Rafe says, walking up behind her. "You have been so brave when facing off with him. There is no shame in wanting to avoid him."

Kara turns to her. "He's right. You know what that means, if I am agreeing with him."

Ana smiles. "Thank you, both of you. I want to go to the library, first. Then we'll train this afternoon," she says. Rafe gives her a nod then flashes her a small smile. She sits at the table and thinks of the upcoming ball. As she pictures dancing with Rafe, she sighs and pushes it down.

Once at the library, Kara sits with Rafe, and they watch Ana grab several books and get out her notebook. She reads page after page, writing furiously and making notes. She works through lunch. Rafe walks over and rests his hand on her shoulder.

"You need to eat."

At the sound of his voice, she gathers up her books and closes them. She puts them in her bag. "I will."

"What are you working on?"

"Nothing," she mutters. She joins Kara and Evren. He's tempted to look in her bag, but after the training center, he doesn't want to risk making her angry and follows her to the table instead.

"How goes your studies?" Kara asks.

"Frustrating," she grumbles.

"What's wrong? Did I not suggest the right books or—"

"No, Evren. It's not you, I promise."

"What are you researching?" Rafe asks.

Evren answers when Ana doesn't respond. "She asked for books on the history of the realm, history of the kingdom, and how it came to be. She's interested in the royal lineage, and the writing of our first laws and treaties."

"I don't understand. What's frustrating you?" Kara asks.

Ana takes a deep breath. "Nothing. I'm still tired from yesterday."

Kara gives her a confused look but stays quiet about it. She turns to Rafe. "Are we doing any sword training today? She may not need it, but I would like to learn."

"That's up to her."

"Yes, we can after dinner."

"Great!" Kara smiles.

When she's done eating, Ana walks back to her table and gets her books out. She gestures Evren over to ask her for a favor. Evren nods and leaves. Ana returns to her studies. After a while, she slams the last book in frustration and stands up, pacing the library as she looks through the stacks.

Kara walks up beside her. "What's wrong?"

"Nothing."

"Can I help?"

"No. It's something I have to do alone."

"Mi'lady, we've talked about this—"

"This is different. Please, leave me alone." Ana scans the shelves for more information, then pulls out a few books and brings them to her table.

Kara walks over to Rafe. "I don't know what she's working on. She won't tell me." She watches Ana flip through one of the books and take notes. "I've never seen her like this. Not even during finals week in college."

Evren returns and whispers something to Ana, who is obviously pleased with whatever news she's brought. They return to her quarters for dinner. There is a desk and chair set up by the window. When Rafe sees it, he realizes this is what Ana had asked Evren to do.

Ana walks over, laying her bag on the desk. It's fully stocked with fountain pens and paper. She smiles as she runs her hand along the wood grain, her smile growing when Rafe walks up beside her.

"I promise, tonight will not be like last night. I still feel so badly for how I acted. I am sorry."

"It's okay, mi'lady. You've already been forgiven. Please, let it go."

"Thank you, Rafe."

She sits at the desk and continues working. Even when dinner is brought in, she takes her plate over to eat while she reads.

Kara leans forward, speaking softly to Evren. "What is she working on? You have to tell us."

"I'm sorry, Kara. I don't really know. She said it's for the good of the kingdom, and that's all she would say."

Kara and Rafe look at each other. "You don't know more?"

Evren shakes her head. "Even if she told me, I would not break her confidence."

"Understandable."

Rafe looks over, happy to see that she is eating while studying. He takes that as a good sign. They finish their meal and go to the training center. Evren works with Kara while Rafe does a few refreshers with Ana, before they get their swords.

Rafe turns to Ana, sword in hand. "Ready?"

"Yes."

They move quickly and smoothly. She sidesteps him when he parries, turning on her heel, and bringing down her sword. He blocks the hit, smiling at her. She steps back, raising her sword.

"Would you like to make a friendly wager?"

"Depends, what are the rewards?" she asks, wiping the sweat from her brow.

"If you win, I'll honestly answer any question you ask me, up to three questions. No exceptions."

"And if I win?"

"You tell me what you are working on."

Thinking for a moment, she realizes just how dangerous her questions would be. "No, let's just continue training." She sees the disappointment on his face. "Rafe, please—"

"Why won't you tell us?"

She drops her sword, heading for the door when Rafe runs to her, grabbing her wrist.

"Really? You'd leave again, after what happened yesterday?" he asks, his voice rife with anger.

"Better to give my life than yours."

"What does that mean?"

"Nothing." She takes a breath. "You're right, I shouldn't leave like this. Still, I wish you would stop bothering me with questions. Why won't you all let me have one thing, just one thing, to myself?"

"Because we worry about you," Kara answers, walking over.

"I'm okay, really. Why won't you all believe me?" She shakes her head and turns away. "Because of last night. You have one little breakdown." She looks at Rafe. "I'm ready to return to my quarters, if you'll accompany me, Guardian."

He swallows at her use of his title. "Yes, mi'lady."

Kara and Evren decide to stay and continue training. Rafe strides with Ana, as she is practically running.

"Your Highness, please slow down. We'll be there soon enough."

She slows her gait, walking with him. Once he clears her quarters, she goes to the washroom. She stands under the water, thinking of their first kiss on Earth. *Ana, I'm going to kiss you. Is that all right?* Her fingers trail over her lips, running down her neck and chest. She longs to be in his arms, to feel his warmth. She aches to be near him, the weight of his absence resting on her heart. The pain consumes her, until she pushes it down and wipes her tears, collecting herself.

Stepping out and drying off, she catches her reflection. She sees how worn out she is, her eyes sunk in and her color pallid. Living in this realm is taking its toll on her. She misses Earth and would give anything to be sitting on the couch, eating popcorn, and laughing with Rafe at some silly movie. She pushes the thoughts away again, focusing instead on what she is working on.

She gets dressed and steps out, only to see Rafe is at her desk, rifling through her notebook. Her blood boils at the sight. "What the hell are you doing?" she yells at him as she grabs her books from him and shoves them into her bag. "Rafe?"

"I'm sorry. I've never seen you like this, and I am concerned for your wellbeing." He looks at the books in her hand. "I still don't know what you're researching, as I can't read your writing."

"That's a good thing." She turns away, clenching her hands as she pushes down her anger. "I can't believe you would violate my privacy like this."

"I'm worried."

"It's just research. Let it go."

"Yes, Your Highness."

The sharpness in his tone angers her. "Guardian!"

Kara and Evren walk in, laughing. The laughter stops when they are overwhelmed by the tension in the room. "Is everything all right?" Kara asks.

Ana turns away from Rafe and walks up to Evren. "Do I have everything I need for the ball tomorrow?"

"Let's take a look, mi'lady."

They go into the closet. Evren pulls out a blue-grey dress with a slight V-neck, lace sleeves, and billowing skirt. Silver stars are embroidered along the bodice and trail down the skirt.

"That's the most beautiful dress I've ever seen."

"Mi'lady, you haven't seen your coronation gown."

"One thing at a time, Evren."

"Yes, mi'lady."

"Now, is this a themed ball, or is a mask and gown sufficient?"

"It is themed for celestial beings."

Ana smiles. "Perfect. I need a few accessories." She tells Evren everything she needs.

"I will see to it first thing in the morning."

"Thank you."

Ana steps out, yawning. She says good night to everyone then crawls into bed.

Rafe gestures Kara over to the window. "I know what she's working on."

"What?"

"She wants to free Evren, to free all slaves."

"Really?"

"Yes. She wants to make the kingdom better. It's like it's become her own personal mission."

"She'll have to bring about peace, first."

"Think about it."

"The treaty. She can free Evren if she writes the treaty."

"Hmm, yes and no," Rafe answers. "She still has to get it past the chancellor."

"Oh, right. Okay, now I feel kind of bad that we know."

He smiles. "Right?"

"Why didn't she tell us?"

"She said she really wanted to have one thing that was her own. I guess she meant it."

Kara yawns. "I need sleep. We have a long couple of days ahead of us."

<hr />

Rafe wakes up and is surprised to see Ana at her desk. He gets up and showers, then approaches her.

"What time did you get up, mi'lady?"

"I've been up a few hours."

"Couldn't sleep?"

"No."

"Because of tonight?" he asks.

"Yes."

He realizes she is trying to concentrate, so he steps away and sits on the chaise, watching her. Evren walks in, carrying a garment bag. Ana jumps up at the sight, grabs her hand, and runs into the closet.

"I went ahead and put in your requests last night."

Ana opens the bag and takes the items out, looking over them and smiling. "Oh, Evren! These are perfect. Thank you so much."

"Of course, mi'lady. I'm glad you're pleased."

"Now to dress for breakfast."

Evren picks out a pale pink gown with long sleeves. Ana slips it on with silver shoes. Evren braids her hair and pins in a silver circlet.

Rafe smiles at her when she steps back in the main chamber. "I like that color on you."

"Thank you." She walks up to him.

"I'm sorry about last night. You're right, I violated your privacy," he says with a sigh. "I had no right to."

"It's okay. Do it again, and I won't be so forgiving." She flashes him a smile.

He chuckles, smiling back. "Yes, mi'lady. Are you ready to go to breakfast?"

"Where is Kara?"

"I'll get her, mi'lady. We'll meet you there," Evren responds.

Rafe holds out his arm, acceptable for an escort, and they go to the dining hall. Ana sees the archduke but quickly avoids looking at him. She sits and concentrates on her breakfast.

"Mi'lady?"

She looks up, seeing a man she doesn't recognize. "Can I help you?" she asks. He is dressed in noble clothing, short with a little weight on him. His hair is light brown, and his face is freshly shaved smooth. He adjusts his glasses as he steps closer.

He bows. "Mi'lady, I am Chancellor Corbin. I apologize that we haven't met sooner. I oversee our laws and work with the council."

Ana's blood runs cold. "Is there a problem?"

"Oh, no, mi'lady. I wanted to come over and introduce myself. I am honored to preside over your coronation. Please, feel free to come and see me anytime. I will happily answer any questions you have."

"Thank you, Chancellor."

Pushing down the terror raging through her body, she watches him walk away. She glances at Rafe before staring down at her plate. She closes her eyes. *I've been such a fool. I thought for sure we had been reported! Once I am crowned queen, I will have to send him away. It's too dangerous to be around him.* She looks over at Rafe. He gives her a reassuring smile, which she tries to return. She pushes the food around on her plate.

Kara walks over. "Are you okay?"

"Fine." She waves her hand, letting them take her plate away. She raises her fist, giving the stop gesture.

"You didn't eat!"

"I'm fine. I need to return to my quarters before studies."

Chapter 15

Back in her quarters she goes into the washroom and sits on the edge of the tub. *I'll see Declan after my coronation. He will assign me a new guardian. If we were caught, and he was killed…*

Unable to finish the thought, she weeps into her hands, then pushes down her fears and returns to her desk. Sitting there, book open, she stares off into space.

"Ana, please, what's wrong?"

She looks up when she realizes Kara is speaking to her. "I'm sorry. Did you say something?"

Kara walks over, kneeling in front of her. "What's wrong? Is it tonight?"

She looks at Rafe then back to Kara. "No."

Kara takes her hands, leading her to the closet. They sit on the ottoman. "Talk to me, please."

"I've decided that tomorrow after my coronation, I'm going to request a new guardian."

"What? Why?" Kara asks, shock in her voice.

"I met Chancellor Corbin today."

"Oh, good. He found you."

"What does that mean? What did you do?"

"I'm sorry. I saw a little bit of your notes, that you want to help Evren. I sent him to you, so you know he's available. Maybe he could help you. Wait, what does this have to do with Rafe?"

"I thought maybe Kane had reported us as another ploy. I thought he was coming over to issue an order of execution. I nearly fainted when he told me who he is."

"I'm so sorry. I was just trying to help. I never meant for that to happen."

"Well, it did. It made me realize it's too dangerous, keeping him by my side."

"You can't be serious! You know that no one else here will protect you the way he will."

"I know. That's part of the problem."

"You don't have to do this," Kara says in frustration, battling the urge to tell Ana the truth behind her spell, realizing she can't. Not yet.

"Yes, I do. Don't you understand? If we are reported, it's a death sentence. I would never forgive myself. I don't care if it's his duty. I will not have his blood on my hands."

"You don't have to decide anything—"

"The decision has been made."

"No!" Kara yells, standing up. "You can't do this!"

"Please, calm down. What is wrong with—"

Rafe runs in, scanning the room. "Are you two okay?"

Ana looks at Kara, begging her not to say anything. Kara looks at Rafe. "We're okay. Just a heated discussion. Sorry."

"Okay." He leaves, shutting the door behind him.

"Kara, why are you getting so upset?"

"He is so good for you. Even if you can't be together romantically. Even as friends, do you not see how much he has helped you grow? Plus, the fact that he can heal you and has saved your life? I won't lose you. I can't. Please, don't send him away. At least think about it."

"Fine," Ana lies. "I'll think about it."

"Thank you." Kara pulls her into a hug. Ana hugs back, fighting the tears at the thought of saying goodbye to him. She loses the battle, weeping in Kara's arms. "You've already made up your mind, haven't you?"

"Yes, I'm sorry."

"I wish you wouldn't. I really wish you wouldn't."

"Kara?"

"Just trust me. Don't do this." She looks at Ana. "He is—"

"You don't know what it's been like. You don't know how many times I've cried for him while in the shower or in here getting dressed. The times he's brought me here, holding me for comfort after one of Kane's attacks, and I know he could be killed for that. It's too much for me."

Kara's shoulders slump. "I understand."

They go back into her chambers. Ana sits at her desk and resumes looking through her book. Kara walks up to Rafe and pulls him in for a hug.

"What was that for?"

"Because you've been so wonderful for her." She walks over and sits with Evren.

Rafe looks at Ana. Taking the chance, he approaches her. "Mi'lady, are you happy with how I've performed my duties?"

She freezes, pen in hand. She looks at Kara. "What did you say to him?" she demands.

"Nothing."

She gets to her feet. "No, Kara. What did you tell him?"

"I swear."

She looks at Rafe. "Why would you ask me that?"

"You're thinking of asking for another guardian, aren't you?"

"How could you possibly know that?"

"I overheard some of your argument. Plus, the pain on your face when you looked at me after. What did I do wrong?"

She sits back down, her head swimming and brings up her hand, resting her head on it. "It's nothing like that."

"Tell me, please."

She stands up, gesturing him to follow her into the closet. She shuts the door behind him, taking a breath as she faces him, stepping up and caressing his cheek. "I love you, Rafe. I love you too much not to be with you. I can't do this anymore. I thought I could, but it's too hard. I'm going to see Declan tomorrow, after the coronation. I'll find a way to keep you out of battle, I promise. I'll tell him it's nothing against you, that I need a different guardian. I'm sorry."

"After everything I've said and done to you, you still love me?"

"Yes. I would never forgive myself if you died because of me."

He turns away, unable to believe what he's hearing. He takes her hand, tracing over the lines of her palm before he releases her. "I'll take care of it for you, mi'lady." He abruptly leaves the room.

Ana struggles to keep the tears at bay. She thought it would be easier to say goodbye since she knows it's for the best. When she leaves the closet, Kara and Evren hurry to her side.

"I'm sorry, mi'lady."

"It's okay, Kara. It had to be done."

"Why?" Evren asks.

"It had to. I would like to be alone to do some research until lunch."

"We'll be right next door in Evren's quarters."

"Thank you."

As soon as they're gone, she cries again. Her heart is heavy with sorrow at the thought of saying goodbye to Rafe. She's grateful he took care of it himself, but she feels like a coward for letting him. She goes to the washroom and cleans her face. Sitting on the chaise and watching the fire, she looks up when Rafe and Declan enter. She stands up.

"Mi'lady," Declan says, bowing.

"Captain, how may I help?"

"May I ask why you are unhappy with Rafe's duties? As far as I've seen, he has done an excellent job of protecting you."

"It's… not him," she says.

"I see. There's no easy way to say this, mi'lady. If I assign you a new guardian, it will be somebody I will have to recall from battle. Rafe would have to take their place. There is no way around it."

"Then I refuse your protection."

"What?" they ask at the same time.

"You heard me. I refuse your protection. Rafe may join you without going into battle."

"It… but… mi'lady, it doesn't work that way," Declan stutters out.

"If I were to command it?"

Rafe sucks his breath in. "Please, Ana, don't. My duty is to protect you. That is my purpose."

"Perhaps it's best if we just pretend none of this conversation ever happened," Declan offers.

Ana hesitates before she nods and turns away. Declan looks at Rafe in relief then leaves. She goes into the closet, knowing Rafe will follow her in.

"Why did you do that? You would refuse protection?"

"I don't want you to die for me or because of me."

"You're getting crowned tomorrow. There will still be danger, but you will have royal guards, and Kane will no longer be a threat. Why now?"

"Meeting Chancellor Corbin at breakfast."

"You thought Kane had reported us?"

"I thought it was possible. I wouldn't put it past him, as desperate as he is. I was terrified."

He walks up, taking her into his arms. "It's not going to happen. There's more to it than someone reporting it. As long as there isn't an eyewitness to anything considered an offense, like me kissing you, and we both deny anything happened, they can't hurt us. I suppose Kane could claim to be an eyewitness, but given that Kara and Evren are with us almost all the time, it would be pretty difficult on his part. Honestly, I think it's why he hasn't tried it yet."

"Why didn't you tell me this before? You and Kara made it seem like even a hint of impropriety would be disastrous."

"We did that so you would be careful around me. We thought it best, to protect you and me. I'm sorry."

"No, I am. Please, forgive me for this?"

"You were looking out for me. There is nothing to forgive," he says, kissing her forehead.

"After tomorrow, my life is going to be so different. I don't think I'm ready for all of this."

"Ana, you are such an amazing, strong woman, only becoming more so in the time we've been here. If anyone can take this on, it's you."

"Thank you, Rafe." She looks up at him. "You'll be there tomorrow, right? When I'm crowned as queen?"

"Nothing will keep me from it."

There's a knock at the door. She pulls away from Rafe, walking over and opening it slightly. At the sight of Kara, she opens it fully.

"Sorry, does this mean he's staying?"

"Yes."

"Oh, thank God!" she exclaims, walking away. Ana shuts the door and walks back to Rafe.

"I don't mean to alarm you, but I think Kara has taken a liking to you."

"I know. It scares me."

Ana laughs then looks up at him. "I don't know what I was thinking."

He pulls her to him. "Because you keep turning inward. Kara asked you to talk with her, with us. Let us help you."

"I'll try."

Back in her chambers, Ana looks at Evren. "What time does the ball start?"

"Seven o'clock."

"Will you help me start getting ready at six?"

"Yes, mi'lady." Evren steps out to request lunch. Kara looks at Ana, taking her hand and leading her to the chaise.

She watches as Rafe walks to the window. "Well, at least he knows for sure how you feel about him."

"That wasn't really in question. I wish I knew how he felt about me," Ana says, uncertainty worming its way through her.

"Is it not obvious?"

"You know it's not. I don't doubt he cares for me, as you and Evren do. I honestly can't tell if there's more to it. I know he could never tell me. It hurts, not knowing."

"I'm sorry. I can't imagine."

"How are you and Evren doing?"

"We are doing well."

"Do you love her?"

"I do," Kara admits, a slight blush in her cheeks.

"Does she love you back?"

"I don't know. I… I haven't told her yet."

"Kara, seeing what I'm dealing with should inspire you to be open."

"You're right. Thank you."

"I'm sorry."

"For what?"

"That your love is forbidden. I worry over the two of you, too. If anything happened to either of you—"

"We are very careful in public."

Chapter 16

They're eating lunch when there's a knock at the door. Kara answers it and lets Declan in. When Ana joins them, Kara gives them privacy.

"Mi'lady, I apologize for the interruption."

"It's no trouble. Is everything all right?"

Declan shakes his head, anger on his face. "Kane has decided that there is only to be members of court, dignitaries, and his own royal guards at the ball."

Her breath stops in her throat. "No guardians?"

"No, mi'lady. I tried to tell him it was against protocol, but he still has all the power, for now. We will be patrolling the halls and exits, but we aren't allowed inside."

"Not even Rafe?"

"I'm afraid not," he says, studying her face. "I'm sorry. I have failed you."

"No, it's just another of his games. I'll attend, do my duty, and try to leave as soon as I can without looking like I'm running away. He won't be able to do anything to me in a room full of people."

"Yes, mi'lady." Giving her an apologetic look, he bows and walks out.

Going into her closet, she shuts the door behind her and sits on the floor with her back resting against the ottoman. Her arms wrap around her knees as she brings her them to her chest, struggling to breathe. The thought of being in the same room with Kane was bad enough. Knowing she will be on her own is more than she can bear. She looks up when Rafe walks in.

"No," she begs softly, looking down. "I don't want you to see me like this."

"We've been over this. What did Declan want?"

She keeps her head down and licks her lips, realizing her whole mouth has gone dry. "Kane has decided only court members, dignitaries, and the royal guard are to attend tonight."

"Wait, no guardians? You can't be serious."

When she buries her head in her legs, he runs over and sits beside her. She looks up at him when he wraps her in his arms.

"I'm sorry I'm not stronger. I'm so scared of him. The thought of being alone—"

"I know. I'll be there, even if it's just in the hall. You know how much I love that post." He smiles when she lets out a quiet laugh. He reaches into his shirt and pulls out a sheathed dagger. "I want you to wear this tonight. It straps to your thigh. I don't want around him unarmed."

"Thank you," she says, taking it. She looks it over, admiring the vines engraved along the hilt. She sets it behind her on the ottoman. "I know we've trained some, but I prefer a sword."

"It will protect you if you need it. Don't hesitate to use it."

"I won't."

He holds her tight as she trembles in his arms. "I'm sorry he has you feeling like this."

"I hate being so afraid of him."

"You do a great job being brave in front of him, just remember that. You'll have to control this, because I'm sure he will make you dance with him. When he does, you can't let him feel the affect he has on you."

"I know. You're the only thing that calms me down," she admits.

"Then think of me, if you have to," he says, helping her to her feet. He leans down by her ear, taking her hand, and slow dancing around the ottoman. "If he takes you in his arms, imagine this. Imagine you're dancing with me. Stay focused in the moment, of course, but convince your body you're with me."

"I'll try. Thank you."

They go into the main chamber. Ana and Evren study while Kara and Rafe talk in the corner. Kara sits up.

"Wait, am I allowed to attend?"

"Yes, of course! How could I forget that? She gave you the title of Sage, making you a member of court. She won't be alone in there."

Kara runs over to tell Ana the good news. She flies from her chair into Kara's arms, overrun with joy.

Rafe looks at the clock. *Three hours until the ball. What is Kane planning? Why did he exclude the guardians? Every decision he makes has a purpose.*

When they have dinner brought in, Rafe makes sure Ana eats. "You'll need your strength to be around him."

Knowing he's right, she reluctantly eats. She gets up at six and showers, then follows Evren into the closet. Evren helps her into her gown and makes sure every detail is perfect, each accessory in place. Ana has chosen a silver mask to accent the gown, and white wings to contrast. She holds her breath as she walks out of the closet, anxious to see Rafe's reaction.

Kara is standing near the chaise in a burgundy gown and black mask, with a sword sheathed at her hip. Ana looks around.

"He's not here," Kara says. "He went to speak with Declan to discuss security for tonight."

Ana's heart sinks. "I see. Thank you."

At six-thirty, there's a knock at the door. Evren opens it, stepping back at the sight of Kane. He is dressed in black slacks with a black uniform jacket. His shoulders are adorned with blue and gold velvet pads with tassels. His face is half covered with a silver and black wolf mask.

"Archduke, please come in," she says, hiding her disdain.

He steps inside. "Slave," he says. He turns to Ana. "Per tradition, I am to escort you to the masquerade ball. You look quite lovely, mi'lady."

She walks over, trying to do as Rafe said, and envision him instead. Kane links his arm with hers and leads the way to the ballroom. He examines her outfit.

"The dress is quite ravishing, but the accessories are a bit much," he says with disdain.

A smug smile plays across her lips. "I had hoped that would be your reaction," she responds. "I thought they were appropriate."

His hand grips her arm tighter. "Don't be coy, mi'lady."

She struggles not to let him see he's hurting her. "Apologies, Archduke."

Inside the ballroom, there are white marble columns, and the walls are covered with navy blue tapestries, each adorned with silver stars. The ceiling is painted with silver stars and gold suns. Ana is taken back by the beauty of it.

"Like it?"

"Yes, it's stunning," she exclaims.

He smiles at her. "Good." The kitchen staff set up the buffet while a few guests meander about. Kane takes Ana to the entrance. "We stand here to welcome our guests. Once everyone has arrived, we will join in the festivities. It's long and boring, I apologize. It is our duty."

"I understand. Thank you for explaining."

She smiles and greets members of court, admiring the various costumes. A countess bows, dressed in royal blue with a blue feathered mask, a raven face over the bridge of her nose. Ana wonders what Rafe would think of it. She smiles at Kane, surprising him.

More guests arrive, some in gowns and masks while others are in more expressive costumes, ones that almost make her laugh. She ignores Kane's arm around her waist as she concentrates on the moment, telling herself she is safe while they are not alone. Once they finish greeting, he takes her hand and leads her to the dance floor. She pulls back.

"No, thank you," she tries.

He steps up, his lips on her ear. "I have Evren. She's quite safe, for now. As long as you do everything tonight I tell you to."

She swallows hard. "Yes, Archduke."

He holds her tight as they dance, while she chokes down the vomit threatening to rise in her throat. She thinks of being in Rafe's arms while they danced in the closet.

Kane shakes off the surprise when she puts her head on his shoulder. The song ends, and he takes her to their table. It's a small table for two, sitting on a platform that overlooks the ballroom. As they sit, two plates are brought over.

"Shall I eat off your plate to prove to you it's not poisoned?"

"No, thank you. I know you wouldn't risk ruining your big night."

He smiles at her. "You're starting to get me. I like that."

She eats, wishing more than anything she were back in her quarters. *All my life, I've longed to be at a masquerade. Reading about them, watching them in musicals, only to long to be away from here now. The irony.* She forces herself to smile and stay polite. A royal guard walks up, needing to see Kane in private.

"Excuse me, mi'lady. I'll only be a moment."

"Of course, Archduke."

As soon as he's gone, she gets up and walks around the ballroom. She watches people dancing, laughing when she sees a dragon is dancing with a cat. A few men ask her to dance, but she politely declines. A tall stranger approaches, dressed in black pants, a white shirt, and a red vest with black embroidery. He has a black cape draped over his shoulders, wearing a simple black mask on his face. His cravat is adorned with a black gemstone. He holds out his hand.

"Mi'lady, may I have this dance?" he asks quietly.

"No, I—"

"Please, mia estrela?"

She takes his hand, leaning up to him. "Rafe?" she asks in disbelief.

"I had to sneak in. They think I'm an ambassador from MoonFrost."

"Oh, I don't think I've ever been happier to see you."

"What's wrong?"

"He has Evren. He told me to be on my best behavior tonight if I want her back, safe and sound."

Rafe tenses up. "I'm sorry," he says, "that he would use her as a pion against you. He is so low." He takes a breath, looking around. "I can't stay long. Kane will have me executed if he catches me here. Declan and I heard some things, and I had to come see you. We need somewhere private to talk."

"Please, dance with me? If only for a minute?"

I would dance with you to every song. Once the music stopped, I would dance with you from sunrise to sunset, to the crescent moon, to the beat of your heart. We would dance to our own music for all eternity. "Yes," is all he can say as her scent overwhelms him and her warmth seeps into his bones.

She relishes being in his arms, knowing she is safe with him. "Thank you."

His fingers brush over her white wings. "I like these. Nice touch." He plays with them.

She smiles at him. "I wore them for you," she admits.

"Really?"

"Yes." She looks over, seeing a set of doors that lead out to an empty balcony. "There," she turns him to see. He leads

334

them over, then leans back against the wall so anyone looking out would only see her.

"We've heard some of his plans. He is not going down without a fight. The transition of power will not go smoothly if he has his way. We are unsure for what, but he has requested an appointment with the chancellor at two o'clock tomorrow—"

"Well, I'm glad I found you. Where have you been?" Kane asks, stepping out onto the balcony.

Ana fans herself with her hand. "I was feeling faint and needed air. This kind ambassador, Stefan, you said?"

"Yes, mi'lady," Rafe answers, sinking down to hide his height while disguising his voice.

"He was kind enough to escort me out here."

"I was just leaving, if you'll pardon me," Rafe says, giving a bow and returning to the ballroom.

Kane steps up beside her, unfazed by Rafe's presence. "We need to discuss tomorrow."

"Please," she says, attempting a smile.

"Your coronation is at ten o'clock. We will have lunch, then be married at two."

"What?" she asks, stepping back in shock. "What are you talking about?"

He smiles at her. "Why else do you think I took your little slave? You will announce our engagement at breakfast tomorrow, or I will snap her neck like I did Brienne. Do you understand?"

"I won't marry you." Fear floods through her, but she knows Evren would never allow Ana to marry him, not even to save herself. She knows how important the kingdom is.

"What?" he asks in surprise. "I honestly thought that's all it would take."

"Then I guess you underestimated me," she says, walking for the door.

"How will you feel when you wake up in the morning to find out Kara murdered her lover in her own quarters?"

She stops in her tracks, her breath trembling as she slowly faces him. "What?"

"That's how it will look. A lover's quarrel gone wrong. Then Kara will be arrested and executed for her death. Be reasonable, Your Highness. Together, we would be good for this kingdom. Join me."

Do I sacrifice my two best friends or the fate of the entire kingdom? I know they would tell me to choose the kingdom. Even so, how could I live with myself? How do I decide? "What guarantees do I have that after we're married, you wouldn't kill them and me as well?"

"None," he answers. "You know I don't give those."

She fights back the tears. "Then my answer stands."

He reaches for her, and she runs inside the ballroom, looking for Rafe or Kara. When she can't find them, she flees from the ballroom and leaves the palace. She collapses at the fountain in the courtyard, crying into her hands, terrified of what will happen to her friends.

Rafe walks forward to comfort her when a hand clamps over his mouth. As he's dragged backwards, he can only watch in horror as Ana is picked up and carried away, kicking and screaming. He struggles and fights to get free to no avail. He gasps at the sharp pain in his neck and loses consciousness.

When Ana and Rafe come to, they're tied up in separate corners of a room she doesn't recognize. He and Evren are tied up together with magical bindings, attached to each other's chain that runs up to a ring on the wall. Rafe looks down, seeing he is only in pants and socks. Ana is still fully dressed, pulling desperately on her restraints.

Kane walks in with his guard behind him. The guard approaches Ana. "Don't touch me," she spits at him. He shakes his head while freeing her of the binds. She runs for Rafe when the guard grips her arms, holding her in place.

"Rafe!" she cries out, trying to break free. She whimpers when his grip only tightens. Gathering her courage, she looks at Kane. "What are you doing?" she demands.

He saunters over, a smirk on his face. "I see the rumors are true, that you... care for your guardian. Good. Here's the deal, Princess. Tomorrow, you will be crowned, then we will marry after." He walks over to Rafe, running a blade along his face. "Or I kill them both. It's your choice."

"Don't do it!" Rafe cries out.

"Don't let him win," Evren says, her tone calm and steady.

Kane nods, and the guard gags them both. He turns back to Ana. "That's better. Now, what is your choice? Will you marry me?"

"No," she says, wiping a tear that falls down her cheek. "They would tell you themselves that their lives aren't as important as an entire kingdom, as the realm itself. Sometimes we must put our duty above ourselves."

Rafe tries to smile at her through the gag around his mouth, pride in his eyes. Ana sees it, smiling back. She looks up when Kane approaches her, pulling out his pistol. "That is quite noble in thoughts and words, until you put action to it. Will you feel the same way once her brains have painted the wall behind her? Will you feel that way when his body is slumped over, drained of blood and cold to the touch?"

"Yes," she whispers. "I have to."

He walks over, putting his pistol to Rafe's head. "His life is now in your hands. Say you'll marry me, or I'll pull this trigger."

She looks at Rafe and Evren, unable to bear the thought of losing them. Shame washing over her, she closes her eyes and hangs her head. "I'll marry you," she says quietly.

"What was that? I didn't catch that." He smiles as he cocks the pistol, pointing it again at Rafe's head. Rafe sits still as Evren struggles in her bindings.

"I said I'll marry you!" she cries out.

Rafe looks at Ana in disbelief while Evren hangs her head in despair. Kane stands up, chuckling and walking up to Ana, taking her in his arms and kissing her. "The throne will finally be mine. I've waited so long for this." He walks to Rafe, clamping a hand down on his bare shoulder. "Thank you for returning her to me. I couldn't have done this without you."

Rafe's eyes close in anger for a moment, then he looks at Evren. He sees the worry on her face and the pain in her eyes. She knows what Ana is sacrificing.

"Come, mi'lady. You need your rest now. You have a big day tomorrow."

"Please, let me have a moment with my friends? Just one moment. Is that too much to ask for?"

He thinks it over. "Fine. Consider it a wedding present." He nods to the guard, who then removes their gags. He steps out to give them privacy, but Kane stands in the doorway to keep an eye on them.

Ana walks over and kneels by them. "I am so sorry."

"No, we are."

"We failed you," Rafe says. "We couldn't protect you."

"Please," Evren begs. "Don't do this."

"I have to. I won't lose you. I won't have your deaths on my hands."

"It's okay, mia estrela. Whatever happens is not your fault."

She looks at him, nodding as she gets to her feet. Kane walks up to her. "I would like a wedding present, too."

Fear in her eyes, she meets his gaze. "What do you want?"

He smiles, pulling out her dagger. She didn't even realize it was gone. "Stab Rafe in the shoulder. Prove your loyalty me."

"I can't hurt anyone. Hurt me, not him. Please."

He pulls out his pistol. "Stab him, or I'll shoot her in the head."

"No, please don't ask me to do this!"

He walks towards Evren when Rafe speaks up. "Do it, Ana. It's okay. Save Evren's life."

Shaking, she takes the dagger from Kane. Her entire body is a bundle of nerves as she kneels beside Rafe. "I'm sorry, my love," she whispers in his ear. Her eyes close as she brings the dagger up. With everything she has, she makes herself stab him in the shoulder, grimacing when the blade penetrates his flesh. She drops the blade, falling backwards as tears stream down her face.

"Hmm. How do you not enjoy that? How does that not put a smile on your face?" Kane asks, the pleasure apparent on his.

"Because I'm not a monster!" she screams at him.

"Oh, darling. We are all monsters. Some of us are just prettier than others."

"You truly delight in death and pain, don't you?"

"Of course. It's more fun than anything I've ever done." He nods to a guard. "Tend to his wound. Can't have him dying before tomorrow, can we?" Before it's too late, Ana brings her hand up and places it on Rafe's arm. He tries pulling away, knowing what she is doing. He's in the corner with nowhere to go. She concentrates as much as she can. Kane walks over and drags her to her feet.

"Hmm, maybe we should give Rafe a sneak peek of the honeymoon. Gag them," He commands the guard, who gags Rafe and Evren again before he cleans Rafe's wound. The guard watches it heal, but he says nothing. Kane pins Ana to the wall, smiling at Rafe. One hand holds her wrists above her head as his other caresses down her neck and chest. "So soft." He leans forward, kissing her neck. He goes lower, kissing the apex of her chest and pressing into her with everything he has.

Rafe pulls against the bindings as hot, angry tears pour out. He swears under the gag, struggling to break free.

Kane steps back, taking a breath. "You are exquisite, my dear. I cannot wait to taste every inch of you. Who says I will wait until tomorrow night?"

She spits at him then cries out when he slaps her. He grips her neck. "Please," she tries.

"Do you really think you can claim the throne and bring peace to the quadrants?" He laughs when she nods. "You still haven't figured it out, have you? All those swords, the armor, the supplies being used by each and every quadrant? Everything is made in my factories. I'm making a killing." He laughs at his own bad joke. "War means gold, Your Highness."

"No," she sputters. "It's more than that. War is separation of families as husbands, wives, fathers, daughters leave their homes, saying goodbye to the only life they've known to fight for the throne, to protect the kingdom. It's bravery, sacrifice, loyalty, and trying to do the right thing. It's honorable and cruel and scary. You wouldn't know any of these things! You are incapable of feeling anything but hatred and greed."

"That was quite a speech." Yawning, he grabs her arm. "Shall we go?"

She looks at Rafe one last time as Kane drags her out.

At the palace, he places her in her quarters and posts a royal guard in the hallway.

"As badly as I want to, I won't hurt you tonight because I need you looking your best for tomorrow. What a beautiful bride you will be. And tomorrow night? Hmm. The pleasure will be all mine." He caresses her cheek. "I need one more taste."

He lays her on the chaise, pinning her down with his body as he kisses her. She lies still, unable to move or think. He pulls back, looking at her longingly.

"Please, don't," she begs.

He moans and kisses her, his fingers tangling themselves in her hair as his other hand caresses along her thigh. Taking his time with her, he forces her mouth open with his tongue. When she gags in response, he slaps her then continues to caress her.

Smiling, he stands up and looks down at her. "Until the morning, darling."

The second the door closes behind him, she runs to the washroom to throw up. She showers and scrubs herself until she is red. Slipping into a robe, she curls up on the chaise, covers herself with the blanket that smells like Rafe, and cries herself to sleep.

She wakes up to Kara screaming at the guard to let her in. "I have every right to be here!" she demands.

He looks at Ana, who is on her feet. "Let her in," Ana commands.

"Yes, mi'lady." He leaves the room, shutting the door behind him.

"What is going on? Where is everyone?" She stops, looking Ana up and down. "What happened to you?"

She wants to fall into Kara's arms and tell her what Kane did, but she pushes it down, knowing she has to in order to save Rafe and Evren. Gesturing Kara to join her, she sits on the chaise. She tells Kara what happened after she left the ballroom, sparing her the disgusting details.

"You know how I feel about Evren, but they're right. You can't do this."

"I don't have a choice. He threatened you three because he knows I care for you. If you weren't here, he would line up innocent people, shooting each one in the head until I agreed. You know that's the truth."

"You're right. You don't have a choice. He is relentless in his pursuit for the throne. Can you tell me where they're being held?"

"It's too dangerous. There are royal guards everywhere. You will only get yourself killed. I won't let you risk it."

"Ana, please."

"No."

"At least let me tell Declan what is going on."

"No one can know. The only reason I told you, is so you aren't surprised at breakfast when I announce my engagement to Kane. Not because I don't trust you but to protect you."

"I understand. Now, let's get you dressed."

"I need another shower," Ana says, hanging her head.

Kara debates asking, but she decides to let it go. "All right. Grab a shower while I get you clothes."

"Thank you, Kara."

She strips down, crying under the shower head as she washes herself vigorously all over again. She dries off as Kara walks in.

"Are you all right?" Kara asks, seeing Ana has practically scrubbed herself red.

"Just worried about today."

She changes into the pale pink gown with silver shoes and circlet that Kara had brought in.

"Are you ready to go for breakfast?"

"No, but I don't have a choice."

Kara gently grips her arm. "How are you holding up?"

"I'm all right now. I understand what must be done."

They enter the dining hall, and Kane gestures her over to his table at the head of the room. She nods, slowly approaching him. "Shall I make the announcement, or will you?" he asks.

"I would appreciate if you would announce it."

"Of course."

He smiles as he stands and gets everyone's attention, quieting them down. "Today is a glorious day for our kingdom. We have the coronation of our lost princess, who has been returned to us. This will hopefully bring about peace throughout the land." He pauses for applause and cheers. "Then we have a wedding." The room is silent. "I asked Princess Maeriana for her hand in marriage last night at the ball. She has graciously accepted. We shall be married this afternoon." More applause and cheers. He sits beside her. "Smile, mi'lady. Think of your friends."

She smiles and gives a polite wave, then she finishes her meal. "Kara will take me to my quarters, so I may get ready for my coronation. With your permission."

"Of course."

She stands up and walks to Kara. They return to her quarters in silence, as Ana tries to calm her racing heart. In the closet, Kara sits her on the ottoman while she picks up the garment bag containing her coronation gown and lifting it out. Ana gasps at the sight. "Evren was right. It truly is the most beautiful gown I've ever seen." She runs her fingers over the royal blue bodice, adorned with silver stars. The sleeves have slits and are cinched up, so they billow down her arms. Kara helps her into her gown and puts her hair into braids that knot at the nape of her neck.

"You look breathtaking."

"Thank you, Kara."

She goes to her dresser and pulls her cross necklace out of a drawer. It rests, heavy but comforting, on her neck, and she goes to the mirror. The sight before her is hard to believe. She looks at Kara, who has tears in her eyes.

"Ana, you will be such a beautiful queen."

Kara escorts Ana to the throne room, with a royal guard following behind. Ana keeps her head high as they pass people who stop and bow. Once at the throne room, the guards open the doors for her. Kara escorts her in and up the stairs, as is tradition for a member of the court to do, before going to her seat. Ana walks up to Chancellor Corbin, who is holding the coronation crown on a velvet pillow. The crown is platinum and adorned with sapphires and diamonds.

"Per a tradition," he starts, addressing the crowd, "that goes back throughout the millennia, it is with great pleasure that I will bestow the crown upon the rightful heir to the throne. Princess Maeriana, do you swear to work in the best interests of the kingdom, to protect its people at any cost, to never forsake them nor put yourself above them?"

"I do," she replies. *Liar,* the voice in her head calls her. *Coward.*

"With this crown, you hereby retain the lawful and rightful title of Queen." He steps up, lifting the crown, and placing it on her head. He turns to the crowd. "I present Her Majesty, Queen Maeriana of the Maristellar Kingdom and Sea-Stellar Realm."

Every person in the room kneels before her. She nods, and they stand up. The chancellor takes a step back, gesturing for her to sit on the throne. Her heart is about to explode in her chest. She takes a breath, walks forward, and sits on the throne, thinking of Rafe clearing his throat and correcting her. She smiles at the crowd, pushing the memory away as her eyes begin to water.

"I want to thank each and every one of you for coming today. You were able to bear witness to an event this kingdom has been long overdue for."

While watching the crowd shuffle out, Ana wonders if Rafe and Evren are all right. Imagining the horrible things Kane could be doing, she clenches her hands and pushes the thoughts away. Kara approaches the throne, kneeling before Ana. "Your Majesty."

"Please, Sage. Rise."

She stands up. "You need lunch, then preparation for your wedding. I'm so sorry. I hate to even bring it up, but we are running out of time."

She nods. "Of course. Thank you, Kara."

They head out to the hall when Declan approaches. "Your Majesty," he says, bowing. He looks around. "Where is your guardian?"

She looks at him, shaking her head. Kara tells him to come with them, and they all return to Ana's quarters, where Kara and Ana tell him everything, including their theory that Kane will kill anyone who stands between him and the throne. Declan nods in understanding.

"Please, tell me where they are. I will not go off on a rescue mission, not until you have said your vows. I swear."

Ana walks over to her desk and writes the information down. She hands it to Declan. "Please, not a moment sooner. He will not hesitate to have them killed."

"I promise."

He takes the paper and leaves. Kara walks to her. "I've arranged a small lunch. I know you'll argue with me, but you need to eat."

"Thank you." She changes into a pale blue gown and circlet. They discuss the upcoming wedding. "Not how I pictured my big day," Ana says, sadness in her voice. "I never wanted to get married. At least, not until I met Rafe."

"Did you imagine it with him?"

She lets out a quiet laugh. "Yes, I did. I walk down the aisle in a beautiful white gown, seeing him in his black tux, then he takes my hands as we say our vows." She looks away, wiping her tears. "It'll never happen. Fate is cruel, and she is set against us. Though I don't know why."

"Ana—"

"I have to get ready."

Kara takes her hand, leading her into the closet, and sitting her on the ottoman while she opens a small wardrobe, full of fancy gowns. She finds a long sleeve white gown with a cinched bodice, and a tulle skirt dotted with silver stars. She holds it up for Ana to see, who smiles at the beauty of it before breaking into tears.

She takes a breath and calms herself. "I can't do that. He will punish them if I do." She wipes her tears away.

Kara nods and helps gets her dressed. Ana removes her cross, putting it in the small drawer and instead pulls out a crystal heart pendant, with a halo of diamonds around the heart. Kara puts it on her, along with a diamond and platinum crown.

"Oh, Ana. You look beautiful."

Kara takes her hand, leading her to the mirror. "I look like something out of a fantasy book," Ana says, with awe in her voice.

Kara squeezes her hand. "I never thought we would be here like this. You look so much like your mother."

Ana bites back the tears. "Shall we?"

———— ✦ ————

Kara escorts her to the Cathedral of Penstrella, goddess of the moon and sea. Kara leads her to the doors, which are opened by the guards as Ana approaches. Kara squeezes her hand and wishes her luck.

Ana swallows down all of her fear, her hate, her love, and focuses on each step. She walks down the aisle and arrives at the archduke, who smiles at how magnificently beautiful she is. Ana looks at Corbin, who gives her a small smile before starting the ceremony.

Kara is watching from the hallway when Declan runs up to her. He pulls her away from the royal guards for privacy and hands her an intelligence report. She skims through it, then looks at him with shock on her face.

"You can't be serious!"

"I've looked into it myself. I am very serious. Want to help me put a stop to it?"

She smiles at him. "I thought you'd never ask."

Outside, Declan looks at Kara and holds out his hand. She looks at him, begrudgingly nodding. He takes her in his arms, his great black wings pulling them to the sky. Kara keeps her eyes closed for the flight, only opening them when they land on a balcony at the citadel. He breaks the window and pulls her in with him.

They unsheathe their swords when Kane's guards approach. "Halt!" one calls out.

"The queen's assigned guardian and her handmaid are here. Release them at once!" Declan commands.

"We don't know what—"

Kara screams, charging forward. The guard steps back in shock before equipping his sword, but Kara kills him quickly. She and Declan fight through the guards, when Declan manages to injure one. Getting the information they need, they rush to where Rafe and Evren are being held. Rafe's eyes go wide at the sight of them.

"Kara, what are you doing here?"

"Rescuing you," she answers, looking him up and down. She cringes at the sight of dried blood and bruises that haven't healed. "You're hurt!"

"I'm fine," he tries.

"Kane tortured him all night," Evren explains.

"Did he hurt you?" Kara asks, kneeling before Evren. She caresses her face.

"No, I'm okay."

"You can't save us. He'll kill her," Rafe says with a hitch in his breath.

"That's the point."

"What are you talking about?" Rafe asks.

Declan steps forward. "There is an assassin somewhere in the cathedral. As soon as they've said their vows, and Kane is crowned, the assassin will kill Her Majesty. He doesn't care about her; he only wants the throne."

"We have to stop him!" Rafe cries out.

Kara rolls her eyes, freeing Evren. "Why do you think we're here?"

Declan gets Rafe free of his bindings, then Rafe quickly dresses. They go to the balcony they had landed on, Declan carrying Kara as Rafe carries Evren back to the palace. They are running out of time, so they land in one of the battlements near the cathedral. Declan and Rafe rush to the rafters to look for the assassin. Kara goes inside the cathedral, desperate to stop Ana before she says her vows. At the thought of it, a chill runs down Kara's spine, forcing her to move faster.

Rafe sees the assassin, his crossbow perched on his arm, and quietly makes his way behind the hooded figure. He lunges at the assassin, who sees him at the last second. As Rafe tries to grab the crossbow away, the bolt is released. Flying through the air, it pierces through Ana's back, exiting through her abdomen, and lodging into a wood pillar several feet away. The force of the impact knocks Ana to the floor, with blood pooling around her white gown. Kara rushes up to the altar, praying she isn't dead. Panic ensues as the royal guards escort Kane to safety.

Looking down, Rafe wants nothing more than to be at Ana's side but knows he must deal with the assassin first. He gets him in bindings, going through his pockets. When he finds the order from Kane, containing his signature and personal wax seal, he sighs in relief, knowing this will be more than enough to finally have him arrested. He slips the evidence into his pocket, gripping the would-be assassin even tighter.

"Even if my bolt only grazed her, she's dead," the assassin snarls at him. "We've won."

Declan runs over. "I've got him. See to Her Majesty."

Rafe steps up to the balcony, extending his wings. Kara watches in awe as he steps off and flies down, landing beside them.

"How bad is it?"

"It went straight through her side, in and out. That's probably good. She's losing a lot of blood, though."

He is kneeling beside her, reaching for her arm when Kara grabs his wrist. "What are you doing?" he demands.

"You can't! You are in no shape. Let's get her to the Medical Center. Besides, we want this documented for evidence, right?"

"Kara—"

"We don't have time! We need to get her there."

He nods, removing his jacket. He wraps Ana in it, then picks her up and starts running to the Medical Center. Kara follows him closely, her sword drawn as she keeps an eye out in case Kane has other plans.

They burst into the Medical Center. "The queen needs help!" Rafe calls out. The room erupts with medical personnel. She's put on a gurney and rushed back. A few minutes later, Winslow walks out.

"What is going on?" he asks.

"Ana was hurt," Kara explains. "They took her already."

He looks at Rafe. "You need attention, too. Come on."

"I'll get you clean clothes," Kara offers, running out.

Winslow takes him into an exam room. Rafe refuses a gown but removes his jacket and shirt. Winslow runs a towel under the tap and hands it to Rafe. "Tortured, were you?"

"Yes," Rafe answers, cleaning up the caked-on blood.

"Kane?"

"How did you know?"

"I've seen his work and heard the stories. You aren't the first I've treated, but I truly hope you are the last."

"Shit," Rafe says, reaching into his pocket. He gets out the evidence he had collected from the assassin. Winslow gets him a small gossamer bag, and Rafe drops everything inside. "Thanks."

A nurse walks in with the change of clothes Kara had gotten. He changes in the washroom then steps out. Winslow looks at him.

"Your bruises are finally healing. I'm not a guardian, but I know what it means that it took so long. He nearly killed you. You need to rest. Do not overdo it any more than you already have. Your body is worn down and needs to recover."

"I'll try. Thank you." He joins Kara in the hallway, and they go to the waiting room. "I appreciate you getting me clothes."

"Of course."

They sit and wait for news, staring at the clock and praying Ana is all right. When the surgeon walks out, Kara stands and helps Rafe do the same.

"It was a clean shot. She lost a lot of blood, but we gave her a transfusion after we stitched her up. Barring any infections, she should make a full recovery. She needs rest, so we'll probably keep her overnight before moving her to her quarters."

"Thank you, Stekkal," Kara says.

"You're welcome." He steps away.

Rafe looks at Kara. "I need to hand the evidence off."

"Only to someone you trust."

"Obviously." He leaves the waiting area as Evren walks in.

"I heard what happened. How is she?"

"She'll be okay. Where were you?"

"With all of the chaos, the royal guards kept everyone away from the cathedral. The crowd took up the hall, and I couldn't get through. What happened to Kane?"

"I'm not sure," Kara says as Rafe walks back in. "Kane?"

He shakes his head. "The guards loyal to him helped him escape. There is an arrest warrant in the works. At least now, he won't be able to set foot in the palace again." He watches as a nurse runs over to Winslow, a silver chart in her hand and panic on her face. He sees Kara watching, too. Winslow and the nurse leave quickly together. "I wonder what that's all about?"

"I don't know."

"I need to see her, to heal her."

"Rafe, I heard what Winslow said to you." When he gives her a look of determination, she shakes her head. "You need to rest now. I will have Declan drag you away if need be."

He smiles at her. "Anyone ever tell you what a pain in the ass you can be?"

She laughs. "Nope, never."

"Bullshit."

Chapter 17

A half hour later, Winslow walks out. "You can see her now."

Kara and Rafe exchange a glance when they see how shaken up Winslow is. They follow him to Ana's room. Rafe walks over and studies Ana's face. Her skin is pallid, her lips blue, as if there is hardly any life left in her. Rafe shakes his head and reaches for her.

Kara grabs his arm, leading him to the chair in the corner. "Sit and rest."

"Yes, Sage."

She sticks her tongue out at him before taking Ana's hand. Ana groans softly, her eyes fluttering open. "Hmm. What happened?" She moves slightly, wincing. "Why does everything hurt?"

"Mi'lady, you were injured."

"Am I married?" she asks, sitting up. She regrets it as pain shoots down her side and back. She clenches the blanket, falling back against the pillow. Kara pushes the button to help her sit up.

"No," Kara says. "We stopped it."

She gasps softly. "Rafe and Evren—"

"They're right here, perfectly safe."

"Oh, I was so worried about you both."

"We're okay," Rafe assures her.

"How was I hurt?"

"What do you remember?" Kara asks.

"We were almost to our vows. I could literally feel the excitement coming off Kane. He couldn't stop smiling at me. Like, creepy smiling. I knew something was wrong. Then my body went numb, and I hit the floor."

"You were hit with a crossbow bolt. It went in and out, a clean shot. The doctor said you need to take it easy while you heal."

Ana looks at Rafe then back at Kara. "What's wrong with him?"

"What do you mean?" Kara asks. Ana gives her a look. Kara glances at Rafe, who nods his head. "He was tortured all night by Kane. He doesn't have the strength to heal you."

"I am so sorry," she says to him.

"Mi'lady," Rafe says, jumping to his feet, "I should be saying that to you."

"Sit and rest, that's an order."

He returns to his chair. "I would say the same for you."

She smiles at him. "Not even queen for one day, and my guardian is giving me orders. The nerve." Her smile grows when he laughs. "Thank you for saving me from Kane. I knew he was going to kill me, but I figured it would be tonight when it was just the two of us." She looks away, biting back tears. Kara walks over with a towel and wipes her tears. "Thank you."

Winslow walks in with a silver chart in hand. "Mi'lady, may I have a moment of your time?"

"Of course."

"I'm sorry. It's… delicate. Could I speak to you in private?"

"Yes, of course. Would you three step out a moment?"

Rafe, Evren, and Kara give them the room. Winslow sighs and approaches her, solemn. "I'm sorry to have to be the one to tell you this. We noticed your vitals were declining even after we'd repaired your wound, so we ran some bloodwork. The assassin used a poisoned bolt. He used Rose's Kiss. There is no treatment or cure. We've pumped medicine into your IV to help clean your blood, but it's only bought you a little time. You have maybe a few hours, at most. I'm so terribly sorry. I didn't know if you wanted me to tell your friends?"

"No, I will. Once we get back to my quarters."

"You shouldn't be moved."

"I want to die there, surrounded by my friends. Please?"

Biting back his emotions, he swallows hard. "We will make arrangements to get you there."

"Thank you for everything you've done."

"I failed you."

"None of you have failed me. You've done everything right, kept our secrets, and earned my trust. I count you among my friends, Winslow. Thank you."

He bows, "Your Majesty." As he's leaving the room, he wipes his eyes.

Ana lies back down, wondering how she will tell them. She watches them walk in, Kara and Evren holding hands, Rafe laughing at something Kara said. She takes a deep breath, wiping away the tears threatening to fall. Kara walks over to her.

"What's wrong?"

"Not here. We'll discuss it in my quarters."

Winslow comes in with a wheelchair. Ana shakes her head. "Majesty, this is the only way you'll get to your quarters. Unless you want one of us to carry you there."

"Fine," she relents.

Kara gets her into the chair, covering her with a blanket. They use back hallways and the hidden corridor to get her inside her room. Winslow examines her wounds and checks her vitals once she's in bed, then gives her a sad smile as he leaves.

Rafe and Evren sit at the table, discussing the day's events while Kara holds Ana's hand. "You're so pale, mi'lady. Are you all right?"

"Will you get the others? I need to tell you something." Kara stands up, gesturing Evren and Rafe to join them. Ana looks at Rafe before staring at her hands, clenching the blanket tight. "My wounds from the crossbow would heal, with time. But…" she hesitates. "The assassin tipped the bolt with poison. He used Rose's Kiss."

"No!" Kara cries out. "That can't be!"

"I'm not familiar with that one," Rafe admits, panic rising in his chest at Kara's outburst.

"It's forbidden to even speak of because it's the most lethal of all poisons. It's extremely rare."

"What does this mean?" Evren asks.

"I don't have much time. The poison is working its way through my blood. I may have a few hours at most."

Rafe pulls the blanket down and opens her gown. The black venom is branching out from the center of her wound and webbing through her veins. He covers her back up, looking at Kara and Evren.

"Guard the door!" he commands.

As they run over, he picks up Ana. With her protesting the whole time, he carries her into the closet, lays her on the ottoman, then runs over to shut the door. As he's returning to her, he strips out of his jacket and shirt. He looks down, seeing she is in a short sleeve gown. He lies down on the ottoman with her.

"Rafe, what are you doing?"

"I'm taking the poison."

"What? No! You need to heal."

"I won't lose you."

"Rafe—"

"I love you, Ana. I always have. I know I don't deserve you, because I'm a coward who lied and hid, who broke your heart. I said I was protecting both of us, but I regret the time we lost because I was too afraid. I shouldn't even be saying it now, but I don't care. You have to know the truth. I love you. I've always loved you."

"I love you, too," she says softly. She watches his face, as he concentrates on taking the poison from her. "You can't do this though."

"I have to."

"I ord—" her words die in her throat as his lips land on hers. His grip on her loosens as he grows weaker from the poison flowing into him. She pulls back, watching him lose his color. "You can't do this!" she cries.

"I'm a guardian. We are immune to poison," he says as the venom is taking him over.

"You're too weak!"

"I am strong enough to save you. I have to do this for you. After everything I have done to you, this is the least I can do."

"Rafe—"

"Do me a favor, Ana?"

"Anything."

"You must forgive yourself."

"What?" she asks, looking down. She cradles his head in her arms. He's trembling, and the last of his color is fading. "You lied to me! The poison is killing you!"

"I'm sorry, mia estrela. I had to save you." He caresses along her cheek. She takes his hand, kissing his palm and crying out when he goes limp.

"You can't leave me!"

"I love you. Rule over this kingdom with love and compassion. Show them what a leader truly looks like."

Kara runs in. "What's happen—" she sees what Rafe is doing.

"I love you, Ana," he says, dying in her arms.

"No!" she cries out, clutching him to her. She screams and struggles when Kara tries to pull her away from him. "You can't leave me! You can't!" She weeps over him, sobbing violently. Kara grabs her arm again, trying to pull her away.

"You can't do anything for him."

"I have to try!" she cries out, as Kara yanks her away.

"You can't heal him. Doing so may kill you. I won't lose both of you! Not today. I can't."

She pulls away from Kara, falling over Rafe. "I don't care. I have to be with him. He loves me, Kara. He loves me!"

Kara walks to him and grips his wrist to search for a pulse. "Ana, he's gone." Her body goes still at Kara's words. Kara gingerly picks her up, holding her to her chest as she backs away from his body. Ana clings to her as she weeps again.

Evren walks in, bringing her hand to her mouth in shock at the sight before her. "No," she says quietly.

Ana collects herself, stepping away from Kara. She sits on the edge of the ottoman, looking at Rafe. "He looks so peaceful," she says, brushing his hair from his face.

"Ana, we need to get Declan. We need to tell him what happened. He needs to know that Rafe is… what Rafe did."

"Not yet. Please, not yet? I'm not ready to say goodbye. Don't make me," she begs.

"We'll go when you're ready."

Kara and Evren hold each other while Ana stares at Rafe. *Please, God, please don't take him. I will give anything, do anything. He is my soulmate; I know this now. Please, bring him back. I can't lose him.* She wipes her tears as they fall.

Rafe's hand twitches. She jumps to her feet, and a grunt escapes his lips. He slowly sits up.

"Rafe," she cries out, jumping onto the ottoman and pulling him into her arms. "Are you really here?"

"Hmm, what happened?"

"What happened was we thought we lost you," Kara answers. "You drew the poison out, went cold, and had no pulse."

"I'm okay now," he says, looking at Ana. He leans up and kisses her softly. She gets to her knees, pulling him tighter into her arms and kissing him back. Kara and Evren give them privacy.

"I thought I had lost you."

"I could say the same, watching you on the ground, laying in a pool of your own blood. I thought you were dead."

She kisses him again. "I'm still here."

"Me, too."

"Did you mean it? You weren't just saying you love me because you were dying? You really love me?"

"With everything I am. I love you so much."

"I love you, too. Rafe."

"This doesn't change anything. We can't be together. It's still forbidden."

She pulls back, tears in her eyes. "What do you mean? I've lost you too much, already. I won't lose you again."

"If we're caught—" he takes a breath. "To hell with it. I've hidden from you long enough. Never again." He pulls her to him, kissing her as if he hasn't seen her in a thousand years. She wraps her arms around his neck, getting lost in his lips, his tongue exploring her mouth. She breathes in relief, finally home. He pulls back. "Ana, will this be enough for you? Stealing away moments in the closet together, never being able to show our affection in public?"

"Even if I could only have five minutes a day with you, having you in my arms and kissing you, it would still be more than enough."

He kisses her again. "I'm sorry. I'm still recovering. I need more sleep."

"So do I."

They lie down together on the ottoman. Kara walks in, covering them with the blanket. "Both of you, get some rest. We'll stand guard."

"Thank you," Ana says.

Kara turns to leave and sees Rafe grab Ana, taking her into his arms as they succumb to the exhaustion from healing. She turns on the small floor lamp on, so they aren't completely in the dark. She smiles and turns the overhead light off before she shuts the door.

Ana wakes up in Rafe's arms. She snuggles into his chest, holding him as tightly as she can and listening to his heartbeat. He opens his eyes when she plants a gentle kiss on his lips.

"Hello, love," she says.

"Hello, mia estrela. How do you feel?"

"Better. I think we healed each other."

"That would explain why I am so drained," he says, yawning.

"I am, too."

"Let's just lay here for now. If we get up, we'll have to deal with everything that's happened today. Or yesterday? I'm not even sure what time it is or if it's the same day," he admits.

"I don't either. Let's get more sleep."

"Good idea."

When Ana wakes again, she walks over and picks out a blue gown with silver shoes. She gets her cross out of the drawer and puts it on. Rafe stands up and dresses.

She walks out first, making sure there are no royal guards or anyone else in her quarters then gestures for him to come out. He walks over and sits on the chaise while she knocks on Evren's door. Evren and Kara walk in.

"How do you both feel?" Kara asks.

"Better," Rafe says.

"Tired," Ana responds.

Kara looks at her. "You have to be careful."

"Kara, we've already discussed it. During the day, I will do my duties and act in accordance. At night, in the privacy of my room, we can be together."

"I worry for the both of you. This will be dangerous."

Rafe stands up and walks to Kara. "As if we both haven't nearly been killed already?"

"Point taken."

"When do I begin?" Ana asks.

"I spoke with Chancellor Corbin. We agree that, while you're healing from your wound, you should stay in here a few days."

"If he only knew," she says with a laugh. "That's okay. With everything that happened, I wasn't really wanting to rush into anything."

"Stay, recover, get better. Physically and mentally."

"What day is it?" Rafe asks.

"Really?"

"Yes, Kara. We were both wiped out."

"Oh, it's Saturday."

"We slept all day and night."

"You needed it. You both nearly died."

"I'll get lunch brought in." Evren leaves.

"I don't suppose there's any word on the archduke?"

Kara turns to Ana. "He's made an alliance with one of the quadrants. They took him in, in exchange for information."

"I wish the assassin had taken him out, instead."

"Don't we all?"

Rafe starts for the door but sways and has to catch himself. "I need to see Declan."

Kara walks over, putting her hand on his arm, and sitting him on the chaise. "You are in no shape to go anywhere. Either of you."

"We need to talk about the royal guard. How will we know who is loyal to her, and who is still loyal to Kane?"

"He's already dealing with that. I met with him, the chancellor, and some advisors last night, while you were both catching up on your beauty sleep. We are taking care of it."

"Thank you, Kara. What would I do without you?" Ana asks.

"How are the other quadrants reacting, since we have a queen now? Any chance of peace?" Rafe asks.

"No. They see her being nearly killed as a sign of weakness. If anything, the fighting has intensified. Kane is getting exactly what he wanted."

The food is brought in then, and Rafe is happy to see Ana eat every bite without prompting. Kara catches it, too. Ana stands up to go to the washroom but has to stop and lean against the wall for support. Rafe starts to stand, but Kara pushes him back down as she makes her way to Ana. She puts her arm around Ana's waist and leads her inside.

"I'm going to take a shower. Would you bring me a nightgown to slip into? I feel like I need more sleep."

"Of course," Kara says.

Ana cleans and changes, then climbs into bed. Rafe sits on the edge. "Do you need more sleep?" she asks. "We could go in the closet."

"No. I'm already much better. Just rest. We'll be here when you wake up."

"Okay." She rolls over and falls asleep.

He joins Kara at the table. "Between her wound and being poisoned, it really took it out of her."

"She'll be okay. She's strong."

There's a knock at the door, and Evren walks over to answer it. She lets Winslow in. He's in shock when he sees Ana asleep.

"How is she still alive?" He looks at Rafe. "You?"

Rafe nods. "Yes."

Winslow thinks for a moment. "I'll alter her file to say it was a lesser poison. There's no other plausible explanation I could give."

"She told me you were on our side. I'm so thankful," Kara says.

He nods and smiles. "She is going to be an incredible queen, I can tell. I can't wait to see what she has in store for our kingdom."

"Yes. Thank you for your help."

"You're welcome." He turns and leaves.

Kara, Rafe, and Evren sit back at the table. Kara looks at Rafe. "So, you told her how you really feel?"

"I couldn't contain it any longer. Not after almost losing her." He smiles at her. "I remember our first talk. Don't worry."

"Good. I mean it just as much now as I did then."

"You don't have to worry about that." He sighs. "What now? She'll heal, then have more responsibility than she'll know how to handle. We'll all have to step up and make sure she's taken care of."

"One of us will be with her, at all times. I won't let her get too overwhelmed, ever again."

"None of us will."

"Rafe?" Ana calls out. He walks over to her. "I'm sorry."

"For what?"

"I forgot you're still recovering, too."

"I told you, I'm much better. What do you need, mi'lady?"

"I'd like to get up and sit at the table. I think I've laid down long enough." He helps her out of bed and walks with her to the table. She sits and looks at Evren. "I would like a sofa brought in here." She points over by the bookshelf. "To go there. Would you please have that arranged?"

"Yes, Majesty."

"I'll go with her."

Kara and Evren step out to fulfill her request. Rafe sits beside Ana. "How are you feeling?" he asks.

"Better. Not as tired."

"But you're still tired?"

"A little. Should I be worried?"

"You lost a lot of blood and were poisoned. I would say no."

"I still can't believe you did that. You gave your life for me."

"You did it first, knowing what Kane would do once you were married."

362

"I couldn't bear the thought of losing you."

He lifts her hand, kissing the back then moving to the palm. "You won't."

She gets up and goes into the closet to pick out clothes. She's going through a drawer when Rafe tilts her head back and kisses her. A moan escapes her lips, and she turns to wrap her arms around him. He leads her over to the ottoman and sits as she wraps her legs around his waist, never breaking the kiss. She brings her arms up around his neck, holding him tight.

He puts his hand on the small of her back, gently pressing in. Her lips part into another moan. He smiles, loving her response. She pulls back, worried. "Kara and Evren aren't here to keep watch."

"All of the doors are locked," he answers.

She brings her lips down, crashing onto his. He lies back on the ottoman, while she stays on top of him. He kisses her, bringing his hands down her gown. He slowly unbuttons it, opening it when she nods, and slides it off. She sits before him, only in undergarments, barely covering her. She looks down, biting her lip as her cheeks flush red.

"You are so beautiful." He leans up and kisses her neck, planting a trail of kisses down her neck and chest. He puts his hand on her side, holding her steady. He rolls to the side, so she is lying beside him as he leans over her, continuing with kisses down her stomach. She brings his head back up to hers so she can kiss him on the mouth while he caresses her waist with his hand.

"Rafe," she says softly. "Wait."

He pulls away. "What's wrong?"

"I'm light-headed."

He helps her sit up, then runs and gets her a glass of water. She slowly sips it down. "Did that help?" he asks.

"Yes. I think I'm still recovering. I'm sorry."

"Don't," he says. "It's okay."

She picks out a gown and shoes. He helps her dress, and she steps up to him, kissing him. "I love you."

"I love you."

Once back in chambers, they are queen and guardian, not lovers or friends. While she sits at her desk and studies, a group of young servants carry in a large, plush sofa, supervised by Kara and Evren. Kara walks over to Ana.

"What made you want that, if you don't mind me asking?"

"I love the library. It's absolutely gorgeous, but I wanted my own little reading space."

"I can understand that. May I ask what you're working on?"

"I have to figure out how to stop the war. Just a little thing, right?"

"Oh, yes. Very simple. Won't take you any time at all. Might I remind you that you are still recovering? You should be resting. Or at the very least, start with something a little easier."

"I can't. I need this war to end."

Kara hears desperation in her voice. "Why do you care so much? I don't mean to sound rude, I'm happy you do. But why now? What's changed?" Ana looks over at Rafe, then back at Kara. "You're afraid he could be called back into battle."

"I won't stop him because I can't show favoritism. I have to end this war."

"We will work on it together," she says, heading for Evren.

"Thank you. I'll also need a fitting for armor and to pick my sword."

Kara freezes, slowly turning back around. "I beg your pardon, mi'lady?"

Ana holds up the book she's reading. "The queen may go into battle."

"That doesn't mean you should!"

"My soldiers have given their blood, their loyalty, their lives, in defense of a queen they haven't even met. Every day, they risk and give everything to protect my throne. I will go into battle with them."

"Over my dead body!" Kara yells.

Rafe and Evren run over. "What is going on?" Rafe demands.

"Do you want to tell them you've lost your mind or should I?"

Ana gets to her feet. "Kara, please—"

Kara turns to Rafe. "She wants to go into battle."

"What?" he asks. "No one should ever want that." His hands clench as his skin grows cold at the thought of her on the battlefield.

"I will not sit in here, like some princess locked in a tower. It is my life. I choose to join my soldiers in battle."

"You don't know what you speak of. It isn't gleaming swords and glory and honor. It's dirty and bloody and damning. Please, don't do it."

She looks at him, then Kara, and sees the fear in her eyes. Without another word, she sits at her desk and continues studying. Kara storms from the room with Evren trailing behind. Rafe thinks on what she said.

"Why do you want to go into battle?"

"I feel like it's my duty. I don't think you brought me across time and space, just to be a pretty face on the throne. I want to defend my kingdom, fighting alongside my soldiers."

"If that is what you choose, I will help you. I will continue to train you. If you don't, there is no shame in that."

"Why would you help me? Of all people, I figured you would be the one most angry, not Kara."

"Because I know what it means to put duty first. I understand the responsibilities, to myself and my squad."

"Thank you."

"You're going to help her?"

They turn and see Kara has walked back in. "Kara—" Ana tries.

"No. Rafe, why? You of all people!"

"She and I are a lot alike. We both believe in fighting for the kingdom, fighting for the people."

Kara looks away. "What if you die out there? What about your people then? You have no heir! The war would rage on. Do you not understand why it's so important for you to stay alive?"

Rafe steps towards her. "Kara—"

"No, Rafe. Not now."

"I do understand, Kara. I also understand how serious this is. We are losing! What's the point of being a queen if I don't have a kingdom?"

"What's a kingdom without it's queen?" Kara shoots back. "You see what has happened here. If you die out there, it would be utter chaos."

"Kara—" Ana starts.

"How many people would die because you wanted to fight beside your soldiers?"

Ana's eyes go wide. "How dare you? I want to fight with them to show them I am as much a part of this realm as they are, to prove my place on the throne. Would you deny me that?"

"No." Kara sighs, looking away. "You're right, mi'lady. Please, forgive me for my anger."

"You were angry because you care. You are forgiven."

"Thank you."

When Ana stands up, she has to grab Rafe's arm. "What's wrong?" he asks, touching her cheek for a moment before realizing his error and pulling his hand away.

"I'm still tired. Will you help me to the chaise? I don't want to lay in bed just yet." He walks her over and helps her sit. "Thank you."

"Now I'm worried about you."

"I'm okay, really. My body went through so much in such a short time."

"Please, keep us updated on how you're feeling. Don't hide anything from us. As you've just said, you've been through a lot."

She smiles at him. "I promise."

Kara walks over and sits beside her. "Do you need to rest tomorrow, or will you be ready to start your new position?"

"I think I'll be ready. No. I know I will be."

Evren leaves to have dinner brought in. Kara turns back to Ana. "I want to train with you, too."

"Kara—"

"Please? I am proficient at hand-to-hand combat, and Evren has been teaching me to use a sword. I could be quite handy on the field."

"Yes, you can train with me."

"Thank you."

Food is brought in. Rafe and Ana discuss her agenda for the next day while they eat. "Breakfast at eight, briefing at ten, lunch at noon, training at two, dinner at five."

"That doesn't sound as bad as I thought it would."

"Your advisors are still taking care of a lot of the daily duties. They know you are still, um, recovering," he says, winking at her.

"Of course," she responds with a smile.

After dinner, Rafe and Ana go into the closet. She changes into a nightgown while he removes his jacket. She walks up to him, putting her arms around his neck. He leans down, planting a soft kiss, then pulling his head back. She looks at him, staring at his lips. Hers part when he brings his head back down, devouring her. She grips him tighter, pulling into the curve of him. He brings his arms around her, lifting her up and onto his chest. She brings her legs around his waist, while he holds her up.

She looks intently into his eyes. "Love?"

"Yes?"

"Will this be enough for you? You asked me that, but I have to know. I want you to be happy, too."

"Being here, with you in my arms, is the only happiness I have ever known."

"That doesn't answer my question, though."

"Yes, it will be enough."

She kisses him again. He sits on the ottoman and holds her in his lap. Planting kisses along his cheek, his chin, his neck, then she kisses his mouth as hard as she can. He traces her lips with his fingertips, staring at her mouth. She looks at him.

"Please, kiss me."

"I'm afraid if I do, I may never stop."

"Do you promise?" she asks. In response, he's consuming her mouth with his. She moans as his hands roam along her stomach and neck. She looks at him.

"I think I'm ready, my love."

He stops. "What?"

"To be with you."

He stands up, gently sitting her on the ottoman and turning away. "We can't."

"What do you mean?"

"If you became pregnant, everyone would know. I would be killed, and you would be punished."

She sucks in her breath. "I didn't think of that." She stands up. "I'll be okay, with not going that far with you. That's not something I've ever really wanted." Rafe looks at her, opening his mouth to ask. "But it's not fair to you. I see what my body does to you."

"There are other ways we can be together," he says.

"It would never be enough for you. You deserve more."

He scoffs at her words. "I don't even deserve you, but you are all I want. Do you not see that?"

"Rafe—"

"No, Ana. We found each other, and we finally have each other. Don't destroy that. Not now, please." He takes her hand and kisses the scar on her wrist. "Maeriana, please."

She nods her head, tears streaming down her cheeks. He gently wipes them away. "I love you, Rafe. Please, don't ever question that."

"I won't." He leans down and kisses her again, tasting the salt from her tears. "I love you, too. You are all I have ever wanted."

He holds her in his arms, giving her the warmth and comfort she has so desperately longed for. Though she doesn't want to, she pulls away. "I need to get some rest. I have a long day tomorrow."

He stands up with her and kisses her before following her out into her room. She goes to the washroom then gets into bed. Rafe tucks her in.

"I hate the thought of you sleeping on that chaise. Are you sure you don't want a bed brought in here?"

"With my wings, that's the most comfortable thing I've slept on." He flashes her a reassuring smile.

"Okay, if you're sure."

"Thank you, though." He starts to lean forward, catching himself and clearing his throat. "Good night, mi'lady," he says, winking at her.

She giggles softly. "Good night, Guardian."

Ana steps into the dining hall, trying not to be self-conscious for her first time coming in since she was crowned queen. Everyone stands in respect. She walks in with Kara, Evren, and Rafe following behind her.

Instead of the table they'd been sitting at, they go up front to the table where Kane used to sit. When Ana takes her seat, everyone sits back down and resumes. The first course is brought out. She's so nervous, she doesn't want to eat. One look from Rafe, though, and she does.

"Your Majesty, may I present Count Bela of the NightFall quadrant," announces the court squire.

She stands as he bows, then she nods. "Count."

"Majesty."

He has sleek gray skin, red eyes, and black hair. She finds herself staring at him, then clears her throat. "How may I help?"

"I would like to join you for dinner tonight."

Thinking of Kane, her heart begins to race. She smiles to hide her fear. "Here, in the dining hall?"

"Of course, Your Majesty."

"That would be fine."

"Thank you." He bows and leaves. She sits back down and catches a look of anger flash across Rafe's face. "What did I do?" she asks.

"Why do you think he wants to dine with you?" Rafe asks.

"I have to keep the peace, here in the palace. I didn't want to be rude."

"Of course. My apologies, mi'lady."

"It's okay. I still have much to learn, apparently. Now I'm embarrassed."

"Actually," Kara speaks up, "it would be good for you to dine with him. His quadrant is the one that allied with Kane. Maybe you could get some information out of him."

"I can try."

In the meeting room, Ana goes up to the desk and begins organizing it. "How in the world did Kane ever find anything on here?" Her dagger falls from between a pile of papers. She gasps and quickly throws it into a drawer before Rafe sees. Walking over to the window to hide her tears, her heart is pounding furiously. They hadn't yet spoken about the night she stabbed him.

Rafe walks up behind her. "Are you okay?"

She nods, refusing to look at him. "Fine," she mumbles.

He grabs her arm and turns her around. "What's wrong?" he asks, wiping her tears.

"I found my dagger on his desk. I can't believe I could forget doing something like that. I'm so sorry I hurt you." She gasps air in and out frantically. Rafe runs over to shut and lock the door, then he returns to her and takes her in his arms.

"You were literally almost killed the next day. You had a very traumatic twenty-four hours, but you did what you had to in order to save Evren. I wasn't angry at you then, and I'm certainly not now. Please, forget it ever happened."

Once calmed down, she wipes her eyes and goes back to rearranging while he opens the door. By the time she's done, there's space for any important reports or intel, a space to sit and work, and anything old or outdated is filed away in a drawer. She looks up as the room begins to fill. The chancellor walks over and bows.

"Mi'lady," he says quietly. "I know this is all still new to you. Would you like me to start the briefing and walk us through? Just until you learn it yourself, of course."

"I would greatly appreciate that."

He smiles at her, then turns to the crowd. He welcomes them, then goes over the agenda. Everyone gives their reports, from supplies, to battle, to the treasury, and the accounts of happenings in the other quadrants. "Lastly," the chancellor says, "it's been brought to my attention that Kane attempted to burn down our armory and factory when he was escaping. Thankfully, he was scared away and only did minimal damage. Everything will be as it was in just a few days."

Ana tries to hide her surprise. Why had no one told her? She looks at Rafe and Kara, wondering if they knew. The chancellor dismisses everyone.

"Thank you for your help today."

"Of course, mi'lady. Is there anything else I could help with?"

"Actually, there is." She looks at Kara and Rafe. "Would you give us some privacy, please?"

Confused, they stand up and go into the hall. Rafe leaves the door open so he can keep an eye on them. He sees Ana pull out a book. She opens it and seems to be asking the chancellor about it, growing upset when he shakes his head. She goes to another page, with the same result. She shuts the book, closing her eyes in exasperation then opens them and turns to him, thanking him for his time. He smiles and leaves. Rafe and Kara go back in.

Ana walks up to them. "Lunch now, right?"

"Are you okay?" Kara asks.

"Fine," she says, smiling. "Let's eat."

Ana does everything but eat. She sends each plate away, finally signaling to stop. She sits there while Rafe and Kara eat and pulls out her book again. She's reading through when she hears Rafe say something. Setting it down, she looks at him.

"What's that?"

"I won't train you if you don't eat. You know that."

"I'm not training tonight."

"What is going on?" Kara asks.

"I have to go to the library next." Rafe and Kara resume eating. Ana stands up when they finish, eager to get to the library, where Rafe and Kara sit in the back, watching her search through tomes.

"Is this still about Evren? Or is it about you?" Kara asks.

"I truly don't know. She won't open up to me about this."

They watch her go to an older section, very carefully handling the papers and books she finds there. She brings them back to her table, gingerly going through them. Shaking her head and muttering, she scribbles notes furiously. Kara decides she's had enough.

She walks over. "What are you working on?"

"Kara, please. Don't interrupt me."

"Your Majesty—"

"Please."

Kara turns and walks back to Rafe, shaking her head. They both look up when Ana jumps to her feet in excitement.

"I knew it!" she cries out. She gathers the books and papers then puts them back on the shelf where she got them from before stuffing her books and notes into her bag. "I'm ready to return to my quarters," she says, approaching them.

"Did you get good news?" Kara asks on the way out.

"I think so. I have to follow up."

"Will you tell us, if it is?"

"No." She practically runs back to her room once her door is in sight. She goes to her desk and pulls out her notebook, then opens a drawer and gets out another book. She flips through the pages until she finds the one she's looking for and compares it to her notes. "Damn it!" She falls down into the chair. "There has to be a way. There just has to."

Kara and Rafe walk over. "Enough, Ana. Tell us what you're working on. We are worried about you," Kara pleads.

"I'm so tired of the looks everyone gives Evren. I know there has to be a way to free her, if I can just figure it out."

"Mi'lady, I'm not worth so much trouble."

Ana hadn't heard Evren come in. She turns to her. "Please, don't take this wrong. It's not just about you. Anyone in this kingdom who is a slave, unless they are a criminal, should be free. I can't believe as well off as this kingdom is, we still use slave labor. I won't stand for it."

"Thank you. No one else has ever spoken to me like that, except your mother."

Ana stands up at her words. "Really? What did she say?"

"She was like you, speaking out against it. I think I know where her journal is. We had been searching for it upon your return. I'll be back."

"Your Majesty," Kara starts, "I'm grateful you've found something to be passionate about. Please, don't let it consume you. Let us help you."

"You're right. I'm sorry." She hugs Kara.

A few minutes later, Evren returns with a book in her hands. "Here, mi'lady."

"Thank you." Ana looks at her mother's journal. She would've given anything to meet her. "I can't believe you both knew my mother."

"I did, too." Rafe says. "I'm a guardian, remember?"

Ana sits down. "I miss her. How can I miss someone I never met?" She opens the journal. They walk away to give her privacy. Her hand trails over the beautiful handwriting in blue ink. She starts to read through it. There are references to what Evren mentioned, entries about wanting to free the slaves. Her mother had even written down some book names, as if working on the same research Ana is undertaking now. A few of the books are ones she's already read, but some are new. Ana writes them down. She comes to the last passage of the journal.

I found out today I am to have a healthy baby girl. For some reason, the name Maeriana popped into my head. In our language, it means "child of the sea." My beloved daughter, Maeriana. I cannot wait to meet you. I cannot wait to hold you in my arms, to tell you how much I love you, to share this beautiful world with you. That is what I want, with all my heart. I will raise up my beautiful princess to be a beacon of hope in the dark times ahead.

Ana sets the journal on the desk, crying into her hands. Rafe picks her up and takes her into the closet, holding her tight and stroking her hair.

"It's okay, mia estrela. I don't know what made you cry, but I'm here."

"My mother was so excited to find out she was pregnant with me. Reading how much she wanted to meet me, it overwhelmed me."

"I can't imagine how you're feeling."

"Just hold me, please." She grips him tighter, as the tears continue to fall. "That's all I need."

"She was so beautiful and so kind. She was the only thing that kept his cruelty in check."

"Rafe, I really don't want to talk about him right now."

"I'm sorry."

He calms her down, and they return to her chamber. She goes to the desk and packs up her books. She looks at the clock.

"I need to start getting ready for dinner." She and Evren go into the closet. She slips on a crimson dress, with gold shoes and crown, trying to push down her worry over dinner.

"Mi'lady, you look amazing in that color," Rafe says when she steps out from the closet.

She smiles at him. "Thank you. I just hope the count likes it." She sees a look of jealousy cross his face. "You know I'm teasing."

"I know."

"Like Kara said, maybe I can work this to our advantage."

"I appreciate you joining me this evening, Your Majesty," Bela says while sitting down.

"The pleasure is mine." The first course is served, and they eat in awkward silence. "I apologize," Ana says, "but I'm not sure if you're aware of the fact that I didn't grow up here. I just returned not too long ago. I'm still learning, so I apologize if I'm rude or ignorant. May I ask about you and your people?"

"Of course, mi'lady. And yes, I had heard about your adventures. To travel to Earth sounds exciting. You will not offend me, I promise."

"Thank you."

"What would you like to know? I'm sure I can guess. You want to know why we are also fighting to attain the throne?"

"That's one of my questions, yes," she admits.

"The MoonFrost quadrant does not like us. They think we are lesser or evil. If they took over, they would wipe us out. We are only fighting for our very survival. If you are able to bring about peace, we will ask for leniency and for help to rebuild, after what they have done to our quadrant."

"Again, I apologize in advance for my ignorance. Are you the capitol leader?" she asks, taking another drink of her wine.

"I am."

"Then why not work towards the peace now? Why not ask for my help? If you allied with us, we could end the war."

"It's not that easy. I can't do it myself. My council would have to approve, and they refuse to do so. They still believe I can take the throne. I assured them that would not happen now, not with a queen upon it. They will not listen to me. They are too power hungry."

"Forgive me, but how do I know that anything you're telling me is true?"

"Because I'm going to give you information on the man who tried to kill you, as a show of my good faith."

"Please, go ahead." She leans in, curious to hear what he has to say.

"Kane came to us, after what he did to you. The council took him in and offered him sanctuary in exchange for his valuable information. I want him gone. He's a vile man. I've heard some rumors of the horrible things he did to you.

Anyone who can do that to royalty is not someone I wish to associate with. Anyway, he is telling my council everything. How many men you have, your supplies, any weaknesses you have. He's told us about your guardians and royal guards."

"Everything you've just said, I can't verify. How do I know you're telling the truth?"

"He told us about your phalanx plan. He showed us techniques and plans used by your army." He gives her some of the information Kane had shared with the council. Ana shakes her head in disbelief.

"What can we do? How can you and I work to end this war?"

"I wish I knew, mi'lady. I'll keep applying pressure to my council, but they see me as a young, ignorant child, who only got his rank because his father died. I've tried to prove myself to them, but no matter what I do, it's never been good enough. They wanted me to assassinate you, but I'm like you, I just want peace in the land."

"I'm so sorry they put that on you. Why would they give you the throne if they think so poorly of you?"

He snickers. "Because I would earn it, killing you myself."

"What will you tell them when you return, and I'm still alive?"

"That I didn't get the chance. Since the recent attempt, there were too many guards. I'll use you being alive as an excuse to push my agenda, that we should be working with you."

"Thank you. I appreciate your support."

"Of course, mi'lady." He looks down at his plate, swallowing hard. "May I ask a favor, Your Majesty?"

"Please, ask."

"May I call upon you again before I leave? Not as a suitor. No offense, you aren't to my... taste. However, if people believe I am pursuing you, it will give us cause to speak in private without raising any red flags."

Ana thinks a moment. "Of course."

"Thank you. Please, let's keep this between the two of us?"

She nods. They finish eating, then say their goodbyes. She returns to her quarters, followed by her entourage, and immediately goes to the washroom to shower. As she steps out, she sees they are all waiting for her.

"What? You want details of how my date went?"

Rafe laughs. "He looked more nervous than you did."

"Ha ha. It actually went really well. However, assuming what he told me is true, we could be in trouble. In exchange for sanctuary, Kane is giving up all of our secrets to their council, who want the count to take the throne."

"I've heard whispers of this. It sounds very plausible," Rafe confirms.

"Speaking of rumors and stories, why did none of you tell me Kane tried to destroy our armory? I felt like an idiot this morning when I didn't know about it."

"That's my fault," Kara says. "I was supposed to tell you. I found out while you and Rafe were still recovering, and it slipped my mind. I'm sorry. I won't fail you like that again."

"It's okay, Kara. Thank you." She gives Rafe a sultry look as she goes into the closet. He joins her a moment later, shutting and locking the door. She runs and practically jumps into his arms, kissing him. "I've been thinking about it. Even if we could be together publicly, what would we do? Make out at breakfast in the dining hall?" She laughs. "It really wouldn't be much different than this, anyway." She leans forward again, when he puts her on her feet, stepping back.

"Who are you trying to convince? Me or yourself?" Rafe asks.

"What?"

"You sound like you are trying to convince yourself that this is enough."

"No!" She looks down. "I'm trying to convince you."

"Ana, why?"

"When you brought me here on our first day, you told me you didn't love me. Honestly, I wasn't really surprised. I mean, how could anyone love me? Damaged, broken, useless, worthless me? I was more angry at myself for believing you when you did say you love me, than for you saying you didn't. The count asked me to dinner, and I saw the look on your face. It made me think this wasn't enough for you. That, I'm not enough for you," she adds softly.

"Ana!" He swoops her into his arms, kissing her with everything he can as his fingers caress her cheek. "Please, believe me. I love you so much. You mean everything to me. I know it must be hard to believe anything I say. I deserve that, to not have your trust, after what I've put you through. Just please, when it comes to this, believe me?"

She looks at him, seeing the pain in his eyes, and nods. "I do. I believe you. I love you, too." She wraps her arms around his neck as he leans in to kiss her. "Just please, don't ever break my heart again. I couldn't bear it. Not again," she says with a hitch in her voice.

"Never, I swear it." He leans down, gently taking her arms. He kisses her scars. He looks at her, making sure she's okay with it. She smiles at him. He takes his finger and runs along the scar. "Will you ever tell me about this?"

She turns to run from the room, but he grabs her arm and pulls her into his chest. She trembles as her tears are soaking his jacket.

"I'm so sorry. I'll never ask again."

"Let me go!" she begs. He releases her. She runs from the closet and goes to the washroom, slamming the door.

"Ana, open the door," Kara begs.

"No! How could he ask about them?"

"What?" Kara asks. Ana hears footsteps walking away. Muffled, she hears, "What the hell is wrong with you?"

She can't make out the response. She wipes her tears and steps out, seeing Kara getting in Rafe's face. They turn and look at her. Rafe pushes past Kara to Ana.

"I'm sorry."

She takes his hand, leads him into the closet, and sits on the ottoman with him. "Why did you ask?"

"I didn't intend to. I was kissing them, then feeling it under my finger, it made me wonder. I won't ask again."

She says nothing for several minutes, and he waits patiently. Finally, she speaks, her voice small. "I don't ever want to talk about these. It's from a dark time in my life, that I barely survived. Let it go, please?"

"I will."

"Just so you know, not even Kara knows why. It's not just you, okay?"

"I know. She told me. Is it okay if I kiss them, from time to time?"

"As long as you never ask again."

"I won't."

She leans up, kissing him as she wraps her arms around his neck, sitting in his lap, his warmth and love bringing comfort to her.

"I need sleep," she says, yawning and pulling away. He helps her to her feet and carries her to bed. Covering her up, he kisses her forehead. "Good night, my love," she whispers to him.

"Mia estrela," he whispers back.

Chapter 18

The next morning, she wakes up, and Rafe is not in his usual spot on the chaise. She sits up and realizes she's alone in the room. On her way to the closet to get dressed, Rafe steps out of the washroom. When she stops and looks at him, he sees the worry on her face and approaches her.

"What's wrong?"

"Nothing," she says, smiling to hide her fear.

"I saw the look on your face."

Swallowing hard, she looks down. "I'm not used to waking up and being alone. I got scared for a moment. It was stupid. I'm sorry."

"You… what? That's nothing for you to be sorry about. You have every right to be a little on edge."

"Thank you." She continues to the closet and turns back in surprise when he follows her in. Grinning, she looks at him. "Hmm, is this going to be a morning thing, too?"

He smirks back. "Don't get excited, Your Majesty."

"But what if I want to be?" she asks, walking up to him. She kisses him, and he wraps his arms around her.

"Seriously, though. We are going to be late for breakfast. I only came in here because—ah," he walks over to the ottoman, "there it is." One of his buttons had come off. "I'll have Evren mend this when she gets a chance." He puts it in his pocket and steps out while she gets dressed.

She walks over to her desk, getting papers and books together, then placing them in her bag.

"Mi'lady, if I may?"

She looks at Rafe. "What?"

"You need a more… appropriate bag."

"But I like my laptop bag."

"I know you do, but you are the queen now, and your bag should be fitting of your status."

She sighs. "Fine. I'll have Evren find me something. I have to use this for now, though."

After breakfast, Kara and Evren go to find a suitable bag for Ana while she and Rafe attend the meeting. Ana walks up to the desk and skims through the latest intelligence briefing. She looks at Rafe.

"MoonFrost struck against NightFall last night. Both sides suffered heavy losses." She sets the paper on her desk, shaking her head. "We have to stop this war."

"We will. It's just going to take time."

Everyone wanders in and takes their seats. The chancellor takes the floor, with Ana's permission. She sits through the briefing, half listening, half wondering what it will take to finally end the war. After the briefing, she asks Rafe to take her to her quarters.

"Lunch, mi'lady?"

"Can we have it brought in?" Ana asks.

"Of course."

He stops a member of staff and passes along the request. They nod and bow, before running off. He takes her arm, and they return to her room. She walks over to her desk, sitting down and pouring through her books. There's a knock at the door. Rafe walks over and opens it, surprised to see the count.

"May I have a moment with the queen?"

"Please, let him in," Ana says, getting to her feet. Rafe gestures for him to come inside.

The count approaches and bows before her. "I apologize, mi'lady. I know this is most inappropriate."

"It's quite all right, Count. How can I help?"

"I have been called back to the capitol. After last night's attack, we have to regroup. I came to tell you the Nightfall army intends to march on the palace Friday morning at dawn. I don't have any other details, but as a sign of trust, I had to tell you."

"You put yourself in great danger telling me this."

"I think the reward is worth the risk," Bela says.

"Thank you. Do not hesitate to reach out to me, for anything you may need. Please, be safe."

"Same to you, Your Majesty." He bows and leaves.

Kara and Evren walk in, carrying a silver bag for Ana. She looks at Evren.

"Please, fetch Declan. Tell him it's urgent and cannot wait."

"Yes, mi'lady." She runs from the room.

"What is going on?" Kara asks.

"You'll all hear, soon enough." She walks over to her desk, moving things from her laptop bag into the new bag. Looking at her laptop bag, she thinks of her time on Earth and pushes the feelings down as she folds up the bag and puts it in a desk drawer. Declan and Evren walk in.

"What is happening, Your Majesty?" Declan asks.

"The Nightfall army plans to march on the palace Friday morning at dawn."

He steps back in disbelief. "We've heard no such thing. Where are you getting your information from?"

She looks at Rafe, who nods. "You cannot repeat this to anyone. The count himself told me, putting himself in danger doing so."

"Why?"

"He doesn't want war or the throne. He says his council wants those things, not him. He's trying to stop it. He gave me information on Kane. He even confessed he had been sent by his council to assassinate me. I've heavily considered everything he has said, and I believe him."

"He was sent to kill you?" Rafe asks. "When were you going to tell us this?"

"Rafe, he never intended to. He could've poisoned me at dinner or stabbed me just now as we were speaking. I believe him. He wants the war to stop."

"We'll have to gather more intelligence. I'll see what I can do to prepare for the assault. Rafe, could you come with me? I promise to return him to you shortly, Your Majesty."

She nods. "Of course, Captain."

Rafe and Declan leave, while Kara goes into Evren's quarters. Ana sits at her desk and eats lunch, worrying over the upcoming battle. She thinks back on her conversations with Kane, realizing she may have to prove herself to stop the war.

"Do you need anything, mi'lady?" Evren asks.

"What is the name of whoever runs the armory?"

"His name is Ridley, he's also called Captain of Arms."

"Will you speak to him for me? See when I can be fitted and armed?"

She steps back. "Mi'lady?"

"I'm going into battle Friday. You cannot say anything to Rafe or Kara. I will tell them when the time is right."

"Of course, Your Majesty." She leaves to speak with Ridley.

———— ⚓ ————

Kara walks in to see Ana is still working at her desk. "Where's Evren?"

"She's doing a favor for me."

"Your Majesty, forgive me for speaking out of turn, but for someone who acts like you don't want a slave, you seem to use her a lot."

Ana jumps to her feet. "What are you saying?"

"Just that you seem to enjoy having someone at your beck and call." Her words cut deep.

"You don't really believe that, do you? I've always treated her as an equal. I've asked her to do things the same way I've asked you and Rafe, with kindness, never demanding or ordering."

"So, you're a kind master?"

Ana steps back, in shock. "Kara!"

"No. You treat her as your inferior. You may think you act like an equal, but you don't. What favor is she doing for you that you couldn't do yourself?"

Ana hangs her head in shame. She is the queen. The Captain of Arms would've made time for her. Why did she send Evren? She turns away and swallows down her tears. "You're right. I'm a horrible person." She runs into the closet and locks the door. Slumping against it and sliding to the floor, she wipes her tears. She orders Evren around like that? How did she not notice what she was doing? Hearing raised voices, she opens the door and peeks out.

"She does not treat me like a slave, Kara. How dare you attack her like that? Out of everyone in the kingdom, she has been the kindest and most loyal to me. The queen herself!"

"I'm sorry. It hurts me to see the way people look at you, how they treat you. I see her sending you on errands, and it makes me so angry."

"Kara, this is my position. I am to do anything the queen asks. Even though I am just a slave, she was going to marry Kane to save me. I know you think she did it for Rafe, but I assure you, she was beside herself when she saw that Kane had me, too. She blamed herself for me being captured. She even stabbed Rafe to save me!"

"What?" Kara asks, horrified at the discovery.

"Kane demanded she stab Rafe, saying he would shoot me in the head if she didn't. She hurt him to protect me."

"I didn't know that," Kara says softly.

"I will always be a slave, it's my lot in life, but I have never been as happy as I am to be in her service. I am grateful every day to have a master like her. I know other girls who aren't as lucky, girls who are whipped, starved, tortured, branded." She looks down a moment before looking back at

Kara. "Just because they can be. The queen values me, cares for me, counts me as a part of her inner circle. Why would you ever think differently?"

Kara pulls her into her arms. "I'm sorry. I don't know what came over me."

Evren holds her, too. "It's okay. I love you, Kara."

"I love you, too."

"Just know this, even if being her handmaid was a choice to be made, and not something I was forced into, I would still be here. I love her, the way you do."

Ana clears her throat, stepping out of the closet. Kara runs to her, kneeling before her with her head hung in shame.

"You aren't the horrible person. I am. Please, Your Highness, forgive me."

She pulls Kara to her feet, then into her arms. "Hush, sis. You were defending the one you love."

"Thank you."

When Kara excuses herself to the washroom, Evren walks up to Ana. "Mi'lady, he can see you at three."

"Thank you."

"If I may, how will you get there? You know Rafe and Kara will not let you out of their sight."

Ana laughs softly. "I know. I'll figure something out. Thanks."

Evren nods and bows just as Rafe walks in. He joins Ana at her desk.

"It looks as though the count may be telling the truth. We are sending out scouts for more information, but there are already rumors of an impending battle."

"Why do you think they are marching on us? Why now, I mean?" Ana asks.

Rafe shakes his head. "We're trying to figure that out, as well. There must be something to this. They wouldn't dare take on the throne without some sort of plan."

"Kane," she says, softly. "He's somehow convinced them he would let the count have the throne, with his help.

But we all know he'll end up betraying them and take the throne for himself."

"They would never believe us, even if we could tell them."

"Let them learn on their own that he is not to be trusted. I have a feeling he will get what he deserves." She finishes her meal. "I would like to train, if you are up for it."

"Of course. Get changed, and we'll go."

Evren takes her into the closet, getting her into dark blue gossamer pants and a white, long sleeve shirt. Ana looks at her reflection. "I feel like a pirate."

"What's a pirate?" Evren asks.

She looks at her. "Seriously? A world covered with water, and you don't have pirates here?"

"What is it?"

"They have ships and crews, pillaging and stealing and drinking."

"No, thank goodness. No pirates here."

"That's a shame." She laughs at the confusion on Evren's face. "It's a long story."

In the training center, Ana and Rafe practice with her dagger for half an hour before switching to swords. They lift their swords to their face, lower them down, then take their stance. As she lunges, she accidentally cuts his arm. She drops her sword and runs to him. "I'm so sorry!" Putting her hand on his, she closes her eyes to focus as she heals him. "Are you okay?"

He looks down at her. "It was just a cut. I'm fine." He takes her arms and looks at her. "Please, mi'lady. Don't do that again."

"I didn't mean to hurt you."

"No, I meant the healing. It was just a minor wound. I could do that myself. I don't need you to hurt yourself or wear yourself out, please."

She nods, not wanting to get into an argument. "Yes, Rafe. Of course."

She walks over and picks up her sword, and they go again. Their swords clang when he parries as she lunges. She pulls back, feinting right then going left. When she knocks the sword from his hands, he falls to his knees. She has her sword at his throat.

"Beg for mercy," she says, her eyebrows raised, a grin on her lips.

He smiles up at her. "Never!" he cries, grabbing his sword and knocking hers back. He jumps to his feet and lunges. They clash and duel, until she's knocked backwards and hits the floor, her head landing with a loud thud. He drops his sword and runs to her. He lifts her onto his lap, feeling around her face and head. "Ana, are you okay?"

"I'm fine. There are two of you, right?"

He closes his eyes, putting his hand on her forehead. She tries to swat it away, but he grabs her wrist with his other hand. Once she's healed, he stands up and holds her tight. "How do you feel?"

"Like I'm going to be sick."

He picks her up and carries her to the washroom off to the side. She throws up in the toilet while he holds her hair back.

"I'm so sorry. That's twice now you've been hurt in training!"

"Things like this will happen. That's why we train, though. So, I don't make the mistake in battle or while defending myself, and truly get hurt."

"I know, but I still feel bad."

He helps her to the vanity, where she runs the faucet and rinses out her mouth. She steals a kiss. "Don't. This is why we train."

"Let's get you back to your quarters. You need to rest."

They gather their things and return. Evren helps her into bed while Rafe tells Kara what happened. Kara sees how upset he is with himself. "Rafe, it was an accident. Don't blame yourself."

He nods his head. "I'll try."

"Rafe?"

He walks over to Ana. "Yes, Your Majesty?"

"Please, tell me you'll continue to train me."

"You know I will."

"Thank you." She turns away to get some sleep.

He walks over to Evren and pulls out the button from his pocket. "I hate to bother you, but—"

"Rafe, it's never a bother." He smiles while he removes his jacket and hands it to her, along with the button.

"Thank you, Evren." Her eyes go down. "What's wrong?"

"Kara and the queen got into it, earlier. Kara was angry at her, acting like she was treating me as a slave for asking me to do things. It broke my heart to know they fought like that about me. I'm nobody important."

"Evren?" He gently tilts her chin, so she's looking at him. "Slave is just another title, like guardian or queen. It does not define who you are."

She smiles at him. "Thank you. You three have always treated me as an equal. I never thought that would be possible."

While Evren sits to fix his jacket, Rafe checks on Ana, who is still asleep. He presses his palm flat on her forehead to make sure she's not running a fever. He sighs in relief, then goes to Kara. "You fought with her about Evren?"

"Rafe, please."

"Why?"

"I got angry. I see the looks Evren gets in the hall or when we're out together. People bump into her or push her back, thinking it's okay because of her status."

"What made you mad at Ana?"

"She sent her out to do her a favor. I know it's her right as queen, and Evren's duty, as handmaid, but it made me angry. Believe me, I feel awful for the things I said to her. I still shake at her reaction."

"Her reaction? What happened?"

"Her face was flush, like she was ashamed of herself. She called herself a horrible person and went into the closet to cry. I was going to apologize when Evren walked in, having overheard some of it. We made up, though."

"She called herself a horrible person?" Rafe shakes his head as his anger flows through him. "Kara, do you not see how much she values your opinion? You have the power to make her or destroy her, with just your words. That is a dangerous power to have over a queen."

"I know. Believe me, I know. My stomach has been in knots ever since our fight. I still feel awful."

They turn as Ana sits up, screaming in horror. They run to her.

"No, Kane! Stop!" she cries out, thrashing her arms and legs. Rafe catches her as she nearly falls out of bed. "Please, don't!"

"Your Majesty!" He tries waking her. "Ana!"

She stops struggling in his arms and looks around. Her heart is pounding in her ears as she tries to calm her mind. She turns and pulls herself into his arms. He carries her into the closet, shutting the door behind him, then sits on the ottoman while her body shakes in fear.

"It was just a nightmare," he reassures her, stroking her hair. "Shh. You're okay now." She says nothing as he holds her, letting his warmth penetrate her ice-cold skin, breathing into it, and making her feel whole. She pushes down her fears and struggles to keep the tears at bay. "You're safe." He wipes away the unshed tears and kisses her softly. He pulls his head up, holding her tighter into his chest and resting his chin on her head. "Listen to my heartbeat. Let it calm yours."

She lays her head against his chest, doing as he says. Her own heart returns to its normal beat. "Thank you, Rafe."

"How do you feel?"

"Tired, but comforted. I still don't know how you do that to me. No one has ever made me feel the way you do." He kisses her again. She caresses his face, wondering how she got so lucky with him. "I love you, Rafe."

"I love you, mia estrela." He sighs. "We should probably get back out there. I'm sure the others are worried about you."

She nods, getting to her feet. He takes her out. Kara walks up to her, taking her hands.

"Are you okay?"

"Yes. Just a nightmare."

"What was he doing to you?"

"No, Kara."

"Please, Ana. What did he do to you?"

"Ask again, I'll reopen my scars," she threatens.

"You don't have to tell us anything," Rafe says, picking her up and carrying her into the closet. Kara follows them in. "But after what you just said, I have to make sure you're all right."

"I'm sorry. It was… it was the night before the masquerade. The things he did to me, and that you had to watch… I'm so ashamed! Then he brought me back here. He laid me on the chaise, kissing and caressing me…" Her eyes squeeze shut as shame flows through her at the memory.

"I'm so sorry I failed to protect you. This was my fault. I love you, more than your scars, more than your pain, more than you'll ever know. Even when you told me you hated me, it did not stop the love I have for you. Nothing could ever do that."

"Rafe, don't. How can you say that? I'm damaged, broken into a million pieces, and irreparable."

"No, mia estrela. You are so much more than you give yourself credit for. You are a warrior, a survivor, and an unstoppable force! I love you as you are. I promise you, I'm not going anywhere. You say you're broken into a million pieces? I love every single one. Don't ever doubt that."

She hangs her head, leaning into his chest. "I love you, too."

He leans down and kisses her, enfolding her in his arms. His wings wrap around them as he comforts her.

Kara stands there, amazed at the sight. She gives them privacy, stepping out of the closet and shutting the door behind her, then walks over to Evren.

"She's okay now. I wish I could kill Kane myself."

"He hasn't fled the realm. Maybe one of us will get the chance."

They look up when Rafe and Ana walk back out. Ana looks at the clock and sees it's almost three.

"Oh, I've got to get ready. Evren, please help me."

"Yes, mi'lady."

They go into the closet, picking out black breeches, a pale blue button up long sleeve shirt, and a circlet. She puts on black boots, loving how they feel.

"I miss wearing boots."

Evren chuckles. "They aren't really appropriate for a queen."

"Is there anything appropriate about me?" Ana asks, laughing.

When they return to the main chamber, Kara and Rafe glance at each other, both equally confused. "What are you doing?" Kara asks.

"Evren and I have somewhere to be. We'll only be about an hour."

"Mi'lady—"

"No, Rafe. Stay here." She sees the concern on his face. "Please," she adds. "I'm not leaving the palace, and Evren will be with me the entire time."

"Yes, majesty," he relents.

She and Evren leave, unaware that Rafe is following behind. He keeps his distance, not wanting to spy on her, but to keep her safe. The palace is mostly empty this time of day, as people are getting ready for dinner or doing their work. He comes around the corner and nearly barges into two young women he doesn't recognize.

"My apologies," he says, flashing a smile. He tries to go around when the woman in blue steps up to him.

"You're a guardian, aren't you?" she asks.

"Yes, ma'am. I am the queen's personal guardian. My name is Rafe." He gives a small bow and looks at her. Her blonde hair is in curls that fold around her shoulders. Her bright blue eyes are staring at his wings, trying not to be obvious. Her sister is shorter, with the same blonde hair and blue eyes.

"I am Azra, this is my sister Amaya. We are ambassadors of the MoonFrost quadrant."

"Pleasure to meet you ladies. If you'll excuse me—"

"Why the rush?" Azra asks, stepping a little closer. "I mean, you don't want to get away from us that quickly, do you?"

He takes a breath, knowing he could cause an interquadrant incident if he offends them. "Of course not. I am simply on my way to aid the queen."

"Hmm. What if am in need of aid?"

"How may I help?" he asks, giving another small bow.

"I need company for dinner. Join me tonight?"

"Mi'lady, please—"

"Unless you're too busy with your... precious queen. Maybe you are more than just her protector, right?"

"Dinner in the dining hall, correct?"

"Of course."

"Yes, mi'lady. I will have dinner with you."

"I'll see you at five." They turn and run off, giggling with excitement. He looks around, realizing he's lost Ana and Evren. He considers using his locator sense but feels guilty for violating Ana's privacy as much as he has. Instead, he returns to her quarters, angry with himself and with Ana for not trusting him.

———————— ❦ ————————

Ana and Evren step into the armory, where Ana is completely out of place being surrounded by weapons and polished armor. She walks up to the smith, who is working on a sword. Upon seeing her approaching, he stops and looks up. He gives her a nod as he finishes his work, wipes his hands, and walks over to her. He towers over them, nearly as wide as he is tall, with strong muscles. His long, dark hair is pulled back with a bandana on his head. He wipes the sweat from his brow.

"Mi'lady, I am Ridley." He bows before her. "I believe there was a misunderstanding. Your handmaid there said you wanted armor and a weapon, to go into battle?"

"There is no misunderstanding. That is correct."

He smiles at her answer. "Well, then. I have something for you." He reaches over to a shelf, bringing down a long, ebony box. He opens it to reveal a sword with moons and stars etched on the hilt and up the blade. "This was made for the queen to use, though only a few ever have."

"May I?" Ana asks.

"It is quite hea—" He stops when she picks it up with one hand and gently swings it around.

She turns to him. "I'm sorry. What did you say?"

"Noth… Nothing, mi'lady," he stammers out. He looks at Evren, who is just as surprised. "I'm sorry. You remind me of the legends of old."

"I'll gladly take the sword." She gently lays it back in the box. "Now, for my armor."

"I apologize, as we have slim pickings. We are in desperate need for metal, which we previously traded with NightFall for, plus Archduke Kane had anything extra sent to the factory to mass produce weapons for our troops."

"I'll see what I can do."

"Mi'lady, you don't need to trouble yourself."

"Ridley, please. It's something we need, correct?" He nods. "I will see you have it. Is there anything else you're in need of?"

"No, mi'lady. Just the metal." He looks her up and down a moment. "I think I have something that will work, at least for now." He walks to a shelf full of crates, pulling one out and setting it on the table between them. Various pieces to a suit of armor rest inside. "It's a whole set. It just needs cleaning and some attention. I believe it should fit you."

"Let's find out."

"Yes, Your Majesty."

He and Evren set forth to get her into the armor. Once every piece is on, they step back. Ana looks down, moving her arms and legs.

"How does it feel?" Ridley asks.

"As if it were made for me."

He looks at Evren. "Do you know who that armor was made for?" She shakes her head. "Queen Celestia, herself. The sword, too."

"Oh, wow," Evren mutters, turning back to Ana.

They help her out of the armor, then he boxes it up. "I'll have this cleaned and ready for you shortly."

"Thank you." Ana looks at Evren. "Please have this discreetly put in my closet while we are at dinner tonight."

"Yes, mi'lady."

"Ridley, thank you. I will let you know what I find out about getting metal shipped here."

"Your Majesty," Ridley says with a bow.

She and Evren are in the hall when Ana looks at her. "I need to send a message to the count. How do I do that?"

Evren escorts her to the Communications Lounge. Ana stands in awe, admiring all the golden wires and silver tubes everywhere. Evren leads her over to a table marked NightFall Quadrant.

"Write what you want to say, put it in an envelope and seal it, then put it in the appropriate tube and hold the button until it lights up. When a response is received, they will deliver it to you, unopened and unread."

She writes as best she can, wishing her handwriting was better, asking the count for help with the metal. Sending it through the tube, it disappears with a flash. She hopes it reaches him.

Ana leaves the closet, dressed in a pale pink gown with silver shoes and a crown adorned with diamonds.

Rafe walks up to her, worry on his face. "Mi'lady."

"Rafe." She steps back at the sight. "What's wrong?"

He bows to her. "I'm so sorry."

"What is going on?"

"I tried to follow you and Evren. I won't apologize for that, I was worried about you. But on the way," he looks down. "On the way, I ran into two women from MoonFrost. They were very curious about me, never having seen or met a guardian. One of them invited me to dinner with her in the dining hall tonight. I said yes to avoid an incident. I'm so sorry." He looks up when she says nothing. He sees a blank look on her face. "Ana—"

She breaks into laughter, hardly able to stop herself. "You have a date tonight? That's so cute."

Kara walks over. "Who has a date?"

"Rafe. With a girl from MoonFrost."

They both laugh. He looks at Kara, then Ana. "You're not mad?"

"We will have to wine and dine with certain people, to keep the peace and to keep our secret. Of course, I'm not mad. I think it's hilarious. I can't wait to hear all about it."

She sees the relief wash over him. "I was afraid you would be hurt or angry."

"No, Rafe. How is this not forbidden?" Ana suddenly asks.

He sighs. "As you said, we are expected to host. I am not courting her but entertaining her and her sister at dinner."

"I understand. Let's go."

Rafe joins Azra, trying not to look miserable and failing. He sits with her while she and Amaya talk about the gowns they've bought and how boring the palace is.

Ana chuckles, eating with Evren and Kara. "I wish I could help him."

"Me, too," Kara says. "It's kind of funny though."

They both laugh. "Still," Ana says. She watches as one of the girls tries to touch his wing. Ana watches him fold them in completely, so you cannot even see them. She laughs harder. "I feel so bad for him!"

"I have to do something."

"Kara, don't. We have to keep the peace."

"Yes, mi'lady." Kara takes a bite and looks at Ana. "So, what did you girls do earlier?"

Ana looks at her plate and takes a breath. "No point in trying to hide it. I'm sure rumor has already started, since it's near impossible to keep a secret in this palace." She looks Kara in the eye. "I am riding into battle on Friday."

Kara nearly drops her fork. "You can't be serious."

"Kara, we've discussed this."

"As a possibility, as something you might do in the future. Not this same week!"

"Please, I need your support, not anger."

Kara opens her mouth to beg, to protest, but she stops. "Yes, mi'lady."

"Please, don't tell Rafe yet. I will tell him, soon."

"Of course." Kara looks over at Rafe. "I think I'd better save him."

The two women are laughing and giggling, while Rafe stares down at his food. Kara approaches the table.

"Kara, is everything okay?" he asks.

"Yes." She clears her throat. "Her Majesty is still recovering and is ready to return to her quarters for rest."

He jumps to his feet. "My apologies, ladies. Thank you for a lovely time." He bows then practically runs with Kara to their table. He helps Ana to her feet and escorts her back to her room. They are almost there when a squire approaches them.

"For Your Majesty," he says, bowing and handing her an envelope.

"Thank you," she replies.

Once inside her quarters, she opens it up and reads the reply from the count. She gestures Evren over. "Please, tell Ridley his metal will be here first thing in the morning."

"Yes, mi'lady." She quickly leaves.

Ana goes to her desk, tucking the letter into one of her books. Rafe and Kara approach her. "Are you going to tell us what's going on?" Kara asks.

"Oh, it's nothing. I arranged for some supplies." She sits down, opening a book. She looks over, realizing they're still there. "What?"

"Anything else?" Kara asks, thinking Ana will tell Rafe her decision.

"No." She thinks for a moment. "Oh, right!" She jumps up and runs past them, going into her closet. Excitement flows through her when she sees the box on the ottoman. She shuts and locks the door behind her before walking over. Carefully lifting the sword out, she takes a few practice swings, feeling the weight and balance of it. She places it back in the box and slides it under the ottoman, grateful it has a ruffle around it to hide the box underneath.

She looks at the crate with her armor in it, then slides it into a nook on the shelf against the wall, where it's hardly noticeable. She smiles as she leaves the closet. Kara and Rafe are sitting at the table in the corner.

Ana returns to her desk, writing notes in her journal when Kara walks up behind her. "When are you going to tell him?"

"Tonight, when we're in the closet. Why do you care?"

"Because I know he wants to help you, but I don't know how he's going to react when he finds out you're actually doing it."

Ana looks over at him, watching him at the bookshelf and looking through one of her books. "He'll be fine. He understands."

"I thought I did, too. It still made me angry."

"I'm sorry. It's something I have to do," Ana explains. Kara shakes her head, going back to the table and sitting down. "Rafe?"

He sets the book on the shelf and walks over. "Yes, mi'lady?"

"How was your date?"

"Please, don't. Those girls were awful."

"They're pretty."

"Uh, no."

"Really?"

"Really. They tried to touch my wings. I thought I was going to vomit right there at the table."

"I saw that."

"I hope I never have to see them again."

She stands up, taking his hand. They go into the closet. She sits him on the ottoman and steps back, looking at him.

"Is something wrong?" Rafe asks.

"I have something to tell you. I'm not sure how you're going to react."

"Okay."

"I had my fitting today. I've got my sword and armor. I'm going into battle on Friday." She studies him as she waits for his reaction.

He sits there, letting her words sink in before he looks at her. "Yes, mi'lady," he says with no emotion.

"Rafe, please. Tell me how you feel."

"You want my honest opinion?" he asks, standing up.

"Yes."

"You need more training. I think you are rushing into this."

"I don't have time. I need to rally my soldiers. I need to be out there with them."

"It's too dangerous. You aren't ready."

"I am. I know I am. I—"

"You're a liability out in the field."

"Rafe!" She steps back in shock, hurt splayed across her face.

"If you freeze out there, like you did in the gym, people will die."

"That was months ago! I've come so far since then."

"I wouldn't want you in my battalion."

"What?" she asks, not believing the words she's hearing. "How could you?"

She turns and runs, trying to get the door open when he comes up behind her, gently grabbing her wrist. She twists her arm free, ducking under him and behind. When she kicks the back of his knee, he falls forward, hitting the wall then the floor. She kneels by his side, pulls out her dagger, and has it pointed at his throat. "You, of all people, should never underestimate me!" she hisses. "Do you not see how much you have taught me?"

She runs to the washroom, turns the water on and strips down. As she steps in, she is trembling in anger at how he and Kara are reacting. She knows they are worried about her, she understands, but how do they not see that this is important to her? They still see her as a scared, lost little girl.

She thought she would tell Rafe, he'd be a little upset, but he'd understand after they discussed it, then they would enjoy some time together. After what he said about her, she wonders if he really loves her. How could you doubt someone you love? He is definitely full of doubt. She shakes her head, trying to clear it.

Wiping her tears, she dries and gets dressed, not really wanting to step out. She takes a breath and opens the door, grateful he's not taking up the door frame like usual. When she glances over, she sees Rafe and Kara at the table in the corner. She debates going over and saying good night, but she's too angry. Instead, she crawls into bed, praying she will fall asleep.

Chapter 19

She wakes up to see Rafe is asleep on the chaise and Kara on the sofa. Confused, she says nothing as she gets up and changes into fresh clothes. She walks to her desk, sitting down and going through her books. Corbin mentioned something that had her curious. He was explaining how the treaty will come about if they are able to end the war. She looks through some of the books on laws and history, researching what he said. She looks up when she realizes Rafe is standing behind her.

"Yes, Guardian?" she asks, her voice chilling him to the core.

"Mi'lady, I just wanted to make sure you are okay."

"Apparently, I'm not."

"What does that mean?"

"Not if I'm a liability."

"Your Majesty—"

"You're dismissed."

He walks to the chaise and sits down. Kara walks over to Ana, deciding to take the chance.

"Your Highness."

"Yes, Kara?"

"Please, understand. We are worried about you. We don't doubt your ability—"

Ana breaks out laughing. "I think you two need to get your stories straight. Rafe didn't tell you? He thinks I'm a liability and wouldn't want me in his battalion." She sees the look of shock and anger on Kara's face. "Now you know how I feel."

"Rafe," Kara turns to him, "what the hell is wrong with you?"

They both look when he doesn't respond. He sits on the chaise with his head buried in his hands. Ana gets to her feet and runs over to him.

"What's wrong?" she asks. When he still doesn't respond, she takes his hand, and they go into the closet. "Please, talk to me."

"I'm scared of losing you. I was hurtful, using anger because I didn't want you to see how scared I am. I'm sorry. I'm so ashamed."

"Oh, Rafe." She lays her head against his chest. "I'm still hurt by what you said, but I understand now."

"I know how incredible you are, at everything you do. I would never question your ability. I've seen you with a sword, with your bare hands, and with a dagger. I know what you are capable of. I just didn't expect you to go into battle so soon, and it scares me." He wraps his arms around her, caressing her back. "Please, don't leave me so soon. I just got you back."

"I have to go into battle. Don't ask me why, it's something I have to do. You and Kara practically beg me to open up, to tell you what I want, what I'm dealing with. Then, the first time I do about something really important to me, you both turn your backs on me!"

"I'm so sorry. You're absolutely right. Please, forgive my cruel words and know I didn't mean them."

She looks at him, seeing his eyes watering up. "Yes, I forgive you, my love. I do." She leans up and kisses him. "I'm sorry I nearly killed you last night."

He smiles at her. "Ah, yes. Dagger to the throat. You'll pay for that." He lifts her up and gently tosses her onto the ottoman. He gets on top of her, smothering her with kisses. She's laughing and crying when he pulls back. "Are you going to be okay?"

She caresses his face. "I am. I am okay."

He buries his face in the crook of her neck, holding her tightly. "Mia estrela, I love you so much."

"I love you, too. We need to go. We have breakfast and briefings."

"The life of a royal," he says, getting off the ottoman and taking her hand to help her up.

They go into her room. She walks over to Kara. "Are you still mad at me?"

"No. I see now how important this is to you. You have my support, one hundred percent. I swear it."

"Thank you," Ana says with a smile.

"As long as you understand, I will be by your side."

"Kara—"

"Don't try. If you're going, I'm going."

When Rafe and Ana enter the briefing room, she's surprised to see Declan there already.

"Is everything okay?" Ana asks, worried he has bad news.

"We need to talk. The count sent over a shipment of metal."

"Did I do something wrong?"

"No, mi'lady. I'm sorry. We are grateful he did. However, he has been arrested by his council, labeled a traitor, and is set to be executed on Friday."

"We have to do something!"

"We can't. We are stretched thin as it is," Declan says.

"You don't understand. He's going to be killed because he helped us. If other people find out that's how someone is treated because of their aid, and we let them die, no one will want to help us. It's why we have to do something."

"I could rescue him," Rafe offers.

"No," she says. She catches herself. "Not alone, at least."

"I have no one to spare. If Rafe is willing to go after the count, I won't stop him."

"When would you leave, Guardian?" she asks.

"After dinner."

"Take anything you may need to assist you."

"Thank you, mi'lady. I'm going to go see Ridley while you have your meeting. Declan, if I'm not back before it's finished—"

"I'll stay with her."

"Thank you."

He bows to Ana and leaves. She turns to Declan, seeing a smile on his face. "Are you okay?" she asks.

"Yes. I'm just grateful you two worked through whatever issues you were having. He truly is the best warrior to protect you."

"I see that now. He wasn't happy when I told him I am going into battle on Friday."

Declan drops the folder he was looking through, sending pages scattering to the floor. "You're what, mi'lady?"

"I'm going into battle on Friday. I've been training, and I'm ready. I want to do this."

He bends down, scooping up the papers and hastily shoving them into the folder. "Your Majesty—"

"Rafe and Kara have already tried. You really think you're going to talk me out of it?"

He sets the folder on the desk, worry on his face and his brow furrowed in concentration. "If it's what you want, Your Majesty."

"It is."

"Do you have armor and a sword?"

"I do."

"We won't tell anyone, yet. We'll announce it at tomorrow's briefing."

"I understand. Thank you. It's also probably best if we don't mention Rafe or the count."

"Yes, agreed."

She goes to her desk as people start coming in and find their seats. The chancellor opens the briefing. Once they get through their reports, the meeting is adjourned, and everyone leaves. Declan turns to Ana.

"Dining hall or your quarters, Your Majesty?"

"My quarters, please."

"May I ask?"

"Yes, Declan."

"Why do you not eat every meal in the dining hall?"

"Between you and me?" she asks. He nods. "Sometimes, it's a little overwhelming for me. I need to retreat, if you will, and recuperate before being around so many people again. I'm ashamed to admit that, but it's true."

"There is no shame in that, Majesty. Not everyone is social."

"Thank you."

He escorts her to her room. "Shall I check inside?"

"Yes, please." She hands him her key.

He unlocks the door and steps inside. He goes to the closet and washroom. "All clear," he says, walking back out into the hall, shocked at the sight.

Ana is battling a man he doesn't know, dressed in black with a sword on his hip. The man reaches for Ana's throat when she grabs his wrist and brings him to the floor. He jumps up and grabs her, holding her above him. She manages to kick him in the stomach, causing him to drop her. He's gasping for air when she hits him again.

Ana manages to bring him to his knees, when he quickly recovers and rushes at her, plunging a dagger into her side. She cries out in pain and lands against the wall when Declan comes up behind him and restrains him. Rafe runs over, shocked at the sight. He picks Ana up and carries her into her quarters while Declan takes the man to the dungeon. Rafe holds her on the chaise and heals her, then starts for the washroom when Kara and Evren run in behind him, taking Ana into the shower while Rafe runs to his quarters to clean up.

He returns to her room as they are bringing her out. Rafe picks her up, carrying her into the closet, and holding her on the ottoman as they both recover.

"Rafe," Ana says softly as she comes to. He's beside her, holding her in his arms.

"Shh. You're okay."

"You saved me?"

"Uh, no, Your Highness. You saved yourself."

"What?"

"You are such an amazing fighter. Declan told me and Kara what happened while you were sleeping in here. Any battalion will be lucky to have you fighting with them."

"Thank you." She smiles at him.

"I'm just grateful you're okay. Declan said it was the man's intention to take you from here and present you to Kane. In return, once Kane was on the throne, he would make him a capitol leader."

"How can someone do that? Kill an innocent woman to be in charge?"

"I've never understood the lust and greed for power. To hurt and kill innocent people and put yourself above them! It's disgusting."

Rafe looks up when the closet door opens, and Declan walks in, freezing in place at the sight of them.

"Guardian, what are you doing?"

Kara rushes over. "He's healing her."

Declan turns to her. "What?"

"We don't know how, but he can heal her."

Rafe pulls away from Ana, sitting beside her. "We didn't tell anyone, for her protection. Kane's assassin used Rose's Kiss on her. It's a wonder he hasn't said anything about her still being alive." He helps Ana sit up.

"See for yourself," Ana says as she stands up and walks to Declan. "No injuries."

Declan shakes his head. "He mentioned it, but I thought perhaps he accidentally used a clean bolt or was lying. I see now, you are telling the truth."

"What are you going to do?" Rafe asks as Ana sits back down.

"About what? There's no law that says a guardian can't heal their ward. As you've said, it's best if no one knows." He clears his throat.

"Thank you, Declan," Rafe says.

"Are you still leaving tonight?"

Rafe looks at Ana, who nods. "Yes, I am."

"All right. Come see me before you leave." He looks at Ana. "I just wish I had someone I could assign while he's gone. Especially after this."

Kara steps forward. "Evren and I are trained. We won't leave her side, even for a second."

"Thank you." He gives a bow and leaves the room.

Ana looks at Kara. "Why was he in here?"

"He wanted to give me more information about your attempted kidnapping. Evren let him in, and I was in the washroom. I didn't know he would come in here! I'm so sorry."

"It's okay," Rafe says, "because he already knows. But we all have to be more careful." He looks at Ana. "I don't want to leave you."

"You have to. He's our ally and could be the key to having peace."

"I know. It doesn't make it any easier."

"We'll try to stay in my quarters as much as possible, until you return."

"Where are you going?" Kara asks.

"I can't give too much information. Just know, it's a rescue mission."

"All right."

Ana yawns. "I need more rest."

"We both do."

"Evren and I are right out here. We will do better, I promise."

⌁

Kara uses the key Ana had given her and lets herself into the closet. She smiles, seeing them asleep together. She hates to wake them, but they've had dinner brought in, and she knows they need to eat. Walking over and gently waking Ana first, she holds her hand as she sits beside her.

Ana slowly sits up, looking at Kara. "What time is it?"

"It's six. We've had food brought in."

Ana leans down and kisses Rafe gently. "Time to eat, love."

He opens his eyes, smiling at her. He gets off the ottoman and escorts her to the table.

"How do you feel?" Evren asks Ana.

"Better. Just tired." She looks at Rafe. "How do you feel?"

"Almost a hundred percent. I'll be okay to leave after we eat."

Worried, she looks down, not wanting him to go but knowing he has to. She won't let the count be executed, not after helping her. When she's finished eating, she goes for the washroom, but loses her balance.

Kara jumps up and runs to Ana, catching her as she nearly falls. She takes her into the washroom then gets her to the bed. Rafe walks over and takes her hand.

"I'm so worried about you."

She smiles at him. "I'll be okay. Just tired, is all." She squeezes his hand. "Please, hurry back. I'll miss you."

"I'll miss you, too."

He gives her a quick kiss, then goes to his quarters, gathering up clothes and weapons, then packing them into a bag. He slings it over his shoulder then heads to the barracks to speak with Declan. He finds him waiting for him.

"What are we going to do with the count, if your mission is a success?"

"Queen Maeriana has already said she will offer him sanctuary. He'll stay here until the war is over. Then we'll see if we can put him back in charge of their capitol."

"How is she doing?"

"Fine. Just exhausted."

"May I ask, how long have you known you can heal her?"

"Since we were on Earth."

"Wow."

"I know. I don't understand it myself. I'm so grateful, though. With everything Kane has done to her."

"Don't get me started on him. I'd be quite happy to execute him myself."

"I know."

"So, you're about to head out?"

"Yes. I'll arrive tomorrow, under cover of darkness. I'd rather fly all the way, but I know they have scouts everywhere. Getting in shouldn't be too hard. It's always getting out that's the problem."

Rafe stops in the kitchen for some bread and dry goods to take on his trip. Walking down the stairs and outside, he glances back at the palace, and says a prayer of protection for Ana. Once he's in wilderness, he spreads his wings and flies over the plains. He heads East, towards NightFall. He lowers down once he's no longer above Maristellar and walks along the river, listening for any scouts or soldiers.

When the sun comes up, he finally rests. He sleeps a few hours, then continues walking, staying in the woods and off the main roads, knowing there will be patrols. Just as the sun is going down, he sees the capitol on the horizon.

He sneaks around the back of the city, under cover of darkness. This will take more time, but he also knows it's his best way to slip in undetected. He flies up the wall, scanning for any soldiers or guards, then lands softly on the roof and admires the view.

The city is mostly constructed of grey brick buildings with gothic windows, the citadel being the tallest building in the quadrant. A few buildings are crumbling and in desperate need of repair. The streets are grey cobblestone. Declan had given him a briefing about the capitol and where it was rumored that the count was being held.

Making his way to the citadel, he is surprised at how empty the streets are. He realizes they're stretched thin because of the war. Quietly, he enters the citadel, staying against the walls and using the shadows where he can. He sees a guard up ahead. He slips behind him, extending his hidden blade when he grabs the guard and pins the blade to his throat.

"Where are they holding the count?"

"Why would I tell you anything?" the guard asks defiantly.

Rafe quickly stabs him in the shoulder then has the tip back at his throat. "Tell me," he snarls.

"I'll show you where he's at. It's just over here."

"Trick me or try anything, you'll find my blade in your back."

"Understood."

The guard walks him over to a locked door, inputs the code, and they go inside. The count is in a cell, badly beaten and wearing some sort of black prisoner jumpsuit. Rafe makes the guard open the cell, then puts the magical bindings and gag on the guard before tossing him inside. He gets the count out.

"You came to save me?" Bela asks in disbelief.

"On the queen's orders. She wouldn't let you die."

"I'll have to thank her, when we see her."

"How badly are you hurt?" Rafe asks.

"I can stand and walk, but they haven't fed me in three days. I'm a little weak."

Rafe opens his pack, getting out some of the food he brought. "Eat this, then we'll go."

Bela quickly eats, then stays behind Rafe as they leave the dungeon. "Wait," he says. "There is something you need to see."

"I need to get you safe."

"I promise you, it's important. You need to see this," he says with urgency in his voice.

Rafe looks at him, worried it could be a trap. He knows Ana trusts him, so he decides he will as well. "Okay. Tell me where we are going." They get into an elevator that takes them to a sublevel. When they step out, Rafe gasps in surprise "What is this?" he asks, scanning what looks like a hundred bodies kept in individual cryosleep chambers.

"They're all guardians. Taken from battle, still alive, and brought here to be studied. Our scientists were trying to unlock your immortality," Bela explains. "I am truly sorry."

Rafe walks up to one of the chambers. He looks at the console, which is easily marked, and presses the buttons, freeing one of the guardians. Helping her out and easing her to the ground, he sits by her, waiting to see if she will wake. A moment later, she opens her eyes.

"Where am I?" she asks, groggy and disoriented.

"You're in NightFall, Melian. What's the last thing you remember?"

"I was on the field, sword in hand, when I was hit from behind." She looks at him. "Rafe? Is that you?"

"Yes. Now, we have to free them. All of them. You have to help me. Can you do that?" Rafe asks, getting her to her feet.

"Yes."

They run through the room, freeing the guardians as fast as they can. Some haven't been gone that long and quickly recover the same as Melian. Others have been there a year or two, or even longer, and need more time to regain their strength. The ones who are in better shape take the others and help them escape.

The sun is starting to come up when they leave the city. Once Rafe and the count are free of the city walls, he spreads his wings, carrying the count and flying as quickly as he can. Archers are on the wall, sending wave after wave of arrows at them. Rafe flinches in pain when one pierces through his left side. He looks down and sees the tip sticking out, but decides to push on, eager to see Declan's reaction to the guardians returning. More than anything, he needs to see Ana.

I'm coming, mia estrela. I'm coming home to you. Please, be all right.

Ana sits on the edge of the bed, knowing the battle is coming in the morning. She hardly ate at dinner, which made Kara even more of a nervous wreck.

"You need to eat," she begs. "You need a good night's sleep and your strength, for in the morning."

Declan had posted a royal guard outside her quarters for the night. Ana looks at Kara. "Did he get dinner, too?"

"Yes, mi'lady. I made sure he ate."

"Good."

"We'll be in Evren's quarters for the night. If you need anything, come, and get us."

"I will."

They say their good nights. Ana is in bed, her mind racing about going into battle the next day. She tosses and turns, worried about Rafe. Eventually, she falls into a restless sleep.

A hand clamps over her mouth, startling her awake. With their other hand, they turn on the lamp. Her eyes go wide at the sight of Kane. She struggles to pull away, but he quickly has his blade at her throat. When she goes still, he smiles at her.

"Did you miss me, darling?"

"No," she says, her voice muffled. He shakes his head.

"I've been looking forward to this." He leans down so his face is inches from hers. "I'm going to move my hand. Speak softly and briefly. If you scream or cry for help, I'll slit your throat then go pay your friends a visit. Understand?"

Once she nods, he removes his hand. "Please," she begs, "don't kill me."

"Oh, no, darling. I'm not here to kill you," he says with a laugh.

"What do you mean?"

"I know you promised your troops you're going into battle with them in the morning. I'm going to wound you, so you won't be able to go. It will break their spirits and make you look weak. It'll make tomorrow go so much easier for me."

"Please, you don't have to do this."

"Hmm, you know I do." He covers her mouth again as he slides the blade into her shoulder, moaning when she cries. Removing the blade, he digs it into her side then kisses her as he rams it into her leg. "Now, just don't die, m'kay? I don't need you to be made into a martyr." He bends down, kissing her again and licking her tears. "I wish I had more time with you. Count to thirty, then scream all you want. I need you alive, remember?" He runs from the room.

The room is going dark as she grows cold, unable to count past ten. She tries again but gives in and cries out. "Kara," she tries, but it only comes out as a mumble. She takes a breath. "Kara!" she yells.

Kara and Evren run in, shocked at the sight of her. Her face is white, and her sheets are soaked in blood. Kara gently picks her up and runs to the Medical Center. Winslow is surprised to see Ana in such shape. He takes her and rushes her into the surgical wing. Evren looks at Kara.

"I'll stay here. Go get cleaned up. You're covered in her blood."

Evren is relieved when Kara meets her in the waiting room and takes her hand. "Who did this to her?" Kara asks, shaking with anger.

"I don't know. I wish I did."

"She needs Rafe."

"He won't be back until tomorrow night," Evren points out.

"Damn it! He never should've left."

"The queen was right; we couldn't leave the count to die. Not after he's helped us," Evren says.

Winslow walks out and sits with them. "She'll be okay. We stopped the bleeding, stitched up the wounds, and bandaged her up. Where is her guardian?"

Kara shakes her head. "He's out on assignment and won't be back for a while."

"I see. So, traditional healing for her. We'll give her pain medicine and make her comfortable. You two can come on back."

As they follow Winslow, Kara looks at Evren. "I managed to find Declan and tell him what's happened on my way back here. They're searching the palace, but I'm not holding my breath. I also arranged for her quarters to be cleaned up."

They walk into her room. Evren goes to the chair in the corner, while Kara sits beside Ana, taking her hand. "I'm so sorry, Ana. We were supposed to guard you, and we failed."

"Kara?" she asks weakly.

"I'm right here."

"Shut up. It's not your fault."

"Who did this to you?"

"Kane," Ana whispers, before she passes out again.

Kara turns to Evren. "That can't be right. Did she say Kane?"

"She did."

"He was in the palace? If that's true, he may still have loyal supporters here. Declan needs to know."

"I'll stay with her while you inform him."

Kara walks over and kisses her. "Thank you."

She leaves, and Evren sits in the chair by Ana's bed. Stroking her hair, Evren shakes her head at how pale Ana is. "Please, be okay," she whispers.

Ana wakes up the next morning and looks at Kara. "What time is it?"

"Early. Go back to sleep."

"Have the troops left yet?" Ana asks.

"No."

"I need to address them."

"You are in no shape."

"Please, if you don't let me, you're letting Kane win. Get me a change of clothes, something gold. Please, Kara. I'm begging you."

"You swear to me right now, as soon as you give your speech, you will come back here, not to your quarters, and rest where they can keep an eye on you?"

"I swear it."

"Fine." Kara jumps up and gets her the things she had requested. She and Evren help her dress. Watching Ana wince getting in the chair, she leans down and looks in her eyes. "This is a bad idea. You need your—"

"I need to do this. Please, don't argue."

Kara lets out a loud sigh and pushes her down to the barracks. She starts to push the chair onto the balcony when Ana holds up her hand, looking at Kara.

"I need to walk out."

"Ana—"

"I have to. They need to see me as strong as I can be." She takes Kara's hand. Kara hits the brakes on the wheelchair and helps her to her feet. Ana smiles at her. "I'll be okay. Really." She slowly makes her way out to the balcony. Corbin is surprised to see her but says nothing. He hands her the sound amplifier, and she brings it to her mouth.

"Good morning, troops," she says. They all stand at attention, watching her in anticipation to hear what she has to say. "I know I was supposed to ride with you into battle this morning. Some of you may have heard, Kane got into the palace and wounded me last night. I am so sorry I am unable to join you. That was his purpose. His goal was not to kill me but to wound me and make me look weak. He wanted you disheartened, to feel betrayed by me. I beg of you, do not let him win.

"This battle today could truly turn the tide in our favor. As you go out there, remember you do not just fight for me. You fight for your loved ones, you fight for your families, and most important, you fight for yourselves. You have all been so brave, and courageous, and admirable, fighting for a queen you do not even know. Believe me when I tell you, I may not be there on that field with you, but my heart and soul goes with each and every one of you! Now, who is with me?"

A hearty round of "ayes" circulates, followed by "long live the queen." She turns to Kara and smiles, then nearly crumples to the ground, grabbing the rail of the balcony to keep herself standing. Kara runs to her, helping her sit in her wheelchair.

"How did I do?"

"Fantastic," Kara says.

"Thank you."

"Let's get you back to the Medical Center."

"Yes, Kara."

Rafe lands about two hundred feet from the palace, meeting with the other guardians. They had agreed it best so the guards didn't think they were invading. He leads the guardians up to the palace when Declan runs out, mouth agape. He looks at Rafe.

"How?" is all he can utter.

"They were being held captive by the NightFall council, being tested and experimented on. They were trying to unlock the key to our immortality."

Declan notices Rafe is wounded. "We need to get you taken care of." He walks over, letting Rafe put his arm around his waist, and escorts him into the palace. They head for the Medical Center.

"How is the queen? Did she... did she survive battle?"

Declan swallows hard, debating how to answer. "She wasn't wounded in battle," he says, honestly. He gets Rafe into the center, and Winslow takes over.

"Let's get him in that room." He gestures over. They get Rafe inside and sitting on the exam table. Declan helps him remove his coat. Winslow cuts the shirt off, examining his side. "Your accelerated healing is closing the wound around the arrow. We'll have to cut it out."

Rafe looks at him. "No." He yanks the arrow out of his side and throws it to the ground. Winslow runs to get towels. Rafe concentrates to stop the bleeding.

"That was a stupid thing to do," Winslow says, sopping up the blood on the exam table.

"But it worked."

Declan chuckles, getting a look from Winslow. "Rafe, you are one of a kind."

"If you only knew." He looks at Winslow. "I need to see the queen. When can I see her?"

Winslow looks at Declan. "I think this is where you come in." He steps back, taking away the bloody rags.

Declan walks up to Rafe. "I'm going to tell you something, but you have to stay calm. Do you understand me, Rafe?"

"Yes."

"Kane managed to sneak in last night. He stabbed the queen—" before he can finish, Rafe jumps off the table. He falls to his knees, as the pain overwhelms him. He makes himself stand, trying to leave the exam room, but stops when there's a sharp prick in his neck. He looks at Winslow, who is holding a syringe in his hand.

"You son of a—" Rafe passes out. Declan grabs him, and with Winslow's help, gets him back on the exam table. Declan leaves to check on Ana.

He goes into her room. "How are you feeling?" He worries that she is so pale. "Mi'lady?"

"I'm okay," she says, giving him a reassuring smile.

"I wanted to let you know, Rafe and the count have returned."

Kara turns to Ana. "Let him see you, please!"

"Mi'lady, if I may," Declan says, "Rafe was wounded. He took an arrow through the side. He'll be okay, but he is also recovering."

Ana shakes her head. "I won't let him see me while he's still recovering. We will wait at least twenty-four hours. That's an order."

"Yes, Your Majesty. Find comfort in knowing he is here."

"Thank you, Declan. Please see that the count is treated well."

"Of course." He bows and leaves.

"Kara, would you check on Rafe? Not right now, I'm sure they are still tending to him. But in a little bit? I'm sure he won't be happy about the situation. A familiar face may help to calm him down."

"Yes, mi'lady, of course."

"Thank you. I'm going to try and get some rest."

"Is the medicine kicking in?"

She yawns. "Yes." Her eyes close as she gives in.

"How do you think he's going to react to her orders?" Evren asks softly.

Kara looks at her. "I don't think. I know. He is going to be pissed. She's right. I'll have to help calm him down. He won't understand."

Rafe opens his eyes. He's still in the exam room, and when he tries to sit up, he realizes his wrists and ankles are in leather restraints. Unable to move his body, he lifts his head, but doesn't see anyone. Winslow walks in a moment later.

"What is the meaning of this?" Rafe tugs on the restraints.

"Those aren't my orders. You'll have to ask Declan about that."

"What is going on? Why won't anyone tell me anything?"

"We tried, but you wouldn't listen."

Rafe closes his eyes, calming his racing mind and pounding heart. He looks at Winslow. "Please, tell me what's happened."

Winslow pulls up the chair and sits next to him. "As Declan was trying to tell you, Kane broke into the palace. He wounded the queen, wanting to stop her from going into battle. He tried to break her spirit. Instead, she gave a rousing speech to the troops, and they rode off to a victorious battle. She is recovering, and she said that if you were wounded when you returned, for you to stay here and recover twenty-four hours before seeing her."

"Winslow, please. Let me go. I need to see her. I need to. Don't you understand?"

"I can't. I'm sorry. Kara is right outside, though. She wants to give you an update on the queen." He steps out, nodding to Kara.

Rafe closes his eyes, wishing more than anything he can see Ana. The pang hits his chest, his breathing shallow, at the thought of waiting.

Kara walks in. "Rafe, are you okay?"

He opens his eyes and looks at her. "I'm fine. I'm recovered. Please, tell her I can see her," he begs.

She shakes her head. "No. I can see how pale you are, see the pain you're still in. She won't allow it."

"I'm in pain because I need to see her! Don't you understand that?"

"Rafe, these are her orders."

A tear slides down his cheek. "I need her," he says, softly.

"I know. She needs you, too."

His body goes tense. "What do you mean?"

"She is healing, and she is recovering, but she's in so much pain. She tries to hide it, putting on a brave face, but I see it."

"Then let me help," he cries, pulling on the restraints. "Damn it, Kara!"

"I can't. You think this isn't killing me, too? I hate seeing her like this."

Rafe shakes his head. "Kara, please. I'm begging you, let me go."

"I'm sorry, Rafe. I can't." She heads for the door.

"Kara, if you really love her, you will let me help her."

"And risk her losing you? She would never forgive either of us. You know that." She turns to him. "Don't ask me to do that."

He looks down, reluctantly nodding. "Please, if she does take a turn for the worse—"

"I'll be in here in a flash."

Once she's gone, he struggles against the restraints and pulls with all his effort, unable to break free. He lays his head back against the pillow and closes his eyes, gathering his strength, then pulls again, still not breaking the restraints. His head falls back against the pillow as the exhaustion begins to seep in.

"No," he says, fighting it while struggling against them. He hangs his head and weeps, praying he can see her soon.

"How is he?" Ana asks as soon as Kara is in the room.

"He's still recovering."

"How is he taking everything?" Evren asks.

Kara shakes her head. "He's not pleased. He begged me to see you." She walks over to Ana. "Are you sure you won't see him? His wound has healed."

"Kara, you know what healing does to him. He needs time."

"He's hurting, mi'lady. He's hurting over not being with you."

"Kara, I can't. You know this."

"How are you feeling?"

"Better. The medicine is helping. The pain's not so bad." She smiles at her.

Kara sees through the smile but says nothing. "Good. Let us know if we can do anything for you."

"When can I return to my quarters?"

"Probably in the morning," Kara replies.

"How is the count doing?" Ana asks.

"Okay. He had been tortured and starved, but he is recovering. He said to thank you for everything." Kara smiles at her. "And you haven't heard the news about the guardians?" At the excitement in her voice, Evren walks over. Ana shakes her head. "Rafe rescued over a hundred guardians! They were being studied by the NightFall council. They're here now, recovering."

"Oh, my God!" Ana exclaims. "Really?"

"Yes. The count showed Rafe where they were, and they freed them."

"Oh, that's incredible. They can rebuild their numbers." She smiles at Kara. "This is wonderful news."

"Yes, the whole kingdom is buzzing about it. They're giving you and Rafe the credit."

"But he did the rescuing."

"Because you sent him. Take the credit. It makes you look like a strong, intelligent leader."

"Yes, Kara. Even if I don't always feel that way."

"Ana—"

"No, it's okay."

"If you're wanting to return to your quarters, you should get more rest," Kara suggests.

"Yes. Thank you."

Kara adjusts the bed and covers her with the blanket. She leans down and kisses her forehead. "You aren't allowed to die on me, mi'lady."

She smiles up at her. "I'm not planning on it."

Rafe looks over when the door opens, and Declan walks in.

"How are you feeling?"

"A hundred percent! I'm ready to see the queen."

Declan scoffs. "No, don't try that with me. I can see how you feel. I didn't understand her orders, at first. Now I see that the healing really takes it out of you."

"Only because I was still recovering from healing her then traveling. I'm just a little tired, but I'm okay. Really."

Declan shakes his head. "No, you're not. You need to continue to rest." He walks up, lifting Rafe's wrist restraint and seeing where it's rubbed from him trying to break free. "Continue in this manner, you're only going to hurt yourself. Then that's more time you have to stay in here."

"No!"

"Then stop trying to break free."

Rafe hangs his head. "Yes, Declan."

"They're getting ready to move her to her quarters. You have—" he looks at the clock on the wall, "twelve more hours, then you can see her. See? Time's already half over. You'll see her in no time."

"Thank you."

"Please, stop trying to free yourself. She needs you," Declan says quietly.

Rafe sees the concern on his face. "I promise."

He watches Declan leave, then tries to rest, but his shoulders and wrists are aching, his legs numb. Winslow walks in.

"How are you feeling this morning?"

"I have a favor to ask, and I know you aren't going to believe me. My body is hurting, being restrained like this. I don't care if you have twenty guards brought in, but please, release me, if only for a minute. I need to stretch and move."

Winslow gets out a syringe. "I will let you go, but the second I think you're making for the door I will not hesitate.

Then I will add time to your recovery, do you understand me?"

Rafe nods. "Yes."

Winslow undoes his ankle restraints first, then his wrists. Rafe sits up, rubbing them before he slowly gets to his feet and paces the room, while Winslow stands against the door. For a flash, he considers making a break for it. He knows he'd never make it, so he continues to pace, turning his head and stretching his arms and wings. He sits on the exam table.

"Thank you."

"Of course." Winslow sets the syringe on the tray and starts to lift the first wrist strap. Rafe snatches up the syringe and aims for his neck, but Winslow slips free as Rafe jumps to his feet.

"I'm sorry," he says. "It's nothing personal. I have to see her."

"Guards!" Winslow cries out. Two royal guards run in. Rafe doesn't hurt them, only deflects and blocks. He's almost to the door, when Winslow has another syringe in hand, and jabs it into Rafe. He falls to the floor, clutching his neck and falls unconscious. The guards get him onto the exam table, while Winslow fixes the restraints. The guards leave. Winslow leans down by Rafe's face. "That was stupid. Why did you do that? Now it's another twelve hours while you're recovering. I have to tell the queen, which I really don't want to do."

Winslow storms from the room, slamming the door. He takes a deep breath to calm himself before stepping into Ana's room.

"Are you ready to return to your quarters?" Winslow asks.

"Yes."

"Good. We'll help with that. Also, I'm sorry to have to tell you this. Rafe had a, um, minor setback. He's going to be okay, but it will be an additional twelve hours of recovery time for him."

Ana nods. "I understand. Whatever he needs, please." Winslow bows and leaves. She looks up when Kara laughs. "What?"

"That stupid son of a bitch. He did something. I don't know what, but he did this to himself."

"Can you blame him?" Ana asks. "He knows I'm right here, wounded, and he can't even see me. Wouldn't you be doing everything you could if that was you and Evren?"

"Yes, I would. Still, he should know better."

"Kara, please."

"I know." Kara takes a deep breath. Anger overwhelms her because she knows Ana needs Rafe sooner than twenty-four hours. She sees it, on her face and in her eyes. In that moment, she decides it won't be that long.

They get Ana moved into her quarters, where Kara and Evren help give her a sponge bath and change into a new gown.

"You're missing him, too. Aren't you?" Kara asks while helping Ana into bed.

"I close my eyes to sleep, and I keep seeing Kane. Rafe is the only one who can comfort me. I won't risk him, though. Not while he is still recovering." She winces and grabs her side.

"Are you okay?"

"Just sore, from the bath and movement." She closes her eyes, letting the medicine take effect.

Kara looks at Evren. "I have an errand to run. Please, stay with her."

"Of course."

Kara sneaks through the palace, making her way into the Medical Center without being seen. She goes to Rafe's room.

"What do you want?" he asks, turning away.

"Look at me," she demands. He obeys. "Tell me, honestly, how are you feeling? Tell me the truth."

"I'm better. I'm a little tired, but I swear, I'm recovered."

She approaches him, placing a hand on his wrist restraint. "Swear to me, Rafe. Swear right now. If I undo one of your restraints, you will wait at least ten minutes before freeing yourself."

"What's going on? Is Ana okay?"

"She's in too much pain. She needs you, but she won't admit it."

"I swear. I will watch the clock, and I will wait at least ten minutes."

"Fine." She undoes one of his restraints then folds it over. "It still looks secured, so if anyone checks on you before your ten minutes are up, they'll never know."

"Thank you."

"You better keep your mouth shut about this."

"I swear."

She opens the door, making sure it's clear, before sneaking out. She stops by Declan's office to give her an excuse for why she was out.

"Is the queen all right?" he asks, walking over to her.

"Yes. I wanted to let you know that she is back in her quarters, resting. I also wanted to see how the count and the guardians who were rescued are doing."

"Everyone is recovering well."

"Thank you. I'll let Her Highness know."

She goes back to Ana's room. She knows she has to distract Evren. If she sees Rafe coming in, she's not sure how she will react. She takes her to the corner of the room, leaning in and kissing her. Kara has Evren's back to the door, so Kara can watch for Rafe. He comes in a few minutes later. She distracts Evren, planting kisses on her cheek and neck while Rafe walks to the bed and climbs in, holding Ana tight.

"Is he with her yet?" Evren asks.

Kara steps back. "What?"

"I love you, but I know why you were doing that." Kara's head goes down. "It's okay. I enjoyed it."

They walk over and see him with his arms around her. Kara fixes the blanket, covering them both. She locks the door then pulls a chair over beside the bed.

"Did you do that?" Evren asks.

"I went to see Declan. I wanted to tell her when she wakes up that the count and the guardians are recovering well."

"Okay."

"Rafe!" Ana cries out as she comes to. "What are you doing in here?"

"Uh-oh," Kara says, rushing to Ana's side.

"I had to see you."

"But you're still recovering. I feel it."

"No, I swear."

"Then what is this pain from you?"

"The pain of separation. I couldn't bear to be away from you."

"Really?"

"Yes. I begged Winslow, Declan, and Kara to release me. They refused. My heart was broken, not being with you."

"What do you mean, release you?"

Kara clears her throat. "We um, had to keep him restrained to keep him from you. It was Declan's idea."

"Kara! Why didn't you tell me that?"

"We knew you would never agree. It was literally the only way to keep you two apart."

She looks at Rafe, "I'm so sorry, my love. I had no idea." She pulls him tighter. "Please, forgive me."

"There's nothing to forgive, mia estrela. They were trying to protect me, to protect both of us." He kisses her as a tear runs down his cheek. "I just missed you so much."

"Let me in!" Declan demands, banging on the door. Rafe jumps to his feet. Evren grabs him, throwing him into her quarters and sliding his boots under the bed, using the blanket to hide them.

Kara opens the door. "The queen is resting. What is wrong with you?"

"Where is he?" Declan demands.

"Who?"

"Rafe! He managed to free himself."

"We haven't seen him." She opens the door, so he can see inside. Ana appears to be sleeping, and Evren is sitting on the sofa with a book in her hand. "I'll let you know if we do."

"Thank you." He leaves in a huff.

Kara returns to Ana. "You have to fix this. He's acting on your orders, you know."

"I know."

Kara tells Rafe he can come back out. He takes Ana's hand. "How are your wounds?"

"Healed."

"Enough that I can move you?"

She smiles at him. "Yes, please."

He scoops her up, taking her to the closet, and locking the door behind him before placing her on the ottoman. He climbs on, taking her in his arms.

"God, I've missed this," he says, breathing in her scent. "I've missed you so much. I love you, Ana."

"I missed you, too, my love."

He leans over, planting gentle kisses on her lips and chin. She looks up at him, smiling. He smiles back. "I'm never leaving you again. I swear."

"This wasn't your fault."

"Will you tell me what happened? Everyone said you were wounded, but no one gave me any details." She trembles in his arms. "I'm sorry. I shouldn't have asked, mia estrela."

"No, it's okay. I'll tell you." She recounts the events of the night before, and how she barely managed to call out Kara's name before she passed out.

"Why wasn't she in here?"

"She slept in Evren's room. This wasn't their fault, either. He slit the throat of my royal guard. Who knows what he would've done to them? I'm thankful they weren't in here."

"They should've been in here to protect you."

"Rafe, I'm just happy to be alive and in your arms. Can we please not fight about this right now? Not while we are both still recovering?"

"Yes, of course. I just worry about you so much."

"I know, love. I know. I worry about you, too."

"Ana, is this still enough for you?" Rafe asks, wanting nothing more than for her to be happy.

She sits up at his tone. "Why? What do you mean?"

"Seeing you dine with the count, to be out in public with a suitor. To not have to hide in a closet. I want you to have everything you want," he says, sitting up with her.

"Don't you understand, Rafe? You are all I've ever wanted. Please, don't question that."

"You just, you deserve so much more."

"Where is this coming from? Why are you asking this now?" She looks at him, tears streaming down her face. "Am I not enough for you anymore? Do you not want me?"

"Oh, mia estrela." He scoops her into his lap, wrapping his arms tightly around her. "You're more than I could've ever dreamt of. I love you more than words can say. If I could give you a kiss for every star in the sky, I still would not be able to show you all my love. I feel so lost and empty when I'm not with you. Please, don't question my love for you."

She turns and brings her legs around his waist, wrapping her arms around his neck. She kisses his cheek, then lays her head on his chest. "Don't scare me like that, please."

"I'm sorry. I just want you to be happy."

"This, right here, is the only time I am truly happy. You are my anchor in the storm. Why do you not see that?" She pulls back when he doesn't answer. She wipes the tear from his face. "What's wrong?"

"I just wish I could give you more."

"Honestly, it wouldn't be much different if we could be together publicly."

"Ana—"

"You know it's the truth."

"I do."

"Then please, don't ask me that again. I will tell you now, and a million times more, this is all I ever needed. I love you."

"I love you, too."

"Rafe?"

"Yes?"

"Shut up and kiss me."

He leans forward, bringing a hand up gently to the back of her head, as his mouth crashes into hers. He devours her lips, tasting her, wanting her while she caresses his face. He takes her hand and plants gentle kisses, then kisses her scar and looks at her.

"I'm sorry," she says. "I'm still tired."

"We both are. Let's get more rest."

Chapter 20

Kara leaves to see Declan. He takes her into his office and shuts the door. She clears her throat, trying to find the words. He looks at her, tilting his head.

"Son of a bitch," he says with a smile across his face. "He was there, wasn't he?"

"Yes. I'm sorry."

"Don't be. Those two are going to be the death of me! Has he healed her?"

"Yes, they're both doing fine now. When he came in, I almost thought about stopping him, but I couldn't."

"I understand." She turns to leave. "Kara?"

"Yes, Declan?"

"I know I shouldn't ask."

"Then don't. Unless you really want to know."

He shakes his head. "I already know too much as it is."

"Hypothetically," she asks, "is there any way? Is it possible to change the law?"

"I've looked. Ever since I saw the way they look at each other, I knew. Hell, I think half the kingdom does. We just, look the other way. I don't see how she can, but I'll tell you this, I have seen the fire in her eyes. If anyone can, it's her. That's what I'm holding onto."

"Thank you, Declan. For everything."

He nods as she leaves. Going to Ana's quarters and thinking on his words, she knows there has to be some way they can be together. It can't be impossible forever. She passes by the chancellor's office when she decides to stop in.

"How is the queen?" Corbin asks, sitting behind his large oak desk.

"She is recovering."

"I don't know how this happened."

"We're still investigating," Kara says.

"How can I help you?"

"I want to know, what power does the queen have? To change laws, I mean?"

"Any specific law?"

"Everything I'm about to say, is in total confidence. It's also one hundred percent hypothetical and does not relate to any actual people in this kingdom. Do I make myself clear?"

He nods in understanding. "You want to know if she can change the law, regarding royals and guardians?"

"Yes. How did you know?"

"It's not hard to guess. If she came before the Celestial Council and tried, they would know why. If it failed, they would both be punished. She's the only royal. She couldn't try to claim it was on someone else's behalf."

"What if it wasn't just about her? What if she wanted the guardians to be free to engage in a relationship with anyone, regardless of status? They were nearly wiped out. What if she claimed it was to help rebuild their numbers?"

"Hmm. Let me put some feelers out, see what kind of reaction I get. If it's mostly positive, I say she should go for it. If not, then at least they would still be safe."

"Thank you for your discretion. We truly appreciate it."

"Is it true that he can heal her? And she can heal him?"

She catches her breath. "Yes."

"Astounding!"

She smiles at him. "Thank you, again."

"Of course. I will send for you, once I've had some feedback."

She gives a slight bow and leaves, feeling better about the situation. She returns to Ana's quarters with a smile on her face. "Evren—" she says, locking the door and turning around. Kane is in the room with a blade to Evren's throat. Kara reaches for her sword.

"Ah, ah, witch. Now, tell me where the queen is, or I'll slit her throat."

Kara's eyes dart to Evren's quarters, trying to trick him. He walks that way with Evren. "Open the door!" he demands. She pushes the button and the door swings out, nearly hitting them. Evren uses it as a chance to break free of his grip. She runs over to Kara. Evren gets out her dagger while Kara unsheathes her sword. Together, they step up to him.

"Archduke Kane, you are under arrest!" Kara cries out, charging at him. He gets his sword out and quickly deflects. Evren can only watch, praying Kara will be okay.

Kara knocks the sword from his hand, pushing him up against the wall. She takes a step back and brings the point of her blade to his chest. Evren walks over, finding a pair of bindings in his pocket. When she goes to put them on, he grabs her wrist and pulls her to him.

He has his dagger at her throat then waves it at Kara. Kara stands there, looking at Evren. She nods, then falls to the floor. Kara rushes forward, only scraping Kane as he turns away. He runs out the door. She chases after him, calling for the guards to help. Evren goes into the closet, seeing Rafe and Ana still asleep from the healing.

She walks to her side and wakes her up. "Mi'lady?"

"Hmm, yes?"

"I hate to bother you. You need to get up and return to your bed. Rafe needs to get dressed. We may have company coming."

Ana's eyes pop open as she sits up. "What do you mean?"

"Kara is pursuing Kane through the palace. Declan or the royal guard may come in here."

Ana hurries to her feet, panic flowing through her. "Love, get up. You need to get up and dressed, right now. Evren is taking me to the bed. Hurry!"

They leave while Rafe gets his shirt and shoes back on. He steps out, as Evren is getting her covered up. He walks over to them.

"What's going on?"

Evren turns to him. "Kane was here."

He steps back in shock. "What?"

"Kara and the guards are pursuing him right now."

"Should I join in?"

"Stay with her. I'm going to see what's happening." Before Evren's at the door, Kara walks back in, shaking her head.

"Son of a bitch! He got away. How is he getting in here?"

Declan walks in. "Sorry to intrude. We lost track of him. Someone here has to be helping him. It's the only way he's getting in and out." He looks around the room. "Is everyone all right?"

"Yes," Kara says. "He didn't get the chance to hurt anyone. I cut him with my sword, but I'm not sure how serious."

"I'll notify Winslow so they can be on guard." He bows and leaves.

Ana looks up at Evren. "Thank you for your fast thinking."

"Of course, mi'lady."

Ana looks at Rafe, knowing how close it could have been. He sees the fear on her face and takes her hand as he sits on the edge of the bed.

"We're okay. Do not dwell on it."

"Rafe—"

"No. We have good friends to protect us. Please, I know how you think. I love that about you, but right now, don't let it do that to you."

"I won't."

He walks over to Kara. "Please, help reassure her. She's worried that we could've been caught."

She nods and sits beside Ana, speaking softly with her. When there's a knock at the door, Evren answers it, seeing a guardian she doesn't recognize.

"Can I help you?" Evren asks.

"I'm looking for Rafe?"

Everyone goes quiet, watching as she walks into the room. Her long auburn hair trails down her back, her face is kissed with just a few freckles. Then Ana sees her turquoise wings, contrasting the dark blue of her uniform. Ana is envious of her beauty. Kara walks over and stands by Rafe.

"Melian," he says, stepping forward. "How are you feeling? Are you recovered from you experience at NightFall?"

"I am. Sorin says I should be returned to duty by tomorrow."

"I'm glad."

"I wanted to thank you for saving me. For saving all of us."

He gives her a slight bow. "It was my duty."

She walks up to him and puts her hand on his shoulder. "I would love if you would have dinner with me tonight, so I may properly thank you."

"I apologize, but my duty is to the queen. She is still recovering."

"Oh, I'm sure she won't mind."

Ana clears her throat. Melian turns to her. "It's an honor to meet you, Your Majesty." She approaches Ana, falling to one knee. "My humblest of apologies."

"It's quite all right, Guardian. Please, rise."

Melian stands up. "You are every bit as beautiful as the rumors I'd heard."

"Thank you."

Melian looks at Rafe, giving him a smile. "Perhaps another time then." She bows and leaves the room.

Rafe walks over to the window, looking out. Ana watches him. *My duty is to the queen. Was he saying that because I was sitting here? Or was he really trying to give himself a polite out?* She stands up, goes into the washroom, and sits on the edge of the tub. *She is so beautiful. I'm sure he saw it, too. They obviously know each other.* She turns on the shower and strips down, then steps in. *If Rafe was with Melian, he wouldn't have to hide. He wouldn't have to be afraid. There are enough guardians now, Declan could give me a new one, and Rafe wouldn't have to go into battle.*

She weeps at the thought. Overwhelmed by her anger and confusion and fear, she finally lets everything out. Getting dressed, she knows her strength is almost gone. Between the healing and the tears, she doesn't have much left in her. She slips her gown back on and opens the door. She leans against the doorframe, trying to gather her courage. All she can think about is asking Rafe how he feels about Melian.

Rafe walks towards her. Suddenly afraid, she doesn't want to know. Rafe sees the fear in her eyes and runs to her.

"What's wrong?" he asks.

Her head instantly goes down. "She's so beautiful," she whispers.

"Who?"

Her head snaps up. "That's not funny."

"I'm being serious. Who are you talking about?"

"Melian."

Rafe sighs, running his hand through his hair. "Really? Is this going to be like Lauren all over again?" He sees her face flush red. "Look, she and I are about the same age. We went through boot camp together. She's a friend, nothing more. I swear to you." He steps back when he sees her eyes are red and swollen. "Were you crying in the shower, thinking that I would be happier with her than with you?"

Her head falls again. "Yes," she admits.

He picks her up and carries her into the closet. "You have to stop this. You have to stop thinking that you're not good enough for me. Or that what we have in here isn't enough for me. You have to stop doubting yourself! How can I convince you? What will it take to prove my love to you?"

"It's… it's not you. You said it yourself, just a minute ago, about how I think. It's how I am. I can't control it. Please, don't be mad at me."

"What makes you think I'm mad at you? I'm telling you how much I love you!"

She pulls away and paces. "I just feel like, now that there are more guardians, maybe you would want to be with them, to not have to hide who you are and be afraid of being caught."

"Do you think I am?" Rafe asks.

"What?"

"I'm not afraid of being caught. I wouldn't want you to get hurt, obviously, but I would rather die, admitting my love for you, than live a lie by saying I didn't."

She stops and looks at him. "What?"

He plants a soft kiss on her forehead. "I mean that. Why do you doubt me?"

"I don't. I doubt myself."

"Please, believe this. You and I are in love with each other. Nothing will ever come between that love. Nothing will ever hurt or destroy it. If you believe nothing else, believe that." He looks at her. "Think of this. What does the soulmates legend say? If one of the people aren't in love, the healing won't work. Has our healing ever not worked?"

"No."

"Even when you thought I didn't love you, even when you said you hated me, it still worked."

She smiles at him. "You're right. Why didn't I think of that? Thank you for your patience with me. I know I'm frustrating."

"You have no idea." He smirks at her, kissing her. She puts her arms around his neck. "I love you, mia estrela."

"I love you, too, Rafe."

They return to the main chamber. She walks over to the table, sitting with Kara and Evren. "Everything okay with you two?" Kara asks.

She looks over, smiling at Rafe. "Yes."

"Good."

There's another knock at the door. Evren walks over, letting Declan in. "I'm sorry again, to intrude. I know you are still recovering."

"What's going on?"

"We're hearing that the NightFall Quadrant will be sending their army in the next few days. They are angry they lost their guardians, and they want the count back."

"There has to be something we can do to stop the conflict."

"No, mi'lady. I've spoken with the count. They are a stubborn race. There is no way to convince them not to fight. We have nothing to offer them or appease them."

"The count told me they are afraid of the MoonFrost Quadrant. He said they are always attacking them. Do you think they would help us?"

"You won't get a truce out of them."

"Even if it's to help fight their sworn enemy?"

"Mi'lady, that's brilliant. It's worth a shot. I'll message Ansel, the leader of their guard. Thank you." He bows and runs out.

"You really have a brilliant mind for this."

Ana looks at Rafe. "I think that's a compliment?"

He laughs. "It is. Now, are you okay?" he asks, arm around her waist as he takes her to the bed.

"Yes. Just tired."

"Okay." He tucks her in then strokes her face as she drifts off to sleep.

Evren goes to see about dinner. Rafe walks over to Kara. "Do you think she will want to fight in the upcoming battle?"

"I didn't even think about that." She lets out a sigh. "I hope she doesn't."

"Whatever her decision, we support her. Understood?"

"Yes, Rafe."

Evren returns. They wake Ana up once the food is set up. She eats quickly and goes back to sleep.

"I'm worried about her," Kara says.

"She's okay," Evren assures her.

"Let's get some rest."

Rafe goes to his chaise, while Kara and Evren go into Evren's room. Rafe looks over at Ana as he sits down, wishing he could lie beside her.

Ana is surprised the next morning when Declan joins them for breakfast. She's grateful she had decided to put on a gown instead of one of the nightgowns she had been wearing. They sit at their table in the corner, Ana, Rafe, and Declan. Kara and Evren are on the chaise.

"MoonFrost is sending a squadron to help with the upcoming battle. It looks like the army from Nightfall will be here in the morning."

"I'll be ready to fight," Ana says.

"Mi'lady, if I may. With the help we have coming, and more guardians, it's not necessary for you to risk your life. Please, let us fight for you."

"I was denied my last battle by Kane. This one is even more important. If we can hurt them enough, maybe we can force them to sign a treaty and finally have peace, possibly even have Kane delivered to us. I want to see him pay for his crimes."

"Of course." Declan looks down at his plate, clearing his throat. "Mi'lady, do you know how to ride a horse?"

"What?"

"It's tradition, you will go out on a steed. Do you know how to ride?"

"I've ridden a few times."

"Good. I had completely forgotten. My apologies."

"It's okay."

"Rafe and Kara will be joining us on the field as well?" Declan asks.

Kara walks over, hearing her name. She looks at Ana. "We'll be with you. You aren't going out there alone."

She looks at them both. "No. You can't."

"Are you ordering us not to?"

"No, of course not. Rafe may join me, but Kara, I need you here. You need to be running things while I'm on the field. I need someone I can trust. Please?"

"Yes, Your Majesty." She returns to Evren, who is grateful Kara will not be going into battle.

They finish eating, and Declan takes his leave. Ana goes into her closet, getting her sword out from under the ottoman and removing it from the box.

"It's beautiful," Rafe says, walking in. He shuts the door, locking it behind him before he walks over to her.

"Apparently, it's meant for the queen, though very few of us have taken it into battle." She swings it around, feeling the weight and checking the balance.

"May I see it?"

She hands it to Rafe, who is surprised by the weight. "It's quite sturdy, isn't it?"

"What do you mean?"

"The weight. It's quite heavy."

"Not to me."

"What do you mean?"

She gestures to the sword, and he hands it back to her. With one hand, she graciously swings it around, then twirls it. He steps back.

"I've only ever heard of one other queen who could wield the sword like that."

"Really?"

"Yes. It's amazing, like it's a part of you."

"It feels like that, yes."

"And you have your armor?"

"I do."

"Ana, if one of us doesn't survive tomorrow—"

"Rafe, please."

"We have to talk about this."

She puts the sword back in the box, then sets it on the floor. She sits on the ottoman, and Rafe sits beside her, taking her hand between his.

"Go ahead," she says, softly.

"Please, promise me, you won't risk yourself for me. That if you see me fall, you won't try and heal me. You have to keep fighting, no matter what you see. Promise me that. Promise me, so I'm not on the field beside myself with worry over you."

"I promise," she says. "Same to you."

"I am your guardian, it is my duty—"

"No, Rafe. You are the love of my life. That is more important. Now, make the same promise to me."

"I promise," he says.

They sit there, holding hands in silence while they are both thinking about the next day, about the battle, about what could happen. She stands up, pulling him with her. She leans up and kisses him. "I love you, Rafe."

"I love you, too, mi estrela." He kisses her harder, pulling her into his arms. He sits on the ottoman, holding her in his lap while he plants kisses all over her face and neck. She wraps her arms around his neck, bringing one hand up behind his head, crushing her lips into his. He smiles at her as he brings his hand up and along her side. He looks at her. "May I touch you somewhere I've never touched you before?"

Her breath catches in her throat, and all she can do is nod. He gently cups her breast, his thumb stroking her through the thin fabric. She writhes and moans. His other hand cups her face, and he kisses her while his hand continues along her chest then down her stomach. He stops when he reaches her thigh and looks at her. She nods again. He pulls the gown up, placing his hand on her bare skin, caressing her thigh. She looks at him, her heart pounding in her chest as she grows flush.

"Ana, I'm going to put my hands all over your body, if you're okay with that."

"Yes, please," she begs.

He fingers brush along the cotton of her undergarment. She writhes as they swirl around, gently touching and stroking. Unable to control herself, she moans as she is hit with waves of pleasure. Her body shudders as he moves faster, teasing and slowing down, then stroking again. She cries out when her body can take no more and grabs his hand, seeing the smile on his face. He leans over and kisses her softly.

"I'd say you quite enjoyed that."

"Oh, my God. What you do to me, do to my body. How is that possible?"

He smiles at her. "I'm glad."

"I want to do the same for you."

"You will. Later." He stands up, taking her hands and helping her off the ottoman. Her legs are still shaking. He pulls her to him. "I'm sorry. I didn't realize you needed a moment."

"That was incredible."

"Another first for us?" He leans down and kisses her. "A good one at that."

"Yes, it was," she says, looking down.

Rafe goes to the washroom, and Ana walks out of the closet in a daze. Kara walks over to her.

"You have got the biggest smile on your face I've ever seen. What were you two doing in there? Did you finally—"

"No."

"Then what? I've never seen you like this." Ana blushes, leaning over and whispering into Kara's ear. Kara laughs. "Oh, my." She pulls her in, hugging her.

"What's that for?"

"I'm so happy for you," Kara says.

"I just wish—"

Kara sighs. "I know. I'm working on that."

When there's a knock at the door, Evren opens it and lets Declan in. He paces in front of the fireplace. "How could this happen? Right under our own nose!"

Ana runs over to him. "Declan, what's wrong?"

"We found the traitor. We know who was helping Kane."

"Who is it?" Ana asks.

"Chancellor Corbin."

Kara's heart stops in her chest. "No. No, that can't be."

"I'm afraid it is."

"Shit!" she yells, turning away. "Oh, how could I be so stupid?"

"What?" Ana asks Kara. "What's wrong?" She looks at Rafe, as he steps out of the washroom.

"He was helping me about," she looks at Declan then back at Ana, "about a question with the law. When we were talking, he asked me if it's true, that you heal each other. I wanted to stay on his good side, since I needed his help. I told him it was. I have failed you. I am so sorry!"

"Kara, you did nothing wrong. The fact that he asked you means he probably already knew. Please, none of us saw this coming."

"What did I miss?" Rafe asks.

She turns to him. "Chancellor Corbin was helping Kane."

"No."

"The evidence against him is overwhelming. He's disappeared. We're still trying to find him. Mi'lady, in the interim, you will have to appoint a new chancellor," Declan says.

"Who would you recommend? Who knows our laws and history like he did?" Ana asks.

"I'll come up with a list of names and give you at dinner. In the meantime, I can oversee it, with your permission, of course."

"Yes, Declan. Thank you."

He bows and leaves the room.

Ana tells Rafe she would like to check on the count. He escorts her to the barracks where he is being temporarily housed.

"Your Majesty," he says as he bows to her.

She nods. "Count, I apologize I haven't been here—"

"Mi'lady, I heard about your attack. I'm just grateful for your guardian rescuing me. Thank you."

"You're very welcome. It was the least I could do. I want to thank you for helping free the guardians. I am sorry that no one is giving you credit for that."

The count smiles. "That's actually a good thing. If I ever want to have a chance at running the capitol again, it's best they don't know."

"I see."

"I hear there is a battle tomorrow? That you got help from MoonFrost?"

"How do you know all of this?"

"Mi'lady, I may not have earned this position, but I will keep it with a few tricks up my sleeve. I pretended to be unconscious when they were moving weapons and armor through."

She laughs. "You are something else!"

"Well, I still haven't assassinated you... yet."

"Would you like the chance to try?"

He laughs. "Oh, no. I don't kill friends."

She smiles at him. "I like that, being your friend."

"Thank you."

"Are you okay in here? I don't want you to feel like you're a prisoner, but with everything going on—"

"It's fine, Your Majesty. They bring me books to read and keep me fed. I have no complaints."

"If you do, ask for me. I will personally see to anything you need."

He gives her a bow. "Thank you, mi'lady."

She returns to her quarters, counting down the time until dinner, then sleep, then battle. She thinks of the week before, when she was supposed to go into battle, of Kane, sticking her over and over with his dagger. Leaning her forehead against the cool glass, she takes deep breaths to try and calm herself. Her face is flush at the memories.

"Mi'lady, do you need to sit down?" Rafe asks.

"No," she says softly. "I'm okay."

"What are you thinking about?"

"I was thinking about tomorrow's battle, and it made me think of the last time I was waiting."

"Kane?"

"Yes."

"He could even be on the battlefield, for all we know."

"I hadn't thought of that."

"Does that scare you?"

She looks at him, smiling. "A little. I would love to simply end him myself, though."

"Ana, you've never taken a life. You don't know how it's going to affect you."

She scoffs. "Who says I haven't?"

"What?" Rafe asks.

Ana sighs and realizes she's ready. She beckons Kara over. She looks at them both, then brings up the sleeves of her dress, exposing her scars. "You want to know about these, right?" They both nod. "I was fourteen and living in a group home, after being taken away from my foster father. There were two boys, one fifteen and one sixteen. They were always grabbing at me, groping me, trying to get me alone.

"One morning, I woke up to find them standing over me. It was just the three of us in the house. They tried to jump me. I fought like hell, kicking and biting and screaming. When they saw they weren't going to be able to pin me down, they hit me instead. The matron, as we called her, returned as they were hurting me." She looks down.

"Ana—" Kara starts.

"No. It's okay. She took me to the hospital and told them I had fallen down the stairs. Once I was treated and sent home, she told me it was just boys being boys. Next time, don't get them excited. I was in the shower, and they were pounding on the door, saying horrible things about what they wanted to do to my body. I took one of the razors, made my cuts, and laid in the tub. The matron unlocked the door and found me. She tried to have me institutionalized. I told the authorities everything those boys did to me, but they never even brought them in for questioning. I was released and returned to the same group home.

"I managed to steal a paring knife from the kitchen and slept with it under my pillow for days. One night, the sixteen-year-old came and tried to climb in bed with me. He put his hands on me, and in the dark, I slashed with the knife. I couldn't see anything. I screamed. The matron ran in and found his body on top of me. I had slit his throat." She looks back out the window. "So yes, Rafe. I have killed before. I will do it again, to defend myself and my kingdom." She steps back when Kara goes to put her hand on her arm. "Please," she says softly, "don't touch me right now. My mind is still in a dark place, remembering that."

Kara looks at Rafe. "Help her, please."

He nods to Kara, as she walks away. "Ana, how did you feel? When you realized you'd killed him?"

"I was so relieved. It meant none of the other boys would ever mess with me again. They tried to charge me and send me to juvie, but between my hospital chart and filing the complaint I did, they ruled it as self-defense. I thought about running away, not sure what it would be like in the home. The matron was replaced, and none of the other kids spoke to me or messed with me again."

"Do you ever feel regret? Or guilt? Since you killed someone."

"No," she says, looking at him. "I don't regret it. Guilt?" She shakes her head. "I wish it had never happened in the first place. Do you feel guilt for the lives you've taken?"

"I do, sometimes. Like you, I've only killed to defend myself."

"Yes, you were battling other soldiers, doing a duty. Of course, you would feel guilt or remorse. I never could regret it, knowing it meant he wouldn't put his nasty hands on me again."

"Ana," Rafe tries, putting his hand on her arm. She pulls away. "Please."

She looks at him. "I can't. I won't take these memories from such a dark time and associate them with a touch of comfort. Please understand."

"I'll give you some space. Come and see me when you're ready."

"I will."

She goes back to looking out the window, reliving that night. She'll never forget the blood spraying over her, the coppery smell invading her nose, or the sight of his lifeless eyes. A chill runs down her spine, and she wraps her arms around her. Fighting the vomit that always threatens to rise, she struggles to push the memory away. Her hands clench into fists. The anger is too much this time, and it boils over. She falls to her knees, screaming, as she sees his dead body on her.

Kara and Rafe rush to her, comforting her. "Shh, sis. You're okay. You're safe now. Those boys will never hurt you again."

"I killed him!" she cries, tears streaming down. "Why do I care now? What's changed?"

"Because you know what you're facing tomorrow," Rafe says. "I went through something similar. I was fine after my first battle. Drank with my fellow guardians, had a great night, so I thought. I was more traumatized than I realized…" He takes a breath as shame washes over him, then clears his throat. "Anyway, the next night, knowing we were going into battle again, I reacted like you are." He pulls her into his arms. "You're going to be fine. We both are." He looks at her. "If you don't want to go into battle, you don't have to."

"No, I will. I have to." She wipes her tears. "I've repressed this so long, that I had to let it out. I'm okay now, really." She looks at Kara. "Would you and Evren sleep in my bed tonight?"

"Of course!" Kara says, walking over to Evren and taking her hand. "Let's get cleaned up and ready for bed."

"Are we sleeping on the ottoman tonight?" Rafe asks Ana, smiling when she blushes.

"Yes."

He leans down and kisses her. "My pleasure." He watches her cheeks grow redder. "You're so damn cute."

She goes into the closet, turns on the lamp in the corner, and turns off the overhead light. While waiting for him to join her, she sits on the ottoman. He steps in, locks the door behind him, and walks over to her. In one flawless move, he picks her up and her legs wrap around his waist.

"Ana, how are you feeling? After letting all of that out?"

She smiles at him, caressing his face and kissing him softly. "Much better, actually. I needed to let that out. Now, what are we doing in here?" she teases.

He leans forward, kissing her. He takes her to the wall, standing her up. "Trust me?" he asks.

"Yes."

He pins her body to the wall with his own. He takes her wrists, grabbing them and holding them above her head. She's nervous, never having seen him like this before. He kisses her, hard and deep. She gasps for breath after he pulls away. His kiss is hungry. He trails his free hand up along her stomach and chest, then moves his hand down, running along her thigh.

"No, love," she says.

He instantly pulls back. "What's wrong?"

She smiles at him. "You deserve the same."

"We will. For tonight, I want this to be about you. Will you let me spoil you?"

"Yes," she whispers.

He picks her up, takes her to the ottoman, and sits her down. He gently removes her gown. She blushes, as she's not wearing a bra or corset. "Do you want your gown back?" he offers when he sees how red her face is.

"No. It's okay." She scoots back and lies down. He leans over her, running his fingers along her bare chest and kissing her, while his fingertips begin to caress lower. She parts her legs for him. He tugs on the undergarment.

"Can I?" he asks.

"Yes," she replies, her cheeks flushing again.

"You don't have to do anything you don't want to do, if you're embarrassed or uncomfortable."

"I'm not, I swear."

"Okay."

He gently pulls them down. "Just so you know, we aren't having sex tonight. Not in the way you think of it."

"I trust you."

"You're okay though?"

"I am." She swallows hard as his fingers stroke her. Her eyelids flutter as the first wave of pleasure rushes through her. "Oh," she cries out, her body shuddering.

He smiles. "This could be a long night."

The next morning, Ana wakes up and realizes she's still completely nude, wrapped in his arms. Trying not to wake him, she gently pulls away and gets her undergarments on. She gets out her battle outfit that Evren had helped her pick out, then turns on the light and wakes him up. He sits on the ottoman, watching as she puts on her shirt.

"I think I like it better when the clothes are coming off."

She smiles at him. "Me, too." This time he looks away. "Rafe, are you blushing?"

He clears his throat. "No, mi'lady."

"Then look at me." Her smile grows at the sight of him. She walks up, running her fingers through his hair. "Now who's cute?"

"Woman, I am 6'1" and 180 pounds of pure muscle. I am not cute."

"You so are." She brings her hand to his chest. "Can I— " she looks down, blushing and takes a breath. "Can I feel your wings?" He chuckles softly and extends them out. She walks behind him, gently ruffling her fingers through the feathers. "Is this okay?"

"It is."

"They're so beautiful."

"Like you," he says as she steps in front of him. He kisses her while his wings wrap around them, comforting her. He pulls back, so they can finish getting ready. Leaving the closet, they are suddenly serious, knowing what they are about to face. Rafe takes her hand and pulls her back into the closet. "I can't do this once we leave here." He holds her tight as he kisses her. "For good luck," he says.

"You, too." She walks across the room and knocks on Evren's door. When she steps out, Kara looks like she's hardly slept. "Are you okay?" Ana asks.

"Yes, mi'lady."

Evren and Kara follow her back into the closet to help her get her tunic and armor on. She picks up her sword, sheathing it then walks out.

"How do I look?" she asks Rafe.

"Like a warrior, Your Majesty," he says with a smile.

In the barracks, royal guards and guardians part as they come through, giving a small bow. She walks over to Declan.

"Are you making a speech, mi'lady?"

"Yes." He hands her the sound amplifier. "Good morning," she starts. "Today, we go into battle, not just to protect a queen, but to defend what is right. The army from NightFall is coming here, intent on taking back the guardians they had previously kidnapped, and to execute one of our closest allies. We fight to show not only do we defend our own, but we defend those who aid us. We fight for what we love, we fight to save the day. Who is with me?"

"Ayes" and "long live the queen" circulate around, before dying off. She gets to her steed, a solid black horse with white eyes and a grey mane and tail. "What is his name?" she asks Declan.

"StarFly."

"StarFly," she repeats. "I like it." She turns to her right and sees Rafe on what looks like a winged unicorn. She struggles to believe what she is seeing. "Is that—"

He smiles at her. "I thought you'd be surprised. It's what the higher-ranking guardians ride when going into battle."

"He's beautiful."

"She. Only the females have horns."

She shakes her head. "You'll have to tell me more, after the battle."

"Yes, mi'lady. That's a promise."

They ride out with everyone staring at her. Her armor is polished silver with gold accents, her dark blue tunic contrasting underneath. She wears a small gold crown upon her head. They arrive at the front of the battalion. Declan raises his sword, waiting for any movement from the other side. When there is none, he lowers it, and they all ride forward. She looks at Rafe, clutching her cross and praying he survives. They stop once they arrive at the flat, empty field.

She looks it over, thinking that any other day it would be picturesque with the wildflowers and weeds. Knowing today it will be soaked in blood, she shakes her head at the thought. The trees off to the side catch her eye, and she smiles a moment as she imagines climbing one, then focuses on the sight before her.

The MoonFrost army, now her closest allies, are adorned in armor trimmed in silver with royal blue accents. Their banner is royal blue with a dragon holding a spear in one claw. They have blue and white paint smeared across their faces. *They may take our freedom*—She stifles the laugh. *This is hardly the time or place!* She shakes her head, losing her smile when she looks at Rafe, and a cold sensation worms down her spine and into her stomach. She looks at him as if it will be the last time she will look upon him.

I love him, knowing it is the end of me, the beginning, unraveling all that I am. Our love will not be denied, nor our hearts kept apart. To hell with fate! If fate won't give me Rafe, I will do it myself. I will not be a pawn of fate!

Arrows fly through the air, signaling the fight has begun. They ride into battle, and she's quickly knocked off her steed. She hits his backside, telling him to return as she runs forward with her sword drawn.

Soldiers from NightFall learn she is on the field and try to take her down. The vampyra armor is crimson and black leather, while their swords have a slight curve to them. Guardians surround Ana, but when enemy soldiers break through, she parries and lunges, deflecting as she fights her away across the field. She looks over, seeing their leaders sitting on horses, staying out of the fray.

Cowards, she thinks as she continues to maim or kill those who would try to stop her. Pausing to catch her breath, she sees Kane. She shakes off the exhaustion and watches him approach her. She brings her sword up, deflecting just as he strikes at her. She deflects again, sending his sword into the ground, his arms and body following the movement. He jerks it out of the earth and faces her.

"Hello, darling. Did you miss me? We need to have a little chat."

"I think our swords will do the talking."

She steps back when he lunges. She feints, then lunges back at him. He parries but barely. His sword nearly flies from his hand, but he regains his grip and steps forward. She quickly backs away, trying to put some distance between them. A squadron runs through, and she can't find Kane as he's swept away with them. She continues through the field, bringing down as many enemy soldiers as she can, when she's hit from behind and brought to her knees.

Ana jumps up and turns just in time to deflect the second blow, then kills the soldier. She watches her fall to the ground. Her breath shudders as her eyes go grey. Ana shakes her head at the sight before continuing forward. She gasps when she looks over to see Rafe lying on the ground, growing concerned when she realizes he's not moving. Swallowing hard and pushing down her fear, she swings her sword up to protect herself, racing towards him but stops when she sees Kane to her left. He looks over, sees Rafe, and starts making his way to him. She realizes Kane is closer to Rafe than she is.

When Kane turns, she rushes to him, but he deflects against her sword. As they fight, she knocks the sword from his hand, sending it flying into the field. He runs to get his sword as she makes her way to Rafe. Kane sees her going after him, so he abandons his sword and instead unsheathes his dagger. He gets to Rafe first, bringing up his blade.

Ana goes to raise her sword, but she is unable as her strength has finally abandoned her. She can't even lift it off the ground. The sword falling from her grip, she gathers what strength she has and runs to them, jumping on Rafe as Kane brings the dagger down. She cries out when the blade goes into her lower back.

Kane grabs her off and drags her away. "No!" she screams. "Take me back to him, now!"

"Oh, I don't think so. Corbin told me all about your little healing powers. No, mi'lady, you will not be saving him." They go into the woods, where Kane realizes how much blood she is losing. "Hmm, you are wounded worse than I thought. This will not do." He drops her to the ground, leaving her behind and running off.

Lying on the forest floor, Ana is alone and dying. Gasping for air, she snatches the breast plate and tunic off, tossing them aside. The world is going dark and cold, her limbs numb. Her heart races, and she closes her eyes, ready for whatever end awaits.

I'm sorry, my love. I failed you. I pray you are still alive. I'm sorry I won't be there with you. I don't know why the stars have aligned against us, but I'm sorry. You were wrong, my love. Fate would be so cruel, when it comes to the two of us.

Her last breath exhales as her heart stops beating. Her body lies in the silence of the woods as the battle rages beyond the trees. The queen is dead. Long live the queen.

Acknowledgements

Emily, my editor, who did a fantastic job.

Kevin, my husband, who supported me and gave me unconditional love on this writing journey.

To my sister Lisa, for everything.

To my beta readers, Traci, Bonita, and Brittany. I could not have done this without your valuable input.

To Austin and Ally, thank you for letting me spend a Saturday afternoon perusing your collection of RPG books to get ideas for characters, armor, and weapons.

To the Kaufer family, for all of your support in my writing endeavors.

To my followers on social media, who helped with cover adjustments and gave me support.

To my readers, thank you.

About the Author

A.R. Kaufer lives in Indiana with her husband and furbabies. When she's not playing video games or watching movies, she is reading or writing. She can be found on Twitter and Pinterest, and she is happy to engage with her readers.

Author Photo By:
Kevin Kaufer

Printed in Great Britain
by Amazon

18588841R00263